# CALLISTA

# CALLISTA

## A TALE OF THE THIRD CENTURY

## Bl. John Henry Newman

### Annotated by Søren Filipski

"Love thy God, and love Him only,
And thy breast will ne'er be lonely.
In that One Great Spirit meet
All things mighty, grave, and sweet.
Vainly strives the soul to mingle
With a being of our kind;
Vainly hearts with hearts are twined:
For the deepest still is single.
An impalpable resistance
Holds like natures still at distance.
Mortal: love that Holy One,
Or dwell for aye alone."

DE VERE

ASSUMPTION PRESS

*2014*

*To*

HENRY WILLIAM WILBERFORCE.

*To you alone, who have known me so long, and who love me so well, could I venture to offer a trifle like this. But you will recognise the author in his work, and take pleasure in the recognition.*

*J. H. N.*

# ADVERTISEMENT

It is hardly necessary to say that the following Tale is a simple fiction from beginning to end. It has little in it of actual history, and not much claim to antiquarian research; yet it has required more reading than may appear at first sight.

It is an attempt to imagine and express, from a Catholic point of view, the feelings and mutual relations of Christians and heathens at the period to which it belongs, and it has been undertaken as the nearest approach which the Author could make to a more important work suggested to him from a high ecclesiastical quarter.

*September 13, 1855.*

This edition features new annotations, defining various
terms  in Latin and other ancient language, by Søren Filipski, MA,
Theology and Christian Ministry, Franciscan University of Steubenville.
Two annotations, however, are by Newman himself, and may be
distinguished by the inclusion of square brackets.

# Contents

# Callista

# Chapter One

# SICCA VENERIA

I N NO PROVINCE OF THE vast Roman empire, as it existed in the middle of the third century, did Nature wear a richer or a more joyous garb than she displayed in Proconsular Africa, a territory of which Carthage was the metropolis, and Sicca might be considered the centre. The latter city, which was the seat of a Roman colony, lay upon a precipitous or steep bank, which led up along a chain of hills to a mountainous track in the direction of the north and east. In striking contrast with this wild and barren region was the view presented by the west and south, where for many miles stretched a smiling champaign, exuberantly wooded, and varied with a thousand hues, till it was terminated at length by the successive tiers of the Atlas, and the dim and fantastic forms of the Numidian mountains. The immediate neighbourhood of the city was occupied by gardens, vineyards, cornfields, and meadows, crossed or encircled here by noble avenues of trees or the remains of primeval forests, there by the clustering groves which wealth and luxury had created. This spacious plain, though level when compared with the northern heights by which the city was backed, and the peaks and crags which skirted the southern and western horizon, was discovered, as light and shadow travelled with the sun, to be diversified with hill and dale, upland and hollow; while orange gardens, orchards, olive and palm plantations held their appropriate sites on the slopes or the bottoms. Through the mass of green, which extended still more thickly from the west round to the north, might be seen at intervals two solid causeways tracking their persevering course to the Mediterranean coast, the one to the ancient rival of Rome, the other to Hippo Regius in Numidia. Tourists might have complained of the absence of water from the scene; but the native peasant would have explained to them that the eye alone had reason to be discontented, and that the thick foliage and the uneven surface did but conceal what mother earth with no niggard bounty supplied. The Bagradas, issuing from the spurs of the Atlas, made up in depth what it wanted in breadth of bed, and ploughed the rich and yielding mould with its rapid stream, till, after passing Sicca in its way, it fell into the sea near Carthage. It was but the largest of a multitude of others, most of them tributaries to it, deepening as much as they increased it. While channels had been cut from the larger rills for the irrigation of the open land, brooks, which sprang up in the gravel which lay against the hills, had been artificially banked with cut stones or paved with pebbles; and where neither springs nor rivulets were to be found, wells had been dug, sometimes to the vast depth of as much as 200 fathoms, with such effect that the spurting column of water had in some instances drowned the zealous workmen who had been the first to reach it. And, while such were the resources of less favoured localities or seasons, profuse rains descended over the whole region for one half of the year, and the thick summer dews compensated by night for the daily tribute extorted by an African sun.

At various distances over the undulating surface, and through the woods, were seen the villas and the hamlets of that happy land. It was an age when the pride of architecture had been indulged to the full; edifices, public and private, mansions and temples, ran off far away from each market-town or borough, as from a centre, some of stone or marble, but most of them of that composite of fine earth, rammed tight by means of frames, for which the Saracens were afterwards famous, and of which specimens remain to this day, as hard in surface, as sharp at the angles, as when they first were finished. Every here and there, on hill or crag, crowned with basilicas and temples, radiant in the sun, might be seen the cities of the province or of its neighbourhood, Thibursicumber, Thugga, Laribus, Siguessa, Sufetula, and many others; while in the far distance, on an elevated table-land under the Atlas, might be discerned the Colonia Scillitana, famous about fifty years before the date of which we write for the martyrdom of Speratus and his companions, who were beheaded at the order of the proconsul for refusing to swear by the genius of Rome and the emperor.

If the spectator now takes his stand, not in Sicca itself, but about a quarter of a mile to the south-east, on the hill or knoll on which was placed the cottage of Agellius, the city itself will enter into the picture. Its name, Sicca Veneria, if it be derived (as some suppose) from the Succoth benoth, or "tents of the daughters," mentioned by the inspired writer as an object of pagan worship in Samaria, shows that it owed its foundation to the Phœnician colonists of the country. At any rate, the Punic deities retained their hold upon the place; the temples of the Tyrian Hercules and of Saturn, the scene of annual human sacrifices, were conspicuous in its outline, though these and all other religious buildings in it looked small beside the mysterious antique shrine devoted to the sensual rites of the Syrian Astarte. Public baths and a theatre, a capitol, imitative of Rome, a gymnasium, the long outline of a portico, an equestrian statue in brass of the Emperor Severus, were grouped together above the streets of a city, which, narrow and winding, ran up and down across the hill. In its centre an extraordinary spring threw up incessantly several tons of water every minute, and was inclosed by the superstitious gratitude of the inhabitants with the peristylium[1] of a sacred place. At the extreme back, towards the north, which could not be seen from the point of view where we last stationed ourselves, there was a sheer descent of rock, bestowing on the city, when it was seen at a distance on the Mediterranean side, the same bold and striking appearance which attaches to Castro Giovanni, the ancient Enna, in the heart of Sicily.

And now, withdrawing our eyes from the panorama, whether in its distant or nearer objects, if we would at length contemplate the spot itself from which we have been last surveying it, we shall find almost as much to repay

---

1    "peristyle," a court surrounded by a collonade

attention, and to elicit admiration. We stand in the midst of a farm of some wealthy proprietor, consisting of a number of fields and gardens, separated from each other by hedges of cactus or the aloe. At the foot of the hill, which sloped down on the side furthest from Sicca to one of the tributaries of the rich and turbid river of which we have spoken, a large yard or garden, intersected with a hundred artificial rills, was devoted to the cultivation of the beautiful and odoriferous *khennah*.[2] A thick grove of palms seemed to triumph in the refreshment of the water's side, and lifted up their thankful boughs towards heaven. The barley harvest in the fields which lay higher up the hill was over, or at least was finishing; and all that remained of the crop was the incessant and importunate chirping of the *cicadæ*,[3] and the rude booths of reeds and bulrushes, now left to wither, in which the peasant boys found shelter from the sun, while in an earlier month they frightened from the grain the myriads of linnets, goldfinches, and other small birds who, as in other countries, contested with the human proprietor the possession of it. On the south-western slope lies a neat and carefully dressed vineyard, the vine-stakes of which, dwarfish as they are, already cast long shadows on the eastern side. Slaves are scattered over it, testifying to the scorching power of the sun by their broad *petasus*,[4] and to its oppressive heat by the scanty *subligarium*,[5] which reached from the belt or girdle to the knees. They are engaged in cutting off useless twigs to which the last showers of spring have given birth, and are twisting those which promise fruit into positions where they will be safe both from the breeze and from the sun. Everything gives token of that gracious and happy season which the great Latin poets have hymned in their beautiful but heathen strains; when, after the heavy rains, and raw mists, and piercing winds, and fitful sun-gleams of a long six months, the mighty mother manifests herself anew, and pours out the resources of her innermost being for the life and enjoyment of every portion of the vast whole;—or, to apply the lines of a modern bard—

---

2 　"henna"
3 　"cicadas"
4 　"cap"
5 　"loincloth"

"When the bare earth, till now
Desert and bare, unsightly, unadorned,
Brings forth the tender grass, whose verdure clads
Her universal face with pleasant green;
Then herbs of every leaf, that sudden flower,
Opening their various colours, and make gay
Her bosom, swelling sweet; and, these scarce blown,
Forth flourishes the clustering vine, forth creeps
The swelling gourd, up stands the corny reed
Embattled in her fields, and the humble shrub,
And bush with frizzled hair implicit; last
Rise, as in dance, the stately trees, and spread
Their branches hung with copious fruit, or gem
Their blossoms; with high woods the hills are crowned
With tufts the valleys, and each fountain side
With borders long the rivers; that earth now
Seems like to heaven, a seat where gods might dwell,
Or wander with delight, and love to haunt
Her sacred shades."

A snatch from some old Greek chant, with something of plaintiveness in the tone, issues from the thicket just across the mule-path, cut deep in the earth, which reaches from the city gate to the streamlet; and a youth, who had the appearance of the assistant bailiff or *procurator* of the farm, leaped from it, and went over to the labourers, who were busy with the vines. His eyes and hair and the cast of his features spoke of Europe; his manner had something of shyness and reserve, rather than of rusticity; and he wore a simple red tunic with half sleeves, descending to the knee, and tightened round him by a belt. His legs and feet were protected by boots which came half up his calf. He addressed one of the slaves, and his voice was gentle and cheerful.

"Ah, Sansar!" he cried, "I don't like your way of managing these branches so well as my own; but it is a difficult thing to move an old fellow like you. You never fasten together the shoots which you don't cut off, they are flying about quite wild, and the first ox that passes through the field next month for the ploughing will break them off."

He spoke in Latin; the man understood it, and answered him in the same language, though with deviations from purity of accent and syntax, not without parallel in the *talkee-talkee* of the West Indian negro.

"Ay, ay, master," he said, "ay, ay; but it's all a mistake to use the plough at all. The fork does the work much better, and no fear for the grape. I hide the tendril under the leaf against the sun, which is the only enemy we have to consider."

"Ah! but the fork does not raise so much dust as the plough and the heavy cattle which draw it," returned Agellius; "and the said dust does more for the protection of the tendril than the shade of the leaf."

"But those huge beasts," retorted the slave, "turn up great ridges, and destroy the yard."

"It's no good arguing with an old vinedresser, who had formed his theory before I was born," said Agellius good-humouredly; and he passed on into a garden beyond.

Here were other indications of the happy month through which the year was now travelling. The garden, so to call it, was a space of several acres in extent; it was one large bed of roses, and preparation was making for extracting their essence, for which various parts of that country are to this day celebrated. Here was another set of labourers, and a man of middle age was surveying them at his leisure. His business-like, severe, and off-hand manner bespoke the *villicus* or bailiff himself.

"Always here," said he, "as if you were a slave, not a Roman, my good fellow; yet slaves have their Saturnalia; always serving, not worshipping the all-bounteous and all-blessed. Why are you not taking holiday in the town?"

"Why should I, sir?" asked Agellius; "don't you recollect old Hiempsal's saying about 'one foot in the slipper, and one in the shoe.' Nothing would be done well if I were a town-goer. You engaged me, I suppose, to be here, not there."

"Ah!" answered he, "but at this season the empire, the genius of Rome, the customs of the country, demand it, and above all the great goddess Astarte and her genial, jocund month. 'Parturit almus ager;'[6] you know the verse; do not be out of tune with Nature, nor clash and jar with the great system of the universe."

A cloud of confusion, or of distress, passed over Agellius's face. He seemed as if he wished to speak; at length he merely said, "It's a fault on the right side in a servant, I suppose."

---

6    The teeming earth brings forth"; Vergil, *Georgic Hymns*, IV.329

"I know the way of your people," Vitricus replied, "Corybantians, Phrygians, Jews, what do you call yourselves? There are so many fantastic religions now-a-days. Hang yourself outright at your house-door, if you are tired of living—and you are a sensible fellow. How can any man, whose head sits right upon his shoulders, say that life is worth having, and not worth enjoying?"

"I am a quiet being," answered Agellius, "I like the country, which you think so tame, and care little for the flaunting town. Tastes differ."

"Town! you need not go to Sicca," answered the bailiff, "all Sicca is out of town. It has poured into the fields, and groves, and river side. Lift up your eyes, man alive, open your ears, and let pleasure flow in. Be passive under the sweet breath of the goddess, and she will fill you with ecstasy."

It was as Vitricus had said; the solemn feast-days of Astarte were in course of celebration; of Astarte, the well-known divinity of Carthage and its dependent cities, whom Heliogabalus had lately introduced to Rome, who in her different aspects was at once Urania, Juno, and Aphrodite, according as she embodied the idea of the philosopher, the statesman, or the vulgar; lofty and intellectual as Urania, majestic and commanding as Juno, seductive as the goddess of sensuality and excess.

"There goes the son of as good and frank a soldier as ever brandished pilum[7]," said Vitricus to himself, "till in his last years some infernal god took umbrage at him, and saddled him and his with one of those absurd superstitions which are as plentiful here as serpents. He indeed was too old himself to get much harm from it; but it shows its sour nature in these young shoots. A good servant, but the plague's in his bones, and he will rot."

His subordinate's reflections were of a different character: "The very air breathes sin to-day," he cried; "oh that I did not find the taint of the city in these works of God! Alas! sweet Nature, the child of the Almighty, is made to do the fiend's work, and does it better than the town. O ye beautiful trees and fair flowers, O bright sun and balmy air, what a bondage ye are in, and

---

7    "javelin"

how do ye groan till you are redeemed from it! Ye are bond-slaves, but not willingly, as man is; but how will you ever be turned to nobler purpose? How is this vast, this solid establishment of error, the incubus of many thousand years, ever to have an end? You yourselves, dear ones, will come to nought first. Anyhow, the public way is no place for me this evening. They'll soon be back from their accursed revelry."

A sound of horns and voices had been heard from time to time through the woods, as if proceeding from parties dispersed through them; and in the growing twilight might be seen lights, glancing and wandering through the foliage. The cottage in which Agellius dwelt was on the other side of the hollow bridle-way which crossed the hill. To make for home he had first to walk some little distance along it; and scarcely had he descended into it for that purpose, when he found himself in the front of a band of revellers, who were returning from some scene of impious festivity. They were arrayed in holiday guise, as far as they studied dress at all; the symbols of idolatry were on their foreheads and arms; some of them were intoxicated, and most of them were women.

"Why have you not been worshipping, young fellow?" said one.

"Comely built," said another, "but struck by the furies. I know the cut of him."

"By Astarte," said a third, "he's one of those sly Gnostics! I have seen the chap before, with his hangdog look. He is one of Pluto's whelps, first cousin to Cerberus, and his name's Channibal."

On which they all began to shout out, "I say, Channibal, Channibal, here's a lad that knows you. Old fellow, come along with us;" and the speaker made a dash at him.

On this Agellius, who was slowly making his way past them on the broken and steep path, leapt up in two or three steps to the ridge, and went away in security; when one woman cried out, "O the toad, I know him now; he is a wizard; he eats little children; didn't you see him make that sign? it's a charm. My sister did it; the fool left me to be one of them. She was ever doing so" (mimicking the sign of the cross). "He's a Christian, blight him! he'll turn us into beasts."

"Cerberus, bite him!" said another, "he sucks blood;" and taking up a stone, she made it whiz past his ear as he disappeared from view. A general scream of contempt and hatred followed. "Where's the ass's head? put out the lights, put out the lights! gibbet him! that's why he has not been with honest people down in the vale." And then they struck up a blasphemous song, the sentiments of which we are not going even to conceive, much less to attempt in words.

# Chapter Two

# CHRISTIANITY IN SICCA

THE REVELLERS WENT ON THEIR WAY; Agellius went on his, and made for his lowly and lonely cottage. He was the elder of the two sons of a Roman legionary of the Secunda Italica,[8] who had settled with them in Sicca, where he lost their mother, and died, having in his old age become a Christian. The fortitude of some confessors at Carthage in the persecution of Severus had been the initial cause of his conversion. He had been posted as one of their guards, and had attended them to the scene of their martyrdom, in addition to the civil force, to whom in the proconsulate the administration of the law was committed. Therefore, happily for him, it could not fall to his duty to be their executioner, a function which, however revolting to his feelings, he might not have had courage to decline. He remained a pagan, though he could not shake off the impression which the martyrs had made upon him; and, after completing his time of service, he retired to the protection of some great friends in Sicca, his brother's home already. Here he took a second wife of the old Numidian stock, and supported himself by the produce of a small piece of land which had been given to him for life by the imperial government. If trial were necessary in order to keep alive the good seed which had been sown in his heart, he found a never-failing supply of that article in the companion of his declining years. In the hey-day of her youth she might have been fitted to throw a sort of sunshine, or rather torchlight, on a military carouse; but now, when poor Strabo, a man well to do in the world, looking for peace, had fallen under her arts, he found he had surrendered his freedom to a malignant, profligate woman, whose passions made her better company for evil spirits than for an invalided soldier. Indeed, as time went on, the popular belief, which she rather encouraged, went to the extent that she actually did hold an intercourse with the unseen world; and certainly she matured in a hatred towards God and man, which would naturally follow, and not unnaturally betoken, such intercourse. The more, then, she inflicted on him her proficiency in these amiable characteristics, the more he looked out for some consolation elsewhere; and the more she involved herself in the guilt or the repute of unlawful arts, the more was he drawn to that religion, where alone to commune with the invisible is to hold intercourse with heaven, not with hell. Whether so great a trial supplied a more human inducement for looking towards Christianity, it is impossible to say. Most men, certainly Roman soldiers, may be considered to act on mixed motives; but so it was in fact, that, on his becoming in his last years a Christian, he found, perhaps discovered, to his great satisfaction, that the Church did not oblige him to continue or renew a tie which bound him to so much misery, and that he might end his days in a tranquillity which his past life required, and his wife's presence would have precluded. He made a good end; he had been allowed to take the blessed sacrament from the altar to his own home on the last time he had been able to attend a *synaxis*[9] of the faithful, and thus had communicated at least six months within his decease; and the priest who anointed him at the beginning of his last illness also took his confession. He died, begging forgiveness of all whom he had injured, and giving large alms to the poor. This was about the year 236, in the midst of that long peace of the Church, which was broken at length by the Decian persecution.

---

9    Greek: a liturgical assembly

This peace of well-nigh fifty years had necessarily a peculiar, and not a happy effect upon the Christians of the proconsulate. They multiplied in the greater and the maritime cities, and made their way into positions of importance, whether in trade or the governmental departments; they extended their family connections, and were on good terms with the heathen. Whatever jealousy might be still cherished against the Christian name, nevertheless, individual Christians were treated with civility, and recognised as citizens; though among the populace there would be occasions, at the time of the more solemn pagan feasts, when accidental outbursts might be expected of the antipathy latent in the community, as we have been recording in the foregoing chapter. Men of sense, however, began to understand them better, and to be more just to the reasonableness of their faith. This would lead them to scorn Christianity less, but it would lead them to fear it more. It was no longer a matter merely for the populace to insult, but for government deliberately to put down. The prevailing and still growing unbelief among the lower classes of the population did but make a religion more formidable, which, as heathen statesmen felt, was able to wield the weapons of enthusiasm and zeal with a force and success unknown even to the most fortunate impostors among the Oriental or Egyptian hierophants. The philosophical schools were impressed with similar apprehensions, and had now for fifty years been employed in creating and systematising a new intellectual basis for the received paganism.

But, while the signs of the times led to the anticipation that a struggle was impending between the heads of the state religion and of the new worship which was taking its place, the great body of Christians, laymen and ecclesiastics, were on better and better terms, individually, with the members of society, or what is now called the public; and without losing their faith or those embers of charity which favourable circumstances would promptly rekindle, were, it must be confessed, in a state of considerable relaxation; they often were on the brink of deplorable sins, and sometimes fell over the brink. And many would join the Church on inferior motives as soon as no great temporal disadvantage attached to the act; or the families of Christian parents might grow up with so little of moral or religious education as to make it difficult to say why they called themselves members of a divine religion. Mixed marriages would increase both the scandal and the confusion.

"A long repose," says St. Cyprian, speaking of this very period, "had corrupted the discipline which had come down to us. Every one was applying himself to the increase of wealth; and, forgetting both the conduct of the faithful under the Apostles, and what ought to be their conduct in every age, with insatiable eagerness for gain devoted himself to the multiplying of possessions. The priests were wanting in religious devotedness, the ministers in entireness of faith; there was no mercy in works, no discipline in manners. Men wore their beards disfigured, and woman dyed their faces. Their eyes were changed from what God made them, and a lying colour was passed upon the hair. The hearts of the simple were misled by treacherous artifices, and brethren became entangled in seductive snares. Ties of marriage were formed with unbelievers; members of Christ abandoned to the heathen. Not only rash swearing was heard, but even false; persons in high place were swollen with contemptuousness; poisoned reproaches fell from their mouths, and men were sundered by unabating quarrels. Numerous bishops, who ought to be an encouragement and example to others, despising their sacred calling, engaged themselves in secular vocations, relinquished their sees, deserted their people, strayed among foreign provinces, hunted the markets for mercantile profits, and tried to amass large sums of money, while they had brethren starving within the Church; took possession of estates by fraudulent proceedings, and multiplied their gains by accumulated usuries."[10]

The relaxation which would extend the profession of Christianity in the larger cities would contract or extinguish it in remote or country places. There would be little zeal to keep up Churches, which could not be served without an effort or without secular loss. Carthage, Utica, Hippo, Milevis, or Curubis, was a more attractive residence than the towns with uncouth Afri-

---

10    [*Vide* Oxford transl. of St. Cyprian.]

can names, which amaze the ecclesiastical student in the Acts of the Coun-
cils. Vocations became scarce; sees remained vacant; congregations died out.
This was pretty much the case with the Church and see of Sicca. At the time
of which we write, history preserves no record of any bishop as exercising
his pastoral functions in that city. In matter of fact there was none. The last
bishop, an amiable old man, had in the course of years acquired a considerable extent of arable land, and employed himself principally, for lack of more
spiritual occupation, in reaping, stacking, selling, and sending off his wheat
for the Roman market. His deacon had been celebrated in early youth for his
boldness in the chase, and took part in the capture of lions and panthers (an
act of charity towards the peasants round Sicca) for the Roman amphitheatre. No priests were to be found, and the bishop became *parochus*[11] till his
death. Afterwards infants and catechumens lost baptism; parents lost faith,
or at least love; wanderers lost repentance and conversion. For a while there
was a flourishing meeting-house of Tertullianists, who had scared more
humble minds by pronouncing the eternal perdition of every Catholic; there
had also been various descriptions of Gnostics, who had carried off the clever youths and restless speculators; and then there had been the lapse of time,
gradually consuming the generation which had survived the flourishing old
days of the African Church. And the result was, that in the year 250 it was
difficult to say of whom the Church of Sicca consisted. There was no bishop,
no priest, no deacon. There was the old *mansionarius* or sacristan; there were
two or three pious women, married or single, who owed their religion to
good mothers; there were some slaves who kept to their faith, no one knew
how or why; there were a vast many persons who ought to be Catholics, but
were heretics, or nothing at all, or all but pagans, and sure to become pagans
on the asking; there were Agellius and his brother Juba, and how far these
two had a claim to the Christian name we now proceed to explain.

They were about the ages of seven and eight when their father died,
and they fell under the guardianship of their uncle, whose residence at Sicca

---

11    "parish priest"

had been one of the reasons which determined Strabo to settle there. This man, being possessed of some capital, drove a thriving trade in idols, large and small, amulets, and the like instruments of the established superstition. His father had come to Carthage in the service of one of the assessors of the proconsul of the day; and his son, finding competition ran too high to give him prospect of remuneration in the metropolis, had opened his statue-shop in Sicca. Those modern arts which enable an English town in this day to be so fertile in the production of ware of this description for the markets of the pagan East, were then unknown; and Jucundus depended on certain artists whom he imported, especially on two Greeks, brother and sister, who came from some isle on the Asian coast, for the supply of his trade. He was a good-natured man, self-indulgent, positive, and warmly attached to the reigning paganism, both as being the law of the land and the vital principle of the state; and, while he was really kind to his orphan nephews, he simply abominated, as in duty bound, the idiotic cant and impudent fee-fa-fum, to which, in his infallible judgment, poor old Strabo had betrayed his children. He would have restored them, you may be quite sure, to their country and to their country's gods, had they acquiesced in the restoration: but in different ways these little chaps, and he shook his head as he said it, were difficult to deal with. Agellius had a very positive opinion of his own on the matter; and as for Juba, though he had no opinion at all, yet he had an equally positive aversion to have thrust on him by another any opinion at all, even in favour of paganism. He had remained in his catechumen state since he grew up, because he found himself in it; and though nothing would make him go forward in his profession of Christianity, no earthly power would be able to make him go back. So there he was, like a mule, struck fast in the door of the Church, and feeling a gratification in his independence of mind. However, whatever his profession might be, still, as time went on, he plainly took after his step-mother, renewed his intercourse with her after his father's death, and at length went so far as to avow that he believed in nothing but the devil, if even he believed in him. It was scarcely safe, however, to affirm that the senses of this hopeful lad were his own.

Agellius, on the other hand, when a boy of six years old, had insisted on receiving baptism; had perplexed his father by a manifestation of zeal to which the old man was a stranger; and had made the good bishop lose the corn-fleet which was starting for Italy from his importunity to learn the Catechism. Baptized he was, confirmed, communicated; but a boy's nature is variable, and by the time Agellius had reached adolescence, the gracious impulses of his childhood had in some measure faded away, though he still retained his faith in its first keenness and vigour. But he had no one to keep him up to his duty; no exhortations, no example, no sympathy. His father's friends had taken him up so far as this, that by an extraordinary favour they had got him a lease for some years of the property which Strabo, a veteran soldier, had held of the imperial government. The care of this small property fell upon him, and another and more serious charge was added to it. The long prosperity of the province had increased the opulence and enlarged the upper class of Sicca. Officials, contractors, and servants of the government had made fortunes, and raised villas in the neighbourhood of the city. Natives of the place, returning from Rome, or from provincial service elsewhere, had invested their gains in long leases of state lands, or of the farms belonging to the imperial *res privata* or privy purse, and had become virtual proprietors of the rich fields or beautiful gardens in which they had played as children. One of such persons, who had had a place in the *officium*[12] of the quæstor, or rather procurator, as he began to be called, was the employer of Agellius. His property adjoined the cottage of the latter; and, having first employed the youth from recollection of his father, he confided to him the place of under-bailiff from the talents he showed for farm-business.

Such was his position at the early age of twenty-two; but honourable as it was in itself, and from the mode in which it was obtained, no one would consider it adapted, under the circumstances, to counteract the religious languor and coldness which had grown upon him. And in truth he did not know where he stood further than that he was firm in faith, as we have said, and

---

12   "public office"

had shrunk from a boy upwards, from the vice and immorality which was the very atmosphere of Sicca. He might any day be betrayed into some fatal inconsistency, which would either lead him into sin, or oblige him abruptly to retrace his steps, and find a truer and safer position. He was not generally known to be a Christian, at least for certain, though he was seen to keep clear of the established religion. It was not that he hid, so much as that the world did not care to know, what he believed. In that day there were many rites and worships which kept to themselves—many forms of moroseness or misanthropy, as they were considered, which withdrew their votaries from the public ceremonial. The Catholic faith seemed to the multitude to be one of these; it was only in critical times, when some idolatrous act was insisted on by the magistrate, that the specific nature of Christianity was tested and detected. Then at length it was seen to differ from all other religious varieties by that irrational and disgusting obstinacy, as it was felt to be, which had rather suffer torments and lose life than submit to some graceful, or touching, or at least trifling observance which the tradition of ages had sanctioned.

# Chapter Three

# AGELLIUS IN HIS COTTAGE

T HE COTTAGE FOR WHICH Agellius was making, when last we had sight of him, was a small brick house consisting of one room, with a loft over it, and a kitchen on the side, not very unlike that holy habitation which once contained the Eternal Word in human form with His Virgin Mother, and Joseph, their guardian. It was situated on the declivity of the hill, and, unlike the gardens of Italy, the space before it was ornamented with a plot of turf. A noble palm on one side, in spite of its distance from the water, and a group of orange-trees on the other, formed a foreground to the rich landscape which was described in our opening chapter. The borders and beds were gay with the lily, the bacchar, amber-coloured and purple, the golden abrotomus, the red chelidonium, and the variegated iris. Against the wall of the house were trained pomegranates, with their crimson blossoms, the star-like pothos or jessamine, and the symbolical passionflower, which well became a Christian dwelling.

And it was an intimation of what would be found within; for on one side of the room was rudely painted a red cross, with doves about it, as is found in early Christian shrines to this day. So long had been the peace of the Church, that the tradition of persecution seemed to have been lost; and Christians allowed themselves in the profession of their faith at home, cautious as they might be in public places; as freely as now in England, where we do not scruple to raise crucifixes within our churches and houses, though we shrink from doing so within sight of the hundred cabs and omnibuses which rattle past them. Under the cross were two or three pictures, or rather sketches. In the centre stood the Blessed Virgin with hands spread out in prayer, attended by the holy Apostles Peter and Paul on her right and left. Under this representation was rudely scratched upon the wall the word, "Advocata,"[13] a title which the earliest antiquity bestows upon her. On a small shelf was placed a case with two or three rolls or sheets of parchment in it. The appearance of them spoke of use indeed, but of reverential treatment. These were the Psalms, the Gospel according to St. Luke, and St. Paul's Epistle to the Romans, in the old Latin version, The Gospel was handsomely covered, and ornamented with gold.

The apartment was otherwise furnished with such implements and materials as might be expected in the cottage of a countryman: one or two stools and benches for sitting, a table, and in one corner a heap of dried leaves and rushes, with a large crimson coverlet, for rest at night. Elsewhere were two millstones fixed in a frame, with a handle attached to the rim of one of them, for grinding corn. Then again, garden tools; boxes of seeds; a vessel containing syrup for assuaging the sting of the scorpion; the *asir-rese* or *anagallis*, a potent medicine of the class of poisons, which was taken in wine for the same mischance. It hung from the beams, with a large bunch of *atsirtiphua*, a sort of camomile, smaller in the flower and more fragrant than our own, which was used as a febrifuge. Thence, too, hung a plentiful gathering of dried grapes, of the kind called *duracinæ*; and near the door a bough of the green *bargut* or *psyllium*, to drive away the smaller insects.

Poor Agellius felt the contrast between the ungodly turmoil from which he had escaped, and the deep stillness into which he now had entered; but neither satisfied him quite. There was no repose out of doors, and no relief within. He was lonely at home, lonely in the crowd. He needed the sympathy of his kind; hearts which might beat with his heart; friends with whom he

---

13 "Advocate"

might share his joys and griefs; advisers whom he might consult; minds like
his own, who would understand him—minds unlike his own, who would
succour and respond to him. A very great trial certainly this, in which the
soul is flung back upon itself; and that especially in the case of the young, for
whom memory and experience do so little, and wayward and excited feelings
do so much. Great gain had it been for Agellius, even in its natural effect,
putting aside higher benefits, to have been able to recur to sacramental confession; but to confession he had never been, though once or twice he had
attended the public *homologesis*[14] of the Church. Shall we wonder that the
poor youth began to be despondent and impatient under his trial? Shall we
not feel for him, though we may be sorry for him, should it turn out that he
was looking restlessly into every corner of the small world of acquaintance
in which his lot lay, for those with whom he could converse easily, and interchange speculation, argument, aspiration, and affection?

"No one cares for me," he said, as he sat down on his rustic bench. "I
am nothing to any one; I am a hermit, like Elias or John, without the call to
be one. Yet even Elias felt the burden of being one against many; even John
asked at length in expostulation, 'Art Thou He that shall come?' Am I for
ever to have the knowledge, without the consolation, of the truth? am I for
ever to belong to a great divine society, yet never see the face of any of its
members?"

He paused in his thoughts, as if drinking in the full taste and measure of
his unhappiness. And then his reflections took a turn, and he said, suddenly,
"Why do I not leave Sicca? What binds me to my father's farm? I am young,
and my interest in it will soon expire. What keeps me from Carthage, Hippo,
Cirtha, where Christians are so many?" But here he stopped as suddenly as
he had begun; and a strange feeling, half pang, half thrill, went through his
heart. And he felt unwilling to pursue his thought, or to answer the question
which he had asked; and he settled into a dull, stagnant condition of mind,
in which he seemed hardly to think at all.

---

14   "confession"

Be of good cheer, solitary one, though thou art not a hero yet! There is One that cares for thee, and loves thee, more than thou canst feel, love, or care for thyself. Cast all thy care upon Him. He sees thee, and is watching thee; He is hanging over thee, and smiles in compassion at thy troubles. His angel, who is thine, is whispering good thoughts to thee. He knows thy weakness; He foresees thy errors; but He holds thee by thy right hand, and thou shalt not, canst not escape Him. By thy faith, which thou hast so simply, resolutely retained in the midst of idolatry; by thy purity, which, like some fair flower, thou hast cherished in the midst of pollution, He will remember thee in thy evil hour, and thine enemy shall not prevail against thee!

What means that smile upon Agellius's face? It is the response of the child to the loving parent. He knows not why, but the cloud is past. He signs himself with the holy cross, and sweet reviving thoughts enliven him. He names the sacred Name, and it is like ointment poured out upon his soul. He rises; he kneels down under the dread symbol of his salvation; and he begins his evening prayer.

# Chapter Four

# JUBA

THERE WAS MORE OF HEART, less of effort, less of mechanical habit, in Agellius's prayers that night, than there had been for a long while before. He got up, struck a light, and communicated it to his small earthen lamp. Its pale rays feebly searched the room and discovered at the other end of it Juba, who had silently opened the door, and sat down near it, while his brother was employed upon his devotions. The countenance of the latter fell, for he was not to go to sleep with the resignation and peace which had just before been poured into his breast. Yet why should he complain? we receive consolation in this world for the very purpose of preparing us against trouble to come. Juba was a tall, swarthy, wild-looking youth. He was holding his head on one side as he sat, and his face towards the roof; he nodded obliquely, arched his eyebrows, pursed up his lips, and crossed his arms, while he gave utterance to a strange, half-whispered laugh.

"He, he, he!" he cried; "so you are on your knees, Agellius."

"Why shouldn't I be at this hour," answered Agellius, "and before I go to bed?"

"O, every one to his taste, of course," said Juba; "but to an unprejudiced mind there is something unworthy in the act."

"Why, Juba?" said his brother somewhat sharply; "don't you profess any religion at all?"

"Perhaps I do, and perhaps I don't," answered Juba; "but never shall it be a bowing and scraping, crawling and cringing religion. You may take your oath of that."

"What ails you to come here at this time of night?" asked Agellius; "who asked for your company?"

"I will come just when I please," said the other, "and go when I please. I won't give an account of my actions to any one, God or man, devil or priest, much less to you. What right have you to ask me?"

"Then," said Agellius, "you'll never get peace or comfort as long as you live, that I can tell you, let alone the life to come."

Juba kept silent for awhile, and bit his nails with a smile on his face, and his eyes looking askance upon the ground. "I want no more than I have; I am well content," he said.

"Contented with yourself," retorted Agellius.

"Of course," Juba replied; "whom ought one to wish rather to content?"

"I suppose, your Creator."

"Creator," answered Juba, tossing back his head with an air of superiority; "Creator;—that, I consider, is an assumption."

"O, my dear brother," cried Agellius, "don't go on in that dreadful way!"

"'Go on!' who began? Is one man to lay down the law, and not the other too? Is it so generally received, this belief of a Creator? Who have brought in the belief? The Christians. 'Tis the Christians that began it. The world went on very well without it before their rise. And now, who began the dispute but you?"

"Well, if I did," answered Agellius; "but I didn't. You began in coming here; what in the world are you come for? by what right do you disturb me at this hour?"

There was no appearance of anger in Juba; he seemed as free from feeling of every kind, from what is called *heart*, as if he had been a stone. In answer to his brother's question, he quietly said, "I have been down there," pointing in the direction of the woods.

An expression of sharp anguish passed over his brother's face, and for a moment he was silent. At length he said, "You don't mean to say you have been down to poor mother?"

"I do," said Juba.

There was again a silence for a little while; then Agellius renewed the conversation. "You have fallen off sadly, Juba, in the course of the last several years."

Juba tossed his head, and crossed his legs.

"At one time I thought you would have been baptized," his brother continued.

"That was my weakness," answered Juba; "it was a weak moment: it was just after the old bishop's death. He had been kind to me as a child; and he said some womanish words to me, and it was excusable in me."

"Oh that you had yielded to your wish!" cried Agellius.

Juba looked superior. "The fit passed," he said. "I have come to a juster view of things. It is not every one who has the strength of mind. I consider that a logical head comes to a very different conclusion;" and he began wagging his own, to the right and left, as if it were coming to a great many.

"Well," said Agellius, gaping, and desiring at least to come to a conclusion of the altercation, "what brings you here so late?"

"I was on my way to Jucundus," he answered, "and have been delayed by the Succoth-benoth[15] in the grove across the river."

Here they were thrown back upon their controversy. Agellius turned quite white. "My poor fellow," he said, "what were you there for?"

"To see the world," answered Juba; "it's unmanly not to see it. Why shouldn't I see it? It was good fun. I despise them all, fools and idiots. There they were, scampering about, or lying like hogs, all in liquor. Apes and swine! However, I will do as others do, if I please. I will be as drunk as they, when I see good. I am my own master, and it would be no kind of harm."

"No harm! why, is it no harm to become an ape or a hog?"

---

15    Hebrew: "Booths of the Daughters," a Babylonian idol

"You don't take just views of human nature," answered Juba, with a self-satisfied air. "Our first duty is to seek our own happiness. If a man thinks it happier to be a hog, why, let him be a hog," and he laughed. "This is where you are narrow-minded. I shall seek my own happiness, and try this way, if I please."

"Happiness!" cried Agellius; "where have you been picking up all this stuff? Can you call such detestable filth happiness?"

"What do you know about such matters?" asked Juba. "Did you ever see them? Did you ever try them? You would be twice the man you are if you had. You will not be a man till you do. You are carried off your legs in your own way. I'd rather get drunk every day than fall down on all fours as you do, crawling on your stomach like a worm, and whining like a hound that has been beaten."

"Now, as I live, you shan't stop here one instant longer!" cried out Agellius, starting up. "Be off with you! get away! what do you come here to blaspheme for? who wants you? who asked for you? Go! go, I say! take yourself off! Why don't you go? Keep your ribaldry for others."

"I am as good as you any day," said Juba.

"I don't set myself up," answered Agellius, "but it's impossible to confound Christian and unbeliever as you do."

"Christian and unbeliever!" said Juba, slowly. "I suppose, when they are a-courting each other, they *are* confounded." He looked hard at Agellius, as if he thought he had hit a blot. Then he continued, "If I *were* a Christian, I'd be so in earnest: else I'd be an honest heathen."

Agellius coloured somewhat, and sat down, as if under embarrassment.

"I despise you," said Juba; "you have not the pluck to be a Christian. Be consistent, and fizz upon a stake; but you're not made of that stuff. You're even afraid of uncle. Nay, you can be caught by those painted wares, about which, when it suits your purpose, you can be so grave. I despise you," he continued, "I despise you, and the whole kit of you. What's the difference between you and another? Your people say, 'Earth's a vanity, life's a dream, riches a deceit, pleasure a snare. Fratres charissimi,[16] the time is short;' but who love earth and life and riches and pleasure better than they? You are all of you as fond of the world, as set upon gain, as chary of reputation, as ambitious of power, as the jolly old heathen, who, you say, is going the way of the pit."

"It is one thing to have a conscience," answered Agellius; "another thing to act upon it. The conscience of these poor people is darkened. You had a conscience once."

"Conscience, conscience," said Juba. "Yes, certainly, once I had a conscience. Yes, and once I had a bad chill, and went about chattering and shivering; and once I had a game leg, and then I went limping; and so, you see, I once on a time had a conscience. O yes, I have had many consciences before now—white, black, yellow, and green; they were all bad; but they are all gone, and now I have none."

Agellius said nothing; his one wish, as may be supposed, was to get rid of so unwelcome a visitor.

"The truth is," continued Juba, with the air of a teacher—"the truth is, that religion was a fashion with me, which is now gone by. It was the complexion of a particular stage of my life. I was neither the better nor the worse for it. It was an accident, like the bloom on my face, which soon," he said, spreading his fingers over his dirty-coloured cheeks, and stroking them, "which soon will disappear. I acted according to the feeling, while it lasted; but I can no more recall it than my first teeth, or the down on my chin. It's among the things that were."

Agellius still keeping silence from weariness and disgust, he looked at him in a significant way, and said, slowly, "I see how it is; I have penetration enough to perceive that you don't believe a bit more about religion than I do."

"You must not say that under my roof," cried Agellius, feeling he must not let his brother's charge pass without a protest. "Many are my sins, but unbelief is not one of them."

---

16   "Dearest brothers"

Juba tossed his head. "I think I can see through a stone slab as well as any one," he said. "It is as I have said; but you're too proud to confess it. It's part of your hypocrisy."

"Well," said Agellius coldly, "let's have done. It's getting late, Juba; you'll be missed at home. Jucundus will be inquiring for you, and some of those revelling friends of yours may do you a mischief by the way. Why, my good fellow," he continued, in surprise, "you have no leggings. The scorpions will catch hold of you to a certainty in the dark. Come, let me tie some straw wisps about you."

"No fear of scorpions for me," answered Juba; "I have some real good amulets for the occasion, which even *boola-kog* and *uffah* will respect."

Saying this, he passed out of the room as unceremoniously as he had entered it, and took the direction of the city, talking to himself, and singing snatches of wild airs as he went along, throwing back and shaking his head, and now and then uttering a sharp internal laugh. Disdaining to follow the ordinary path, he dived down into the thick and wet grass, and scrambled through the ravine, which the public road crossed before it ascended the hill. Meanwhile he accompanied his quickened pace with a louder strain, and it ran as follows:—

> "The little black Moor is the mate for me,
> When the night is dark, and the earth is free,
> Under the limbs of the broad yew-tree.
>
> "'Twas Father Cham that planted that yew,
> And he fed it fat with the bloody dew
> Of a score of brats, as his lineage grew.
>
> "Footing and flaunting it, all in the night,
> Each lock flings fire, each heel strikes light;
> No lamps need they, whose breath is bright."

Here he was interrupted by a sudden growl, which sounded almost under his feet, and some wild animal was seen to slink away. Juba showed no surprise; he had taken out a small metal idol, and whispering some words to it, had presented it to the animal. He clambered up the bank, gained the city gate, and made his way for his uncle's dwelling, which was near the temple of Astarte.

# Chapter Five

# JUCUNDUS AT SUPPER

THE HOUSE OF JUCUNDUS was closed for the night when Juba reached it, or you would see, were you his companion, that it was one of the most showy shops in Sicca. It was the image-store of the place, and set out for sale, not articles of statuary alone, but of metal, of mosaic work, and of jewellery, as far as they were dedicated to the service of paganism. It was bright with the many colours adopted in the embellishment of images, and the many lights which silver and gold, brass and ivory, alabaster, gypsum, talc, and glass reflected. Shelves and cabinets were laden with wares; both the precious material, and the elaborated trinket. All tastes were suited, the popular and the refined, the fashion of the day and the love of the antique, the classical and the barbarian devotion. There you might see the rude symbols of invisible powers, which, originating in deficiency of art, had been perpetuated by reverence for the past: the mysterious cube of marble sacred among the Arabs, the pillar which was the emblem of Mercury or Bacchus, the broad-based cone of Heliogabalus, the pyramid of Paphos, and the tile or brick of Juno.

There, too, were the unmeaning blocks of stone with human heads, which were to be dressed out in rich robes, and to simulate the human form. There were other articles besides, as portable as these were unmanageable: little Junos, Mercuries, Dianas, and Fortunas, for the bosom or the girdle. Household gods were there, and the objects of personal devotion: Minerva or Vesta, with handsome niches or shrines in which they might reside. There, too, were the brass crowns, or *nimbi* which were intended to protect the heads of the gods from bats and birds. There you might buy, were you a heathen, rings with heads on them of Jupiter, Mars, the Sun, Serapis, and above all Astarte. You would find there the rings and signets of the Basilidians; amulets too of wood or ivory: figures of demons, preternaturally ugly; little skeletons, and other superstitious devices. It would be hard, indeed, if you could not be pleased, whatever your religious denomination—unless indeed you were determined to reject all the appliances and objects of idolatry indiscriminately—and in that case you would rejoice that it was night when you arrived there, and, in particular, that darkness swallowed up other appliances and objects of pagan worship, which to darkness were due by a particular title, and by darkness were best shrouded, till the coming of that day when all things, good and evil, shall be made light.

The shop, as we have said, was closed, concealed from view by large lumbering shutters, and made secure by heavy bars of wood. So we must enter by the passage or vestibule on the right side, and that will conduct us into a modest *atrium*,[17] with an *impluvium*[18] on one side, and on the other the *triclinium* or supper-room, backing the shop. Jucundus had been pleasantly engaged in a small supper-party; and, mindful that a *symposium*[19] should lie within the number of the Graces and of the Muses, he had confined his guests to two, the young Greek Aristo, who was one of his principal artists, and Cornelius the son of a freedman of a Roman of distinction, who had lately got a place in one of the *scrinia*[20] of the proconsular *officium*,[21] and had migrated into the province from the imperial city where he had spent his best days.

The dinner had not been altogether suitable to modern ideas of good living. The grapes from Tacape, and the dates from the lake Tritonis, the white

---

17  "court"
18  "pool" in an atrium
19  "drinking party"
20  "cabinets"
21  "public office"

and black figs, the nectarines and peaches, and the watermelons, address themselves to the imagination of an Englishman, as well as of an African of the third century. So also might the liquor derived from the sap or honey of the Getulian palm, and the sweet wine, called *melilotus*, made from the poetical fruit found upon the coast of the Syrtis. He would have been struck, too, with the sweetness of the mutton; but he would have asked what the sheep's tails were before he tasted them, and found how like marrow the firm substance ate of which they consisted. He would have felt he ought to admire the roes of mullets, pressed and dried, from Mauritania; but he would have thought twice before he tried the lion cutlets though they had the flavour of veal, and the additional *goût*[22] of being imperial property, and poached from a preserve. But when he saw the indigenous dish, the very haggis and cock-a-leekie of Africa, in the shape of—(alas! alas! it *must* be said, with whatever apology for its introduction)—in shape, then, of a delicate puppy, served up with tomatoes, with its head between its fore-paws, we consider he would have risen from the unholy table, and thought he had fallen upon the hospitality of some sorceress of the neighbouring forest. However, to that festive board our Briton was not invited, for he had some previous engagement that evening, either of painting himself with woad, or of hiding himself to the chin in the fens; so that nothing occurred to disturb the harmony of the party, and the good humour and easy conversation which was the effect of such excellent cheer.

Cornelius had been present at the Secular Games in the foregoing year, and was full of them, of Rome, and of himself in connection with it, as became so genuine a cockney of the imperial period. He was full of the high patriotic thoughts which so solemn a celebration had kindled within him. "O great Rome!" he said, "thou art first, and there is no second. In that wonderful pageant which these eyes saw last year was embodied her majesty, was promised her eternity. We die, she lives. I say, *let* a man die. It's well for him to take hemlock, or open a vein, after having seen the Secular Games. What

---

22    French: "savour"

was there to live for? I felt it; life was gone; its best gifts flat and insipid after that great day. Excellent—Tauromenian, I suppose? We know it in Rome. Fill up my cup. I drink to the genius of the emperor."

He was full of his subject, and soon resumed it. "Fancy the Campus Martius lighted up from one end to the other. It was the finest thing in the world. A large plain, covered, not with streets, not with woods, but broken and crossed with superb buildings in the midst of groves, avenues of trees, and green grass, down to the water's edge. There's nothing that isn't there. Do you want the grandest temples in the world, the most spacious porticoes, the longest racecourses? there they are. Do you want *gymnasia?*[23] there they are. Do you want arches, statues, obelisks? you find them there. There you have at one end the stupendous mausoleum of Augustus, cased with white marble, and just across the river the huge towering mound of Hadrian. At the other end you have the noble Pantheon of Agrippa, with its splendid Syracusan columns, and its dome glittering with silver tiles. Hard by are the baths of Alexander, with their beautiful groves. Ah! my good friend! I shall have no time to drink if I go on. Beyond are the numerous chapels and fanes which fringe the base of the Capitoline hill; the tall column of Antoninus comes next, with its adjacent basilica, where is kept the authentic list of the provinces of the empire, and of the governors, each a king in power and dominion, who are sent out to them. Well, I am now only beginning. Fancy, I say, this magnificent region all lighted up; every temple to and fro, every bath, every grove, gleaming with innumerable lamps and torches. No, not even the gods of Olympus have anything that comes near it. Rome is the greatest of all divinities. In the dead of night all was alive; then it was, when nature sleeps exhausted, Rome began the solemn sacrifices to commemorate her thousand years. On the banks of the Tiber, which had seen Æneas land, and Romulus ascend to the gods, the clear red flame shot up as the victims burned. The music of ten thousand horns and flutes burst forth, and the sacred dances began upon the greensward. I am too old to dance; but, I protest, even I

---

23  "schools"

stood up and threw off. We danced through three nights, dancing the old millenary out, dancing the new millenary in. We were all Romans, no strangers, no slaves. It was a solemn family feast, the feast of all the Romans."

"Then we came in for the feast," said Aristo; "for Caracalla gave Roman citizenship to all freemen all over the world. We are all of us Romans, recollect, Cornelius."

"Ah! that was another matter—a condescension," answered Cornelius. "Yes, in a certain sense, I grant it; but it was a political act."

"I warrant you," retorted Aristo, "most political. We were to be fleeced, do you see? so your imperial government made us Romans, that we might have the taxes of Romans, and that in addition to our own. You've taxed us double; and as for the privilege of citizenship, much it is, by Hercules, when every snob has it who can wear a *pileus*[24] or cherish his hair."

"Ah! but you should have seen the procession from the Capitol," continued Cornelius, "on, I think, the second day; from the Capitol to the Circus, all down the Via Sacra. Hosts of strangers there, and provincials from the four corners of the earth, but not in the procession. There you saw, all in one *coup-d'œil*,[25] the real good blood of Rome, the young blood of the new generation, and promise of the future; the sons of patrician and consular families, of imperators, orators, conquerors, statesmen. They rode at the head of the procession, fine young fellows, six abreast; and still more of them on foot. Then came the running horses and the chariots, the boxers, the wrestlers, and other combatants, all ready for the competition. The whole school of gladiators then turned out, boys and all, with their masters, dressed in red tunics, and splendidly armed. They formed three bands, and they went forward gaily, dancing and singing the Pyrrhic. By-the-bye, a thousand pair of gladiators fought during the games—a round thousand, and such clean-made, well-built fellows, and they came against each other so gallantly! You should have seen it; *I* can't go through it. There was a lot of satyrs, jumping and frisking, in burlesque of the martial dances which preceded them. There

---

24   "cap"
25   French: "glance" or "shot of the eyes"

was a crowd of trumpeters and horn-blowers; ministers of the sacrifices with their victims, bulls and rams, dressed up with gay wreaths; drivers, butchers, haruspices, heralds; images of gods with their cars of ivory or silver, drawn by tame lions and elephants. I can't recollect the order. O! but the grandest thing of all was the Carmen, sung by twenty-seven noble youths, and as many noble maidens, taken for the purpose from the bosoms of their families to propitiate the gods of Rome. The flamens, augurs, colleges of priests, it was endless. Last of all came the emperor himself."

"That's the late man," observed Jucundus, "Philip; no bad riddance his death, if all's true that's said of him."

"All emperors are good in their time and way," answered Cornelius; "Philip was good then, and Decius is good now;—whom the gods preserve!"

"True," said Aristo, "I understand; an emperor cannot do wrong, except in dying, and then everything goes wrong with him. His death is his first bad deed; he ought to be ashamed of it; it somehow turns all his great virtues into vices."

"Ah! no one was so good an emperor as our man, Gordianus," said Jucundus, "a princely old man, living and dead; patron of trade and of the arts; such villas! he had enormous revenues. Poor old gentleman! and his son too. I never shall forget the day when the news came that he was gone. Let me see, it was shortly after that old fool Strabo's death—I mean my brother; a good thirteen years ago. All Africa was in tears; there was no one like Gordianus."

"That's old world philosophy," said Aristo; "Jucundus, you must go to school. Don't you see that all that is, is right; and all that was, is wrong? 'Te nos facimus, Fortuna, deam,'[26] says your poet; well, I drink 'to the fortunes of Rome,'—while it lasts."

"You're a young man," answered Cornelius, "a very young man, and a Greek. Greeks never understand Rome. It's most difficult to understand us. It's a science. Look at this medal, young gentleman; it was one of those struck at the games. Is it not grand? 'Novum sæculum,'[27] and on the reverse, 'Æterni-

26    "It is we, oh Furtuna, who make you a goddess," Juvenal, *Satire X*, 366
27    "A New Age"

tati.'[28] Always changing, always imperishable. Emperors rise and fall; Rome remains. The eternal city! Isn't this good philosophy?"

"Truly, a most beautiful medal," said Aristo, examining it, and handing it on to his host. "You might make an amulet of it, Jucundus. But as to eternity, why, that is a very great word; and, if I mistake not, other states have been eternal before Rome. Ten centuries is a very respectable eternity; be content, Rome is eternal already, and may die without prejudice to the medal."

"Blaspheme not," replied Cornelius: "Rome is healthier, more full of life, and promises more, than at any former time, you may rely upon it. 'Novum sæculum!' she has the age of the eagle, and will but cast her feathers to begin a fresh thousand."

"But Egypt," interposed Aristo, "if old Herodotus speaks true, scarcely had a beginning. Up and up, the higher you go, the more dynasties of Egyptian kings do you find. And we hear strange reports of the nations in the far east, beyond the Ganges."

"But I tell you, man," rejoined Cornelius, "Rome is a city of kings. That one city, in this one year, has as many kings at once as those of all the kings of all the dynasties of Egypt put together. Sesostris, and the rest of them, what are they to imperators, prefects, proconsuls, *vicarii*,[29] and *rationales*[30]? Look back at Lucullus, Cæsar, Pompey, Sylla, Titus, Trajan. What's old Cheops' pyramid to the Flavian amphitheatre? What is the many-gated Thebes to Nero's golden house, while it was? What the grandest palace of Sesostris or Ptolemy but a second-rate villa of any one of ten thousand Roman citizens? Our houses stand on acres of ground, they ascend as high as the Tower of Babylon; they swarm with columns like a forest; they pullulate into statues and pictures. The walls, pavements, and ceilings are dazzling from the lustre of the rarest marble, red and yellow, green and mottled. Fountains of perfumed water shoot aloft from the floor, and fish swim in rocky channels round about the room, waiting to be caught and killed for the banquet. We

---

28   "For Eternity"
29   "under-servants"
30   "men of reason"

dine; and we feast on the head of the ostrich, the brains of the peacock, the liver of the bream, the milk of the murena, and the tongue of the flamingo. A flight of doves, nightingales, beccaficoes are concentrated into one dish. On great occasions we eat a phœnix. Our saucepans are of silver, our dishes of gold, our vases of onyx, and our cups of precious stones. Hangings and carpets of Tyrian purple are around us and beneath us, and we lie on ivory couches. The choicest wines of Greece and Italy crown our goblets, and exotic flowers crown our heads. In come troops of dancers from Lydia, or pantomimes from Alexandria, to entertain both eye and mind; or our noble dames and maidens take a place at our tables; they wash in asses' milk, they dress by mirrors as large as fish-ponds, and they glitter from head to foot with combs, brooches, necklaces, collars, ear-rings, armlets, bracelets, finger-rings, girdles, stomachers, and anklets, all of diamond and emerald. Our slaves may be counted by thousands, and they come from all parts of the world. Everything rare and precious is brought to Rome: the gum of Arabia, the nard of Assyria, the papyrus of Egypt, the citron-wood of Mauretania, the bronze of Ægina, the pearls of Britain, the cloth of gold of Phrygia, the fine webs of Cos, the embroidery of Babylon, the silks of Persia, the lionskins of Getulia, the wool of Miletus, the plaids of Gaul. Thus we live, an imperial people, who do nothing but enjoy themselves and keep festival the whole year; and at length we die—and then we burn: we burn—in stacks of cinnamon and cassia, and in shrouds of *asbestos*, making emphatically a good end of it. Such are we Romans, a great people. Why, we are honoured wherever we go. There's my master, there's myself; as we came here from Italy, I protest we were nearly worshipped as demi-gods."

"And perhaps some fine morning," said Aristo, "Rome herself will burn in cinnamon and cassia, and in all her burnished Corinthian brass and scarlet bravery, the old mother following her children to the funeral pyre. One has heard something of Babylon, and its drained moat, and the soldiers of the Persian."

A pause occurred in the conversation as one of Jucundus's slaves entered with fresh wine, larger goblets, and a vase of snow from the Atlas.

# Chapter Six

# GOTHS AND CHRISTIANS

ORNELIUS WAS FULL of his subject, and did not attend to the Greek. "The wild-beasts hunts," he continued, "ah, those hunts during the games, Aristo! they were a spectacle for the gods. Twenty-two elephants, ten panthers, ten hyænas (by-the-bye, a new beast, not strange, however, to you here, I suppose), ten camelopards, a hippopotamus, a rhinoceros—I can't go through the list. Fancy the circus planted throughout for the occasion, and turned into a park, and then another set of wild animals, Getes and Sarmatians, Celts and Goths, sent in against them, to hunt down, capture and kill them, or to be killed themselves."

"Ah, the Goths!" answered Aristo; "those fellows give you trouble, though, now and then. Perhaps they will give you more. There is a report in the prætorium to-day that they have crossed the Danube."

"Yes, they *will* give us trouble," said Cornelius, drily; "they *have* given us trouble, and they will give us more. The Samnites gave us trouble, and our friends of Carthage here, and Jugurtha, and Mithridates; trouble, yes, that is the long and the short of it; they will give us trouble. Is trouble a new thing to Rome?" he asked, stretching out his arm, as if he were making a speech after dinner, and giving a toast.

"The Goths give trouble, and take a bribe," retorted Aristo; "this is what trouble means in their case: it's a troublesome fellow who hammers at our

door till we pay his reckoning. It is troublesome to raise the means to buy
them off. And the example of these troublesome savages is catching; it was
lately rumoured that the Carpians had been asking the same terms for keeping quiet."

"It would ill become the majesty of Rome to soil her fingers with the
blood of such vermin," said Cornelius; "she ignores them."

"And therefore she most majestically bleeds us instead," answered Aristo,
"that she may have treasure to give them. We are not so troublesome as they;
the more's the pity. No offence to you, however, or to the emperor, or to
great Rome, Cornelius. We are over our cups; it's only a game of politics, you
know, like chess or the *cottabus*.[31] Maro bids you 'parcere subjectis, et debel-
lare superbos;'[32] but you have changed your manners. You coax the Goths
and bully the poor African."

"Africa can show fight, too," interposed Jucundus, who had been calmly
listening and enjoying his own wine; "witness Thysdrus. That was giving
every rapacious Quæstor a lesson that he may go too far, and find a dagger
when he demands a purse."

He was alluding to the revolt of Africa, which led to the downfall of the
tyrant Maximin and the exaltation of the Gordians, when the native land-
lords armed their peasantry, killed the imperial officer, and raised the standard of rebellion in the neighbouring town from impatience of exactions
under which they suffered.

"No offence, I say, Cornelius, no offence to eternal Rome," said Aristo, "but
you have explained to us why you weigh so heavy on us. I've always heard it
was a fortune at Rome for a man to have found out a new tax. Vespasian did
his best; but now you tax our smoke, and our very shadow; and Pescennius
threatened to tax the air we breathe. We'll play at riddles, and you shall solve
the following:—Say who is she that eats her own limbs, and grows eternal
upon them? Ah, the Goths will take the measure of her eternity!"

---

31    A Sicilain game in which reclining supper-guests attempt to toss the remains of
their wine into a bowl without spilling.
32    "to spare the humble and subdue the proud," Virgil, *Aeneid*, VI.853.

"The Goths!" said Jucundus, who was warming into conversational life, "the Goths! no fear of the Goths; but," and he nodded significantly, "look at home; we have more to fear indoors than abroad."

"He means the prætorians," said Cornelius to Aristo, condescendingly; "I grant you that there have been several untoward affairs; we have had our problem, but it's a thing of the past, it never can come again. I venture to say that the power of the prætorians is at an end. That murder of the two emperors the other day was the worst job they ever did; it has turned the public opinion of the whole world against them. I have no fear of the prætorians."

"I don't mean prætorians more than Goths," said Jucundus; "no, give me the old weapons, the old maxims of Rome, and I defy the scythe of Saturn. Do the soldiers march under the old ensign? do they swear by the old gods? do they interchange the good old signals and watchwords? do they worship the fortune of Rome; then I say we are safe. But do we take to new ways? do we trifle with religion? do we make light of Jupiter, Mars, Romulus, the augurs, and the ancilia[33]? then I say, not all our shows and games, our elephants, hyænas, and hippopotamuses, will do us any good. It was not the best thing, no, not the best thing that the soldiers did, when they invested that Philip with the purple. But he is dead and gone." And he sat up and leant on his elbow.

"Ah! but it will be all set right now," said Cornelius, "*you'll* see."

"He'd be a reformer, that Philip," continued Jucundus, "and put down an enormity. Well, they call it an enormity; let it be an enormity. He'd put it down; but why? there's the point; why? It's no secret at all," and his voice grew angry, "that that hoary-headed Atheist Fabian was at the bottom of it; Fabian, the Christian. I hate reforms."

"Well, we had long wished to do it," answered Cornelius, "but could not manage it. Alexander attempted it near twenty years ago. It's what philosophers have always aimed at."

"The gods consume philosophers and the Christians together!" said

---

33  "ancillary gods"

Jucundus devoutly. "There's little to choose between them, except that the Christians are the filthier animal of the two. But both are ruining the most glorious political structure that the world ever saw. I am not over-fond of Alexander either."

"Thank you in the name of philosophy," said the Greek.

"And thank you in the name of the Christians," chimed in Juba.

"That's good!" cried Jucundus; "the first word that hopeful youth has spoken since he came in, and he takes on him to call himself a Christian."

"I've a right to do so, if I choose," said Juba; "I've a right to be a Christian."

"Right! O yes, right! ha, ha!" answered Jucundus, "right! Jove help the lad! by all manner of means. Of course, you have a right to go *in malam rem*[34] in whatever way you please."

"I am my own master," said Juba; "my father was a Christian. I suppose it depends on myself to follow him or not, according to my fancy, and as long as I think fit."

"Fancy! think fit!" answered Jucundus, "you pompous little mule! Yes, go and be a Christian, my dear child, as your doting father went. Go, like him, to the priest of their mysteries; be spit on, stripped, dipped; feed on little boys' marrow and brains; worship the ass; and learn all the foul magic of the sect. And then be delated and taken up, and torn to shreds on the rack, or thrown to the lions and so go to Tartarus, if Tartarus there be, in the way you think fit. You'll harm none but yourself, my boy. I don't fear such as you, but the deeper heads."

Juba stood up with a look of offended dignity, and, as on former occasions, tossed the head which had been by implication disparaged. "I despise you," he said.

"Well, but you are hard on the Christians," said Aristo. "I have heard them maintain that their superstition, if adopted, would be the salvation of Rome. They maintain that the old religion is gone or going out; that some-

---

34    "to a bad place," in effect, "Go hang!"

thing new is wanted to keep the empire together; and that their worship is just fitted to the times."

"All I say to the vipers," said Jucundus, "is, 'Let well alone. We did well enough without you; we did well enough till you sprang up.' A plague on their insolence; as if Jew or Egyptian could do aught for us when Numa and the Sibyl fail. That is what I say, Let Rome be true to herself and nothing can harm her; let her shift her foundation, and I would not buy her for this water-melon," he said, taking a suck at it. "Rome alone can harm Rome. Recollect old Horace, 'Suis et ipsa Roma viribus ruit.'[35] He was a prophet. If she falls, it is by her own hand."

"I agree," said Cornelius; "certainly, to set up any new worship is treason; not a doubt of it. The gods keep us from such ingratitude! We have grown great by means of them, and they are part and parcel of the law of Rome. But there is no great chance of our forgetting this; Decius won't; that's a fact. You will see. Time will show; perhaps to-morrow, perhaps next day," he added, mysteriously.

"Why in the world should you have this frantic dread of these poor scarecrows of Christians," said Aristo, "all because they hold an opinion? Why are you not afraid of the bats and the moles? It's an opinion: there have been other opinions before them, and there will be other opinions after. Let them alone and they'll die away; make a hubbub about them and they'll spread."

"Spread?" cried Jucundus, who was under the twofold excitement of personal feeling and of wine, "spread, they'll spread? yes, they'll spread. Yes, grow, like scorpions, twenty at a birth. The country already swarms with them; they are as many as frogs or grasshoppers; they start up everywhere under one's nose, when one least expects them. The air breeds them like plague-flies; the wind drifts them like locusts. No one's safe; any one may be a Christian; it's an epidemic. Great Jove! I may be a Christian before I know where I am. Heaven and earth! is it not monstrous?" he continued, with increasing fierceness. "Yes, Jucundus, my poor man, you may wake and find

---

35   "Rome herself is destroyed by her own strength," Horace, *Epodes* XVI.2

yourself a Christian, without knowing it, against your will. Ah! my friends, pity me! I may find myself a beast, and obliged to suck blood and live among the tombs as if I liked it, without power to tell you how I loathe it, all through their sorcery. By the genius of Rome something must be done. I say, no one is safe. You call on your friend; he is sitting in the dark, unwashed, uncombed, undressed. What is the matter? Ah! his son has turned Christian. Your wedding-day is fixed, you are expecting your bride; she does not come; why? she will not have you; she has become a Christian. Where's young Nomentanus? Who has seen Nomentanus? in the forum, or the campus, in the circus, in the bath? Has he caught the plague or got a sunstroke? Nothing of the kind; the Christians have caught hold of him. Young and old, rich and poor, my lady in her litter and her slave, modest maid and Lydia at the Thermæ, nothing comes amiss to them. All confidence is gone; there's no one we can reckon on. I go to my tailor's: 'Nergal,' I say to him, 'Nergal, I want a new tunic,' The wretched hypocrite bows, and runs to and fro, and unpacks his stuffs and cloths, like another man. A word in your ear. The man's a Christian, dressed up like a tailor. They have no dress of their own. If I were emperor, I'd make the sneaking curs wear a badge, I would; a dog's collar, a fox's tail, or a pair of ass's ears. Then we should know friends from foes when we meet them."

"We should think that dangerous," said Cornelius; "however, you are taking it too much to heart; you are making too much of them, my good friend. They have not even got the present, and you are giving them the future, which is just what they want."

"If Jucundus will listen to me," said Aristo, "I could satisfy him that the Christians are actually falling off. They once were numerous in this very place; now there are hardly any. They have been declining for these fifty years; the danger from them is past. Do you want to know how to revive them? Put out an imperial edict, forbid them, denounce them. Do you want them to drop away like autumn leaves? Take no notice of them."

"I can't deny that in Italy they *have* grown," said Cornelius; "they *have* grown in numbers and in wealth, and they intermarry with us. Thus the upper class becomes to a certain extent infected. We may find it necessary to repress them; but, as you would repress vermin, without fearing them."

"The worshippers of the gods are the many, and the Christians are the few," persisted Aristo; "if the two parties intermarry, the weaker will get the worst of it. You will find the statues of the gods gradually creeping back into the Christian chapel; and a man must be an honest fellow who buys our images, eh, Jucundus?"

"Well, Aristo," said the paterfamilias, whose violence never lasted long, "if your sister's bright eyes win back my poor Agellius you will have something more to say for yourself than, at present, I grant."

"I see," said Cornelius, gravely, "I begin to understand it. I could not make out why our good host had such great fear for the stability of Rome. But it is one of those things which the experience of life has taught me. I have often seen it in the imperial city itself. Whenever you find a man show special earnestness against these fanatics, depend on it there is something that touches him personally in the matter. There was a very great man, the present Flamen Dialis, for whom I have unbounded respect; for a long time I was at a loss to conceive why a person of his weight, sound, sensible, well-judging, should have such a fear of the Christians. One day he made an oration against them in the senate-house; he wanted to send them to the rack. But the secret came out; the good man was on the rack himself about his daughter, who persisted in calling herself a Christian, and refused to paint her face or go to the amphitheatre. To be sure, a most trying affair this for the old gentleman. The venerable Pater Patratus, too, what suppers he gave! a fine specimen of the Lucullus type; yet he was always advocating the lictor[36] and the *commentariensis*[37] in the instance of the Christian. No wonder; his wife and son were disgracing him in the eyes of the whole world by frequenting the meetings of these Christians. However, I agree with Decius, they must be put down. They are not formidable, but they are an eyesore."

Here the rushing of the water-clock which measured time in the neighbouring square, ceased, signifying thereby that the night was getting on. Juba

36  "policeman"
37  "secretary"

had already crept into the dark closet which served him for a sleeping-place; had taken off his sandals, and loosened his belt; had wrapt the serpent he had about him round his neck, and was breathing heavily. Jucundus made the parting libation, and Cornelius took his leave. Aristo rose too; and Jucundus, accompanying them to the entrance, paid the not uncommon penalty of his potations, for the wine mounted to his head, and he returned into the room, and sat him down again with an impression that Aristo was still at table.

"My dear boy," he said, "Agellius is but a wet Christian; that's all, not obstinate, like his brother there. 'Twas his father; the less we say about him the better; he's gone. The Furies make his bed for him! an odious set! Their priests, little ugly men. I saw one when I was a boy at Carthage. So unlike your noble Roman Saliares,[38] or your fine portly priest of Isis, clad in white, breathing odours like spring flowers; men who enjoyed this life, not like that sour hypocrite. He was as black as an Ethiopian, and as withered as a Saracen, and he never looked you in the face. And, after all, the fellow must die for his religion, rather than put a few grains of golden incense on the altar of great Jove. Jove's the god for me; a glorious, handsome, curly god—but they are all good, all the gods are good. There's Bacchus, he's a good, comfortable god, though a sly, treacherous fellow—a treacherous fellow. There's Ceres, too; Pomona; the Muses; Astarte, too, as they call her here; all good;—and Apollo, though he's somewhat too hot in this season, and too free with his bow. He gave me a bad fever once. Ah! life's precious, most precious; so I felt it then, when I was all but gone to Pluto. Life never returns, it's like water spilt; you can't gather it up. It is dispersed into the elements, to the four winds. Ah! there's something more there than I can tell; more than all your philosophers can determine."

He seemed to think awhile, and began again: "Enjoyment's the great rule; ask yourself, 'Have I made the most of things?' that's what I say to the rising generation. Many and many's the time when I have not turned them to the best account. Oh, if I had now to begin life again, how many things should

---

38 "Priests of Mars"

I correct! I might have done better this evening. Those abominable pears! I might have known they would not be worth the eating. Mutton, that was all well; doves, good again; crane, kid; well, I don't see that I could have done much better."

After a few minutes he got up half asleep, and put out all the lights but one small lamp, with which he made his way into his own bed-closet. "All is vanity," he continued, with a slow, grave utterance, "all is vanity but eating and drinking. It does not pay to serve the gods except for this. What's fame? what's glory? what's power? smoke. I've often thought the hog is the only really wise animal. We should be happier if we were all hogs. Hogs keep the end of life steadily in view; that's why those toads of Christians will not eat them, lest they should get like them. Quiet, respectable, sensible enjoyment; not riot, or revel, or excess, or quarrelling. Life is short." And with this undeniable sentiment he fell asleep.

# Chapter Seven

# PERSECUTION IN THE OFFING

NEXT MORNING, as Jucundus was dusting and polishing his statues and other articles of taste and devotion, supplying the gaps in their ranks, and grouping a number of new ones which had come in from his workmen, Juba strutted into the shop, and indulged himself from time to time in an inward laugh or snigger at the various specimens of idolatry which grinned or frowned or frisked or languished on all sides of him.

"Don't sneer at that Anubis," said his uncle; "it is the work of the divine Callista."

"That, I suppose, is why she brings into existence so many demons," answered Juba; "nothing more can be done in the divine line; like the queen who fell in love with a baboon."

"Now I come to think," retorted Jucundus, "that god of hers is something like *you*. She must be in love with you, Juba."

The youth, as was usual with him, tossed his head with an air of lofty displeasure; at length he said, "And why should she not fall in love with me, pray?"

"Why, because you are too good or too bad to need her plastic hand. She could not make anything out of you. 'Non ex quovis ligno.'[39] But she'd be doing a good work if she wiled back your brother."

---

39   "[The God Mercury] cannot be made from just any log."

"*He* does not want wiling any more than I," said Juba, "*I* dare say! he's no Christian."

"What's that?" said his uncle, looking round at him in surprise; "Agellius no Christian?"

"Not a bit of it," answered Juba; "rest assured. I taxed him with it only last night; let him alone, *he'll* come round. He's too proud to change, that's all. Preach to him, entreat him, worry him, try to turn him, work at the bit, whip him, and he will turn restive, start aside, or run away; but let him have his head, pretend not to look, seem indifferent to the whole matter, and he will quietly sit down in the midst of your images there. Callista has an easy task; she'll bribe him to do what he would else do for nothing."

"The very best news I have heard since your silly old father died," cried Jucundus; "the very best—if true. Juba, I'll give you an handsome present the first sow your brother sacrifices to Ceres. Ha, ha, what fine fun to see the young farmer over his cups at the Nundinæ[40]! Ha, ha, no Christian! bravo, Juba! ha, ha, I'll make you a present, I say, an Apollo to teach you manners, or a Mercury to give you wit."

"It's quite true," said Juba; "he would not be thinking of Callista, if he were thinking of his saints and angels."

"Ha, ha! to be sure!" returned Jucundus; "to be sure! yet why shouldn't he worship a handsome Greek girl as well as any of those mummies and death's heads and bogies of his, which I should blush to put up here alongside even of Anubis, or a scarabæus[41]?"

"Mother thinks she is not altogether the girl you take her for," said his nephew.

"No matter, no matter," answered Jucundus, "no matter at all; she may be a Lais or Phryne for me; the surer to make a man of him."

"Why," said Juba, "mother thinks her head is turning in the opposite way. D'you see? Strange, isn't it?" he added, annoyed himself yet not unwilling to annoy his uncle.

---

40   "Marketplace"
41   "beetle"

"Hm!" exclaimed Jucundus, making a wry face and looking round at him, as if to say, "What on earth is going to turn up now?"

"To tell the truth," said Juba, gloomily, "I did once think of her myself. I don't see why I have not as much right to do so as Agellius, if I please. So I thought old mother might do something for me; and I asked her for a charm or love potion, which would bring her from her brother down to the forest yonder. Gurta took to it kindly, for she has a mortal hatred of Callista, because of her good looks, though she won't say so, and because she's a Greek! and she liked the notion of humbling the haughty minx. So she began one of the most tremendous spells," he shrieked out with a laugh, "one of the most tremendous spells in her whole budget. All and everything in the most exact religious way: wine, milk, blood, meal, wax, old rags, gods, Numidian as well as Punic; such names; one must be barbarian to boot, as well as witch, to pronounce them: a score of things there were besides. And then to see the old woman, with her streaming grey hair, twinkling eyes, and grim look, twirl about as some flute girl at a banquet; it was enough to dance down, not only the moon, but the whole milky way. But it did not dance down Callista; at which mother got savage, and protested that Callista was a Christian."

Jucundus looked much perplexed. "Medius fidius!"[42] he said, "why, unless we look sharp, she will be converting him the wrong way;" and he began pacing up and down the small room.

Juba on his part began singing—

> "Gurta the witch would have part in the jest;
> Though lame as a gull, by his highness possessed,
> She shouldered her crutch, and danced with the rest.
>
> "Sporting and snorting, deep in the night,
> Their beards flashing fire, and their hoofs striking light,
> And their tails whisking round in the heat of their flight."

By this time Jucundus had recovered from the qualm which Juba's intelligence had caused him, and he cried out, "Cease your rubbish; old Gurta's

---

42  "By Hercules!"

jealous; I know her spite; Christian is the most blackguard word in her vocabulary, its Barbar for toad or adder. I see it all; no, Callista, the divine Callista, must take in hand this piece of wax, sing a charm, and mould him into
a Vertumnus. She'll show herself the more potent witch of the two. The new
emperor too will help the incantation."

"What! something is coming?" asked Juba, with a grin.

"Coming, boy? yes, I warrant you," answered his uncle. "*We'll* make them
squeak. If gentle means don't do, then we'll just throw in another ingredient
or two: an axe, or a wild cat, or a firebrand."

"Take care what you are about, if you deal with Agellius," said Juba. "He's
a sawney, but you must not drive him to bay. Don't threaten; keep to the
other line; he's weak-hearted."

"Only as a background to bring out the painting; the Muse singing, all
in light, relieved by sardix or sepia. It *must* come; but perhaps Agellius will
come first."

It was indeed as Jucundus had hinted; a new policy, a new era was coming upon Christianity, together with the new emperor. Christians had hitherto been for the most part the objects of popular fury rather than of imperial jealousy. Nero, indeed, from his very love of cruelty, had taken pleasure in
torturing them: but statesmen and philosophers, though at times perplexed
and inconsistent, yet on the whole had despised them; and the superstition
of priests and people, with their "Christianos ad leones,"[43] had been the most
formidable enemy of the faith. Accordingly, atrocious as the persecution had
been at times, it had been conducted on no plan, and had been local and
fitful. But even this trial had been suspended, with but few interruptions,
during the last thirty, nay, fifty years. So favourable a state of things had been
more or less brought about by a succession of emperors, who had shown an
actual leaning to Christianity. While the vigorous rule of the five good emperors, as they are called, had had many passages in its history of an adverse

---

43    "[Throw] the Christians to the lions."

character, those who followed after, being untaught in the traditions, and strangers to the spirit of old Rome, foreigners, or adventurers, or sensualists, were protectors of the new religion. The favourite mistress of Commodus is even said to have been a Christian; so is the nurse of Caracalla. The wretched Heliogabalus, by his taste for Oriental superstitions, both weakened the influence of the established hierarchy, and encouraged the toleration of a faith which came from Palestine. The virtuous Alexander, who followed him, was a philosopher more than a statesman; and, in pursuance of the syncretism which he had adopted, placed the images of Abraham and our Lord among the objects of devotion which his private chapel contained. What is told us of the Emperor Philip is still more to the point: the gravest authorities report that he was actually a Christian; and, since it cannot be doubted that Christians were persuaded of the fact, the leaning of his government must have been emphatically in their favour to account for such a belief. In consequence, Christians showed themselves without fear; they emerged from the catacombs, and built churches in public view; and, though in certain localities, as in the instance of Africa, they had suffered from the contact of the world, they spread far and wide, and faith became the instrument at least of political power, even where it was wanting in charity, or momentarily disowned by cowardice. In a word, though Celsus a hundred years before had pronounced "a man weak who should hope to unite the three portions of the earth in a common religion," that common Catholic faith had been found, and a principle of empire was created which had never before existed. The phenomenon could not be mistaken; and the Roman statesman saw he had to deal with a rival. Nor must we suppose, because on the surface of the history we read so much of the vicissitudes of imperial power, and of the profligacy of its possessors, that the fabric of government was not sustained by traditions of the strongest temper, and by officials of the highest sagacity. It was the age of lawyers and politicians; and they saw more and more clearly that if Christianity was not to revolutionize the empire, they must follow out the line of action which Trajan and Antoninus had pointed out.

Decius then had scarcely assumed the purple, when he commenced that new policy against the Church which was reserved to Diocletian, fifty years later, to carry out to its own final refutation. He entered on his power at the end of the year 249; and on the January 20th following, the day on which the Church still celebrates the event, St. Fabian, Bishop of Rome, obtained the crown of martyrdom. He had been pope for the unusually long space of fourteen years, having been elected in consequence of one of those remarkable interpositions of Divine Providence of which we now and then read in the first centuries of the Church. He had come up to Rome from the country, in order to be present at the election of a successor to Pope Anteros. A dove was seen to settle on his head, and the assembly rose up and forced him, to his surprise, upon the episcopal throne. After bringing back the relics of St. Pontian, his martyred predecessor, from Sardinia, and having become the apostle of great part of Gaul, he seemed destined to end his history in the same happy quiet and obscurity in which he had lived; but it did not become a pope of that primitive time to die upon his bed, and he was reserved at length to inaugurate in his own person, as chief pastor of the Church, a fresh company of martyrs.

Suddenly an edict appeared for the extermination of the name and religion of Christ. It was addressed to the proconsuls and other governors of provinces; and alleged or implied that the emperors, Decius and his son, being determined to give peace to their subjects, found the Christians alone an impediment to the fulfilment of their purpose; and that, by reason of the enmity which those sectaries entertained towards the gods of Rome,—an enmity which was bringing down upon the world multiplied misfortunes. Desirous, then, above all things, of appeasing the divine anger, they made an irrevocable ordinance that every Christian, without exception of rank, sex, or age, should be obliged to sacrifice. Those who refused were to be thrown into prison, and in the first instance submitted to moderate punishments. If they conformed to the established religion, they were to be rewarded; if not, they were to be drowned, burned alive, exposed to the beasts, hung upon the trees, or otherwise put to death. This edict was read in the camp of the prætorians, posted up in the Capitol, and sent over the empire by government couriers. The authorities in each province were themselves threatened with heavy penalties, if they did not succeed in frightening or tormenting the Christians into the profession of paganism.

St. Fabian, as we have said, was the first-fruits of the persecution, and eighteen months passed before his successor could be appointed. In the course of the next two months St. Pionius was burned alive at Smyrna, and St. Nestor crucified in Pamphylia. At Carthage some perplexity and delay were occasioned by the absence of the proconsul. St. Cyprian, its bishop, took advantage of the delay, and retired into a place of concealment. The populace had joined with the imperial government in seeking his life, and had cried out furiously in the circus, demanding him "ad leonem," for the lion. A panic seized the Christian body, and for a while there were far more persons found to compromise their faith than to confess it. It seemed as if Aristo's anticipation was justified, that Christianity was losing its hold upon the mind of its subjects, and that nothing more was needed for those who had feared it, than to let it die a natural death. And at Sicca the Roman officials, as far as ever they dared, seemed to act on this view. Here Christians did no harm, they made no show, and there was little or nothing in the place to provoke the anger of the mob or to necessitate the interference of the magistrate. The proconsul's absence from Carthage was both an encouragement and an excuse for delay; and hence it was that, though we are towards the middle of the year 250, and the edict was published at Rome at its commencement, the good people of Sicca had, as we have said, little knowledge of what was taking place in the political world, and whispered about vague presages of an intended measure, which had been in some places in operation for many months. Communication with the seat of government was not so very frequent or rapid in those days, and public curiosity had not been stimulated by the facilities of gratifying it. And thus we must account for a phenomenon, which we uphold to be a fact in the instance of Sicca, in the early summer of A.D. 250, even though it prove unaccountable, and history has nothing to say about it, and in spite of the *Acta Diurna*.[44]

---

44   "Daily Chronicle"

The case, indeed, is different now. In these times, newspapers, railroads, and magnetic telegraphs make us independent of government messengers. The proceedings at Rome would have been generally and accurately known in a few seconds; and then, by way of urging forward the magistracy, a question of course would have been asked in the parliament of Carthage by the member for Sicca, or Laribus, or Thugga, or by some one of the pagani, or country party, whether the popular report was true, that an edict had been promulgated at Rome against the Christians, and what steps had been taken by the local authorities throughout the proconsulate to carry out its provisions. And then the "Colonia Siccensis"[45] would have presented some good or bad reason for the delay: that it arose from the absence of the proconsul from the seat of government, or from the unaccountable loss of the despatch on its way from the coast; or, perhaps, on the other hand, the under-secretary would have maintained, amid the cheers of his supporters, that the edict had been promulgated and carried out at Sicca to the full, that crowds of Christians had at once sacrificed, and that, in short, there was no one to punish; assertions which at that moment were too likely to be verified by the event.

In truth, there were many reasons to make the magistrates, both Roman and native, unwilling to proceed in the matter, till they were obliged. No doubt they one and all detested Christianity, and would have put it down, if they could; but the question was, when they came to the point, *what* they should put down. If, indeed, they could have got hold of the ringleaders, the bishops of the Church, they would have tortured and smashed them *con amore*,[46] as you would kill a wasp; and with the greater warmth and satisfaction, just because it was so difficult to get at them. Those bishops were a set of fellows as mischievous as they were cowardly; they would not come out and be killed, but they skulked in the desert, and hid in masquerade. But why should gentlemen in office, opulent and happy, set about worrying a handful of idiots, old, or poor, or boys, or women, or obscure, or amiable and

---

45　"Colony of Sicca"
46　Italian: "with love"

well-meaning men, who were but a remnant of a former generation, and as little connected with the fanatics of Carthage, Alexandria, or Rome, as the English freemasons may seem to be with their namesakes on the continent? True, Christianity was a secret society, and an illegal religion; but would it cease to be so when those harmless or respectable inhabitants of the place had been mounted on the rack or the gibbet?

And then, too, it was a most dangerous thing to open the door to popular excitement;—who would be able to shut it? Once rouse the populace, and it was all over with the place. It could not be denied that the bigoted and ignorant majority, not only of the common people, but of the better classes, was steeped in a bitter prejudice, and an intense, though latent, hatred of Christianity. Besides the antipathy which arose from the extremely different views of life and duty taken by pagans and Christians, which would give a natural impulse to persecution in the hearts of the former, there were the many persons who wished to curry favour at Rome with the government, and had an eye to preferment or reward. There was the pagan interest, extended and powerful, of that numerous class which was attached to the established religions by habit, position, interest, or the prospect of advantage. There were all the great institutions or establishments of the place; the law courts, the schools of grammar and rhetoric, the philosophic *exedræ*[47] and lecture-rooms, the theatre, the amphitheatre, the market—all were, for one reason or another, opposed to Christianity; and who could tell where they would stop in their onward course, if they were set in motion? "Quieta non movenda"[48] was the motto of the local government, native and imperial, and that the more, because it was an age of revolutions, and they might be most unpleasantly compromised or embarrassed by the direction which the movement took. Besides, Decius was not immortal; in the last twelve years eight emperors had been cut off, six of them in a few months; and who could tell but the successor of the present might revert to the policy of Philip, and feel no thanks to those who had suddenly left it for a policy of blood.

---

47 "auditoriums"
48 "At rest and undisturbed"

In this cautious course they would be powerfully supported by the influence of personal considerations. The Roman *officia*, the city magistrates, the heads of the established religions, the lawyers, and the philosophers, all would have punished the Christians, if they could; but they could not agree whom to punish. They would have agreed with great satisfaction, as we have said, to inflict condign and capital punishment upon the heads of the sect; and they would have had no objection, if driven to do something, to get hold of some strangers or slaves, who might be a sort of scapegoats for the rest; but it was impossible, when they once began to persecute, to make distinctions, and not a few of them had relations who were Christians, or at least were on that border-land which the mob might mistake for the domain of Christianity—Marcionites, Tertullianists, Montanists, or Gnostics. When once the cry of "the gods of Rome" was fairly up, it would apply to tolerated religions as well as to illicit, and an unhappy votary of Isis or Mithras might suffer, merely because there were few Christians forthcoming. A duumvir of the place had a daughter whom he had turned out of his house for receiving baptism, and who had taken refuge at Vacca. Several of the decurions, the *tabularius*[49] of the district, the *scriba*,[50] one of the exactors, who lived in Sicca, various of the retired gentry, whom we spoke of in a former chapter, and various *attachés* of the prætorium, were in not dissimilar circumstances. Nay, the priest of Esculapius had a wife, whom he was very fond of, who, though she promised to keep quiet, if things continued as they were, nevertheless had the madness to vow that, if there were any severe proceedings instituted against her people, she would at once come forward, confess herself a Christian, and throw water, instead of incense, upon the sacrificial flame. Not to speak of the venerable man's tenderness for her, such an exposure would seriously compromise his respectability, and, as he was infirm and apoplectic, it was a question whether Esculapius himself could save him from the shock which would be the consequence.

The same sort of feeling operated with our good friend Jucundus. He

---

49   "registrar"
50   "notary"

was attached to his nephew; but, be it said without disrespect to him, he was more attached to his own reputation; and, while he would have been seriously annoyed at seeing Agellius exposed to one of the panthers of the neighbouring forest, or hung up by the feet, with the blood streaming from his nose and mouth, as one of the dogs or kids of the market, he would have disliked the *éclat* of the thing still more. He felt both anger and alarm at the prospect; he was conscious he did not understand his nephew, or (to use a common phrase) know where to find him; he was aware that a great deal of tact was necessary to manage him; and he had an instinctive feeling that Juba was right in saying that it would not do to threaten him with the utmost severity of the law. He considered Callista's hold on him was the most promising quarter of the horizon; so he came to a resolution to do as little as he could personally, but to hold Agellius's head, as far as he could, steadily in the direction of that lady, and to see what came of it. As to Juba's assurance that Agellius was not a Christian at heart, it was too good news to be true; but still it might be only an anticipation of what would be, when the sun of Greece shone out upon him, and dispersed the remaining mists of Oriental superstition.

In this state of mind the old gentleman determined one afternoon to leave his shop to the care of a slave, and to walk down to his nephew, to judge for himself of his state of mind; to bait his hook with Callista, and to see if Agellius bit. There was no time to be lost, for the publication of the edict might be made any day; and then disasters might ensue which no skill could remedy.

# Chapter Eight

# THE NEW GENERATION

JUCUNDUS, THEN, SET OUT to see how the land lay with his nephew, and to do what he could to prosper the tillage. His way led him by the temple of Mercury, which at that time subserved the purpose of a boy's school, and was connected with some academical buildings, the property of the city, which lay beyond it. It cannot be said that our friend was any warm patron of literature or education, though he had not neglected the schooling of his nephews. Letters seemed to him in fact to unsettle the mind; and he had never known much good come of them. Rhetoricians and philosophers did not know where they stood, or what were their bearings. They did not know what they held, and what they did not. He knew his own position perfectly well, and, though the words "belief" or "knowledge" did not come into his religious vocabulary, he could at once, without hesitation, state what he professed and maintained. He stood upon the established order of things, on the traditions of Rome, and the laws of the empire; but as to Greek sophists and declaimers, he thought very much as old Cato did about them. The Greeks were a very clever people, unrivalled in the fine arts; let them keep to their strong point; they were inimitable with the chisel, the brush, the trowel, and the fingers; but he was not prepared to think much of their *calamus*[51] or *stylus*,[52] poetry excepted.

---

51  "penmanship"
52  "writing style"

What did they ever do but subvert received principles without substituting any others? And then they were so likely to take some odd turn themselves; you never could be sure of them. Socrates, their patriarch, what was he after all but a culprit, a convict, who had been obliged to drink hemlock, dying under the hands of justice? Was this a reputable end, a respectable commencement of the philosophic family? It was very well for Plato or Xenophon to throw a veil of romance over the transaction, but this was the plain matter of fact. Then Anaxagoras had been driven out of Athens for his revolutionary notions; and Diogenes had been accused, like the Christians, of atheism. The case had been the same in more recent times. There had been that madman, Apollonius, roaming about the world; Apuleius, too, their neighbour, fifty years before, a man of respectable station, a gentleman, but a follower of the Greek philosophy, a dabbler in magic, and a pretender to miracles. And so, in fact, of letters generally; as in their own country Minucius, a contemporary of Apuleius, became a Christian. Such, too, had been his friend Octavius; such Cæcilius, who even became one of the priests of the sect, and seduced others from the religion he had left. One of them had been the public talk for several years, and he too originally a rhetorician, Thascius Cyprianus of Carthage. It was the one thing which gave him some misgiving about that little Callista, that she was a Greek.

As he passed the temple, the metal plate was sounding as a signal for the termination of the school, and on looking towards the portico with an ill-natured curiosity, he saw a young acquaintance of his, a youth of about twenty, coming out of it, leading a boy of about half that age, with his satchel thrown over his shoulder.

"Well, Arnobius,"[53] he cried, "how does rhetoric proceed? are we to take the law line, or turn professor? Who's the boy? some younger brother?"

"I've taken pity on the little fool," answered Arnobius; "these schoolmasters are a savage lot. I suffered enough from them myself, and 'miseris succur-

---

53    [Here is an anachronism, as regards Arnobius and Lactantius of some twenty or thirty years.]

rere disco.'[54] So I took him from under the roof of friend Rupilius, and he's under my tutelage. How did he treat thee, boy?"

"He treated me like a slave or a Christian," answered he.

"He deserved it, I'll warrant," said Jucundus; "a pert, forward imp. 'Twas Gete against Briton. Much good comes of schooling! He's a wicked one already. Ah, the new generation! I don't know where the world's going."

"Tell the gentleman," said Arnobius, "what he did first to you, my boy."

"As the good gentleman says," answered the boy, "first I did something to him, and then he did something to me."

"I told you so," said Jucundus; "a sensible boy, after all; but the schoolmaster had the best of it, I'll wager."

"First," answered he, "I grinned in his face, and he took off his wooden shoe, and knocked out one of my teeth."

"Good," said Jucundus, "the justice of Pythagoras. Zaleuchus could not have done better. The mouth sins, and the mouth suffers."

"Next," continued he, "I talked in school-time to my chum; and Rupilius put a gag in my jaws, and kept them open for an hour."

"The very Rhadamanthus of schoolmasters!" cried Jucundus: "and thereupon you struck up a chant, divine though inarticulate, like the statue of Memnon."

"Then," said the boy, "I could not say my Virgil, and he tore the shirt from off my back, and gave it me with the leather."

"Ay," answered Jucundus, "arma virumque[55] branded on your hide."

"Afterwards I ate his dinner for him," continued the boy, "and then he screwed my head, and kept me without food for two days."

"Your throat, you mean," said Jucundus; "a cautious man! lest you should steal a draught or two of good strong air."

"And lastly," said he, "I did not bring my pence, and then he tied my hands to a gibbet, and hung me up *in terrorem.*[56]"

---

54    "I learn to aid the unfortunate."
55    "arms and the man," Vergil, *Aeneid*, I.i.
56    "in terror"

"There I came in," said Arnobius; "he seemed a pretty boy, so I cut him down, paid his æra,[57] and took him home."

"And now he is your pupil?" asked Jucundus.

"Not yet," answered Arnobius; "he is still a day-scholar of the old wolf's; one is like another; he could not change for the better: but I am his bully, and shall tutorize him some day. He's a sharp lad, isn't he, Firmian?" turning to the boy; "a great hand at composition for his years; better than I am, who never shall write Latin decently. Yet what can I do? I must profess and teach, for Rome is the only place for the law, and these city professorships are not to be despised."

"Whom are you attending here?" asked Jucundus, drily.

"You are the only man in Sicca who needs to ask the question. What! not know the great Polemo of Rhodes, the friend of Plotinus, the pupil of Theagenes, the disciple of Thrasyllus, the hearer of Nicomachus, who was of the school of Secundus, the doctor of the new Pythagoreans? Not feel the presence in Sicca of Polemo, the most celebrated, the most intolerable of men? That, however, is not his title, but the 'godlike,' or the 'oracular,' or the 'portentous,' or something else as impressive. Every one goes to him. He is the rage. I should not have a chance of success if I could not say that I had attended his lectures; though I'd be bound our little Firmian here would deliver as good. He's the very cariophyllus[58] of human nature. He comes to the schools in a litter of cedar, ornamented with silver and covered with a lion's skin, slaves carrying him, and a crowd of friends attending, with the state of a proconsul. He is dressed in the most exact style; his pallium[59] is of the finest wool, white, picked out with purple; his tresses flow with unguent, his fingers glitter with rings, and he smells like Idalium. As soon as he puts foot on earth, a great hubbub of congratulation and homage breaks forth. He takes no notice; his favourite pupils form a circle round him, and conduct him into one of the *exedræ*, till the dial shows the time for lecture. Here

---

57   "copper coins"
58   Greek: "carnation"
59   "cloak"

he sits in silence, looking at nothing, or at the wall opposite him, talking to himself, a hum of admiration filling the room. Presently one of his pupils, as if he were præco[60] to the duumvir,[61] cries out, 'Hush, gentlemen, hush! the godlike'—no, it is not that. I've not got it. What *is* his title? 'the Bottomless,' that's it—'the Bottomless speaks.' A dead silence ensues; a clear voice and a measured elocution are the sure token that it is the outpouring of the oracle. 'Pray,' says the little man, 'pray, which existed first, the egg or the chick? Did the chick lay the egg, or the egg hatch the chick?' Then there ensues a whispering, a disputing, and after a while a dead silence. At the end of a quarter of an hour or so, our præco speaks again, and this time to the oracle. 'Bottomless man,' he says, 'I have to represent to you that no one of the present company finds himself equal to answer the question, which your condescension has proposed to our consideration!' On this there is a fresh silence, and at length a fresh *effatum*[62] from the hierophant: 'Which comes first, the egg or the chick? The egg comes first in relation to the causativity of the chick, and the chick comes first in relation to the causativity of the egg,' on which there is a burst of applause; the ring of adorers is broken through, and the shrinking professor is carried in the arms or on the shoulders of the literary crowd to his chair in the lecture-room."

Much as there was in Arnobius's description which gratified Jucundus's prejudices, he had suspicions of his young acquaintance, and was not in the humour to be pleased unreservedly with those who satirized anything whatever that was established, or was appointed by government, even affectation and pretence. He said something about the wisdom of ages, the reverence due to authority, the institutions of Rome, and the magistrates of Sicca. "Do not go after novelties," he said to Arnobius; "make a daily libation to Jove, the preserver, and to the genius of the emperor, and then let other things take their course."

"But you don't mean I must believe all this man says, because the decu-

---

60   "herald"
61   "[government of] two men"
62   "pronouncement"

rions[63] have put him here?" cried Arnobius. "Here is this Polemo saying that Proteus is matter, and that minerals and vegetables are his flock; that Proserpine is the vital influence, and Ceres the efficacy of the heavenly bodies; that there are mundane spirits, and supramundane; and then his doctrine about triads, monads, and progressions of the celestial gods?"

"Hm!" said Jucundus; "they did not say so when I went to school; but keep to my rule, my boy, and swear by the genius of Rome and the emperor."

"I don't believe in god or goddess, emperor or Rome, or in any philosophy, or in any religion at all," said Arnobius.

"What!" cried Jucundus, "you're not going to desert the gods of your ancestors?"

"Ancestors?" said Arnobius; "I've no ancestors. I'm not African certainly, not Punic, not Libophœnician, not Canaanite, not Numidian, not Gætulian. I'm half Greek, but what the other half is I don't know. My good old gaffer, you're one of the old world. I believe nothing. Who can? There is such a racket and whirl of religions on all sides of me that I am sick of the subject."

"Ah, the rising generation!" groaned Jucundus; "you young men! I cannot prophesy what you will become, when we old fellows are removed from the scene. Perhaps you're a Christian?"

Arnobius laughed. "At least I can give you comfort on that head, old grandfather. A pretty Christian *I* should make, indeed! seeing visions, to be sure, and rejoicing in the rack and dungeon! I wish to enjoy life; I see wealth, power, rank, and pleasure to be worth living for, and I see nothing else."

"Well said, my lad," cried Jucundus, "well said; stick to that. I declare you frightened me. Give up all visions, speculations, conjectures, fancies, novelties, discoveries; nothing comes of them but confusion."

"No, no," answered the youth; "I'm not so wild as you seem to think, Jucundus. It is true I don't believe one single word about the gods; but in their worship was I born, and in their worship I will die."

---

63    cavalry officers

"Admirable!" cried Jucundus in a transport; "well, I'm surprised; you have taken me by surprise. You're a fine fellow; you are a boy after my heart. I've a good mind to adopt you."

"You see I can't believe one syllable of all the priests' trash," said Arnobius; "who does? not they. I don't believe in Jupiter or Juno, or in Astarte or in Isis; but where shall I go for anything better? or why need I seek anything good or bad in that line? Nothing's known anywhere, and life would go while I attempted what is impossible. No, better stay where I am; I may go further, and gain a loss for my pains. So you see I am for myself, and for the genius of Rome."

"That's the true principle," answered the delighted Jucundus. "Why, really, for so young a man, surprising! Where *did* you get so much good sense, my dear fellow? *I've* seen very little of you. Well, this I'll say, you are a youth of most mature mind. To be sure! Well! Such youths are rare now-a-days. I congratulate you with all my heart on your strong sense and your admirable wisdom. Who'd have thought it? I've always, to tell the truth, had a little suspicion of you; but you've come out nobly. Capital! I don't wish you to believe in the gods if you can't; but it's your duty, dear boy, your duty to Rome to maintain them, and to rally round them when attacked." Then with a changed voice, he added, "Ah, that a young friend of mine had your view of the matter!" and then, fearing he had said too much, he stopped abruptly.

"You mean Agellius," said Arnobius. "You've heard, by-the-bye," he continued in a lower tone, "what's the talk in the Capitol, that at Rome they are proceeding on a new plan against the Christians with great success. They don't put to death, at least at once; they keep in prison, and threaten the torture. It's surprising how many come over."

"The Furies seize them!" exclaimed Jucundus: "they deserve everything bad, always excepting my poor boy. So they are cheating the hangman by giving up their atheism, the vile reptiles, giving in to a threat. However," he added gravely, "I wish threats would answer with Agellius; but I greatly fear that menace would only make him stubborn. That stubbornness of a Chris-

tian! O Arnobius!" he said, shaking his head and looking solemn, "it's a visitation from the gods, a sort of *nympholepsia.*[64]"

"It's going out," said Arnobius, "mark my words; the frenzy is dying. It's
only wonderful it should have lasted for three centuries. The report runs
that in some places, when the edict was published, the Christians did not
wait for a summons, but swept up to the temples to sacrifice, like a shoal
of tunnies. The magistrates were obliged to take so many a day; and, as the
days went on, none so eager to bring over the rest as those who have already
become honest men. Nay, not a few of their mystic or esoteric class have
conformed."

"If so, unless Agellius looks sharp," said Jucundus, "his sect will give him
up before he gives up his sect. Christianity will be converted before him."

"Oh, don't fear for him!" said Arnobius; "I knew him at school. Boys
differ; some are bold and open. They like to be men, and to dare the deeds
of men; they talk freely, and take their swing in broad day. Others are shy,
reserved, bashful, and are afraid to do what they love quite as much as the
others. Agellius never could rub off this shame, and it has taken this turn.
He's sure to outgrow it in a year or two. I should not wonder if, when once
he had got over it, he went into the opposite fault. You'll find him a drinker
and a swaggerer and a spendthrift before many years are over."

"Well, that's good news," said Jucundus; "I mean, I am glad you think he
will shake off these fancies. I don't believe they sit very close to him myself."

He walked on for a while in silence; then he said, "That seems a sharp
child, Arnobius. Could he do me a service if I wanted it? Does he know
Agellius?"

"Know him?" answered the other; "yes, and his farm too. He has rambled
round Sicca, many is the mile. And he knows the short cuts, and the blind
ways, and safe circuits."

"What's the boy's name?" asked Jucundus.

"Firmian," answered Arnobius. "Firmian Lactantius."

---

64    "nymphic ectasy"

"I say, Firmian," said Jucundus to him, "where are you to be found of a day, my boy?"

"At class morning and afternoon," answered Firmian, "sleeping in the porticoes in midday, nowhere in the evening, and roosting with Arnobius at night."

"And you can keep a secret, should it so happen?" asked Jucundus, "and do an errand, if I gave you one?"

"I'll give him the stick worse than Rupilius, if he does not," said Arnobius.

"A bargain," cried Jucundus; and, waving his hand to them, he stept through the city gate, and they returned to their afternoon amusements.

# Chapter Nine

# JUCUNDUS BAITS HIS TRAP

AGELLIUS IS BUSILY employed upon his farm. While the enemies of his faith are laying their toils for him and his brethren in the imperial city, in the proconsular *officium*, and in the municipal curia,—while Jucundus is scheming against him personally in another way and with other intentions,—the unconscious object of these machinations is busy about his master's crops, housing the corn in caves or pits, distilling the roses, irrigating the *khennah*, and training and sheltering the vines. And he does so, not only from a sense of duty, but the more assiduously, because he finds in constant employment a protection against himself, against idle thoughts, wayward wishes, discontent, and despondency. It is doubtless very strange to the reader how any one who professed himself a Christian in good earnest should be open to the imputation of resting his hopes and his heart in the tents of paganism; but we do not see why Agellius has not quite as much right to be inconsistent in one way as Christians of the present time in another, and perhaps he has more to say for himself than they. They have not had the trial of solitude, nor the consequent temptation to which he has been exposed, of seeking relief from his own thoughts in the company of unbelievers. When a boy he had received his education at that school in the Temple of Mercury of which we heard in the foregoing chapter; and though happily he had preserved himself from the contagion of idolatry and sin, he had on that very account formed no friendships with his schoolfellows. Whether there were any Christians there besides himself he did not know; but while the worst of his schoolfellows were what heathen boys may be supposed to be, the lightest censure which could be passed on any was that they were greedy, or quarrelsome, or otherwise unamiable. He had learned there enough to open his mind, and to give him materials for thinking, and instruments for reflecting on his own religion, and for drawing out into shape his own reflections. He had received just that discipline which makes solitude most pleasant to the old, and most insupportable to the young. He had got a thousand questions which needed answers, a thousand feelings which needed sympathy. He wanted to know whether his guesses, his perplexities, his trials of mind, were peculiar to himself, or how far they were shared by others, and what they were worth. He had capabilities for intellectual enjoyment unexercised, and a thirst after knowledge unsatisfied. And the channels of supernatural assistance were removed from him at a time when nature was most impetuous and most clamorous.

It was under circumstances such as these that two young Greeks, brother and sister, the brother older, the sister younger, than Agellius, came to Sicca at the invitation of Jucundus, who wanted them for his trade. His nephew in time got acquainted with them, and found in them what he had sought in vain elsewhere. It is not that they were oracles of wisdom or repositories of philosophical learning; their age and their calling forbade it, nor did he require it. For an oracle, of course, he would have looked in another direction; but he desiderated something more on a level with himself, and that they abundantly supplied. He found, from his conversations with them, that a great number of the questions which had been a difficulty to him had already been agitated in the schools of Greece. He found what solutions were possible, what the hinge was on which questions turned, what the issue to which they led, and what the principle which lay at the bottom of them. He began better to understand the position of Christianity in the world of thought, and the view which was taken of it by the advocates of other religions or philosophies. He gained some insight into its logic, and advanced, without knowing it, in the investigation of its evidences.

Nor was this all; he acquired by means of his new friends a great deal also of secular knowledge as well as philosophical. He learned much of the history of foreign countries, especially of Greece, of its heroes and sages, its poets and its statesmen, of Alexander, of the Syro-Macedonic empire, of the Jews, and of the series of conquests through which Rome advanced to universal dominion.

To impart knowledge is as interesting as to acquire it; and Agellius was called upon to give as well as to take. The brother and sister, without showing any great religious earnestness, were curious to know about Christianity, and listened with the more patience that they had no special attachment to any other worship. In the debates which ensued, though there was no agreement, there was the pleasure of mental exercise and excitement; he found enough to tell them without touching upon the more sacred mysteries; and while he never felt his personal faith at all endangered by their free conversation, his charity, or at least his good-will and his gratitude, led him to hope, or even to think, that they were in the way of conversion themselves. In this thought he was aided by his own innocence and simplicity; and though, on looking back afterwards to this eventful season, he recognized many trivial occurrences which ought to have put him on his guard, yet he had no suspicion at the time that those who conversed so winningly, and sustained so gracefully and happily the commerce of thought and sentiment, might in their actual state, nay, in their governing principles, be in utter contrariety to himself when the veil was removed from off their hearts.

Nor was it in serious matters alone, but still more on lighter occasions of intercourse, that Aristo and Callista were attractive to the solitary Agellius. She had a sweet thrilling voice, and accompanied herself on the lyre. She could act the *improvisatrice*,[65] and her expressive features were a running commentary on the varied meaning, the sunshine and the shade, of her ode

---

65    "improviser"

or her epic. She could relate how the profane Pentheus and the self-glorious Hippolytus gave a lesson to the world of the feebleness of human virtue when it placed itself in opposition to divine power. She could teach how the chaste Diana manifests herself to the simple shepherd Endymion, not to the great or learned; and how Tithonus, the spouse of the Morn, adumbrates the fate of those who revel in their youth, as if it were to last for ever; and who, when old, do nothing but talk of the days when they were young, wearying others with tales of "their amours or their exploits, like grasshoppers that show their vigour only by their chirping."[66] The very allegories which sickened and irritated Arnobius when spouted out by Polemo, touched the very chords of poor Agellius's heart when breathed forth from the lips of the beautiful Greek.

She could act also; and suddenly, when conversation flagged or suggested it, she could throw herself into the part of Medea or Antigone, with a force and truth which far surpassed the effect produced by the male and masked representations of those characters at the theatre. Brother and sister were Œdipus and Antigone, Electra and Orestes, Cassandra and the Chorus. Once or twice they attempted a scene in Menander; but there was something which made Agellius shrink from the comedy, beautiful as it was, and clever as was the representation. Callista could act Thais as truly as Iphigenia, but Agellius could not listen as composedly. There are certain most delicate instincts and perceptions in us which act as first principles, and which, once effaced, can never, except from some supernatural source, be restored to the mind. When men are in a state of nature, these are sinned against, and vanish very soon, at so early a date in the history of the individual that perhaps he does not recollect that he ever possessed them; and since, like other first principles, they are but very partially capable of proof, a general scepticism prevails both as to their existence and their truth. The Greeks, partly from the vivacity of their intellect, partly from their passion for the beautiful, lost these celestial adumbrations sooner than other nations. When a collision

---

66   Bacon.

arose on such matters between Agellius and his friends, Callista kept silence; but Aristo was not slow to express his wonder that the young Christian should think customs or practices wrong which, in his view of the matter, were as unblamable and natural as eating, drinking, or sleeping. His own face became almost satirical as Agellius's became grave; however, he was too companionable and good-natured to force another to be happy in his own way; he imputed to the extravagance of his friend's religion what in any but a Christian he would have called moroseness and misanthropy; and he bade his sister give over representations which, instead of enlivening the passing hour, did but inflict pain.

This friendly intercourse had now gone on for some months, as the leisure of both parties admitted. Once or twice brother and sister had come to the suburban farm; but for the most part, in spite of his intense dislike of the city, he had for their sake threaded its crowded and narrow thoroughfares, crossed its open places, and presented himself at their apartments. And was it very strange that a youth so utterly ignorant of the world, and unsuspicious of evil, should not have heard the warning voice which called him to separate himself from heathenism, even in its most specious form? Was it very strange, under these circumstances, that a sanguine hope, the hope of the youthful, should have led Agellius to overlook obstacles, and beguile himself into the notion that Callista might be converted, and make a good Christian wife? Well, we have nothing more to say for him; if we have not already succeeded in extenuating his offence, we must leave him to the mercy, or rather to the justice, of his severely virtuous censors.

But all this while Jucundus had been conversing with him; and, unless we are quick about it, we shall lose several particulars which are necessary for those who wish to pursue without a break the thread of his history. His uncle had brought the conversation round to the delicate point which had occasioned his visit, and had just broken the ice. With greater tact, and more ample poetical resources than we should have given him credit for, he had been led from the scene before him to those prospects of a moral and social character which ought soon to employ the thoughts of his dear Agellius. He had spoken of vines and of their culture, *apropos* of the dwarf vines around him, which stood about the height of a currant-bush. Thence he had proceeded to the subject of the more common vine of Africa, which crept and crawled along the ground, the extremity of each plant resting in succession on the stock of that which immediately preceded it. And now, being well into his subject, he called to mind the high vine of Italy, which mounts by the support of the slim tree to which it clings. Then he quoted Horace on the subject of the marriage of the elm and the vine. This lodged him *in medias res*; and Agellius's heart beat when he found his uncle proposing to him, as a thought of his own, the very step which he had fancied was almost a secret of his own breast, though Juba had seemed to have some suspicion of it.

"My dear Agellius," said Jucundus, "it would be a most suitable proceeding. I have never taken to marrying myself; it has not lain in my way, or been to my taste. Your father did not set me an encouraging example; but here you are living by yourself, in this odd fashion, unlike any one else. Perhaps you may come in time and live in Sicca. We shall find some way of employing you, and it will be pleasant to have you near me as I get old. However, I mean it to be some time yet before Charon makes a prize of me; not that I believe all that rubbish more than you, Agellius, I assure you."

"It strikes me," Agellius began, "that perhaps you may think it inconsistent in me taking such a step, but—"

"Ay, ay, that's the rub," thought Jucundus; then aloud, "Inconsistent, my boy! who talks of inconsistency? what superfine jackanapes dares to call it inconsistent? You seem made for each other, Agellius—she town, you country; she so clever and attractive, and up to the world, you so fresh and Arcadian. You'll be quite the talk of the place."

"That's just what I don't want to be," said Agellius. "I mean to say," he continued, "that if I thought it inconsistent with my religion to think of Callista—"

"Of course, of course," interrupted his uncle, who took his cue from Juba, and was afraid of the workings of Agellius's human respect; "but who knows you have been a Christian? no one knows anything about it. I'll be bound they all think you an honest fellow like themselves, a worshipper of the gods, without crotchets or hobbies of any kind. I never told them to the contrary. My opinion is, that if you were to make your libation to Jove, and throw incense upon the imperial altar to-morrow, no one would think it extraordinary. They would say for certain that they had seen you do it again and again. Don't fancy for an instant, my dear Agellius, that you have anything whatever to get over."

Agellius was getting awkward and mortified, as may be easily conceived, and Jucundus saw it, but could not make out why. "My dear uncle," said the youth, "you are reproaching me."

"Not a bit of it," said Jucundus, confidently, "not a shadow of reproach; why should I reproach you? We can't be wise all at once; *I* had my follies once, as you may have had yours. It's natural you should grow more attached to things as they are,—things as they are, you know,—as time goes on. Marriage, and the preparation for marriage, sobers a man. You've been a little headstrong, I can't deny, and had your fling in your own way; but 'nuces pueris,'[67] as you will soon be saying yourself on a certain occasion. Your next business is to consider what kind of a marriage you propose. I suppose the Roman, but there is great room for choice even there."

It is a proverb how different things are in theory and when reduced to practice. Agellius had thought of the end more than of the means, and had had a vision of Callista as a Christian, when the question of rites and forms would have been answered by the decision of the Church without his trouble. He *was* somewhat sobered by the question, though in a different way from what his uncle wished and intended.

Jucundus proceeded—"First, there is *matrimonium confarreationis*.[68] You have nothing to do with that: strictly speaking, it is obsolete; it went out with the exclusiveness of the old patricians. I say 'strictly speaking'; for the ceremonies remain, waiving the formal religious rite. Well, my dear Agellius, I don't recommend this ceremonial to you. You'd have to kill a porker, to take

---

67   Catullus, *Carmina*, LVIII.128
68   "marriage of ceremony"

out the entrails, to put away the gall, and to present it to Juno Pronuba. And there's fire, too, and water, and frankincense, and a great deal of the same kind, which I think undesirable, and you would too; for there, I am sure, we are agreed. We put this aside then, the religious marriage. Next comes the marriage *ex coemptione*,[69] a sort of mercantile transaction. In this case the parties buy each other, and become each other's property. Well, every man to his taste; but for me, I don't like to be bought and sold. I like to be my own master, and am suspicious of anything irrevocable. Why should you commit yourself (do you see?) for ever, *for ever*, to a girl you know so little of? Don't look surprised: it's common sense. It's very well to buy *her*; but to be bought, that's quite another matter. And I don't know that you can. Being a Roman citizen yourself, you can only make a marriage with a citizen; now the quest ion is whether Callista is a citizen at all. I know perfectly well the sweeping measure some years back of Caracalla, which made all freemen citizens of Rome, whatever might be their country; but that measure has never been carried out in fact. You'd have very great difficulty with the law and the customs of the country; and then, after all, if the world were willing to gratify you, where's your proof she is a freewoman? My dear boy, I must speak out for your good, though you're offended with me. I wish you to have her, I do; but you can't do impossibilities—you can't alter facts. The laws of the empire allow you to have her in a certain definite way, and no other; and you cannot help the law being what it is. I say all this, even on the supposition of her being a freewoman; but it is just possible she may be in law a slave. Don't start in that way; the pretty thing is neither better nor worse for what she cannot help. I say it for your good. Well, now I'm coming to my point. There is a third kind of marriage, and that is what I should recommend for you. It's the *matrimonium ex usu*,[70] or *consuetudine*;[71] the great advantage here is, that you have no ceremonies whatever, nothing which can in any way startle your sensitive mind. In that case, a couple are at length man and wife *præscriptione*.[72]

---

69   "by purchase"
70   "marriage of utility"
71   "by custom"
72   "by prescription"

You are afraid of making a stir in Sicca; in this case you would make none. You would simply take her home here; if, as time went on, you got on well together, it would be a marriage; if not,"—and he shrugged his shoulders—"no harm's done; you are both free."

Agellius had been sitting on a gate of one of the vineyards; he started on his feet, threw up his arms, and made an exclamation.

"Listen, listen, my dear boy!" cried Jucundus, hastening to explain what he considered the cause of his sudden annoyance; "listen, just one moment, Agellius, if you can. Dear, dear, how I wish I knew where to find you! What *is* the matter? I'm not treating her ill, I'm not indeed. I have not had any notion at all even of hinting that you should leave her, unless you both wished the bargain rescinded. No, but it is a great rise for her; you are a Roman, with property, with position in the place; she's a stranger, and without a dower: nobody knows whence she came, or anything about her. She ought to have no difficulty about it, and I am confident will have none."

"O my good, dear uncle! O Jucundus, Jucundus!" cried Agellius, "is it possible? do my ears hear right? What is it you ask me to do?" and he burst into tears. "Is it conceivable," he said, with energy, "that you are in earnest in recommending me—I say in recommending me—a marriage which really would be no marriage at all?"

"Here is some very great mistake," said Jucundus, angrily; "it arises, Agellius, from your ignorance of the world. You must be thinking I recommend you mere *contubernium*,[73] as the lawyers call it. Well, I confess I did think of that for a moment, it occurred to me; I should have liked to have mentioned it, but knowing how preposterously touchy and skittish you are on supposed points of honour, or sentiment, or romance, or of something or other indescribable, I said not one word about that. I have only wished to consult for your comfort, present and future. You don't do me justice, Agellius. I have been attempting to smooth your way. You *must* act according to the received usages of society! you cannot make a world for yourself. Here have I pro-

---

73   "concubinage"

posed three or four ways for your proceeding: you will have none of them. What *will* you have? I thought you didn't like ceremonies; I thought you did not like the established ways. Go, then, do it in the old fashion; kill your sheep, knead your meal, light your torches, sing your song, summon your flamen,[74] if he'll come. Any how, take your choice; do it either with religion or without."

"O Jucundus!" said the poor fellow, "am I then come to this?" and he could say no more.

His distress was not greater than his uncle's disappointment, perplexity, and annoyance. The latter had been making everything easy for Agellius, and he was striking, do what he would, on hidden, inexplicable impediments, whichever way he moved. He got more and more angry the more he thought about it. An unreasonable, irrational coxcomb! He had heard a great deal of the portentous stubbornness of a Christian, and now he understood what it was. It was in his blood, he saw; an offensive, sour humour, tainting him from head to foot. A very different recompense had he deserved. There had he come all the way from his home from purely disinterested feelings. He had no motive whatever, but a simple desire of his nephew's welfare; what other motive could he have? "Let Agellius go to the crows," he thought, "if he will; what is it to me if he is seized for a Christian, hung up like a dog, or thrown like a dead rat into the *cloaca* of the prison? What care I if he is made a hyæna's breakfast in the amphitheatre, all Sicca looking on, or if he is nailed on a cross for the birds to peck at before my door? Ungrateful puppy! it is no earthly concern of mine what becomes of him. I shall be neither better nor worse. No one will say a word against Jucundus; he will not lose a single customer, or be shunned by a single jolly companion, for the exposure of his nephew. But a man can't be saved against his will. Here am I, full of expedients and resources for his good; there is he, throwing cold water on everything, and making difficulties as if he loved them. It's his abominable pride, that's the pith of the matter. He could not have behaved worse though

---

74   "priest"

I had played the bully with him, and had reproached him with his Christianity. But I have studiously avoided every subject which could put his back up. He's a very Typhon or Enceladus for pride. Here he'd give his ears to have done with Christianity; he wants to have this Callista; he wants to buy her at the price of his religion; but he'd rather be burned than say, I've changed! Let him reap as he has sown; why should I coax him further to be merciful to himself? Well Agellius," he said aloud, "I'm going back."

Agellius, on the other hand, had his own thoughts; and the most urgent of them at the moment was sorrow that he had hurt his uncle. He was sincerely attached to him, in consequence of his faithful guardianship, his many acts of kindness, the reminiscences of childhood, nay, the love he bore to the good points of his character. To him he owed his education and his respectable position. He could not bear his anger, and he had a fear of his authority; but what was to be done? Jucundus, in utter insensibility to certain instincts and rules which in Christianity are first principles, had, without intending it, been greatly dishonouring Agellius, and his passion, and the object of it. Uncle and nephew had been treading on each other's toes, and each was wincing under the mischance. It was Agellius's place, as the younger, to make advances, if he could, to an adjustment of the misunderstanding; and he wished to find some middle way. And, also, it is evident he had another inducement besides his tenderness to Jucundus to urge him to do so. In truth, Callista exerted a tremendous sway over him. The conversation which had just passed ought to have opened his eyes, and made him understand that the very first step in any negotiations between them was her *bonâ fide* conversion. It was evident he could not, he literally had not the power of marrying her as a heathen. Roman might marry a Roman; but a degradation of each party in the transaction was the only way by which a Roman could make any sort of marriage with a Greek. If she were converted, they would be both of them under the rules of the Catholic Church. But what prospect was there of so happy an event? What had ever fallen from her lips which looked that way? Could not a clever girl throw herself into the part of Alcestis, or chant the majestic verses of Cleanthes, or extemporize a hymn upon the spring, or hold an argument on the *pulchrum* and *utile*, [75] without having any leaning towards Christianity? A calm, sweet voice, a noble air, an expressive countenance, refined and decorous manners, were these specific indications of heavenly grace? Ah, poor Agellius! a fascination is upon you; and so you are thinking of some middle term, which is to reconcile your uncle and you; and therefore you begin as follows:—

"I see by your silence, Jucundus, that you are displeased with me, you who are always so kind. Well, it comes from my ignorance of things; it does indeed. I ask your forgiveness for anything which seemed ungrateful in my behaviour, though there is not ingratitude in my heart. I am too much of a boy to see things beforehand, and to see them in all their bearings. You took me by surprise by talking on the subject which led to our misunderstanding. I will not conceal for an instant that I like Callista very much; and that the more I see her, I like her the more. It strikes me that, if you break the matter to Aristo, he and I might have some talk together, and understand each other."

Jucundus was hot-tempered, but easily pacified; and he really did wish to be on confidential terms with his nephew at the present crisis; so he caught at his apology. "Now you speak like a reasonable fellow, Agellius," he answered. "Certainly, I will speak to Aristo, as you wish; and on this question of *consuetudo* or prescription. Well, don't begin looking queer again. I mean I will speak to him on the whole question and its details. He and I will talk together for our respective principals. We shall soon come to terms, I warrant you; and then *you* shall talk with him. Come, show me round your fields," he continued, "and let me see how you will be able to present things to your bride. A very pretty property it is. I it was who was the means of your father thinking of it. You have heard me say so before now, and all the circumstances.

"He was at Carthage at this time, undecided what to do with himself. It so happened that Julia Clara's estates were just then in the market. An enormous windfall her estates were. Old Didius was emperor just before my

---

75   "the beautiful and the useful"

time; he gave all his estates to his daughter as soon as he assumed the purple. Poor lady! she did not enjoy them long; Severus confiscated the whole, not, however, for the benefit of the state, but of the *res privata*.[76] They are so large in Africa alone, that, as you know, you are under a special procurator. Well, they did not come into the market at once; the existing farmers were retained. Marcus Juventius farmed a very considerable portion of them; they were contiguous, and dovetailed into his own lands, and accordingly, when he got into trouble, and had to sell his leases, there were certain odds and ends about Sicca which it was proposed to lease piecemeal. Your employer, Varius, would have given any money for them, but I was beforehand with him. Nothing like being on the spot; he was on business of the proconsul at Adrumetum. I sent off Hispa instantly to Strabo; not an hour's delay after I heard of it. The sale was at Carthage; he went to his old commander, who used his influence, and the thing was done.

"I venture to say there's not such a snug little farm in all Africa; and I am sanguine we shall get a renewal, though Varius will do his utmost to outbid us. Ah, my dear Agellius, if there is but a suspicion you are not a thorough-going Roman! Well, well,—here! ease me through this gate, Agellius; I don't know what's come to the gate since I was here. Indeed!—yes! you have improved this very much. That small arbour is delicious; but you want an image, an Apollo or a Diana. Ah! do now stop for a moment; why are you going forward at such a pace? I'll give you an image: it shall be one that you will really like. Well, you won't have it? I beg you ten thousand pardons. Ha, ha! I mean nothing. Ha, ha, ha! Oh, what an odd world it is! Ha, ha, ha, ha, ha! Well, I am keeping you from your labourers. Ha, ha, ha!"

And having thus smoothed his own ruffled temper, and set things right, as he considered, with Agellius, the old pagan took his journey homewards, assuring Agellius that he would make all things clear for him in a very short time, and telling him to be sure to make a call upon Aristo before the ensuing calends.

---

76    "private good"

# Chapter Ten

# THE DIVINE CALLISTA

THE DAY CAME WHICH Agellius had fixed for paying his promised visit to Aristo. It is not to be denied that, in the interval, the
difficulties of the business which occasioned his visit had increased
upon his apprehensions. Callista was not yet a Christian, nor was there
any reason for saying that a proposal of marriage would make her one;
and a strange sort of convert she would be, if it did. He would not suffer
himself to dwell upon difficulties which he was determined never should
be realized. No; of course a heathen he could not marry, but a heathen
Callista should not be. He did not see the process, but he was convinced
she would become a Christian. Yet somehow so it was, that, if he was
able to stultify his reason, he did not quite succeed to his satisfaction
with his conscience. Every morning found him less satisfied with himself, and more disposed to repent of having allowed his uncle to enter
on the subject with Aristo. But it was a thing done and over; he must
either awkwardly back out, or he must go on. His middle term, as he
hastily had considered it, was nothing else than siding with his uncle,
and committing himself to go all lengths, unless some difficulty rose
with the other party. Yet could he really wish that the step had not been
taken? Was it not plain that if he was to put away Callista from his affections, he must never go near her? And was he to fall back on his drear
solitude, and lose that outlet of thought and relief of mind which he

had lately found in the society of his Greek friends?

We may easily believe that he was not very peaceful in heart when he set out on that morning to call upon Aristo; yet he would not allow that he was doing wrong. He recurred to the pleasant imagination that Callista would certainly become a Christian, and dwelt pertinaciously upon it. He could not tell on what it was founded; he knew enough of his religion not to mean that she was too good to be a heathen; so it is to be supposed he meant that he discerned what he hoped were traces of some supernatural influence operating upon her mind. He had a perception, which he could not justify by argument, that there was in Callista a promise of something higher than anything she yet was. He felt a strange sympathy with her, which certainly unless he utterly deceived himself, was not based on anything merely natural or human,—a sympathy the more remarkable from the contrariety which existed between them in matters of religious belief. And hope having blown this large and splendid bubble, sent it sailing away, and it rose upon the buoyant atmosphere of youth, beautiful to behold.

And yet, as Agellius ascended the long flight of marble steps which led the foot-passenger up into that fair city, while the morning sun was glancing across them, and surveyed the outline of the many sumptuous buildings which crested and encircled the hill, did he not know full well that iniquity was written on its very walls, and spoke a solemn warning to a Christian heart to go out of it, to flee it, not to take up a home in it, not to make alliance with anything in it? Did he not know from experience full well that, when he got into it, his glance could no longer be unrestrained, or his air free; but that it would be necessary for him to keep a control upon his senses, and painfully guard himself against what must either be a terror to him and an abhorrence, or a temptation? Enter in imagination into a town like Sicca, and you will understand the great Apostle's anguish at seeing a noble and beautiful city given up to idolatry. Enter it, and you will understand why it was that the poor priest, of whom Jucundus spoke so bitterly, hung his head, and walked with timid eyes and clouded brow through the joyous streets of Carthage. Hitherto we have only been conducting heathens through it, boys or men, Jucundus, Arnobius, and Firmian; but now a Christian enters it with a Christian's heart and a Christian's hope.

Well is it for us, dear reader, that we in this age do not experience—nay, a blessed thing that we cannot even frame to ourselves in imagination—the actual details of evil which hung as an atmosphere over the cities of Pagan Rome. An Apostle calls the tongue "a fire, a world of iniquity, untameable, a restless evil, a deadly poison;" and surely what he says applies to hideous thoughts represented to the eye, as well as when they are made to strike upon the ear. Unfortunate Agellius! what takes you into the city this morning? Doubtless some urgent, compulsive duty; otherwise you would not surely be threading its lanes or taking the circuit of its porticoes, amid sights which now shock and now allure; fearful sights—not here and there, but on the stateliest structures and in the meanest hovels, in public offices and private houses, in central spots and at the corners of the streets, in bazaars and shops and house-doors, in the rudest workmanship and in the highest art, in letters or in emblems or in paintings—the insignia and the pomp of Satan and of Belial, of a reign of corruption and a revel of idolatry which you can neither endure nor escape. Wherever you go it is all the same; in the police-court on the right, in the military station on the left, in the crowd around the temple, in the procession with its victims and its worshippers who walk to music, in the language of the noisy market-people; wherever you go, you are accosted, confronted, publicly, shamelessly, now as if a precept of religion, now as if a homage to nature, by all which, as a Christian, you shrink from and abjure.

It is no accident of the season or of the day; it is the continuous tradition of some thousands of years; it is the very orthodoxy of the myriads who have lived and died there. There was a region once, in an early age, lying upon the Eastern Sea, which is said at length to have vomited out its inhabitants for their frightful iniquity. They, thus cast forth, took ship, and passed over to the southern coast; and then, gradually settling and spreading into the interior, they peopled the woody plains and fertile slopes of Africa, and filled it with their cities. Sicca is one of these set up in sin; and at the time of which we write that sin was basking under the sun, and rioting and extending itself to its amplest dimensions, like some glittering serpent or spotted pard of the neighbourhood, without interposition from heaven or earth in correction of so awful a degradation. In such scenes of unspeakable pollution, our Christian forefathers perforce lived; through such a scene, though not taking part in it, Agellius, blessed with a country home, is unnecessarily passing.

He has reached the house, or rather the floor, to which he has been making his way. It is at the back of the city, where the rock is steep; and it looks out upon the plain and the mountain range to the north. Its inmates, Aristo and Callista, are engaged in their ordinary work of moulding or carving, painting or gilding the various articles which the temples or the private shrines of the established religion required. Aristo has received from Jucundus the overtures which Agellius had commissioned him to make, and finds, as he anticipated, that they are no great news to his sister. She perfectly understands what is going on, but does not care to speak much upon it, till Agellius makes his appearance. As they sit at work, Aristo speaks:—

"Agellius will make his appearance here this morning. I say, Callista, what can he be coming for?"

"Why, if your news be true, that the Christians are coming into trouble, of course he means to purchase, as a blessing on him, some of these bits of gods."

"You are sharp enough, my little sister," answered Aristo, "to know perfectly well who is the goddess he is desirous of purchasing."

Callista laughed carelessly, but made no reply.

"Come, child," Aristo continued, "don't be cruel to him. Wreath a garland for him by the time he comes. He's well to do, and modest withal, and needs encouragement."

"He's well enough," said Callista.

"I say he's a fellow too well off to be despised as a lover," proceeded her brother, "and it would be a merit with the gods to rid him of his superstition."

"Not much of a Christian," she made answer, "if he is set upon me."

"For whose sake has he been coming here so often, mine or yours, Callista?"

"I am tired of such engagements," she replied. She went on with her painting, and several times seemed as if she would have spoken, but did not. Then, without interrupting her work, she said calmly, "Time was, it gratified my conceit and my feelings to have hangers on. Indeed, without them, how should we have had means to come here? But there's a weariness in all things."

"A weariness! Where is this bad humour to end?" cried Aristo; "it has been a long fit; shake it off while you can, or it will be too much for you. What can you mean? a weariness! You are over young to bid youth farewell. Aching hearts for aching bones. So young and so perverse! We must take things as the gods give them. You will ask for them in vain when you are old. One day above, another day beneath; one while young, another while old. Enjoy life while you have it in your hand." He had said this as he worked. Then he stopped, and turned round to her, with his graving-tool in his hand. "Recollect old Lesbia, how she used to squeak out to me, with her nodding head and trembling limbs"—here he mimicked the old crone—"'My boy, take your pleasure while you can. I can't take pleasure—my day is over; but I don't reproach myself. I had a merry time of it while it lasted. Time stops for no one, but I did my best; I don't reproach myself.' There's the true philosopher, though a slave; more outspoken than Æsop, more practical than Epictetus."

Callista began singing to herself:—

> "I wander by that river's brink
> Which circles Pluto's drear domain;
> I feel the chill night breeze, and think
> Of joys which ne'er shall be again.
>
> "I count the weeds that fringe the shore,
> Each sluggish wave that rolls and rolls;
> I hear the ever-splashing oar
> Of Charon, ferryman of souls.

"Heigho!" she continued, "little regret, but much dread. The young have to fear more than the old have to mourn over. The future outweighs the past. Life is not so sweet as death is bitter. It is hard to quit the light, the light of heaven."

"Callistidion!" he said, impatiently; "my girl, this is preposterous. How long is this to go on? We must take you to Carthage; there is more trade there, if we can get it; and it will be on the bright, far-resounding sea. And I will turn rhetorician, and you shall feed my classes."

"O beautiful, divine light," she continued, "what a loss! O, to think that one day I must lose you for ever! At home I used to lie awake at night longing for the morning, and crying out for the god of day. It was like choice wine to me, a cup of Chian, the first streaks of the Aurora, and I could hardly bear his bright coming, when he came to me like Semele, for rapture. How gloriously did he shoot over the hills! and then anon he rested awhile on the snowy summit of Olympus, as in some luminous shrine, gladdening the Phrygian plain. Fair, bright-haired god! thou art my worship, if Callista worships aught: but somehow I worship nothing now. I am weary."

"Well," said her brother in a soothing tone, "it is a change. That light, elastic air, that transparent heaven, that fresh temperate breeze, that majestic sea! Africa is not Greece; O, the difference! That's it, Callista; it is the *nostalgia*; you are home-sick."

"It may be so," she said; "I do not well know what I would have. Yes, the poisonous dews, the heavy heat, the hideous beasts, the green fever-gendering swamps. This vast thickly-wooded plain, like some mysterious labyrinth, oppresses and disquiets me with its very richness. The luxuriant foliage, the tall, rank plants, the deep, close lanes, I do not see my way through them, and I pant for breath. I only breathe freely on this hill. O, how unlike Greece, with the clear, soft, delicate colouring of its mountains, and the pure azure or the purple of its waters!"

"But, my dear Callista," interrupted her brother, "recollect you are not in those oppressive, gloomy forests, but in Sicca, and no one asks you to penetrate them. And if you want mountains, I think those on the horizon are bare enough."

"And the race of man," she continued, "is worse than all. Where is the genius of our bright land? where its intelligence, playfulness, grace, and noble bearing? Here hearts are as black as brows, and smiles as treacherous as the adders of the wood. The natives are crafty and remorseless; they never relax; they have no cheerfulness or mirth; their very love is a furnace, and their sole ecstasy is revenge."

"No country like home to any of us," said Aristo; "yet here you are. Habit would be a second nature if you were here long enough; your feelings would become acclimated, and would find a new home. People get to like the darkness of the extreme north in course of time. The painted Britons, the Cimmerians, the Hyperboreans, are content never to see the sun at all, which is your god. Here your own god reigns; why quarrel with him?"

"The sun of Greece is light," answered Callista; "the sun of Africa is fire. I am no fire-worshipper."

"I suspect even Styx and Phlegethon are tolerable, at length," said her brother, "if Phlegethon and Styx there be, as the poets tell us."

"The cold, foggy Styx is the north," said Callista, "and the south is the scorching, blasting Phlegethon, and Greece, clear, sweet, and sunny, is the Elysian fields." And she continued her improvisations:—

> "Where are the islands of the blest?
>   They stud the Ægean sea;
> And where the deep Elysian rest?
> It haunts the vale where Peneus strong
> Pours his incessant stream along,
> While craggy ridge and mountain bare
> Cut keenly through the liquid air,
> And, in their own pure tints arrayed,
> Scorn earth's green robes which change and fade,
> And stand in beauty undecayed,
>   Guards of the bold and free."

"A lower flight, if you please, just now," said Aristo, interrupting her. "I do really wish a serious word with you about Agellius. He's a fellow I can't help liking, in spite of his misanthropy. Let me plead his cause. Like him or not yourself, still he has a full purse; and you will do a service to yourself and to the gods of Greece, and to him too, if you will smile on him. Smile on him at least for a time; we will go to Carthage when you are tired. His looks have very little in them of a Christian left; you may blow it away with your breath."

"One might do worse than be a Christian," she answered slowly, "if all is true that I have heard of them."

Aristo started up in irritation. "By all the gods of Olympus," he said, "this is intolerable! If a man wants a tormentor, I commend him to a girl like you. What has ailed thee some time past, you silly child? What have I done to you that you should have got so cross and contrary and so hard to please?"

"I mean," she said, "if I were a Christian, life would be more bearable."

"Bearable!" he echoed; "bearable! ye gods! more bearable to have Styx and Tartarus, the Furies and their snakes, in this world as well as in the next? to have evil within and without, to hate one's self and to be hated of all men! to live the life of an ass, and to die the death of a dog! Bearable! But hark! I hear Agellius's step on the staircase. Callista, dear Callista, be yourself. Listen to reason."

But Callista would not listen to reason, if her brother was its embodiment; but went on with her singing:—

> "For what is Afric but the home
>     Of burning Phlegethon?
> What the low beach and silent gloom,
> And chilling mists of that dull river,
> Along whose bank the thin ghosts shiver,
> The thin, wan ghosts that once were men,
> But Tauris, isle of moor and fen;
> Or, dimly traced by seaman's ken,
>     The pale-cliffed Albion?"

Here she stopped, looked down, and busied herself with her work.

# Chapter Eleven

# CALLISTA'S PREACHING, AND WHAT CAME OF IT

It is undeniably a solemn moment, under any circumstances, and requires a strong heart, when any one deliberately surrenders himself, soul and body, to the keeping of another while life shall last; and this, or something like this, reserving the supreme claim of duty to the Creator, is the matrimonial contract. In individual cases it may be made without thought or distress, but surveyed objectively, and as carried out into a sufficient range of instances, it is so tremendous an undertaking that nature seems to sink under its responsibilities. When the Christian binds himself by vows to a religious life, he makes a surrender to Him who is all-perfect, and whom he may unreservedly trust. Moreover, looking at that surrender on its human side, he has the safeguard of distinct *provisos* and regulations, and of the principles of theology, to secure him against tyranny on the part of his superiors. But what shall be his encouragement to make himself over, without condition or stipulation, as an absolute property, to a fallible being, and that not for a season, but for life? The mind shrinks from such a sacrifice, and demands that, as religion enjoins it, religion should sanction and bless it. It instinctively desires that either the bond should be dissoluble, or that the subjects of it should be sacramentally strengthened to maintain it. "So help me God," the formula of every oath, is emphatically necessary here.

But Agellius is contemplating a superhuman engagement without superhuman assistance; and that in a state of society in which public opinion, which in some sense compensates for the absence of religion, supplied human motives, not for, but against keeping it, and with one who had given no indication that she understood what marriage meant. No wonder then, that, in spite of his simplicity, his sanguine temperament, and his delusion, the more he thought of the step he had taken, the more unsatisfactory he found it, and the nearer he grew to the time when he must open the subject with Aristo, the less he felt able to do so. In consequence he was in a distress of mind, as he ascended the staircase which led to his friend's lodging, to which his anxiety, as he mounted the hill on the other side of the city, was tranquillity itself; and, except that he was coming by engagement, he would have turned back, and for the time at least have put the whole subject from his thoughts. Yet even then, as often as Callista rose in his mind's eye, his scruples and misgivings vanished before the beauty of that image, as mists before the sun; and when he actually stood in her sweet presence, it seemed as if some secret emanation from her flowed in upon his heart, and he stood breathless and giddy under the intensity of the fascination.

However, the reader must not suppose that in the third century of our era such negotiations as that which now seems to be on the point of coming off between Callista and Agellius, were embellished with those transcendental sentiments and that magnificent ceremonial with which chivalry has invested them in these latter ages. There was little occasion then for fine speaking or exquisite deportment; and if there had been, we, who are the narrators of these hitherto unrecorded transactions, should have been utterly unable to do justice to them. At that time of day the Christian had too much simplicity, the heathen too little of real delicacy, to indulge in the sublimities of modern love-making, at least as it is found in novels; and in the case before us both gentleman and lady will be thought, we consider, sadly matter-of-fact, or rather semi-barbarous, by the votaries of what is just now called European civilization.

On Agellius's entering the room, Aristo was pacing to and fro in some discomposure; however, he ran up to his friend, embraced him, and, looking at him with significance, congratulated him on his good looks. "There is more fire in your eye," he said, "dear Agellius, and more eloquence in the turn of your lip, than I have ever yet seen. A new spirit is in you. So you are determined to come out of your solitude? That you should have been able to exist in it so long is the wonderment to me."

Agellius had recovered himself, yet he dared not look again on Callista. "Do not jest, Aristo," he said; "I am come, as you know, to talk to you about your sister. I have brought her a present of flowers; they are my best present, or rather not mine, but the birth of the opening year, as fair and fragrant as herself."

"We will offer them to our Pallas Athene," said his friend, "to whom we artists are especially devout." And he would have led Agellius on, and made him place them in her niche in the opposite wall.

"I am more serious than you are," said Agellius; "and I have brought the best my garden contains as an offering to your sister. *She* will not think I bring them for any other purpose. Where are you going?" he continued, as he saw his friend take down his broad *petasus*.[77]

"Why," answered Aristo, "since I am so poor an interpreter of your meaning, you can dispense with me altogether. I will leave you to speak for yourself, and meanwhile will go and see what old Dromo has to tell, before the sun is too high in the heavens."

Saying this, with a half-imploring, half-satirical look at his sister, he set off to the barber's at the Forum.

Agellius took up the flowers, and laid them on the table before her, as she sat at work. "Do you accept my flowers, Callista?" he asked.

"Fair and fragrant, like myself, are they?" she made reply. "Give them to me." She took them, and bent over them. "The blushing rose," she said, gravely, "the stately lily, the royal carnation, the golden moly, the purple amaranth,

---

77    "hat"

the green bryon, the diosanthos, the sertula, the sweet modest saliunca, fit emblems of Callista. Well, in a few hours they will have faded; yes, they will get more and more like her."

She paused and looked him steadily in the face, and then continued: "Agellius, I once had a slave who belonged to your religion. She had been born in a Christian family, and came into my possession on her master's death. She was unlike any one I have seen before or since; she cared for nothing, yet was not morose or peevish or hard-hearted. She died young in my service. Shortly before her end she had a dream. She saw a company of bright shades, clothed in white, like the hours which circle round the god of day. They were crowned with flowers, and they said to each other, 'She ought to have a token too.' So they took her hand, and led her to a most beautiful lady, as stately as Juno and as sweet as Ariadne, so radiant in countenance that they themselves suddenly looked like Ethiopians by the side of her. She, too, was crowned with flowers, and these so dazzling that they might be the stars of heaven or the gems of Asia for what Chione could tell. And that fair goddess (angel you call her) said, 'My dear, here is something for you from my Son. He sends you by me a red rose for your love, a white lily for your chastity, purple violets to strew your grave, and green palms to flourish over it.' Is this the reason why you give me flowers, Agellius, that I may rank with Chione? and is this their interpretation?"

"Callista," he answered, "it is my heart's most fervent wish, it is my mind's vivid anticipation, that the day may come when you will receive such a crown, nay, a brighter one."

"And you are come, of course, to philosophize to me, and to put me in the way of dying like Chione," she made answer. "I implore your pardon. You are offering me flowers, it seems, not for a bridal wreath, but for a funeral urn."

"Is it wonderful," said Agellius, "that the two wishes should have gone together in my heart; and that while I trusted and prayed that you might have the same Master in heaven as I have myself, I also hoped you would have the same service, the same aims, the same home upon earth?"

"And that you should speak one word for your Master and two for yourself!" she retorted.

"It has been by feeling how much you could be to me," he answered, "that I have been led to think how much my Master may be doing for you already, and how much in time to come you might do for Him. Callista, do not urge me with your Greek subtlety, or expect me to analyze my feelings more precisely than I have the ability to do. May I calmly tell you the state of my mind, as I do know it, and will you patiently listen?"

She signified her willingness, and he continued—"This only I know," he said, "what I have experienced ever since I first heard you converse, that there is between you and me a unity of thought so strange that I should have deemed it could not have been, before I found it actually to exist, between any two persons whatever; and which, widely as we are separated in opinion and habit, and differently as we have been brought up, is to me inexplicable. I find it difficult to explain what I mean; we disagree certainly on the most important subjects, yet there is an unaccountable correspondence in the views we take of things, in our impressions, in the line in which our minds move, and the issues to which they come, in our judgment of what is great and little, and the manner in which objects affect our feelings. When I speak to my uncle, when I speak to your brother, I do not understand them, nor they me. We are moving in different spheres, and I am solitary, however much they talk. But to my astonishment, I find between you and me one language. Is it wonderful that, in proportion to my astonishment, I am led to refer it to one cause, and think that one Master Hand must have engraven those lines on the soul of each of us? Is it wonderful that I should fancy that He who has made us alike has made us for each other, and that the very same persuasives by which I bring you to cast your eyes on me, may draw you also to cast yourself in adoration at the feet of my Master?"

For an instant tears seemed about to start from Callista's eyes, but she repressed the emotion, if it were such, and answered with impetuosity, "Your Master! who is your Master? what know I of your Master? what have you ever told me of your Master? I suppose it is an esoteric doctrine which I am not worthy to know; but so it is, here you have been again and again, and talked freely of many things, yet I am in as much darkness about your Master as if I had never seen you. I know He died; I know too that Christians say He lives. In some fortunate island, I suppose; for, when I have asked, you have got rid of the subject as best you could. You have talked about your law and your various duties, and what you consider right, and what is forbidden, and of some of the old writers of your sect, and of the Jews before them; but if, as you imply, my wants and aspirations are the same as yours, what have you done towards satisfying them? what have you done for that Master towards whom you now propose to lead me? No!" she continued, starting up, "you have watched those wants and aspirations for yourself, not for Him; you have taken interest in them, you have cherished them, as if you were the author, you the object of them. You profess to believe in One True God, and to reject every other; and now you are implying that the Hand, the Shadow of that God is on my mind and heart. Who is this God? where? how? in what? O Agellius, you have stood in the way of Him, ready to speak for yourself, using Him as a means to an end."

"O Callista," said Agellius, in an agitated voice, when he could speak, "do my ears hear aright? do you really wish to be taught who the true God is?"

"No, mistake me not," she cried passionately, "I have no such wish. I could not be of your religion. Ye Gods! how have I been deceived! I thought every Christian was like Chione. I thought there could not be a cold Christian. Chione spoke as if a Christian's first thoughts were goodwill to others; as if his state were of such blessedness, that his dearest heart's wish was to bring others into it. Here is a man who, so far from feeling himself blest, thinks I can bless him! comes to me—me, Callista, a herb of the field, a poor weed, exposed to every wind of heaven, and shrivelling before the fierce sun—to me he comes to repose his heart upon. But as for any blessedness he has to show me, why, since he does not feel any himself, no wonder he has none to give away. I thought a Christian was superior to time and place; but all is hollow. Alas, alas, I am young in life to feel the force of that saying, with which sages go out of it, 'Vanity and hollowness!' Agellius, when I first heard you were a Christian, how my heart beat! I thought of her who was gone; and at first I thought I saw her in you, as if there had been some magical sympathy between you and her; and I hoped that from you I might have learned more of that strange strength which my nature needs, and which she told me she possessed. Your words, your manner, your looks were altogether different from others who came near me. But so it was; you came, and you went, and came again; I thought it reserve, I thought it timidity, I thought it the caution of a persecuted sect; but O, my disappointment, when first I saw in you indications that you were thinking of me only as others think, and felt towards me as others may feel; that you were aiming at me, not at your God; that you had much to tell of yourself, but nothing of Him! Time was I might have been led to worship you, Agellius; you have hindered it by worshipping *me*."

It is not often, we suppose, that such deep offence is given to a lady by the sort of admiration of which Agellius had been guilty in the case of Callista; however, startled as he might be, and startled and stung he was, there was too much earnestness in her distress, too much of truth in her representations, too much which came home to his heart and conscience, to allow of his being affronted or irritated. She had but supplied the true interpretation of the misgiving which had haunted him that morning, from the time he set out till the moment of his entering the room. Jucundus some days back had readily acquiesced in his assurance that he was not inconsistent; but Callista had not been so indulgent, though really more merciful. There was a pause in the conversation, or rather in her outpouring; each had bitter thoughts, and silently devoured them. At length, she began again:—

"So the religion of Chione is a dream; now for four years I had hoped it was a reality. All things again are vanity; I had hoped there was something somewhere more than I could see; but there is nothing. Here am I a living, breathing woman, with an over-flowing heart, with keen affections, with a yearning after some object which may possess me. I cannot exist without something to rest upon. I cannot fall back upon that drear, forlorn state, which philosophers call wisdom, and moralists call virtue. I cannot enrol myself a votary of that cold Moon, whose arrows do but freeze me. I cannot sympathize in that majestic band of sisters whom Rome has placed under the tutelage of Vesta. I must have something to love; love is my life. Why do you come to me, Agellius, with your every-day gallantry. Can you compete with the noble Grecian forms which have passed before my eyes? Is your voice more manly, are its tones more eloquent, than those which have thrilled through my ears since I ceased to be a child? Can you add perfume to the feast by your wit, or pour sunshine over grot and rushing stream by your smile? *What* can you give me? There was one thing which I thought you *could* have given me, better than anything else; but it is a shadow. You have nothing to give. You have thrown me back upon my dreary, dismal self, and the deep wounds of my memory.... Poor, poor Agellius! but it was not his fault, it could not be helped," she continued, as if in thought; "it could not be helped; for, if he had nothing to give, how could he give it? After all, he wanted something to love, just as I did; and he could find nothing better than me.... And they thought to persuade her to spend herself upon him, as she had spent herself upon others. Yes, it was Jucundus and Aristo—my brother, even my own brother. They thought not of *me*." Here her tears gushed out violently, and she abandoned herself to a burst of emotion. "They were thinking of *him*. I had hoped he could lead me to what was higher; but woe, woe!" she cried, wringing her hands, "they thought I was only fit to bring him low. Well; after all, *is* Callista really good for much more than the work they have set her to do?"

She was absorbed in her own misery in an intense sense of degradation, in a keen consciousness of the bondage of nature, in a despair of ever finding what alone could give meaning to her existence, and an object to her intellect and affections. And Agellius on the other hand, what surprise, remorse, and humiliation came upon him! It was a strange contrast, the complaint of nature unregenerate on the one hand, the self-reproach of nature regenerate and lapsing on the other. At last he spoke, and they were his last words.

"Callista," he said, "whatever injury I may have unwillingly inflicted upon you, you at least have returned me good for evil, and have made yourself my benefactress. Certainly, I now know myself better than I did; and He who has made use of you as His instrument of mercy towards me, will not forget to reward you tenfold. One word will I say for myself; nay, not for myself, but for my Master. Do not for an instant suppose that what you thought of the Christian religion is not true. It reveals a present God, who satisfies every affection of the heart, yet keeps it pure. I serve a Master," he continued, blushing from modesty and earnestness as he spoke, "I serve a Master whose love is stronger than created love. God help my inconsistency! but I never meant to love you as I love Him. You are destined for His love. I commit you to Him, your true Lord, whom I never ought to have rivalled, for whom I ought simply to have pleaded. Though I am not worthy to approach you, I shall trace you at a distance, who knows where? perhaps even to the prison and to the arena of those who confess the Saviour of men, and dare to suffer and die for His name. And now, farewell; to His keeping and that of His holy martyrs I commit you."

He did not trust himself to look at her as he turned to the door, and left the room.

# Chapter Twelve

# A DEATH

THE FIRST STAGES of repentance are but a fever, in which there is restlessness and thirst, hot and cold fits, vague, dreary dreams, long darkness which seems destined never to have a morning, effort without result, and collapse without reaction. These symptoms had already manifested themselves in Agellius; he spoke calmly to Callista, and sustained himself by the claims of the moment; but no sooner had he left the room and was thrown upon himself, than his self-possession left him, and he fell into an agony, or rather anarchy of tumultuous feelings. Then rose up before his mind a hundred evil spectres, not less scaring and more real than the dreams of the delirious. He thought of the singular favour which had been shown him in his reception into the Christian fold, and that at so early a date; of the myriads all around who continued in heathenism as they had been born, and of his utter insensibility to his own privilege. He felt how much would be required of him, and how little hitherto had been forthcoming. He thought of the parable of the barren fig-tree, and the question was whispered in his ear whether it would not be fulfilled in him. He asked himself in what his heart and his conduct differed from the condition of a fairly virtuous heathen. And then he thought of Callista in contrast with himself, as having done more with the mite which she possessed than he had done with many pounds. He felt that Tyre and Sidon were rising up against him in her person; or rather how the saying seemed about to be verified in her, that strangers should sit down in the kingdom from far countries, while those who were the heirs should be thrust out. He had been rebuked by one to whom he rather ought to have brought self-knowledge and compunction, and she was sensitively alive to his want of charity. She had felt bitterly that she was left in ignorance and sin by one who had what she had not. She had accused him of being zealous enough to win her to himself, when he had shown no zeal at all to win her to her Maker. If she was brought to the truth at length, there would be no thanks to him for the happy change; yet on the other hand, though he had predicted it, alas! was it likely that it would be granted? Had she not had her opportunity, which was lost because he had not improved it? Yes, she had with a deliberate mind and in set words put aside and taken leave of that which she once desired and hoped might have been her own, sorrowfully indeed, but peremptorily, as firmly persisting in rejecting it, as she might have persisted in maintaining it; and, if she died in infidelity, horrible thought! would not the burden lie on him, and was this to be the token of the love which he pretended to entertain for her?

What was he living for? what was the work he had set himself to do? Did he live to plant flowers, or to rear fruit, to maintain himself and to make money? Was that a time to pride himself on vineyards and oliveyards, when, like Eliseus, he was one among myriads who were in unbelief? Ah, the difference between a saint and him? Of what good was he on earth; why should not he die? why so chary of his life? why preserve his wretched life at all? Could he not do more by giving it than by keeping it? Might it not have been given him perchance for the very purpose that he might sacrifice it for Him who had given it? He had been timid about making a profession of his faith, which might have led to prison and death; but perhaps the very object of his life in the divine purpose, the very reason of his birth, had been that, as soon as he was grown, he should die for the truth. He might have been cut off by disease; he was not; and why, except that he might merit in his death, and that what, in the ordinary course of things, was a mere suffering, might in his case be an act of service? His death might have been the conversion of thousands, of Callista; and the fewness of his days here would have been his claim to a blessed eternity hereafter.

Nor Callista alone; he had natural friends, with nearer claims upon his charity. Had he been other than he was, he might have prevailed with his uncle; at least he might have taught him to respect the Christian Faith and Name, and restrained him from daring to attempt, for he now saw that it was an attempt, to seduce him into sin. He might have lodged a good seed in his heart, which in the hour of sickness might have germinated. And his brother again had learned to despise him; indeed he had raised in every one who came near him the suspicion that he was not really a Christian, that he was an apostate (he could not help uttering a cry of anguish as he used the word), an apostate from that which was his real life and supreme worship.

Why did he not at once go into the Basilica or the Gymnasium, and proclaim himself a Christian? There were rumours abroad that the new emperor was beginning a new policy towards his religion; let him inaugurate it in Agellius. Might he not thus perchance wash out his sin? He would be led into the amphitheatre, as his betters had been led before him; the crowds would yell, and the lion would be let loose upon him. He would confront the edict, tear it down, be seized by the apparitor, and hurried to the rack or the slow fire. Callista would hear of it, and would learn at length he was not quite the craven and the recreant which she thought him.

Then his thoughts took a turn. Callista! what was Callista to him? Why should he think of her, when she was girding him to martyrdom? Was she to be the motive which was to animate him, and her praise his reward? Alas, alas! could he gain heaven by pleasing a heathen? "But to whom then," he continued, "am I to look up? who is to give me sympathy? who is to encourage, to advise me? O my Father, pity me! a feeble child, a poor, outcast, wandering sheep, away from the fold, torn by the briars and thorns, and no one to bind his wounds and retrace his steps for him. Why am I thus alone in the world? why am I without a pastor and guide? Ah, was not this my fault in remaining in Sicca? I have no tie here; let me go to Carthage, or to Tagaste, or to Madaura, or to Hippo. I am not fit to walk the world by myself; I am too simple, and am no match for its artifices."

Here another thought took possession of him, which had as yet but crossed his mind, and it made him colour up with confusion and terror. "They were laying a plot for me," he said, "my uncle and Aristo; and it is Callista who has defeated it." And as he spoke, he felt how much he owed to her, and how dangerous too it was to think of his debt. Yet it would not be wrong to pray for her; she had marred the device of which she was to have been the agent. "Laqueus contritus est, et nos liberati sumus:"[78] the net was broken and he was delivered. She had refused his devotion, that he might give it to his God; and now he would only think of her, and whisper her name, when he was kneeling before the Blessed Mary, his advocate. O that that second and better Eve, who brought salvation into the world, as our first mother brought death, O that she might bear Callista's name in remembrance, and get it written in the Book of life!

It was high noon; and all this time Agellius was walking in his present excited mood, without covering to his head, under the burning rays of the sun, not knowing which way he went, and retracing his steps, as he wandered about at random, with a vague notion he was going homewards. The few persons whom he met, creeping about under the shadow of the lofty houses, or under the porticoes of the temples, looked at him with wonder, and thought him furious or deranged. The shafts of the sun were not so hot as his own thoughts, or as the blood which shot to and fro so fiercely in his veins; but they were working fearfully on his physical frame, though they could not increase the fever of his mind. He had come to the Forum; the market people were crouching under their booths or the shelter of their baskets. The riffraff of the city, who lived by their wits, or by odd jobs, or on the windfalls of the market; lazy fellows who did nothing, who did not move till hunger urged them, like the brute; half-idiotic chewers of opium, ragged

---

78   "The snare is broken, and we are delivered," Ps 124:7

or rather naked children, the butcher boys and scavengers of the temples, lay at their length at the mouth of the caverns formed by the precipitous rock, or under the Arch of Triumph, or amid the columns of the Gymnasium and the Heracleum, or in the doorways of the shops. A scattering of beggars were lying, poor creatures, on their backs in the blazing sun, reckless of the awful maladies, the fits, the seizures, and the sudden death, which might be the consequence.

Numbers out of this mixed multitude were asleep; some were looking with dull listless eyes at the still scene, or at any accidental movements which might vary it. They saw a figure coming nearer and nearer and wildly passing by. Just then Agellius was diverted from his painful meditations by hearing one of these fellows say to another, as he roused from a sort of doze, "That's one of them. We know them all, but very poor pickings can be got out of them; but he has more than most. They're a low set in Sicca." And then the man cried out, "Look sharp, young chap! the Furies are at your heels, and the Fates are going before you. Look there at the emperor; he is looking at you, as grim and sour as you could wish him." He spoke of the equestrian statue of Severus before the Basilica on the right; and, attracted by his words, Agellius went up to a board which was fixed to its base. It was an imperial edict, and it ran as follows:—

"Cneius Trajanus Decius, Augustus; and Quintus Herennius Etruscus Decius, Cæsar; Emperors, unconquerable and pious; by united council these:—

"Whereas we have experienced the benefits and the gifts of the gods, and do also enjoy the victory which they have given us over our enemies, and moreover salubrity of seasons, and abundance in the fruits of the earth;

"Therefore, acknowledging the aforesaid as our benefactors and the providers of those things which are necessary for the commonwealth, we make this our decree, that every class of the state, freemen and slaves, the army and civilians, offer to the gods expiatory sacrifices, falling down in supplication before them;

"And if any one shall presume to disobey this our divine command, which we unite in promulgating, we order that man to be thrown into chains, and to be subjected to various tortures;

"And should he thereupon be persuaded to reverse his disobedience, he shall receive from us no slight honours;

"But should he hold out in opposition, first he shall have many tortures, and then shall be executed by the sword, or thrown into the deep sea, or given as a prey to birds and dogs;

"And more than all if such a person be a professor of the Christian religion.

"Farewell, and live happy."

The old man in the fable called on Death, and Death made his appearance. We are very far indeed from meaning that Agellius uttered random words, or spoke impatiently, when he just now expressed a wish to have the opportunity of dying for the Faith. Nevertheless, what now met his eyes and was transmitted through them, sentence by sentence, into his mind, was not certainly of a nature to calm the tumult which was busy in breast and brain; a sickness came over him, and he staggered away. The words of the edict still met his eyes, and were of a bright red colour. The sun was right before him, but the letters were in the sun, and the sun in his brain. He reeled and fell heavily on the pavement. No notice was taken of the occurrence by the spectators around him. They lazily or curiously looked on, and waited to see if he would recover.

How long he lay there he could not tell, when he came to himself; if it could really be said to be coming to himself to have the power of motion, and an instinct that he must move, and move in one direction. He managed to rise and lean against the pedestal of the statue, and its shade by this time protected him. Then an intense desire came upon him to get home, and that desire gave him a temporary preternatural strength. It came upon him as a duty to leave Sicca for his cottage, and he set off. He had a confused notion that he must do his duty, and go straight forward, and turn neither to the right, nor the left, and stop nowhere, but move on steadily for his true home. But next an impression came upon him that he was running away from persecution, and that this ought not to be, and that he ought to face the enemy, or at least not to hide from him, but meekly wait for him.

As he went along the narrow streets which led down the hill towards the city gate this thought came so powerfully upon him that at length he sat down on a stone which projected from an open shop, and thought of surrendering himself. He felt the benefit of the rest, and this he fancied to be the calm of conscience consequent upon self-surrender and resignation. It was a fruiterer's stall, and the owner, seeing his exhaustion, offered him some slices of a water-melon for his refreshment. He ate one of them, and then again a vague feeling came on him that he was in danger of idolatry, and must protest against idolatry, and that he ought not to remain in the neighbourhood of temptation. So, throwing down the small coin which was sufficient for payment, he continued his journey. The rest and the refreshment of the fruit, and the continued shade which the narrow street allowed him, allayed the fever, and for the time recruited him, and he moved on languidly. The sun, however, was still high in heaven, and when he got beyond the city beat down upon his head from a cloudless sky. He painfully toiled up the ascent which led to his cottage. He had nearly gained the gate of his homestead; he saw his old household slave, born in his father's house, a Christian like himself, coming to meet him. A dizziness came over him, he lost his senses, and fell down helplessly upon the bank.

# Chapter Thirteen

# AND RESURRECTION

JUCUNDUS WAS QUITE as much amused as provoked at the result of the delicate negotiation in which he had entangled his nephew. It was a gratification to him to find that its ill success had been owing in no respect to any fault on the side of Agellius. He had done his part without shrinking, and the view which he, Jucundus, had taken of his state of mind, was satisfactorily confirmed. He had nothing to fear from Agellius, and though he had failed in securing the guarantee which he had hoped for his attachment to things as they were, yet in the process of failure it had been proved that his nephew might be trusted without it. And it was a question, whether a girl so full of whims and caprices as Callista might after all have done him any permanent good. The absurd notion, indeed, of her having a leaning for Christianity had been refuted by her conduct on the occasion; still, who could rely on a clever and accomplished Greek? There were secret societies and conspiracies in abundance, and she might have involved so weak and innocent a fellow in some plans against the government, now or at a future time; or might have alienated him from his uncle, or in some way or other made a fool of him, if she had consented to have him for her slave. Why she had rejected so eligible a suitor it was now useless and idle to inquire; it might be that the haughty or greedy Greek had required him to bid higher for her favourable notice. If the negotiation had taken such a turn, then indeed there was still more gratifying evidence of Agellius having broken from his fantastic and peevish superstition.

Still, however, he was not without anxiety, now that the severe measures directed against the Christians were in progress. No overt act, indeed, beyond the publication of the edict, had been taken in Sicca—probably would be taken at all. The worst was, that something must be done to make a show; he could have wished that some of the multitude of townspeople, half suspected of Christianity, had stood firm, and suffered themselves to be tortured and executed. One or two would have been enough; but the magistracy got no credit with the central government for zeal and activity if no Christians were made an example of. Yet still it was a question whether the strong acts at Carthage and elsewhere would not suffice, though the lesser towns did nothing. At least, while the populace was quiet, there was nothing to press for severity. There were no rich Christians in Sicca to tempt the cupidity of the informer or of the magistrate; no political partisans among them, who had made enemies with this or that class of the community. But, supposing a bad feeling to rise in the populace, supposing the magistrates to have ill-wishers and rivals—and what men in power had not?—who might be glad to catch them tripping, and make a case against them at Rome, why, it must be confessed that Agellius was nearly the only victim who could be pitched upon. He wished Callista no harm, but, if a Christian must be found and held up *in terrorem*, he would rather it was a person like her, without connections and home, than the member of any decent family of Sicca, whose fair fame would be compromised by a catastrophe. However, she was *not* a Christian, and Agellius *was*, at least by profession; and his fear was lest Juba should be right in his estimate of his brother's character. Juba had said that Agellius could be as obstinate as he was ordinarily indolent and yielding, and Jucundus dreaded lest, if he were rudely charged with Christianity, and bidden to renounce it under pain of punishment, he would rebel against the tyrannical order, and go to prison and to death out of sheer perverseness or sense of honour.

With these perplexities before him, he could find nothing better than the following plan of action, which had been in his mind for some time. While the edict remained inoperative, he would do nothing at all, and let Agellius go on with his country occupations, which would keep him out of the way. But if any disposition appeared of a popular commotion, or a movement on the part of the magistracy, he determined to get possession of Agellius, and forcibly confine him in his own house in Sicca. He hoped that in the case of one so young, so uncommitted, he should have influence with the municipal authorities, or at the prætorium, or in the camp (for the camp and the prætorium were under different jurisdictions in the proconsulate), to shelter Agellius from a public inquiry into his religious tenets, or if this could not be, to smuggle him out of the city. He was ready to affirm solemnly that his nephew was no Christian, though he was touched in the head, and, from an affection parallel to hydrophobia, to which the disciples of Galen ought to turn their attention, was sent into convulsions on the sight of an altar. His father, indeed, was a malignant old atheist—there was no harm in being angry with the dead—but it was very hard the son should suffer for his father's offence. If he must be judged of by his parents, let him rather have the advantage of the thorough loyalty and religiousness of his mother, a most zealous old lady, in high repute in the neighbourhood of Sicca for her theurgic knowledge, a staunch friend of the imperial government, which had before now been indebted to her for important information, and as staunch a hater of the Christians. Such was the plan of proceedings resolved on by Jucundus before he received the news of his nephew's serious malady. It did not reach him till many days after; and then he did not go to see him, first, lest he should be supposed to be in communication with him, next, as having no respect for that romantic sort of generosity which risks the chances of contagion for the absurd ceremony of paying a compliment.

It was thus that Jucundus addressed himself to the present state of affairs, and anticipated the chances of the future. As to Aristo, he had very little personal interest in the matter. His sister might have thwarted him in affairs which lay nearer his heart than the moral emancipation of Agellius; and as she generally complied with his suggestions and wishes, whatever they were, he did not grudge her her liberty of action in this instance. Nor had the occurrence which had taken place any great visible effect upon Callista herself. She had lost her right to be indignant with her brother, and she resigned or rather abandoned herself to her destiny. Her better feelings had been brought out for the moment in her conversation with Agellius; but they were not ordinary ones. True, she was tired, but she was the slave of the world; and Agellius had only made her more sceptical than before that there was any service better. So at least she said to herself; she said it was fantastic to go elsewhere for good, and that, if life was short, then, as her brother said, it was necessary to make the most of it.

And meanwhile, what of Agellius himself? Why, it will be some little time before Agellius will be in a condition to moralize upon anything. His faithful slave half-carried, half-drew him into the cottage, and stretched him upon his bed. Then, having sufficient skill for the ordinary illnesses of the country, though this was more than an ordinary fever, he drew blood from him, gave him a draught of herbs, and left him to the slow but safe processes of nature to restore him. It could not be affirmed that he was not in considerable danger of life, yet youth carries hope with it, and his attendant had little to fear for his recovery. For some days certainly Agellius had no apprehension of anything, except of restlessness and distress, of sleepless nights, or dreary, miserable dreams. At length one morning, as he was lying on his back with his eyes shut, it came into his mind to ask himself whether Sunday would ever come. He had been accustomed upon the first day of the week to say some particular prayers and psalms, and unite himself in spirit with his brethren beyond seas. And then he tried to remember the last Sunday; and the more he thought, the less he could remember it, till he began to think that months had gone without a Sunday. This he was certain of, that he had lost reckoning, for he had made no notches for the days for a long while past, and unless his slave Asper knew, there was no one to tell him. Here he got so puzzled, that it was like one of the bad dreams which had worried him. He felt it affect his head, and he was obliged to give up the inquiry.

From this time his sleep was better and more refreshing for several days; he was more collected when he was awake, and was able to ask himself why he lay there, and what had happened to him. Then gradually his memory began to return like the dawning of the day; the cause and the circumstances of his recent visit to the city, point after point came up, and he felt first wonder, and then certainty. He recollected the Forum, and then the edict; a solemn, overpowering emotion here seized him, and for a while he dared not think more. When he recovered, and tried to pursue the events of the day, he found himself unequal to the task; all was dark, except that he had some vague remembrance of thirsting, and some one giving him to drink, and then his saying with the Psalmist, "Transivimus per ignem et aquam."[79]

He opened his eyes and looked about him. He was at home. There was some one at the bed-head whom he could not see hanging over him, and he was too weak to raise himself and so command a view of him. He waited patiently, being too feeble to have any great anxiety on the subject. Presently a voice addressed him: "You are recovering, my son," it said.

"Who are *you?*" said Agellius abruptly. The person spoken to applied his mouth to Agellius's ear, and uttered lowly several sacred names.

Agellius would have started up had he been strong enough; he could but sink down upon his rushes in agitation.

"Be content to know no more at present," said the stranger, "praise God, as I do. You know enough for your present strength. It is your act of obedience for the day."

It was a deep, clear, peaceful, authoritative voice. In his present state, as we have said, it cost Agellius no great effort to mortify curiosity; and the accents of that voice soothed him, and the mystery employed his mind, and had something pleasing and attractive in it. Moreover, about the main point there was no mystery, and could be no mistake, that he was in the hands of a Christian ecclesiastic.

---

79    "We have passed through fire and water," Ps. 66:12

The stranger occupied himself for a time with a book of prayers which he carried about him, and then again with the duties of a sick-bed. He sprinkled vinegar over Agellius's face and about the room, and supplied him with the refreshment of cooling fruit. He kept the flies from tormenting him, and did his best so to arrange his posture that he might suffer least from his long lying. In the morning and evening he let in the air, and he excluded the sultry noon. In these various occupations he was from time to time removed to a distance from the patient, who thus had an opportunity of observing him. The stranger was of middle height, upright, and well proportioned; he was dressed in a peasant's or slave's dark tunic. His face was rather round than long; his hair black, yet with the promise of greyness, with what might be baldness in the crown, or a priest's tonsure. His short beard curled round his chin; his complexion was very clear. But the most striking point about him was his eyes; they were of a light or greyish blue, transparent, and shining like precious stones.

From the day that they first interchanged words, the priest said some short prayers from time to time with Agellius—the Lord's Prayer, and portions of the Psalms. Afterwards, when he was well enough to converse, Agellius was struck with the inexpressible peculiarity of his manner. It was self-collected, serene, gentle, tender, unobtrusive, unstudied. It enabled him to say things severe and even stern, without startling, offending, or repelling the hearer. He spoke very little about himself, though from time to time points of detail were elicited of his history in the course of conversation. He said that his name was Cæcilius. Asper, when he entered the room, would kneel down and offer to kiss the stranger's sandal, though the latter generally managed to prevent it.

Cæcilius did not speak much about himself; but Agellius, on the other hand, found it a relief to tell out his own history, and reflect upon and describe his own feelings. As he lay on his bed, he half soliloquized, half addressed himself to the stranger. Sometimes he required an answer; sometimes he seemed to require none. Once he asked suddenly, after a long silence, whether a man could be baptized twice; and when the priest answered distinctly in the negative, Agellius replied that if so, he thought it would be best never to be baptized till the hour of death. It was a question, he said, which had perplexed him a good deal, but he never had had any one to converse with on the subject.

Cæcilius answered, "But how could you promise yourself that you would be able to obtain the sacrament at the last moment? The water and the administrator might come just too late; and then where would you be, my son? And then again, how do you know you would wish it? Is your will simply in your own power? 'Carpe diem;'[80] take God's gift while you can."

"The benefit is so immense," answered Agellius, "that one would wish, if one could, to enter into the unseen world without losing its fulness. This cannot be, if a long time elapses between baptism and death."

"You are, then, of the number of those," said Cæcilius, "who would cheat their Maker of His claim on their life, provided they could (as it is said) in their last moment cheat the devil."

Agellius continuing silent, Cæcilius added, "You want to enjoy this world, and to inherit the next; is it so?"

"I am puzzled, my head is weak, father; I do not see my way to speak." Presently he said, "Sin after baptism is so awful a matter; there is no second laver for sin; and then again, to sin against baptism is so great a sin."

The priest said, "In baptism God becomes your Father; your own God; your worship; your love—can you give up this great gift all through your life? Would you live 'without God in this world'?"

Tears came into Agellius's eyes, and his throat became oppressed. At last he said, distinctly and tenderly, "No."

After a while the priest said, "I suppose what you fear is the fire of judgment, and the prison; not lest you should fall away and be lost."

"I know, my dear father," answered the sick youth, "that I have no right to reckon on anything, or promise myself anything; yet somehow I have never feared hell—though I ought, I know I ought; but I have not. I deserve the

---

80    "Seize the day," Horace, *Odes*, I.11

worst, but somehow I have thought that God would lead me on. He ever has done so."

"Then you fear the fire of judgment," said Cæcilius; "you'd put off baptism for fear of that fire."

"I did not say I *would*," answered Agellius; "I wanted *you* to explain the thing to me."

"Which would you rather, Agellius, be without God here, or suffer the fire there?"

Agellius smiled; he said faintly, "I take Him for my portion here *and* there: *He* will be in the fire with me."

Agellius lay quiet for some hours, and seemed asleep. Suddenly he began again, "I was baptized when I was only six years old. I'm glad you do not think it was wilful in me, and wrong. I cannot tell what took me," he presently continued. "It was a fervour; I have had nothing of the kind since. What does our Lord say? I can't remember: 'Novissima pejora prioribus.'"[81]

He continued the train of thought another day, or rather the course of his argument; for on the thought itself his mind seemed ever to be working. "My spring is gone," he said, "and I have no summer. Nay, I have had no spring; it was a day, not a season. It came, and it went; where am I now? Can spring ever return? I wish to begin again in right earnest."

"Thank God, my son, for this great mercy," said Cæcilius, "that, though you have relaxed, you have never severed yourself from the peace of the Church, you have not denied your God."

Agellius sighed bitterly. "O my father," he said, "'Erravi, sicut ovis quæ periit.'[82] I have been very near denying Him, at least by outward act. You do not know me; you cannot know what has come on me lately. And I dare not look back on it, my heart is so weak. My father, how am I to repent of what is past, when I dare not think of it? To think of it is to renew the sin."

"'Puer meus, noli timere,'"[83] answered the priest; "'si transieris per ignem,

---

81  "The last state is worse than the first," Luke 11:26.
82  "Like a lost sheep, I have gone astray," Ps 119:176.
83  "Do not fear my child," .

odor ejus non erit in te.'[84] In penance, the grace of God carries you without harm through thoughts and words which *would* harm you apart from it."

"Ah, penance!" said Agellius; "I recollect the catechism. What is it, father? a new grace, I know; a plank after baptism. May I have it?"

"You are not strong enough yet to think of these things, Agellius," answered Cæcilius. "Please God, you shall get well. Then you shall review all your life, and bring it out in order before Him; and He, through me, will wipe away all that has been amiss. Praise Him who has spared you for this."

It was too much for the patient in his weak state; he could but shed happy tears.

Another day he had sat up in bed. He looked at his hands, from which the skin was peeling; he felt his lips, and it was with them the same; and his hair seemed coming off also. He smiled and said, "Renovabitur, ut aquila, juventus mea."[85]

Cæcilius responded, as before, with sacred words which were new to Agellius: "Qui sperant in Domino mutabunt fortitudinem; assument pennas, sicut aquilæ,'[86] 'Sursum corda!'[87] you must soar, Agellius."

"'Sursum corda!'" answered he; "I know those words. They are old friends; where have I heard them? I can't recollect; but they are in my earliest memories. Ah! but, my father, my heart is below, not above. I want to tell you all. I want to tell you about one who has enthralled my heart; who has divided it with my True Love. But I daren't speak of her, as I have said; I dare not speak, lest I be carried away. O, I blush to say it; she is a heathen! May God save her soul! Will He come to me, and not to her? 'Investigabiles viæ ejus.'"[88]

He remained silent for some time; then he said, "Father, I mean to dedicate myself to God, simply, absolutely, with His grace. I will be His, and He shall be mine. No one shall come between us. But O this weak heart!"

---

84   "If you pass throught thre fire, the odor of it will not be upon you," .
85   "My youth shall be renewed as the eagle," Ps 103:5.
86   "But those who trust in the Lord will renew their strength, like eagles new-fledged," Is 40:31.
87   "Lift up your hearts!"
88   "His ways are unsearchable," Rom 11:33

"Keep your good resolves till you are stronger," said the priest. "It is easy to make them on a sick-bed. You must first reckon the charges."

Agellius smiled. "I know the passage, father," he said, and he repeated the sacred words: "If any man come to Me, and hate not his father and mother, and wife, and children, and brethren, and sisters, yea, and his own life also, he cannot be My disciple."

Another time Agellius said: "The Martyrs; surely the old bishop used to say something about the Martyrs. He spoke of a second baptism, and called it a baptism of blood; and said, 'Might his soul be with the Martyrs!' Father, would not this wash out every thing, as the first?"

It was now Cæcilius who smiled, and his eyes shone like the sapphires of the Holy City; and he seemed the ideal of him who, when

> "Called upon to face
> Some awful moment to which heaven has joined
> Great issues, good or bad for humankind,
> Is happy as a lover, and attired
> With sudden brightness, like a man inspired."

However, he soon controlled himself, and said, "Quo ego vado, non potes me modo sequi; sequeris autem postea."[89]

---

89　"Where I go, you cannot follow me, but you will follow me afterward," John 13:36.

# Chapter Fourteen

# A SMALL CLOUD

THIS SORT OF INTERCOURSE, growing in frequency and fulness, went on for about a week, till Agellius was able to walk with support, and to leave the cottage. The priest and his own slave took him between them, and seated him one evening in sight of the glorious prospect, traversed by the long shadow of the far mountains, behind which the sun was making its way. The air was filled with a thousand odours; the brilliant colouring of the western heavens was contrasted with the more sober but varied tints of the rich country. The wheat and barley harvest was over; but the beans were late, and still stood in the fields. The olives and chestnut-trees were full of fruit; the early fig was supplying the markets with food; and the numerous vineyards were patiently awaiting the suns of the next month slowly to perfect their present promise. The beautiful scene had a moral dignity, from its associations with human sustenance and well-being. The inexpressible calmness of evening was flung, like a robe, over it. Its sweetness was too much for one who had been confined to the monotony of a sick-room, and was still an invalid. He sat silent, and in tears. It was life from the dead; and he felt he had risen to a different life. And thus he came out evening after evening convalescent, gradually and surely advancing to perfect restoration of his health.

One evening he said, after feeding his eyes and thoughts for some time with the prospect, "'Mansueti hereditabunt terram.'[90] They alone have real enjoyment of this earth who believe in its Maker. Every breath of air seems to whisper how good He is to me."

Cæcilius answered, "These sights are the shadows of that fairer Paradise which is our home, where there is no beast of prey, no venomous reptile, no sin. My child, should *I* not feel this more than you? Those who are shut up in crowded cities see but the work of man, which is evil. It is the compensation of my flight from Carthage that I am brought before the face of God."

"The heathen worship all this, as if God Himself," said Agellius; "how strange it seems to me that any one can forget the Creator in His works!"

Cæcilius was silent for a moment, and sighed; he then said, "You have ever been a Christian, Agellius."

"And you have not, my father?" answered he; "well, you have earned that grace which came to me freely."

"Agellius," said the priest, "it comes freely to all; and is only merited when it has already prevailed. Yet I think you earned it too, else why the difference between you and your brother?"

"What do you know of us?" asked Agellius quickly.

"Not a great deal," answered he, "yet something. Three or four years back an effort was made to rekindle the Christian spirit in these parts, and to do something for the churches of the proconsulate, and to fill up the vacant sees. Nothing has come of it as yet; but steps were taken towards it: one was to obtain a recovery of the Christians who remained in them. I was sent here for that purpose, and in this way heard of you and your brother. When my life was threatened by the persecution, and I had to flee, I thought of your cottage. I was obliged to act secretly, as we did not know friends from foes."

"You were led here for other purposes towards *me*, my father," said Agellius; "yet you cannot have a safer refuge. There is nothing to disturb, nothing to cause suspicion here. In this harvest time numbers of strangers pour in from the mountains, of various races; there is nothing to distinguish you

---

90    "The meek shall in herit the earth," Ps 36:11.

from one of them, and my brother is away convoying some grain to Carthage. Persecution drove you hither, but you have not been suffered to be idle, my father, you have brought home a wanderer." He added, after a pause, "I am well enough to go to confession to you now. May it be this evening?"

"It will be well," answered Cæcilius; "how long I shall still be here, I cannot tell. I am expecting my trusty messenger with despatches. It is now three days since he was here. However, this I say without misgiving, we do not part for long. What do you here longer? you must come to me. I must prepare you, and send you back to Sicca, to collect and restore this scattered flock."

Agellius turned, and leaned against the priest's shoulder, and laughed. "I am laughing," he said, "not from lightness of mind, but from the depth of surprise and of joy that you should so think of me. It was a dream which once I had; but impossible! you do not think that I, weak I, shall ever be able to do more than save my own soul?"

"You will save your own soul by saving the souls of others," said Cæcilius; "my child, I could tell you more things if I thought it good for you."

"But, my father, I have so weak, so soft a heart," cried Agellius; "what am I to do with myself? I am not of the temper of which heroes are made."

"'Virtus in infirmitate perficitur,'"[91] said the priest. "What! are you to do *any* thing of yourself? or are you to be simply the instrument of Another? We shall have the same termination, you and myself, but you long after me."

"Ah, father, because *you* will burn out so much more quickly!" said Agellius.

"I think," said Cæcilius, "I see my messenger; there is some one who has made his way by stealth into the garden, or at least not by the beaten way."

There *was* a visitor, as Cæcilius had said; however, it was not his messenger, but Juba, who approached, looking with great curiosity at Cæcilius, and absorbed in the sight. Cæcilius in turn regarded him steadfastly, and then said to Agellius, "It is your brother."

"What brings you here, Juba?" said the latter.

"I have been away on a distant errand," said Juba; "and find you have

---

91   "Power is made perfect in weakness," 2 Cor 12:9.

been ill. Is this your nurse?" he eyed him almost sternly, and added, "'Tis a Christian priest."

"Has Agellius no acquaintance but Christians?" asked Cæcilius.

"Acquaintance! O surely!" answered Juba; "agreeable, innocent, sweet acquaintance of another sort; myself to begin with. My lad," he continued, "you did not rise to their price, but you did your best."

"Juba," said his brother, "if you have any business here, say it, and have done. I am not strong enough to hold any altercation with you."

"Business!" said Juba, "I can find quite business enough here, if I choose. This is a priest of the Christians. I am sure of it."

Cæcilius looked at him with such calmness and benevolence, that at length Juba turned away his eyes with something of irritation. He said, "If I *am* a priest, I am here to claim you as one of my children."

Juba winced, but said scornfully, "You are mistaken there, father; speak to those who own you. I am a free man."

"My son," Cæcilius answered, "you have been under instruction; it is your duty to go forward, not back."

"What do you know about me?" said Juba; "he has been telling."

"Your face, your manner, your voice, tells a tale; I need no information from others. I have heard of you years ago; now I see you."

"What do you see in me?" said Juba.

"I see pride in bodily shape, treading down faith and conviction," said Cæcilius.

Juba neighed rather than laughed, so fierce and scornful was its expression. "What you slaves call pride," he said, "I call dignity."

"You believe in a God, Creator of heaven and earth, as certainly as I do," said the priest, "but you deliberately set yourself against Him."

Juba smiled. "I am as free," he said, "in *my* place, as He in His."

"You mean," answered Cæcilius, "free to do wrong, and free to suffer for it."

"You may call it wrong, and call it suffering," replied Juba; "but for me, *I* do not call wrong what He calls wrong; and if He puts me to pain, it is because He is the stronger."

The priest stopped awhile; there was no emotion on either side. It was strange to see them so passionless, so antagonistic, like St. Michael and his adversary.

"There is that within you," said Cæcilius, "which speaks as I speak. That inward voice takes the part of the Creator, and condemns you."

"*He* put it there," said Juba; "and *I* will take care to put it out."

"Then He will have justice as well as power on His side," said the priest.

"I will never fawn or crouch," said Juba; "I will be lord and master in my own soul. Every faculty shall be mine; there shall be no divided allegiance."

Cæcilius paused again; he said at length, "My son, my soul tells me, or rather my Maker tells me, and your Maker, that some heavy judgment is impending over you. Do penance while you may."

"Tell your forebodings to women and children," said Juba; "I am prepared for anything. I will not be crushed."

Agellius was not strong enough to bear a part in such a scene. "Father," he said, "it is his way, but don't believe him. He has better thoughts. Away with you, Juba, you are not wanted here."

"Agellius," said the priest, "such words are not strange to me. I am not young, and have seen much of the world; and my very office and position elicits blasphemies from others from time to time. I knew a man who carried out his bad thoughts and words into act. Abjuring his Maker, he abandoned himself to the service of the evil one. He betrayed his brethren to death. He lived on year after year, and became old. He was smitten with illness; then I first saw him. I made him contemplate a picture; it was the picture of the Good Shepherd. I dwelt on the vain efforts of the poor sheep to get out of the fold; its irrational aversion to its home, and its desperate resolution to force a way through the prickly fence. It was pierced and torn with the sharp aloe; at last it lay imprisoned in its stern embrace, motionless and bleeding. Then the Shepherd, though He had to wound His own hands in the work, disengaged it, and brought it back. God has His own times; His power went along with the picture, and the man was moved. I said, '*This* is His return for your enmity: He is determined to have you, cost Him what it will.' I need not go through the many things that followed, but the issue may be told in few words. He came back; he lived a life of penance at the Church's door; he received the peace of the Church in immediate prospect of the persecution, and has within the last ten days died a martyr's death."

Juba had listened as if he was constrained against his will. When the priest stopped he started, and began to speak impetuously, and unlike his ordinary tone. He placed his hands violently against his ears. "Stop!" he said, "no more. *I* will not betray them; no: I *need* not betray them;" he laughed; "the black moor does the work himself. Look," he cried, seizing the priest's arm, and pointing to a part of the forest, which happened to be to windward. "You are in their number, priest, who can foretell the destinies of others, and are blind to their own. Read there, the task is not hard, your coming fortunes."

His finger was directed to a spot where, amid the thick foliage, the gleam of a pool or of a marsh was visible. The various waters round about issuing from the gravel, or drained from the nightly damps, had run into a hollow, filled with the decaying vegetation of former years, and were languidly filtered out into a brook, more healthy than the vast reservoir itself. Its banks were bordered with a deep, broad layer of mud, a transition substance between the rich vegetable matter which it once had been, and the multitudinous world of insect life which it was becoming. A cloud or mist at this time was hanging over it, high in air. A harsh and shrill sound, a whizzing or a chirping, proceeded from that cloud to the ear of the attentive listener. What these indications portended was plain. "There," said Juba, "is what will tell more against you than imperial edict, informer, or proconsular apparitor; and no work of mine."

He turned down the bank and disappeared. Agellius and his guest looked at each other in dismay. "It is the locusts," they whispered to each other, as they went back into the cottage.

# Chapter Fifteen

# A VISITATION

THE PLAGUE OF LOCUSTS, one of the most awful visitations to which the countries included in the Roman empire were exposed, extended from the Atlantic to Ethiopia, from Arabia to India, and from the Nile and Red Sea to Greece and the north of Asia Minor. Instances are recorded in history of clouds of the devastating insect crossing the Black Sea to Poland, and the Mediterranean to Lombardy. It is as numerous in its species as it is wide in its range of territory. Brood follows brood, with a sort of family likeness, yet with distinct attributes, as we read in the prophets of the Old Testament, from whom Bochart tells us it is possible to enumerate as many as ten kinds. It wakens into existence and activity as early as the month of March; but instances are not wanting, as in our present history, of its appearance as late as June. Even one flight comprises myriads upon myriads passing imagination, to which the drops of rain or the sands of the sea are the only fit comparison; and hence it is almost a proverbial mode of expression in the East (as may be illustrated by the sacred pages to which we just now referred), by way of describing a vast invading army, to liken it to the locusts. So dense are they, when upon the wing, that it is no exaggeration to say that they hide the sun, from which circumstance indeed their name in Arabic is derived. And so ubiquitous are they when they have alighted on the earth, that they simply cover or clothe its surface.

This last characteristic is stated in the sacred account of the plagues of Egypt, where their faculty of devastation is also mentioned. The corrupting fly and the bruising and prostrating hail had preceded them in that series of visitations, but *they* came to do the work of ruin more thoroughly. For not only the crops and fruits, but the foliage of the forest itself, nay, the small twigs and the bark of the trees are the victims of their curious and energetic rapacity. They have been known even to gnaw the door-posts of the houses. Nor do they execute their task in so slovenly a way, that, as they have succeeded other plagues so they may have successors themselves. They take pains to spoil what they leave. Like the Harpies, they smear every thing that they touch with a miserable slime, which has the effect of a virus in corroding, or, as some say, in scorching and burning it. And then, as if all this were little, when they can do nothing else, they die;—as if out of sheer malevolence to man, for the poisonous elements of their nature are then let loose, and dispersed abroad, and create a pestilence; and they manage to destroy many more by their death than in their life.

Such are the locusts,—whose existence the ancient heretics brought forward as their palmary proof that there was an evil creator, and of whom an Arabian writer shows his national horror, when he says that they have the head of a horse, the eyes of an elephant, the neck of a bull, the horns of a stag, the breast of a lion, the belly of a scorpion, the wings of an eagle, the legs of a camel, the feet of an ostrich, and the tail of a serpent.

And now they are rushing upon a considerable tract of that beautiful region of which we have spoken with such admiration. The swarm to which Juba pointed grew and grew till it became a compact body, as much as a furlong square; yet it was but the vanguard of a series of similar hosts, formed one after another out of the hot mould or sand, rising into the air like clouds, enlarging into a dusky canopy, and then discharged against the fruitful plain. At length the huge innumerous mass was put into motion, and began its career, darkening the face of day. As became an instrument of divine power, it seemed to have no volition of its own; it was set off, it drifted, with the wind, and thus made northwards, straight for Sicca. Thus they advanced, host after host, for a time wafted on the air, and gradually declining to the earth, while fresh broods were carried over the first, and neared the earth, after a longer flight, in their turn. For twelve miles did they extend from front to rear, and their whizzing and hissing could be heard for six miles on every side of them. The bright sun, though hidden by them, illumined their bodies, and was reflected from their quivering wings; and as they heavily fell earthward, they seemed like the innumerable flakes of a yellow-coloured snow. And like snow did they descend, a living carpet, or rather pall, upon fields, crops, gardens, copses, groves, orchards, vineyards, olive woods, orangeries, palm plantations, and the deep forests, sparing nothing within their reach, and where there was nothing to devour, lying helpless in drifts, or crawling forward obstinately, as they best might, with the hope of prey. They could spare their hundred thousand soldiers twice or thrice over, and not miss them; their masses filled the bottoms of the ravines and hollow ways, impeding the traveller as he rode forward on his journey, and trampled by thousands under his horse-hoofs. In vain was all this overthrow and waste by the road-side; in vain their loss in river, pool, and watercourse. The poor peasants hastily dug pits and trenches as their enemy came on; in vain they filled them from the wells or with lighted stubble. Heavily and thickly did the locusts fall: they were lavish of their lives; they choked the flame and the water, which destroyed them the while, and the vast living hostile armament still moved on.

They moved right on like soldiers in their ranks, stopping at nothing, and straggling for nothing: they carried a broad furrow or wheal all across the country, black and loathsome, while it was as green and smiling on each side of them and in front, as it had been before they came. Before them, in the language of prophets, was a paradise; and behind them a desert. They are daunted by nothing; they surmount walls and hedges, and enter enclosed gardens or inhabited houses. A rare and experimental vineyard has been planted in a sheltered grove. The high winds of Africa will not commonly allow the light trellis or the slim pole; but here the lofty poplar of Campania has been possible, on which the vine plant mounts so many yards into the air, that the poor grape-gatherers bargain for a funeral pile and a tomb as one of the conditions of their engagement. The locusts have done what the winds and lightning could not do, and the whole promise of the vintage, leaves and all, is gone, and the slender stems are left bare. There is another yard, less uncommon, but still tended with more than common care; each plant is kept within due bounds by a circular trench round it, and by upright canes on which it is to trail; in an hour the solicitude and long toil of the vine-dresser are lost, and his pride humbled. There is a smiling farm; another sort of vine, of remarkable character, is found against the farm-house. This vine springs from one root, and has clothed and matted with its many branches the four walls; the whole of it is covered thick with long clusters, which another month will ripen:—on every grape and leaf there is a locust. Into the dry caves and pits, carefully strewed with straw, the harvest-men have (safely, as they thought just now) been lodging the far-famed African wheat. One grain or root shoots up into ten, twenty, fifty, eighty, nay, three or four hundred stalks: sometimes the stalks have two ears apiece, and these again shoot into a number of lesser ones. These stores are intended for the Roman populace, but the locusts have been beforehand with them. The small patches of ground belonging to the poor peasants up and down the country, for raising the turnips, garlic, barley, watermelons, on which they live, are the prey of these glutton invaders as much as the choicest vines and olives. Nor have they any reverence for the villa of the civic decurion or the Roman official. The neatly arranged kitchen-garden, with its cherries, plums, peaches, and apricots, is a waste; as the slaves sit round, in the kitchen in the first court, at their coarse evening meal, the room is filled with the invading force, and news comes to them that the enemy has fallen upon the apples and pears in the basement, and is at the same time plundering and sacking the preserves of quince and pomegranate, and revelling in the jars of precious oil of Cyprus and Mendes in the store-rooms.

They come up to the walls of Sicca, and are flung against them into the ditch. Not a moment's hesitation or delay; they recover their footing, they climb up the wood or stucco, they surmount the parapet, or they have entered in at the windows, filling the apartments, and the most private and luxurious chambers, not one or two, like stragglers at forage or rioters after a victory, but in order of battle, and with the array of an army. Choice plants or flowers about the *impluvia*[92] and *xysti*,[93] for ornament or refreshment, myrtles, oranges, pomegranates, the rose and the carnation, have disappeared. They dim the bright marbles of the walls and the gilding of the ceilings. They enter the triclinium in the midst of the banquet; they crawl over the viands and spoil what they do not devour. Unrelaxed by success and by enjoyment, onward they go; a secret mysterious instinct keeps them together, as if they had a king over them. They move along the floor in so strange an order that they seem to be a tesselated pavement themselves, and to be the artificial embellishment of the place; so true are their lines, and so perfect is the pattern they describe. Onward they go, to the market, to the temple sacrifices, to the baker's stores, to the cook-shops, to the confectioner's, to the druggists; nothing comes amiss to them; wherever man has aught to eat or drink, there are they, reckless of death, strong of appetite, certain of conquest.

They have passed on; the men of Sicca sadly congratulate themselves, and begin to look about them, and to sum up their losses. Being the proprietors of the neighbouring districts, or the purchasers of its produce, they lament over the devastation, not because the fair country is disfigured, but because income is becoming scanty, and prices are becoming high. How is a population of many thousands to be fed? where is the grain, where the melons, the figs, the dates, the gourds, the beans, the grapes, to sustain and solace the multitudes in their lanes, caverns, and garrets? This is another weighty consideration for the class well-to-do in the world. The taxes, too, and contributions, the capitation tax, the percentage upon corn, the various articles of revenues due to Rome, how are they to be paid? How are cattle to be provided for the sacrifices and for the tables of the wealthy? One-half, at least, of the supply of Sicca is cut off. No longer slaves are seen coming into the city from the country in troops with their baskets on their shoulders,

---

92   "pools"
93   Greek: "porticos"

or beating forward the horse, or mule, or ox, overladen with its burden, or driving in the dangerous cow, or the unresisting sheep. The animation of the place is gone; a gloom hangs over the Forum; and if its frequenters are still merry there is something of sullenness and recklessness in their mirth. The gods have given the city up; something or other has angered them. Locusts, indeed, are no uncommon visitation, but at an earlier season. Perhaps some temple has been polluted, or some unholy rite practised, or some secret conspiracy has spread.

Another and a still worse calamity. The invaders, as we have already intimated, could be more terrible still in their overthrow than in their ravages. The inhabitants of the country had attempted, where they could, to destroy them by fire and water. It would seem as if the malignant animals had resolved that the sufferers should have the benefit of this policy to the full; for they had not got more than twenty miles beyond Sicca when they suddenly sickened and died. Thus after they had done all the mischief they could by their living, when they had made their foul maws the grave of every living thing, then they died themselves, and made the desolated land their own grave. They took from it its hundred forms and varieties of beautiful life, and left it their own fetid and poisonous carcases in payment. It was a sudden catastrophe; they seemed making for the Mediterranean, as if, like other great conquerors, they had other worlds to subdue beyond it; but whether they were overgorged, or struck by some atmospheric change, or that their time was come and they paid the debt of nature, so it was that suddenly they fell, and their glory came to nought, and all was vanity to them as to others, and "their stench rose up, and their corruption rose up, because they had done proudly."

The hideous swarms lay dead in the moist steaming underwoods, in the green swamps, in the sheltered valleys, in the ditches and furrows of the fields, amid the monuments of their own prowess, the ruined crops and the dishonoured vineyards. A poisonous element, issuing from their remains, mingled with the atmosphere, and corrupted it. The dismayed peasant found that a pestilence had begun; a new visitation, not confined to the territory which the enemy had made its own, but extending far and wide, as the atmosphere extends, in all directions. Their daily toil, no longer claimed by the produce of the earth, which has ceased to exist, is now devoted to the object of ridding themselves of the deadly legacy which they have received in its stead. In vain; it is their last toil; they are digging pits, they are raising piles, for their own corpses, as well as for the bodies of their enemies. Invader and victim lie in the same grave, burn in the same heap; they sicken while they work, and the pestilence spreads. A new invasion is menacing Sicca, in the shape of companies of peasants and slaves, (the panic having broken the bonds of discipline,) with their employers and overseers, nay the farmers themselves and proprietors, rushing thither from famine and infection as to a place of safety. The inhabitants of the city are as frightened as they, and more energetic. They determine to keep them at a distance; the gates are closed; a strict *cordon* is drawn; however, by the continued pressure, numbers contrive to make an entrance, as water into a vessel, or light through the closed shutters, and anyhow the air cannot be put into quarantine; so the pestilence has the better of it, and at last appears in the alleys, and in the cellars of Sicca.

# Chapter Sixteen

# WORSE AND WORSE

"O WRETCHED MINDS OF MEN! O blind hearts!" truly cries out a great heathen poet, but on grounds far other than the true ones. The true ground of such a lamentation is, that men do not interpret the signs of the times and of the world as He intends who has placed these signs in the heavens; that when Mane, Thecel, Phares, is written upon the ethereal wall, they have no inward faculty to read them withal; and that when they go elsewhere for one learned in tongues, instead of taking Daniel, who is used to converse with Angels, they rely on Magi or Chaldeans, who know only the languages of earth. So it was with the miserable population of Sicca now; half famished, seized with a pestilence which was sure to rage before it assuaged, perplexed and oppressed by the recoil upon them of the population whom they had from time to time sent out into the surrounding territory, or from whom they had supplied their markets, they never fancied that the real cause of the visitation which we have been describing was their own iniquity in their Maker's sight, that His arm inflicted it, and that its natural and direct interpretation was, "Do penance, and be converted." On the contrary, they looked only at their own vain idols, and at the vain rites which these idols demanded, and they thought there was no surer escape from their misery than by upholding a lie, and putting down all who revolted from it; and thus the visitation which was sent to do them good turned through their wilful blindness to their greater condemnation.

The Forum, which at all times was the resort of idleness and dissipation, now became more and more the haunt of famine and sickness, of robust frames without work, of slavish natures virtually and for the time emancipated and uncontrolled, of youth and passion houseless and shelterless. In groups and companies, in and out of the porticoes, on the steps of the temples, and about the booths and stalls of the market, a multitude grows day by day, from the town and from the country, and of all the various races which town and country contain. The civil magistracy and the civil force to which the peace of the city was committed, were not equal to such an emergency as the present; and the *milites stationarii*,[94] a sort of garrison who represented the Roman power, though they were ready to act against either magistrates or mob impartially, had no tenderness for either, when in collision with each other. Indeed the bonds of society were broken, and every political element was at war with every other, in a case of such great common calamity, when every one was angry with every one else, for want of some clearly defined object against which the common anger might be discharged with unanimity.

They had almost given over sacrificing and consulting the flame or the entrails; for no reversal or respite of their sufferings had followed their most assiduous acts of deprecation. Moreover the omens were generally considered by the priests to have been unpropitious or adverse. A sheep had been discovered to have, instead of a liver, something very like a gizzard; a sow had chewed and swallowed the flowers with which it had been embellished for the sacrifice; and a calf, after receiving the fatal blow, instead of lying down and dying, dashed into the temple, dripping blood upon the pavement as it went, and at last fell and expired just before the sacred *adytum*. In despair the people took to fortune-telling and its attendant arts. Old crones were found in plenty with their strange rites, the stranger the more welcome. Trenches were dug in by-places for sacrifices to the infernal gods; amulets, rings, counters, tablets,

---

94 "guards"

pebbles, nails, bones, feathers, Ephesian or Egyptian legends, were in request, and raised the hopes, or beguiled and occupied the thoughts, of those who else would have been directly dwelling on their sufferings, present or in prospect.

Others were occupied, whether they would or no, with diversions fiercer and more earnest. There were continual altercations between farmers, small proprietors of land, government and city officials,—altercations so manifold and violent, that, even were there no hubbub of voices, and no incoherence of wrath and fear to complicate them, we should despair of setting them before the reader. An officer from the camp was expostulating with one of the municipal authorities that no corn had been sent thither for the last six or seven days, and the functionary attacked had thrown the blame on the farmer, and he in turn had protested that he could not get cattle to bring the waggons into Sicca; those which he had set out with had died of exhaustion on the journey. A clerk, as we now speak, in the *Officium* of the society of publicans or collectors of *annona* was threatening a number of small tenants with ejection for not sending in their rated portion of corn for the Roman people:—the *Officium* of the *Notarius*, or assistant prefect, had written up to Sicca from Carthage in violent terms; and come it must, though the locusts had eaten up every stack and granary. A number of half-starved peasants had been summoned for payment of their taxes, and in spite of their ignorance of Latin, they had been made to understand that death was the stern penalty of neglecting to bring the coin. They, on the other hand, by their fierce doggedness of manner, seemed to signify by way of answer that death was not a penalty, unless life was a boon.

The *villicus*[95] of one of the decurions, who had an estate in the neighbourhood, was laying his miseries before the man of business of his employer. "What are we to do?" he said. "Half the gang of slaves is dead, and the other half is so feeble, that I can't get through the work of the month. We ought to be sheep-shearing; you have no chance of wool. We ought to be swarming the bees, pressing the honey, boiling and purifying the wax. We ought to be plucking the white leaves of the camomile, and steeping the golden flowers

---

95    "manager"

in oil. We ought to be gathering the wild grapes, sifting off the flowers, and preserving the residue in honey. We ought to be sowing brassicum, parsley, and coriander against next spring. We ought to be cheese-making. We ought to be baking white and red bricks and tiles in the sun; we have no hands for the purpose. The *villicus* is not to blame, but the anger of the gods." The country *employé* of the procurator of the imperial *Baphia*[96] protests that the insect cannot be found from which the dye is extracted; and argues that the locusts must have devoured them, or the plant on which they feed, or that they have been carried off by the pestilence. Here is old Corbulus in agonies for his febrifuge, and a slave of his is in high words with the market-carrier, who tells him that Mago, who supplied it, is dead of a worse fever than his master's. "The rogue," cried the slave, "my master has contracted with him for the year, and has paid him the money in advance." A jeering and mocking from the crowd assailed the unfortunate domestic, who so truly foreboded that his return without the medicine would be the signal for his summary committal to the *pistrinum*.[97] "Let old Corbulus follow Mago in his passage to perdition," said one of the rabble; "let him take his physic with Pluto, and leave us the bread and wine on which he's grown gouty." "Bread, bread!" was the response elicited by this denunciation, and it spread into a circle larger than that of which the slave and the carrier were part.

"Wine and bread, Ceres and Liber!" cried a young legionary, who, after a night of revelry, was emerging still half-intoxicated from one of the low wine-shops in the vaults which formed the basement of the *Thermæ* or hot baths; "make way there, you filthy slime of the earth, you half-kneaded, half-fermented Africans, who never yet have quite been men, but have ever smelt strong of the baboon, who are three quarters *must*, and two vinegar, and a fifth water,—as I was saying, you are like bad liquor, and the sight of you disagrees with the stomach and affects the eyes."

The crowd looked sullenly, and without wincing, at his shield, which was the only portion of his military accoutrements which he had preserved after

---

96    a type of small shrub
97    "drudge work"

his carouse. The white surface, with a silver boss in the centre, surrounded by first a white and then a red circle, and the purple border, showed that he belonged to the Tertiani or third Italic Legion, which had been stationed in Africa since the time of Augustus. "Vile double-tongued mongrels," he continued, "what are you fit for but to gather the fruits of the earth for your owners and lords, 'Romanos dominos rerum'[98]? And if there are now no fruits to reap, why your service is gone. Go home and die, and drown yourselves, for what are you fit for now, except to take your dead corpses away from the nostrils of a Roman, the cream of humankind? Ye base-born apes, that's why you catch the pestilence, because our blood mantles and foams in our ruddy veins like new milk in the wine cup, which is too strong for this clime, and my blood is up, and I drink a full measure of it to great Rome; for what does old Horace say, but 'Nunc est bibendum'[99]? and so get out of my way."

To a good part of the multitude, both peasantry and town rabble, Latin was unintelligible; but they all understood vocabulary and syntax and logic, as soon as he drew his knuckles across one fellow's face who refused to move from his path, and as soon as his insult was returned by the latter with a thrust of the dagger. A rush was made upon him, on which he made a face at them, shook his fist, and leaping on one side, ran with great swiftness to an open space in advance. From his quarrelsome humour rather than from fear, he raised a cry of alarm; on which two or three fellow-soldiers made their appearance from similar dens of intoxication and vice, and came up to the rescue. The mob assailed them with stones, and the cream of human nature was likely to be roughly churned, when, seeing matters were becoming serious, they suddenly took to their heels, and got into the Temple of Esculapius on one side of the Forum. The mob followed, the ministers of the sacred place attempted to shut the gates, a scuffle ensued, and a riot was in progress. Self-preservation is the first law of man; trembling for the safety of his noble buildings, and considering that it was a bread riot, as it really was, the priest of the god came forward, rebuked the mob for its impiety, and showed the

---

98    "the Romans, lords of the world," Vergil, *Aeneid*, I.282
99    "It is time to drink," Horace, *Odes*, I.37.1.

absurdity of supposing that there were loaves in his enclosure to satisfy its wants; but he reminded them that there was a baker's shop at the other end of the Forum, which was one of the most considerable in Sicca.

A slight impulse determines the movements of an excited multitude. Off they went to the quarter in question, where certainly there was the very large and handsome store of a substantial dealer in grain of all sorts, and in other produce. The shop, however, seemed on this occasion to be but poorly furnished; for the baker was a prudent man, and feared a display of provisions which would be an invitation to a hungry multitude. The assailants, however, were not to be baffled; some one cried out that the man had withdrawn his corn from the market for his own ends, and that great stores were accumulated within. They avail themselves of the hint; they pour in through the open front, the baker escapes as he may, his mills and ovens are smashed, the house is ransacked; whatever is found is seized, thrown about, wasted, eaten, as the case may be; and the mob gains strength and appetite for fresh exploits.

However, the rioters have no definite plan of action yet. Some of them have penetrated into the stable behind the house in search of corn. They find the mill-ass which ground for the baker, and bring it out. It is a beast of more than ordinary pretensions, such as you would not often see in a mill, showing both the wealth of the owner and the flourishing condition of his trade. The asses of Africa are finer than those in the north; but this is fine for an African. One fellow mounts upon it, and sets off with the world before him, like a knight-errant, seeking an adventure, the rabble at his tail acting as squire. He begins the circuit of the Forum, and picks up its riff-raff as he goes along—here some rascal boys, there some drunken women, here again a number of half-brutalized country slaves and peasants. Partly out of curiosity, partly from idleness, from ill temper, from hope of spoil, from a vague desire to be doing something or other, every one who has nothing to lose by the adventure crowds around and behind him. And on the contrary, as he advances, and the noise and commotion increase, every one who has a position of any sort, the confidential *vernæ*[100] of great families, farmers, shopkeepers, men of business, officials, vanish from the scene of action without delay.

"Africa, Africa!" is now the cry; the signal in that country, as an ancient writer tells us, that the parties raising it have something new in hand, and have a mind to do it.

Suddenly, as they march on, a low and awful growl is heard. It comes from the booth of a servant of the imperial court. He is employed as a transporter of wild beasts from the interior to the coast, where they are shipped for Rome; and he has charge at present of a noble lion, who is sitting majestically, looking through the bars of his cage at the rabble, who now begin to look at him. In demeanour and in mental endowments he has the advantage of them. It was at this moment, while they were closing, hustling each other, staring at the beast, and hoping to provoke him, that a shrill voice cried out, "Christianos ad leones, Christianos ad leones!" the Christians to the lions! A sudden and dead silence ensued, as if the words had struck the breath out of the promiscuous throng. An interval passed; and then the same voice was heard again, "Christianos ad leones!" This time the whole Forum took it up from one end to the other. The fate of the day, the direction of the movement, was decided; a distinct object was obtained, and the only wonder was that the multitude had been so long to seek and so slow to find so obvious a cause of their misfortunes, so adequate a subject of their vengeance. "Christianos ad leones!" was shouted out by town and country, priests and people. "Long live the emperor! long live Decius! he told us this long ago. There's the edict; it never has been obeyed. Death to the magistrates! To the Christians! to the Christians! Up with great Jove, down with the atheists!"

They were commencing their march when the ass caught their eye. "The Christians' god!" they shouted out; "the god of the Christians!" Their first impulse was to give the poor beast to the lion, their next to sacrifice it, but they did not know to whom. Then they said they would make the Christians worship it; and dressing it up in tawdry finery, they retained it at the head of their procession.

---

100  "home-born slaves"

# Chapter Seventeen

# CHRISTIANOS AD LEONES

B Y THE TIME that they had got round again to the unlucky baker's, the mob had been swollen to a size which even the area of the Forum would not contain, and it filled the adjacent streets. And by the same time it had come home to its leaders, and, indeed, to every one who used his reason at all, that it was very far from certain that there were any Christians in Sicca, and if so, still very far from easy to say where they were. And the difficulty was of so practical a character as to keep them inactive for the space of several hours. Meanwhile their passions were excited to the boiling point by the very presence of the difficulty, as men go mad of thirst when water is denied them. At length, after a long season of such violent commotion, such restless pain, such curses, shrieks, and blasphemies, such bootless gesticulations, such aimless contests with each other, that they seemed to be already inmates of the prison beneath, they set off in a blind way to make the circuit of the city as before they had paraded round the Forum, still in the knight-errant line, looking out for what might turn up where they were sure of nothing, and relieving the intense irritation of their passions by locomotion, if nothing more substantial was offered to them.

It was an awful day for the respectable inhabitants of the place; worse than anything that even the most timid of them had anticipated, when they had showed their jealousy of a popular movement against the proscribed religion; for the stimulus of famine and pestilence was added to hatred of Christianity, in that unreasoning multitude. The magistrates shut themselves up in dismay; the small body of Roman soldiery reserved their strength for the defence of themselves; and the poor wretches, not a few, who had fallen from the faith, and offered sacrifice, hung out from their doors sinful heathen symbols, to avert a storm against which apostasy was no sufficient safeguard. In this conduct the Gnostics and other sectaries imitated them, while the Tertullianists took a more manly part, from principle or pride.

It would require the brazen voice which Homer speaks of, or the magic pen of Sir Walter, to catalogue and to picture, as far as it is lawful to do either, the figures and groups of that most miserable procession. As it went forward it gained a variety and strength, which the circuit of the Forum could not furnish. The more respectable religious establishments shut their gates, and would have nothing to do with it. The priests of Jupiter, the educational establishments of the Temple of Mercury, the Temple of the Genius of Rome near the Capitol, the hierophants of Isis, the Minerva, the Juno, the Esculapius, viewed the popular rising with terror and disgust; but these were not the popular worships. The vast homestead of Astarte, which in the number and vowed profligacy of its inhabitants rivalled the vaults upon the Forum; the old rites, many and diversified, if separately obscure, which came from Punic times; the new importations from Syria and Phrygia, and a number of other haunts and schools of depravity and crime, did their part in swelling or giving character to the concourse. The hungry and idle rabble, the filthy beggars who fed on the offal of the sacrifices, the drivers and slaughterers of the beasts sacrificed; the tumblers and mountebanks who amused the gaping market-people; dancers, singers, pipers from low taverns and drinking-houses; infamous creatures, young and old, men and boys, half naked and not half sober; brutal blacks, the aboriginal race of the Atlas, with their appetites written on their skulls and features; Canaanites, as they called themselves, from the coast; the wild beast-keepers from the amphitheatre; troops of labourers from the fields, to whom the epidemic was a time of Saturnalia; and the degraded company, alas! how numerous and how pitiable, who took their nightly stand in long succession at the doors of their several cells in the deep galleries under the Thermæ; all these, and many others, had their part and place in the procession. There you might see the devilish emblems of idolatry borne aloft by wretches from the great Punic Temple, while frantic forms, ragged and famished, wasted and shameless, leapt and pranced around them. There too was a choir of Bacchanals, ready at a moment with songs as noisy as they were unutterable. And there was the priest of the Punic Saturn, the child-devourer, a sort of Moloch, to whom the martyrdom of Christians was a sacred rite; he and all his attendants in fiery-coloured garments, as became a sanguinary religion. And there, moreover, was a band of fanatics, devotees of Cybele or of the Syrian goddess, if indeed the two rites were distinct. They were bedizened with ribbons and rags of various colours, and smeared over with paint. They had long hair like women, and turbans on their heads. They pushed their way to the head of the procession, being quite worthy of the post of honour, and, seizing the baker's ass, put their goddess on the back of it. Some of them were playing the fife, others clashing cymbals, others danced, others yelled, others rolled their heads, and others flogged themselves. Such was the character of the frenzied host, which progressed slowly through the streets, while every now and then, when there was an interval in the hubbub, the words "Christianos ad leones" were thundered out by some ruffian voice, and a thousand others fiercely responded.

Still no Christian was forthcoming; and it was plain that the rage of the multitude must be discharged in other quarters, if the difficulty continued in satisfying it. At length some one recollected the site of the Christian chapel, when it existed; thither went the multitude, and effected an entrance without delay. It had long been turned to other purposes, and was now a store of casks and leather bottles. The miserable sacristan had long given up any practical observance of his faith, and remained on the spot a keeper of the premises for the trader who owned them. They found him, and dragged him into the street, and brought him forward to the ass, and to the idol on its back, and bade him worship the one and the other. The poor wretch obeyed; he worshipped the ass, he worshipped the idol, and he worshipped the genius of the emperor; but his persecutors wanted blood; they would not submit to be cheated of their draught; so when they had made him do whatever they exacted, they flung him under the feet of the multitude, who, as they passed on, soon trod all life and breath out of him, and sent him to the powers below, to whom he had just before been making his profession.

Their next adventure was with a Tertullianist, who stationed himself at his shop-door, displayed the sign of the cross, and walking leisurely forward, seized the idol on the ass's back, broke it over his knee, and flung the portions into the crowd. For a few minutes they stared on him with astonishment, then some women fell upon him with their nails and teeth, and tore the poor fanatic till he fell bleeding and lifeless upon the ground.

In the higher and better part of the city, which they now approached, lived the widow of a Duumvir, who in his day had made a bold profession of Christianity. The well connected lady was a Christian also, and was sheltered by her great friends from the persecution. She was bringing up a family in great privacy, and with straitened means, and with as much religious strictness as was possible under the circumstances of the place. She kept them from all bad sights and bad company, was careful as to the character of the slaves she placed about them, and taught them all she knew of her religion, which was quite sufficient for their salvation. They had all been baptized, some by herself in default of the proper minister, and, as far as they could show at their tender ages, which lay between thirteen and seven, the three girls and the two boys were advancing in the love of truth and sanctity. Her husband, some years back, when presiding in the Forum, had punished with just severity an act of ungrateful fraud; and the perpetrator had always cherished a malignant hatred of him and his. The moment of gratifying it had now arrived, and he pointed out to the infuriated rabble the secluded mansion where the Christian household dwelt. He could not offer to them a more acceptable service, and the lady's modest apartment was soon swarming with enemies of her God and His followers. In spite of her heartrending cries and supplications, her children were seized, and when the youngest boy clung to her, the mother was thrown senseless upon the pavement. The whole five were carried off in triumph; it was the greatest success of the day. There was some hesitation how to dispose of them; at last the girls were handed over to the priestesses of Astarte, and the boys to the loathsome votaries of Cybele.

Revenge upon Christians was the motive principle of the riot; but the prospect of plunder stimulated numbers, and here Christians could not minister to their desires. They began the day by the attack upon the provision-shop, and now they had reached the aristocratic quarter of the city, and they gazed with envy and cupidity at the noble mansions which occupied it. They began to shout out, "Bread, bread!" while they uttered threats against the Christians; they violently beat at the closed gates, and looked about for means of scaling the high walls which defended them in front. The cravings of famished men soon take form and organization; they began to ask relief from house to house. Nothing came amiss; and loaves, figs, grapes, wine, found their way into the hands and mouths of those who were the least exhausted and the least enfeebled. A second line of fierce supplicants succeeded to the first; and it was plain that, unless some diversion were effected, the respectable quarter of Sicca had found a worse enemy than the locust.

The houses of the government *susceptor*, or tax collector, of the *tabularius* or registrar, of the *defensor* or city counsel, and one or two others, had already been the scene of collisions between the domestic slaves and the multitude, when a demand was made upon the household of another of the Curia, who held the office of Flamen Dialis.[101] He was a wealthy, easy-going man, generally popular, with no appetite for persecution at all, but still no desire to be persecuted. He had more than tolerated the Christians, and had at this time a Christian among his slaves. This was a Greek, a splendid cook and perfumer, and he would not have lost him for a large sum of money. However, life and limb were nearer to him even than his dinner, and a Jonah must be cast overboard to save the ship. In trepidation, yet with greater satisfaction, his fellow-domestics thrust the poor helpless man out of the

---

101 "Priest of Jupiter"

house, and secured the door behind him. He was a man of middle age, of a grave aspect, and he looked silently and calmly upon the infuriated and yelling multitude, who were swarming up the hill about him, and swelling the number of his persecutors. What had been his prospects, had he remained in his earthly master's service? his fill of meat and drink while he was strong and skilful, the stocks or scourge if he ever failed to please him, and the old age and death of the worn-out hack who once has caracoled in the procession, or snorted at the coming fight. What are his prospects now? a moment's agony, a martyr's death, and the everlasting beatific vision of Him for whom he died. The multitude cry out, "To the ass or to the lion!" worship the ass, or fight the lion. He was dragged to the ass's head and commanded to kneel down before the irrational beast. In the course of a minute he had lifted up his eyes to heaven, had signed himself with the cross, had confessed his Saviour, and had been torn to pieces by the multitude. They anticipated the lion of the amphitheatre.

A lull followed, sure to be succeeded by a fresh storm. Not every household had a Christian cook to make a victim of. Plunder, riot, and outrage were becoming the order of the day; successive messengers were sent up in breathless haste to the capitol and the camp for aid, but the Romans returned for answer that they had enough to do in defending the government buildings and offices. They suggested measures, however, for putting the mob on a false scent, or involving them in some difficult or tedious enterprise, which would give the authorities time for deliberation, and for taking the rioters at disadvantage. If the magistrates could get them out of the city, it would be a great point; they could then shut the gates upon them, and deal with them as they would. In that case, too, the insurgents would straggle, and divide, and then they might be disposed of in detail. They were showing symptoms of returning fury, when a voice suddenly cried out, "Agellius the Christian! Agellius the sorcerer! Agellius to the lions! To the farm of Varius—to the cottage of Agellius—to the south-west gate!" A sudden yell burst forth from the vast multitude when the voice ceased. The impulse had been given as at the first; the tide of human beings ebbed and retreated, and, licking the base of the hill, rushed vehemently on one side, and roared like a torrent towards the south-west. Juba, thy prophecy is soon to be fulfilled! The locusts will bring more harm on thy brother's home than imperial edict or local magistrate. The decline of day will hardly prevent the visitation.

# Chapter Eighteen

# AGELLIUS FLITS

A CHANGE HAD PASSED over the fair face of Nature, as seen from the cottage of Agellius, since that evening on which our story opened; and it is so painful to contemplate waste, decay, and disappointment, that we mean to say little about it. There was the same cloudless sky as then; and the sun travelled in its silent and certain course, with even a more intense desire than then to ripen grain and fruit for the use of man; but its occupation was gone, for fruit and grain were not, nor man to collect and to enjoy them. A dark broad shadow passed across the beautiful prospect and disfigured it. When you looked more closely, it was as if a fire had burned up the whole surface included under that shadow, and had stripped the earth of its clothing. Nothing had escaped; not a head of khennah, not a rose or carnation, not an orange or an orange blossom, not a *boccone*,[102] not a cluster of unripe grapes, not a berry of the olive, not a blade of grass. Gardens, meadows, vineyards, orchards, copses, instead of rejoicing in the rich variety of hue which lately was their characteristic, were now reduced to one dreary cinder-colour. The smoke of fires was actually rising from many points, where the spoilt and poisonous vegetation was burning in heaps, or the countless corpses of the invading foe, or of the cattle, or of the human beings whom the pestilence

---

102  Italian: "morsel"

had carried off. The most furious inroad of savage hordes, of Vandals, or of Saracens, who were destined at successive eras to come and waste that country, could not have spread such thorough desolation. The slaves of the farm of Varius were sorrowfully turning to a new employment, that of clearing away the wreck and disappointment of the bright spring from flower-bed, vineyard, and field.

It was on the forenoon of the eventful day whose course we have been tracing in the preceding Chapters, that a sharp-looking boy presented himself to Agellius, who was directing his labourers in their work. "I am come from Jucundus," he said; "he has instant need of you. You are to go with me, and by my way; and this is the proof I tell you truth. He sends you this note, and wishes you in a bad time the best gifts of Bacchus and Ceres."

Agellius took the tablets, and went with them across the road to the place where Cæcilius was at work, in appearance a slave. The letter ran thus:—"Jucundus to Agellius. I trust you are well enough to move; you are not safe for many days in your cottage; there is a rising this morning against the Christians, and you may be visited. Unless you are ambitious of Styx and Tartarus, follow the boy without questioning." Agellius showed the letter to the priest.

"We are no longer safe here, my father," he said; "whither shall we go? Let us go together. Can you take me to Carthage?"

"Carthage is quite as dangerous," answered Cæcilius, "and Sicca is more central. We can but leap into the sea at Carthage; here there are many lines to retreat upon. I am known there, I am not known here. Here, too, I hear all that goes on through the proconsulate and Numidia."

"But what can we do?" asked Agellius; "here we cannot remain, and you at least cannot venture into the city. Somewhither we must go, and where is that?"

The priest thought. "We must separate," he said. The tears came into Agellius's eyes.

"Though I am a stranger," continued Cæcilius, "I know more of the neighbourhood of Sicca than you who are a native. There is a famous Christian retreat on the north of the city, and by this time, I doubt not, or rather I know, it is full of refugees. The fury of the enemy is extending on all hands, and our brethren, from as far as Cirta round to Curubis, are falling back upon it. The only difficulty is how to get round to it without going through Sicca."

"Let us go together," said Agellius.

Cæcilius showed signs of perplexity, and his mind retired into itself. He seemed for the moment to be simply absent from the scene about him, but soon his intelligence returned. "No," he said, "we must separate,—for the time; it will not be for long. That is, I suppose, your uncle will take good care of you, and he has influence. We are safest just now when most independent of each other. It is only for a while. We shall meet again soon; I tell you so. Did we keep together just now, it would be the worse for each of us. You go with the boy; I will go off to the place I mentioned."

"O my father," said the youth, "how will you get there? What shall I suffer from my fears about you?"

"Fear not," answered Cæcilius, "mind, I tell you so. It will be a trying time, but my hour is not yet come. I am good for years yet; so are you, for many more than mine. He will protect and rescue me, though I know not how. Go, leave me to myself, Agellius!"

"O my father, my only stay upon earth, whom God sent me in my extreme need, to whom I owe myself, must I then quit you; must a layman desert a priest; the young the old?... Ah! it is I really, not you, who am without protection. Angels surround you, father; but I am a poor wanderer. Give me your blessing that evil may not touch me. I go."

"Do not kneel," said the priest; "they will see you. Stop, I have got to tell you how and where to find me." He then proceeded to give him the necessary instructions. "Walk out," he said, "along the road to Thibursicumbur to the third milestone, you will come to a country road; pursue it; walk a thousand steps; then again for the space of seven *paternosters*; and then speak to the man upon your right hand. And now away with you, God speed you, we shall not long be parted," and he made the sign of the cross over him.

"That old chap gives himself airs," said the boy, when Agellius joined him; "what may he be? one of your slaves, Agellius?"

"You're a pert boy," answered he, "for asking me the question."

"They say the Christians brought the locusts," said Firmian, "by their enchantments; and there's a jolly row beginning in the Forum just now. The report goes that you are a Christian."

"That's because your people have nothing better to do than talk against their neighbours."

"Because you are so soft, rather," said the boy. "Another man would have knocked me down for saying it; but you are lackadaisical folk, who bear insults tamely. Arnobius says your father was a Christian."

"Father and son are not always the same religion now-a-days," said Agellius.

"Ay, ay," answered Firmian, "but the Christians came from Egypt: and as cook there is the son of cook, and soldier is son of soldier, so Christian, take my word for it, is the son of a Christian."

"Christians boast, I believe," answered Agellius, "that they are of no one race or country, but are members of a large unpatriotic family, whose home is in the sky."

"Christians," answered the boy, "would never have framed the great Roman empire; that was the work of heroes. Great Cæsar, Marius, Marcus Brutus, Camillus, Cicero, Sylla, Lucullus, Scipio, could never have been Christians. Arnobius says they are a skulking set of fellows."

"I suppose you wish to be a hero," said Agellius.

"I am to be a pleader," answered Firmian; "I should like to be a great orator like Cicero, and every one listening to me."

They were walking along the top of a mud wall, which separated Varius's farm from his neighbour's, when suddenly Firmian, who led the way, leapt down into a copse, which reached as far as the ravine in which the knoll terminated towards Sicca. The boy still went forward by devious paths, till they had mounted as high as the city wall.

"You are bringing me where there is no entrance," said Agellius.

The boy laughed. "Jucundus told me to bring you by a blind way," he said. "You know best why. This is one of our ways in and out."

There was an aperture in the wall, and the bricks and stones about it were loose, and admitted of removal. It was such a private way of passage as schoolboys know of. On getting through, Agellius found himself in a neglected garden or small close. Everything was silent about them, as if the inhabitants were away; there was a great noise in the distance, as if something unusual were going on in the heart of the town. The boy told him to follow him as fast as he could without exciting remark; and, leading him by lanes and alleys unknown to Agellius, at last brought him close upon the scene of riot. At this time the expedition in search of Christians had just commenced; to cross the Forum was to shorten his journey, and perhaps was safer than to risk meeting the mob in the streets. Firmian took the step; and while their attention was directed elsewhere, brought Agellius safely through it. They then proceeded cautiously as before, till they stood before the back door of the house of Jucundus.

"Say a good word for me to your uncle," said the boy, "I have done my job. He must remember me handsomely at the Augustalia," and he ran away.

Meanwhile Cæcilius had been anxiously considering the course which it was safest for him to pursue. He must move, but he must wait till dusk, when the ways were clear, and the light uncertain. Till then he must keep close indoors. There was a remarkable cavern in the mountains above Sicca, which had been used as a place of refuge for Christians from the very time they had first suffered persecution in Roman Africa. No spot in its whole territory seemed more fit for what is called a base of operations, from which the soldiers of the Cross might advance, or to which they might retire, according as the fury of their enemy grew or diminished. While it was in the midst of a wilderness difficult of access, and feared as the resort of ghosts and evil influences, it was not far from a city near to which the high roads met from Hippo and from Carthage. A branch of the Bagradas, navigable for boats, opened a way from it through the woods, where flight and concealment were easy on a surprise, as far as Madaura, Vacca, and other places; at the same time it commanded the vast plain on the south which extended to the roots of the Atlas. Just now, the persecution growing, many deacons, other ecclesiastics, and prominent laymen from all parts of the country had fallen back upon this cavern or grotto; and in no place could Cæcilius have better means than here of learning the general state of affairs, and of communicating with countries beyond the seas. He was indeed on his way thither, when the illness of Agellius made it a duty for him to stop and restore him, and attend to his spiritual needs; and he had received an inward intimation, on which he implicitly relied, to do so.

The problem at this moment was how to reach the refuge in question. His direct road lay through Sicca; this being impracticable at present, he had to descend into the ravine which lay between him and the city, and, turning to the left, to traverse the broad plain, the Campus Martius of Sicca, into which it opened. Here the mountain would rise abruptly on his right with those steep cliffs which we have already described as rounding the north side of Sicca. He must traverse many miles before he could reach the point at which the rock lost its precipitous character, and changed into a declivity allowing the traveller to ascend. It was a bold undertaking; for all this he had to accomplish in the dark before the morning broke, a stranger too to the locality, and directing his movements only by the information of others, which, however accurate and distinct, could scarcely be followed, even if without risk of error, at least without misgiving. However, could he master this point before the morning he was comparatively safe; he then had to strike into the solitary mountains, and to retrace his steps for a while towards Sicca along the road, till he came to a place where he knew that Christian scouts or *videttes* (as they may be called) were always stationed.

This being his plan, and there being no way of mending it, our confessor retired into the cottage, and devoted the intervening hours to intercourse with that world from which his succour must come. He set himself to intercede for the Holy Catholic Church throughout the world, now for the most part under persecution, and for the Roman Empire, not yet holy, which was the instrument of the evil powers against her. He had to pray for the proconsulate, for Numidia, Mauretania, and the whole of Africa; for the Christian communities throughout it, for the cessation of the trial then present, and for the fortitude and perseverance of all who were tried. He had to pray for his own personal friends, his penitents, converts, enemies; for children, catechumens, neophytes; for those who were approaching the Church, for those who had fallen away, or were falling away from her; for all heretics, for all troublers of unity, that they might be reclaimed. He had to confess, bewail and deprecate the many sins and offences which he knew of, foreboded, or saw in prospect as to come. Scarcely had he entered on his charge at Carthage four years before, when he had had to denounce one portentous scandal in which a sacred order of the ministry was implicated. What internal laxity did not that scandal imply! And then again what a low standard of religion, what niggardly faith, and what worn-out, used-up sanctity in the community at large, was revealed in the fact of those frequent apostasies of individuals which then were occurring! He prayed fervently that both from the bright pattern of martyrs, and from the warning afforded by the lapsed, the Christian body might be edified and invigorated. He saw with great anxiety two schisms in prospect, when the persecution should come to an end, one from the perverseness of those who were too rigid, the other from those who were too indulgent towards the fallen; and in proportion to his gift of prescience was the earnestness of his intercession that the wounds of the Church might be healed with the least possible delay. He then turned to the thought of his own correspondence then in progress with the Holy Roman Church, which had lately lost its bishop by martyrdom. This indeed was no unusual event with the see of Peter, in which the successors of Peter followed Peter's steps, as Peter had been bidden to follow the King and Exemplar of Martyrs. But the special trouble was, that months had passed, full five, since the vacancy occurred, and it had not yet been supplied. Then he thought of Fabian, who made the vacancy, and who had already passed through that trial which was to bring to so many Christians life or condemnation, and he commended himself to his prayers against the hour of his own combat. He thought of Fabian's work, and went on to intercede for the remnant of the seven apostles whom that Pope had sent into Gaul, and some of whom had already obtained the martyr's crown. He prayed that the day might come, when not the cities only of that fair country, but its rich champaigns and sunny slopes should hear the voice of the missionary. He prayed in like manner for Britain, that the successful work of another Pope, St. Eleutherius, might be extended even to its four seas. And then he prayed for the neighbouring island on the west, still in heathen darkness, and for the endless expanse of Germany on the east, that there too the one saving name and glorious Faith might be known and accepted.

His thoughts then travelled back to Rome and Italy, and to the martyrdoms which had followed that of St. Fabian. Two Persians had already suffered in the imperial city; Maximus had lost his life, and Felix had been imprisoned, at Nola. Asia Minor, Syria, and Egypt had already afforded victims to the persecution, and cried aloud to all Christians for their most earnest prayers and for repeated Masses in behalf of those who remained under the trial. Babylas, Bishop of Antioch, the third see in Christendom, was already martyred in that city. Here again Cæcilius had a strong call on him for intercession, for a subtle form of freethinking was there manifesting itself, the issue of which was as uncertain as it might be frightful. The Bishop of Alexandria, that second of the large divisions or patriarchates of the Church, the great Dionysius, the pupil of Origen, was an exile from his see, like himself. The messenger who brought this news to Carthage had heard at Alexandria a report from Neocæsarea, that Gregory, another pupil of Origen's, the Apostle of Pontus, had also been obliged to conceal himself from the persecution. As for Origen himself, the aged, laborious, gifted, zealous teacher of his time, he was just then engaged in answering the works of an Epicurean called Celsus, and on him too the persecution was likely to fall; and Cæcilius prayed earnestly that so great a soul might be kept from such high untrue speculations as were threatening evil at Antioch, and from every deceit and snare which might endanger his inheriting that bright crown which ought to be his portion in heaven. Another remarkable report had come, viz., that some young men of Egypt had retired to the deserts up the country under the stress of the persecution,—Paul was the name of one of them,—and that they were there living in the practice of mortification and prayer so singular, and had combats with the powers of darkness and visitations from above so special, as to open quite a new era in the spiritual history of the Church.

And then his thoughts came back to his poor Agellius, and all those hundred private matters of anxiety which the foes of the Church, occupied only with her external aspect, little suspected. For Agellius, he prayed, and for his; for the strange wayward Juba, for Jucundus, for Callista; ah! that Callista might be brought on to that glorious consummation, for which she seemed marked out! But the ways of the Most High are not as our ways, and those who to us seem nearest are often furthest from Him; and so our holy priest left the whole matter in the hands of Him to whom he prayed, satisfied that he had done his part in praying.

This was the course of thought which occupied him for many hours, after (as we have said) he had closed the door upon him, and knelt down before the cross. Not merely before the symbol of redemption did he kneel; for he opened his tunic at the neck, and drew thence a small golden pyx which was there suspended. In that carefully fastened case he possessed the Holiest, his Lord and his God. That Everlasting Presence was his stay and guide amid his weary wanderings, his joy and consolation amid his overpowering anxieties. Behold the secret of his sweet serenity, and his clear unclouded determination. He had placed it upon the small table at which he knelt, and was soon absorbed in meditation and intercession.

# Chapter Nineteen

# A PASSAGE OF ARMS

H OW MANY HOURS passed while Cæcilius was thus employed, he did not know. The sun was declining when he was roused by a noise at the door. He hastily restored the sacred treasure to its hiding-place in his breast, and rose up from his knees. The door was thrown back, and a female form presented itself at the opening. She looked in at the priest, and said, "Then Agellius is not here?"

The woman was young, tall, and graceful in person. She was clad in a yellow cotton tunic, reaching to her feet, on which were shoes. The clasps at her shoulders, partly visible under the short cloak or shawl which was thrown over them, and which might, if necessary, be drawn over her head, seemed to serve the purpose, not only of fastening her dress, but of providing her with sharp prongs or minute stilettos for her defence, in case she fell in with ruffians by the way; and though the expression of her face was most feminine, there was that about it which implied she could use them for that purpose on an emergency. That face was clear in complexion, regular in outline, and at the present time pale, whatever might be its ordinary tint. Its charm was a noble and majestic calm. There is the calm of divine peace and joy; there is the calm of heartlessness; there is the calm of reckless desperation; there is the calm of death. None of these was the calm which breathed from the features of the stranger who intruded upon the solitude of Cæcilius. It was the calm of Greek sculpture; it imaged a soul nourished upon the visions of genius, and subdued and attuned by the power of a strong will. There was no appearance of timidity in her manner; very little of modesty. The evening sun gleamed across her amber robe, and lit it up till it glowed like fire, as if she were invested in the marriage *flammeum*,[103] and was to be claimed that evening as the bride of her own bright god of day.

She looked at Cæcilius, first with surprise, then with anxiety; and her words were, "You, I fear, are of his people. If so, make the most of these hours. The foe may be on you to-morrow morning. Fly while you can."

"If I am a Christian," answered Cæcilius, "what are you who are so careful of us? Have you come all the way from Sicca to give the alarm to mere atheists and magic-mongers?"

"Stranger," she said, "if you had seen what I have seen, what I have heard of to-day, you would not wonder at my wish to save from a like fate the vilest being on earth. A hideous mob is rioting in the city, thirsting for the blood of Christians; an accident may turn it in the direction of Agellius. He is gone; where is he? Murderous outrages have already been perpetrated; you remain."

"She who is so tender of Christians," answered the priest, "must herself have some sparks of the Christian flame in her own breast."

Callista sat down half unconsciously upon the bench or stool near the door; but she at once suddenly started up again, and said, "Away, fly! perhaps they are coming; where is he?"

"Fear not," said Cæcilius; "Agellius has been conveyed away to a safe hiding-place; for me, I shall be taken care of; there is no need for hurry; sit down again. But you," he continued, "you must not be found here."

"They know *me*," she said; "I am well known here. I work for the temples. I have nothing to fear. I am no Christian;" and, as if from an inexplicable overruling influence, she sat down again.

"Not a Christian yet, you mean," answered Cæcilius.

---

103 "bridal veil"

"A person must be born a Christian, sir," she replied, "in order to take up the religion. It is a very beautiful idea, as far as I have heard anything about it; but one must suck it in with one's mother's milk."

"If so, it never could have come into the world," said the priest.

She paused for a while. "It is true," she answered at length; "but a new religion begins by appealing to what is peculiar in the minds of a few. The doctrine, floating on the winds, finds its own; it takes possession of their minds; they answer its call; they are brought together by that common influence; they are strong in each other's sympathy; they create and throw around them an external form, and thus they found a religion. The sons are brought up in their fathers' faith; and what was the idea of a few becomes at length the profession of a race. Such is Judaism; such the religion of Zoroaster, or of the Egyptians."

"You will find," said the priest, "that the greater number of African Christians at this moment, for of them I speak confidently, are converts in manhood, not the sons of Christians. On the other hand, if there be those who have left the faith, and gone up to the capitol to sacrifice, these were Christians by hereditary profession. Such is my experience, and I think the case is the same elsewhere."

She seemed to be speaking more for the sake of getting answers than of objecting arguments. She paused again, and thought; then she said, "Mankind is made up of classes of very various mental complexion, as distinct from each other as the colours which meet the eye. Red and blue are incommensurable; and in like manner, a Magian never can become a Greek, nor a Greek a Cœlicolist. They do but make themselves fools when they attempt it."

"Perhaps the most deeply convinced, the most tranquil-minded in the Christian body," answered Cæcilius, "will tell you, on the contrary, that there was a time when they hated Christianity, and despised and ill-treated its professors."

"I never did any such thing," cried Callista, "since the day I first heard of it. I am not its enemy, but I cannot believe in it. I am sure I never could; I never, never should be able."

"What is it you cannot believe?" asked the priest.

"It seems too beautiful," she said, "to be anything else than a dream. It is a thing to talk about, but when you come near its professors you see it is impossible. A most beautiful imagination, *that* is what it is. Most beautiful its precepts, as far as I have heard of them; so beautiful, that in idea there is no difficulty. The mind runs along with them, as if it could accomplish them without an effort. Well, its maxims are too beautiful to be realized; and then on the other hand, its dogmas are too dismal, too shocking, too odious to be believed. They revolt me."

"Such as what?" asked Cæcilius.

"Such as this," answered Callista. "Nothing will ever make me believe that all my people have gone and will go to an eternal Tartarus."

"Had we not better confine ourselves to something more specific, more tangible?" asked Cæcilius, gravely. "I suppose if one individual may have that terrible lot, another may—both may, many may. Suppose I understand you to say that you never will believe that *you* will go to an eternal Tartarus."

Callista gave a slight start, and showed some uneasiness or displeasure.

"Is it not likely," continued he, "that you are better able to speak of yourself, and to form a judgment about yourself, than about others? Perhaps if you could first speak confidently about yourself, you would be in a better position to speak about others also."

"Do you mean," she said, in a calm tone, "that my place, after this life, is an everlasting Tartarus?"

"Are you happy?" he asked in turn.

She paused, looked down, and in a deep clear voice said, "No." There was a silence.

The priest began again: "Perhaps you have been growing in unhappiness for years; is it so? you assent. You have a heavy burden at your heart, you don't well know what. And the chance is, that you *will* grow in unhappiness for the next ten years to come. You will be more and more unhappy the longer you live. Did you live till you were an old woman, you would not know how to bear your existence."

Callista cried out as if in bodily pain, "It is true, sir, whoever told you. But how can you have the heart to say it, to insult and mock me!"

"God forbid!" exclaimed Cæcilius, "but let me go on. Listen, my child. Be brave, and dare to look at things as they are. Every day adds to your burden. This is a law of your present being, somewhat more certain than the assertion which you just now so confidently made, the impossibility of your believing in that law. You cannot refuse to accept what is not an opinion, but a fact. I say this burden which I speak of is not simply a dogma of our creed, it is an undeniable fact of nature. You cannot change it by wishing; if you were to live on earth two hundred years, it would not be reversed, it would be more and more true. At the end of two hundred years you would be too miserable even for your worst enemy to rejoice in it."

Cæcilius spoke, as if half in soliloquy or meditation, though he was looking towards Callista. The contrast between them was singular: he thus abstracted; she too, utterly forgetful of self, but absorbed in him, and showing it by her eager eyes, her hushed breath, her anxious attitude. At last she said impatiently, "Father, you are speaking to yourself; you despise me."

The priest looked straight at her with an open, untroubled smile, and said, "Callista, do not doubt me, my poor child; you are in my heart. I was praying for you shortly before you appeared. No; but, in so serious a matter as attempting to save a soul, I like to speak to you in my Lord's sight. I am speaking to you, indeed I am, my child; but I am also pleading with you on His behalf, and before His throne."

His voice trembled as he spoke, but he soon recovered himself. "Suffer me," he said. "I was saying that if you lived five hundred years on earth, you would but have a heavier load on you as time went on. But you will not live, you will die. Perhaps you will tell me that you will then cease to be. I don't believe you think so. I may take for granted that you think with me, and with the multitude of men, that you will still live, that you will still be *you*. You will still be the same being, but deprived of those outward stays and reliefs and solaces, which, such as they are, you now enjoy. You will be yourself, shut up in yourself. I have heard that people go mad at length when placed in solitary confinement. If, then, on passing hence, you are cut off from what you had here, and have only the company of yourself, I think your burden will be, so far, greater, not less than it is now.

"Suppose, for instance, you had still your love of conversing, and could not converse; your love of the poets of your race, and no means of recalling them; your love of music, and no instrument to play upon; your love of knowledge, and nothing to learn; your desire of sympathy, and no one to love: would not that be still greater misery?

"Let me proceed a step further: supposing you were among those whom you actually did *not* love; supposing you did *not* like them, nor their occupations, and could not understand their aims; suppose there be, as Christians say, one Almighty God, and you did not like Him, and had no taste for thinking of Him, and no interest in what He was and what He did; and supposing you found that there was nothing else anywhere but He, whom you did not love and whom you wished away: would you not be still more wretched?

"And if this went on for ever, would you not be in great inexpressible pain for ever?

"Assuming then, first, that the soul always needs external objects to rest upon; next, that it has no prospect of any such when it leaves this visible scene; and thirdly, that the hunger and thirst, the gnawing of the heart, where it occurs, is as keen and piercing as a flame; it will follow there is nothing irrational in the notion of an eternal Tartarus."

"I cannot answer you, sir," said Callista, "but I do not believe the dogma on that account a whit the more. My mind revolts from the notion. There *must* be some way out of it."

"If, on the other hand," continued Cæcilius, not noticing her interruption, "if all your thoughts go one way; if you have needs, desires, aims, aspirations, all of which demand an Object, and imply, by their very existence, that such an Object does exist also; and if nothing here does satisfy them, and if there be a message which professes to come from that Object, of whom you already have the presentiment, and to teach you about Him, and to bring the remedy you crave; and if those who try that remedy say with one voice that the remedy answers; are you not bound, Callista, at least to look that way, to inquire into what you hear about it, and to ask for His help, if He be, to enable you to believe in Him?"

"This is what a slave of mine used to say," cried Callista, abruptly; "... and another, Agellius, hinted the same thing.... What is your remedy, what your Object, what your love, O Christian teacher? Why are you all so mysterious, so reserved in your communications?"

Cæcilius was silent for a moment, and seemed at a loss for an answer. At length he said, "Every man is in that state which you confess of yourself. We have no love for Him who alone lasts. We love those things which do not last, but come to an end. Things being thus, He whom we ought to love has determined to win us back to Him. With this object He has come into His own world, in the form of one of us men. And in that human form He opens His arms and woos us to return to Him, our Maker. This is our Worship, this is our Love, Callista."

"You talk as Chione," Callista answered; "only that she felt, and you teach. She could not speak of her Master without blushing for joy.... And Agellius, when he said one word about his Master, he too began to blush...."

It was plain that the priest could hardly command his feelings, and they sat for a short while in silence. Then Callista began, as if musing on what she had heard.

"A loved One," she said, "yet ideal; a passion so potent, so fresh, so innocent, so absorbing, so expulsive of other loves, so enduring, yet of One never beheld;—mysterious! It is our own notion of the First and only Fair, yet embodied in a substance, yet dissolving again into a sort of imagination.... It is beyond me."

"There is but one Lover of souls," cried Cæcilius, "and He loves each one of us, as though there were no one else to love. He died for each one of us, as if there were no one else to die for. He died on the shameful cross. 'Amor meus crucifixus est.'[104] The love which he inspires lasts, for it is the love of

---

104  "My Love is crucified."

the Unchangeable. It satisfies, for He is inexhaustible. The nearer we draw to Him, the more triumphantly does He enter into us; the longer He dwells in us, the more intimately have we possession of Him. It is an espousal for eternity. This is why it is so easy for us to die for our faith, at which the world marvels."

Presently he said, "Why will not *you* approach Him? why will not you leave the creature for the Creator?"

Callista seldom lost her self-possession; for a moment she lost it now; tears gushed from her eyes. "Impossible!" she said, "what, I? you do not know me, father!" She paused, and then resumed in a different tone, "No! *my* lot is one way, yours another. I am a child of Greece, and have no happiness but that, such as it is, which my own bright land, my own glorious race, give me. I may well be content, I may well be resigned, I may well be proud, if I possess *that* happiness. I must live and die where I have been born. I am a tree which will not bear transplanting. The Assyrians, the Jews, the Egyptians, have their own mystical teaching. They follow their happiness in their own way; mine is a different one. The pride of mind, the revel of the intellect, the voice and eyes of genius, and the fond beating heart, I cannot do without them. I cannot do without what you, Christian, call sin. Let me alone; such as nature made me I will be. I cannot change."

This sudden revulsion of her feelings quite overcame Cæcilius; yet, while the disappointment thrilled through him, he felt a most strange sympathy for the poor lost girl, and his reply was full of emotion. "Am *I* a Jew?" he exclaimed; "am *I* an Egyptian, or an Assyrian? Have I from my youth believed and possessed what now is my Life, my Hope, and my Love? Child, *what* was once my life? Am not *I* too a brand plucked out of the fire? Do *I* deserve anything but evil? Is it not the Power, the Mighty Power of the only Strong, the only Merciful, the grace of Emmanuel, which has changed and won me? If He can change me, an old man, could He not change a child like you? I, a proud, stern Roman; I, a lover of pleasure, a man of letters, of political station, with formed habits, and life-long associations, and complicated relations; was it *I* who wrought this great change in me, who gained for myself the power of hating what I once loved, of unlearning what I once knew, nay, of even forgetting what once I was? Who has made you and me to differ, but He who can, when He will, make us to agree? It is His same Omnipotence which will transform *you*, if you will but come to be transformed."

But a reaction had come over the proud and sensitive mind of the Greek girl. "So after all, priest," she said, "you are but a man like others; a frail, guilty person like myself. I can find plenty of persons who do as I do; I want some one who does not; I want some one to worship. I thought there was something in you special and extraordinary. There was a gentleness and tenderness mingled with your strength which was new to me. I said, Here is at last a god. My own gods are earthly, sensual; I have no respect for them, no faith in them. But there is nothing better anywhere else.... Alas!..." She started up, and said with vehemence, "I thought you sinless; you confess to crime.... Ah! how do I know," she continued with a shudder, "that you are better than those base hypocrites, priests of Isis or Mithras, whose lustrations, initiations, new birth, white robes, and laurel crowns, are but the instrument and cloak of their intense depravity?" And she felt for the clasp upon her shoulder.

Here her speech was interrupted by a hoarse sound, borne upon the wind as of many voices blended into one and softened by the distance, but which, under the circumstances, neither of the parties to the above conversation had any difficulty in assigning to its real cause. "Dear father," she said, "the enemy is upon you."

# Chapter Twenty

# HE SHALL NOT LOSE HIS REWARD

THERE WAS NO ROOM for doubt or for delay. "What is to become of you, Callista?" he said; "they will tear you to pieces."

"Fear nothing for me, father," she answered; "I am one of them. They know me. Alas, *I* am no Christian! *I* have not abjured their rites! but you, lose not a moment."

"They are still at some distance," he said, "though the wind gives us merciful warning of their coming." He looked about the room, and took up the books of Holy Scripture which were on the shelf. "There is nothing else," he said, "of special value here. Agellius could not take them. Here, my child, I am going to show you a great confidence. To few persons not Christians would I show it. Take this blessed parchment; it contains the earthly history of our Divine Master. Here you will see whom we Christians love. Read it; keep it safely; surrender it, when you have the opportunity, into Christian keeping. My mind tells me I am not wrong in lending it to you." He handed to her the Gospel of St. Luke, while he put the two other volumes into the folds of his own tunic.

"One word more," she said; "your name, should I want you."

He took up a piece of chalk from the shelf, and wrote upon the wall in distinct characters,

"Thascius Cæcilius Cyprianus, Bishop of Carthage."

Hardly had she read the inscription when the voices of several men were heard in the very neighbourhood of the cottage; and hoping to effect a diver-

sion in favour of Cæcilius, and being at once unsuspicious of danger to herself, and careless of her life, she ran quickly forward to meet them. Cæcilius
ought to have taken to flight without a moment's delay, but a last sacred duty
detained him. He knelt down and took the pyx from his bosom. He had
eaten nothing that day; but even if otherwise, it was a crisis which allowed
him to consume the sacred species without fasting. He hastily opened the
golden case, adored the blessed sacrament, and consumed it, purifying its
receptacle, and restoring it to its hiding-place. Then he rose at once and left
the cottage.

He looked about; Callista was nowhere to be seen. She was gone; so
much was certain, no enemy was in sight; it only remained for him to make
off too. In the confusion he turned in the wrong direction; instead of making
off at the back of the cottage from which the voices had scared him, he ran
across the garden into the hollow way. It was all over with him in an instant;
he fell at once into the hands of the vanguard of the mob.

Many mouths were opened upon him all at once. "The sorcerer!" cried
one; "tear him to shreds; *we'll* teach him to brew his spells against the city."
"Give us back our grapes and corn," said a second. "Have a guard," said a
third; "he can turn you into swine or asses while there is breath in him,"
"Then be the quicker with him," said a fourth, who was lifting up a crow-
bar to discharge upon his head. "Hold!" said a tall swarthy youth, who had
already warded off several blows from him, "hold, will you? don't you see, if
you kill him he can't undo the spell. Make him first reverse it all; make him
take the curse off us. Bring him along; take him to Astarte, Hercules, or old
Saturn. We'll broil him on a gridiron till he turns all these canes into vines,
and makes olive berries of the pebbles, and turns the dust of the earth into
fine flour for our eating. When he has done all this he shall dance a jig with
a wild cow, and sit down to supper with an hyena."

A loud scream of exultation broke forth from the drunken and frantic
multitude. "Along with him!" continued the same speaker in a jeering tone.
"Here, put him on the ass and tie his hands behind his back. He shall go
back in triumph to the city which he loves. Mind, and don't touch him before

the time. If you kill him, you'll never get the curse off. Come here, you priests of Cybele," he added, "and be his body-guard." And he continued to keep a vigilant eye and hand over the old man, in spite of them.

The ass, though naturally a good-tempered beast, had been most sadly tried through the day. He had been fed, indeed, out of mockery, as being the Christians' god; but he did not understand the shouts and caprices of the crowd, and he only waited for an opportunity to show that he by no means acquiesced in the proceedings of the day. And now the difficulty was to move at all. The people kept crowding up the hollow road, and blocked the passage, and though the greater part of the rioters had either been left behind exhausted in Sicca itself, or had poured over the fields on each side of Agellius's cottage, or gone right over the hill down into the valley beyond, yet still it was some time before the ass could move a step, and a time of nervous suspense it was both to Cæcilius and the youth who befriended him. At length what remained of the procession was persuaded to turn about and make for Sicca, but in a reversed order. It could not be brought round in so confined a space, so its rear went first and the ass and its burden came last. As they descended the hill back again, Cæcilius, who was mounted upon the linen and silk which had adorned the Dea Syra[105] before the Tertullianist had destroyed the idol, saw before him the whole line of march. In front were flaunted the dreadful emblems of idolatry, so far as their bearers were able still to raise them. Drunken women, ragged boys mounted on men's shoulders, ruffians and bullies, savage-looking Getulians, half-human monsters from the Atlas, monkeys and curs jabbering and howling, mummers, bacchanals, satyrs, and gesticulators, formed the staple of the procession. Midway between the hill which he was descending and the city lay the ravine, of which we have several times spoken, widening out into the plain or Campus Martius, which reached round to the steep cliffs on the north. The bridle-path, along which he was moving, crossed it just where it was opening and became level, so as to present no abrupt descent and ascent at the

---

105 "Syrian Goddess"

place where the path was lowest. On the left every vestige of the ravine soon ceased, and a free passage extended to the plain.

The youth who had placed Cæcilius on the ass still kept close to him and sung at the pitch of his voice, in imitation of the rest—

> "Sporting and snorting in shades of the night,
> His ears pricking up, and his hoofs striking light,
> And his tail whisking round, in the speed of his flight."

"Old man," he continued to Cæcilius in a low voice, and in Latin, "your curse has not worked on me yet."

"My son," answered the priest, "you are granted one day more for repentance."

"Lucky for you as well as for me," was the reply: and he continued his song:—

> "Gurta, the witch, was out with the rest;
> Though as lame as a gull, by his highness possessed,
> She shouldered her crutch, and danced with the best.
>
> "She stamped and she twirled in the shade of the yew,
> Till her gossips and chums of the city danced too;
> They never are slack when there's mischief to do.
>
> "She danced and she coaxed, but he was no fool;
> He'd be his own master, he'd not be her tool:
> Not the little black moor should send him to school."

He then turned to Cæcilius and whispered, "You see, old father, that others, besides Christians, can forgive and forget. Henceforth call me generous Juba." And he tossed his head.

By this time they had got to the bottom of the hill, and the deep shadows which filled the hollow showed that the sun was rapidly sinking in the west. Suddenly, as they were crossing the bottom as it opened into the plain, Juba seized and broke the thong which bound Cæcilius's arms, and bestowing a tremendous cut with it upon the side of the ass, sent him forward upon the plain at his greatest speed. The youth's manœuvre was successful to the full. The asses of Africa can do more on an occasion of this kind than our own. Cæcilius for the moment lost his seat; but, instantly recovering it, took care to keep the animal from flagging; and the cries of the mob, and the howl-ings of the priests of Cybele cooperated in the task. At length the gloom, increasing every minute, hid him from their view; and even in daylight his recapture would have been a difficult matter for a wearied-out, famished, and intoxicated rabble. Before Cæcilius well had time to return thanks for this unexpected turn of events, he was out of pursuit, and was ambling at a pace more suitable to the habits of the beast of burden that carried him, over an expanse of plain which would have been a formidable night-march to a fasting man.

We must not conclude the day without relating what was its issue to the persecutors, as well as to their intended victim. It is almost a proverb that punishment is slow in overtaking crime; but the present instance was an exception to the rule. While the exiled Bishop of Carthage escaped, the crowd, on the other hand, were caught in the trap which had been laid for them. We have already said it was a *ruse* on the part of the governing authori-ties of the place to get the rioters out of the city, that they might at once be relieved of them, and then deal with them just as they might think fit. When the mob was once outside the walls, they might be refused re-admittance, and put down with a strong hand. The Roman garrison, who, powerless to quell the tumult in the narrow and winding streets and multiplied alleys of the city, had been the authors of the manœuvre, now took on themselves the stern completion of it, and determined to do so in the sternest way. Not a single head of all those who poured out in the afternoon should return at night. It was not to be supposed that the soldiers had any tenderness for the Christians, but they abominated and despised the rabble of the town. They were indignant at their rising, thought it a personal insult to themselves, and resolved they should never do so again. The gates were commonly in the cus-tody of the city guard, but the Porta Septimiana,[106] by which the mob passed out, was on this occasion claimed by the Romans. It was most suitably cir-

---

106 "Septimian Gate"

cumstanced for the use they intended to make of it. Immediately outside of it was a large court of the same level as the ground inside, bordered on the right and left by substantial walls, which after a time were drawn to meet each other, and contracted the space to the usual breadth of a road. The walls continued to run along this road for some distance, till they joined the way which led to the Campus Martius, and from this point the ground was open till it reached the head of the ravine. The soldiers drew up at the gate, and as the worn-out and disappointed, brutalized and half-idiotic multitudes returned towards it from the country, those who were behind pushed on between the border walls those who were in front, and, while they jammed together their ranks, also made escape impossible. It was now that the Roman soldiers began their barbarous, not to say cowardly, assault upon them. With heavy maces, with the pike, with iron gauntlets, with stones and bricks, with clubs, with scourge, with the sword, with the helmet, with whatever came to hand, they commenced the massacre of that large concourse of human beings, who did not offer one blow in return. They slaughtered them like sheep; they trampled them down; they threw the bodies of the wounded over the walls. Attempting to run back, numbers of the poor wretches came into conflict with the ranks behind them, and an additional scene of confusion and overthrow took place; many of them straggled over to the open country or woods, and perished, either from the weather, or from hunger, or even from the wild beasts. Others, weakened by excess and famine, fell a prey to the pestilence that was raging. After some days a remnant of them was allowed silently and timidly to steal back into the city as best they could. It was a long day before the Plebs Siccensis[107] ventured to have any opinion of its own upon the subject of Christianity, or any other political, social, or ecclesiastical topic whatever.

---

107 "Masses of Sicca"

# Chapter Twenty-one

# STARTLING RUMOURS

W HEN JUCUNDUS rose next morning, and heard the news, he considered it to be more satisfactory than he could have supposed possible. He was a zealous imperialist, and a lover of tranquillity, a despiser of the natives and a hater of the Christians. The Christians had suffered enough to vindicate the Roman name, to deter those who were playing at Christianity, and to show that the people of Sicca had their eyes about them. And the mob had received a severe lesson too; and the cause of public order had triumphed, and civic peace was re-established. His anxiety, too, about Agellius had terminated, or was terminating. He had privately denounced him to the government, come to an understanding with the military authorities, and obtained the custody of him. He had met him at the very door to which the boy Firmian brought him, with an apparitor[108] of the military staff (or what answered to it), and had clapped him into prison in an underground cellar in which he kept damaged images, and those which had gone out of fashion, and were otherwise unsaleable. He was not at all sorry, by some suffering, and by some fright, to aid the more potent incantation which Callista was singing in his ears. He did not, however, at all forget Juba's hint, and was careful not to overdo the rack-and-gridiron dodge, if we may so designate it; yet he thought just a flavour or a thought of the inconveniences which the profession of Christianity involved might be a salutary reflection in the midst of the persuasives which the voice and eyes of Callista would kindle in his heart. There was nothing glorious or heroic in being confined in a lumber cellar, no one knowing anything about it; and he did not mean to keep him there for ever.

As the next day wore on towards evening, rumour brought a piece of news which he was at first utterly unable to credit, and which for the moment seemed likely to spoil the appetite which promised so well for his evening repast. He could hardly believe his ears when he was told that Callista was in arrest on a charge of Christianity, and at first it made him look as black as some of those Egyptian gods which he had on one shelf of his shop. However, he rallied, and was very much amused at the report. The imprisonment indeed was a fact, account for it as one could; but who *could* account for it? "Varium et mutabile:"[109] who could answer for the whims and fancies of womankind? If she had fallen in love with the owl of Minerva, or cut off her auburn tresses, or turned rope-dancer, there might have been some shrugging of shoulders, but no one would have tried to analyze the motive; but so much his profound sagacity enabled him to see, that, if there was one thing more than another likely to sicken Agellius of Christianity, it was to find one who was so precious to him suffering from the suspicion of it. It was bad enough to have suffered one's self in such a cause; still he could conceive, he was large-minded enough to grant, that Agellius might have some secret satisfaction in the antagonist feeling of resentment and obstinacy which that suffering might engender: but it was carrying matters too far, and no comfort in any point of view, to find Callista, his beloved, the object of a similar punishment. It was all very well to profess Christianity as a matter of sentiment, mystery, and singularity; but when it was found to compromise the life or limbs of another, and that other Callista, why it was plain that Agellius would be the very first to try and entreat the wayward girl to keep

---

109 "Fickle and changeable"

her good looks for him, and to be loyal to the gods of her country; and he chuckled over the thought, as others have done in other states of society, of a love-scene or a marriage being the termination of so much high romance and fine acting.

However, the next day Aristo came down to him himself, and gave him an account at once more authentic and more extended on the matter which interested him. Callista had been called up before the tribunal, and had not been discharged, but remanded. The meaning of it was as obscure as ever; Aristo could give no account of it; it almost led him to believe in the evil eye; some unholy practices, some spells such as only potent wizards know, some deplorable delusion or hallucination, had for the time got the mastery of his sister's mind. No one seemed quite to know how she had found her way into the hands of the officers; but there she was, and the problem was how to get her out of them.

However, whatever mystery, whatever anxiety, attached to the case, it was only still more urgent to bring the matter home to Agellius without delay. If time went on before the parties were brought together, she might grow more obstinate, and kindle a like spirit in him. Oh that boys and girls *would* be giving old people, who wish them well, so much trouble! However, it was no good thinking of that just then. He considered that, at the present moment, they would not be able to bear the sight of each other in suffering and peril; that mutual tenderness would make them plead with each other in each other's behalf, and that each would be obliged to set the example to each of a concession, to which each exhorted each; and on this fine philosophical view he proceeded to act.

# Chapter Twenty-two

# JUCUNDUS PROPOUNDS HIS VIEW OF THE SITUATION

For thirty-six hours Agellius had been confined in his underground receptacle, light being almost excluded, a bench and a rug being his means of repose, and a full measure of bread, wine, and olives being his dole. The shrieks and yells of the rioters could be distinctly heard in his prison, as the day of his seizure went on, and they passed by the temple of Astarte; but what happened at his farm, and how it fared with Cæcilius, he had no means of conjecturing; nor indeed how it was to fare with himself, for on the face of the transaction, as was in form the fact, he was in the hands of the law, and only indulged with the house of a relative for his prison. On the second night he was released by his uncle's confidential slave, who brought him up to a small back closet on the ground floor, which was lighted from the roof, and next morning, being the second day after the riot, Jucundus came in to have his confidential conversation with him.

His uncle began by telling him that he was a government prisoner, but that he hoped by his influence in high places to get him off and out of Sicca without any prejudice to his honour. He told him that he had managed it privately, and if he had treated him with apparent harshness up to the evening before, it was in order to save appearances with the apparitors who had attended him. He then went on to inform him that the mob had visited his cottage, and had caught some man there; he supposed some accomplice or ally of his nephew's. They had seized him, and were bringing him off, but the fellow had been clever enough to effect his escape. He did not know more than this, but it had happened very fortunately, for the general belief in the place was, that it was Agellius who had been taken, and who had managed to give them the slip. Since it could not any longer be safely denied that he was a Christian, though he (Jucundus) did not think so himself, he had encouraged or rather had given his confirmation to the report; and when some persons who had means of knowing had asserted that the culprit was double the age of his nephew and more, and not at all of his make or description, but a sort of slave, or rather that he was the slave of Agellius who had belonged to his father Strabo, Jucundus had boldly asserted that Agellius, in the emergency, had availed himself of some of the remarkably powerful charms which Christians were known to possess, and had made himself seem what he really was not, in order to escape detection. It had not indeed answered the purpose entirely, for he had actually been taken; but no blame in the charm, which perhaps, after all, had enabled him to escape. However, Agellius was gone, he told people, and a good riddance, and he hoped never to see him again. "But you see, my dear boy," he concluded, "this was all talk for the occasion, for I hope you will live here many years in respectability and credit. I intend you should close my eyes when my time comes, and inherit whatever I have to leave you; for as to that fellow Juba, he inspires me with no confidence in him at all."

Agellius thanked his uncle with all his heart for his kind and successful efforts on his behalf; he did not think there was a word he had said, in the future he had sketched for him, which he could have wished altered. But he thought Jucundus over-sanguine; much as he should like to live with him and tend him in his old age, he did not think he should ever be permitted to return to Sicca. He was a Christian, and must seek some remote corner of the world, or at least some city where he was unknown. Every one in Sicca would point at him as the Christian; he would experience a thousand rubs and collisions, even if the mob did not rise against him, without corresponding advantage; on the other hand, he would have no influence. But were he in the midst of a powerful and widely-extended community of Christians, he might in his place do work, and might extend the faith as one of a number, unknown himself, and strong in his brethren. He therefore proposed as soon as possible to sell his effects and stock, and retire from the sight of men, at least for a time.

"You think this persecution, then, will be soon at an end?" asked Jucundus.

"I judge by the past," answered Agellius; "there have been times of trial and of rest hitherto, and I suppose it will be so again. And one place has hitherto been exempt from the violence of our enemies, when another has been the scene of it."

"A new time is coming, trust me," said Jucundus, gravely. "Those popular commotions are all over. What happened two days ago is a sample of what will come of them; they have received their *coup-de-grâce*. The State is taking up the matter, Rome itself, thank the gods! a tougher sort of customer than these villain ratcatchers and offal-eaters, whom you had to do with two days since. Great Rome is now at length in earnest, my boy, which she ought to have been a long time back, before you were born; and then you know," and he nodded, "you would have had no choice; you wouldn't have had the temptation to make a fool of yourself."

"Well, then," answered Agellius, "if a new time is really coming, there is less chance than ever of my continuing here."

"Now be a sensible fellow, as you are when you choose," said his uncle; "look the matter in the face, do. You cannot wrestle with impossibilities, you cannot make facts to pattern. There are lawful religions, there are illicit. Christianity is illicit; it is not tolerated; that's not your fault; you cannot help it; you would, if you could; you can't. Now you have observed your point of honour; you have shown you can stand up like a man, and suffer for your own fancy. Still Rome does not give way; and you must make the best of it. You must give in, and you are far too good (I don't compliment, I speak my mind), far too amiable, excellent, sweet a boy for so rascally a superstition."

"There is something stronger than Rome," said the nephew almost sternly.

Jucundus cut him short. "Agellius!" he said, "you must not say that in this house. You shall not use that language under my roof. I'll not put up with it, I tell you. Take your treason elsewhere.... This accursed obstinacy!" he said to himself; "but I must take care what I am doing;" then aloud, "Well, we both of us have been railing; no good comes of railing; railing is not argument. But now, I say, do be sensible, if you can. Is not the imperial government in earnest now? better late than never, but it is now in earnest. And now mark my words, by this day five years, five years at the utmost,— I say by this day five years there will not be a single ragamuffin Christian in the whole Roman world." And he looked fierce. "Ye gods! Rome, Rome has swept from the earth by her very breath conspiracies, confederacies, plots against her, without ever failing; she will do so now with this contemptible, Jew-begotten foe."

"In what are we enemies to Rome, Jucundus?" said Agellius; "why will you always take it for granted?"

"Take it for granted!" answered he, "is it not on the face of the matter? I suppose *they* are enemies to a state, whom the state *calls* its enemies. Besides, why a pother of words? Swear by the genius of the emperor, invoke the Dea Roma,[110] sacrifice to Jove; no, not a bit of it, not a whisper, not a sign, not a grain of incense. You go out of your way to insult us; and then you come with a grave face, and say you are loyal. You kick our shins, and you wish us to kiss you on both cheeks for it. A few harmless ceremonies; we are not entrapping you; we are not using your words against yourselves; we tell you the meaning beforehand, the whole meaning of them. It is not as if we tied you to the belief of the nursery: we don't say, 'If you burn incense, you profess to believe that old Jupiter is shivering atop of Olympus;' we don't say, 'You swear by the genius of Cæsar, therefore he has a genius, black, or white, or piebald,' No, we give you the meaning of the act; it is a mere expression of loyalty to the empire. If then you won't do it, you confess yourself *ipso facto* disloyal. It is incomprehensible." And he had become quite red.

---

110 "Goddess of Rome"

"My dear uncle," said Agellius, "I give you my solemn word, that the people whom you so detest do pray for the welfare of the imperial power continually, as a matter of duty and as a matter of interest."

"Pray! pray! fudge and nonsense!" cried Jucundus, almost mimicking him in his indignation; "pray! who thanks you for your prayers? what's the good of prayers? Prayers, indeed! ha, ha! A little loyalty is worth all the praying in the world. I'll tell you what, Agellius; you are, I am sorry to say it, but you are hand and glove with a set of traitors, who shall and will be smoked out like a nest of wasps. *You* don't know; *you* are not in the secret, nor the wretched slave, poor beast, who was pulled to pieces yesterday (ah! you don't know of him) at the Flamen's, nor a multitude of other idiots. But, d'ye see," and he chucked up his head significantly, "there are puppets, and there are wires. Few know what is going on. They won't have done (unless we put them down; but we will) till they have toppled down the state. But Rome will put them down. Come, be sensible, listen to reason; now I am going to put facts before my poor, dear, well-meaning boy. Oh that you saw things as I do! What a trouble you are to me! Here am I"——

"My dearest uncle, Jucundus," cried Agellius, "I assure you, it is the most intense pain to me"——

"Very well, very well," interrupted the uncle in turn, "I believe it, of course I believe it; but listen, listen. Every now and then," he continued in a more measured and lower tone, "every now and then the secret is blabbed— blabbed. There was that Tertullianus of Carthage, some fifty years since. He wrote books; books have done a great deal of harm before now; but *read* his books—read and ponder. The fellow has the insolence to tell the proconsul that he and the whole government, the whole city and province, the whole Roman world, the emperors, all but the pitiful *clique* to which he belongs, are destined, after death, to flames for ever and ever. There's loyalty! but the absurdity is greater than the malevolence. Rightly are the fellows called atheists and men-haters. Our soldiers, our statesmen, our magistrates, and judges, and senators, and the whole community, all worshippers of the gods, every one who crowns his head, every one who loves a joke, and all our great historic names, heroes, and worthies,—the Scipios, the Decii, Brutus, Cæsar, Cato, Titus, Trajan, Antoninus,—are inmates, not of the Elysian fields, if Elysian fields there be, but of Tartarus, and will never find a way out of it."

"That man, Tertullianus, is nothing to us, uncle," answered Agellius; "a man of great ability, but he quarrelled with us, and left us."

"I can't draw nice distinctions," said Jucundus. "Your people have quarrelled among themselves perhaps on an understanding; we can't split hairs. It's the same with your present hierophant at Carthage, Cyprianus. Nothing can exaggerate, I am told, the foulness of his attack upon the gods of Rome, upon Romulus, the Augurs, the Ancilia, the consuls, and whatever a Roman is proud of. As to the imperial city itself, there's hardly one of their high priests that has not died under the hands of the executioner, as a convict. The precious fellows take the title of Pontifex Maximus; bless their impudence! Well, my boy, this is what I say; be, if you will, so preternaturally sour and morose as to misconceive and mislike the innocent, graceful, humanising, time-honoured usages of society; be so, for what I care, if this is all; but it isn't all. Such misanthropy is wisdom, absolute wisdom, compared with the Titanic presumption and audacity of challenging to single combat the sovereign of the world. Go and kick down Mount Atlas first."

"You have it all your own way, Jucundus," answered his nephew, "and so you must move in your own circle, round and round. There is no touching you, if you first assume your premisses, and then prove them by means of your conclusion."

"My dear Agellius," said his uncle, giving his head a very solemn shake, "take the advice of an old man. When you are older than you are, you will see better who is right and who is wrong. You'll be sorry you despised me, a true, a prudent, an experienced friend; you will. Shake yourself, come do. Why should you link your fortunes, in the morning of life, with desperate men, only because your father, in his last feeble days, was entrapped into doing so? I really will not believe that you are going to throw away hope and life on so bad a bargain. Can't you speak a word? Here you've let me speak, and won't say one syllable for yourself. I don't think it kind of you."

Thus adjured, Agellius began. "Well," he said, "it's a long history; you see, we start, my dear uncle, from different points. How am I possibly to join issue with you? I can only tell you my conclusion. Hope and life, you say. Why, my only hope, my only life, my only joy, desire, consolation, and treasure is that I am a Christian."

"Hope and life!" interrupted Jucundus, "immortal gods! life and hope in being a Christian! do I hear aright? Why, man, a prison brings despair, not hope; and the sword brings death, not life. By Esculapius! life and hope! you choke me, Agellius. Life and hope! you are beyond three Anticyras. Life and hope! if you were old, if you were diseased, if you were given over, and had but one puff of life left in you, then you might be what you would, for me; but your hair is black, your cheek is round, your limbs are strong, your voice is full; and you are going to make all these a sacrifice to Hecate! has your good genius fed that plump frame, ripened those goods looks, nerved your arm, bestowed that breadth of chest, that strength of loins, that straightness of spine, that vigour of step, only that you may feed the crows? or to be torn on the rack, scorched in the flame, or hung on the gibbet? is this your gratitude to nature? What has been your price? for what have you sold yourself? Speak, man, speak. Are you dumb as well as dement? Are you dumb, I say, are you dumb?"

"O Jucundus," cried Agellius, irritated at his own inability to express himself or hold an argument, "if you did but know what it was to have the Truth! The Christian has found the Truth, the eternal Truth, in a world of error. That is his bargain, that is his hire; can there be a greater? Can I give up the Truth? But all this is Punic or Barbar to you."

It certainly did pose Jucundus for half a minute, as if he was trying to take in, not so much the sense, as the words of his nephew's speech. He looked bewildered, and though he began to answer him at once, it took several sentences to bring him into his usual flow of language. After one or two exclamations, "The truth!" he cried, "*this* is what I understand you to say,— the truth. The *truth* is your bargain; I think I'm right, the truth; Hm; what is truth? What in heaven and earth do you mean by truth? where did you

get that cant? What oriental tomfoolery is bamboozling you? The truth!" he
cried, staring at him with eyes, half of triumph, half of impatience, "the truth!
Jove help the boy!—the truth! can truth pour me out a cup of melilotus? can
truth crown me with flowers? can it sing to me? can it bring Glyceris to me?
drop gold into my girdle? or cool my brows when fever visits me? Can truth
give me a handsome suburban with some five hundred slaves, or raise me to
the duumvirate? Let it do this, and I will worship it; it shall be my god; it
shall be more to me than Fortune, Fate, Rome, or any other goddess on the
list. But *I* like to see, and touch, and feel, and handle, and weigh, and measure
what is promised me. I wish to have a sample and an instalment. I am too old
for chaff. Eat, drink, and be merry, that's my philosophy, that's my religion;
and I know no better. To-day is ours, to-morrow is our children's."

After a pause, he added, bitterly, "If truth could get Callista out of prison,
instead of getting her into it, I should have something to say to truth."

"Callista in prison!" cried Agellius with surprise and distress, "what do
you mean, Jucundus?"

"Yes, it's a fact; Callista *is* in prison," answered he, "and on suspicion of
Christianity."

"Callista! Christianity!" said Agellius, bewildered, "do I hear aright? She
a Christian! oh, impossible, uncle! you don't mean to say that she is in prison.
Tell me, tell me, my dear, dear Jucundus, what this wonderful news means."

"You ought to know more about it than I," answered he, "if there is any
meaning in it. But if you want my opinion, here it is. I don't believe she is
more a Christian than I am; but I think she is over head and ears in love
with you, and she has some notion that she is paying you a compliment, or
interesting you in her, or sharing your fate—(*I* can't pretend to unravel the
vagaries and tantarums of the female mind)—by saying that she is what she
is *not*. If not, perhaps she has done it out of spite and contradiction. You can
never answer for a woman."

"Whom should she spite? whom contradict?" cried Agellius, thrown for
the moment off his balance. "O Callista! Callista in prison for Christianity!
Oh if it's true that she is a Christian! but what if she is not?" he added with

great terror, "what if she's not, and yet in prison, as if she were? How are we to get her out, uncle? Impossible! no, she's not a Christian—she is not at all. She ought not to be there! Yet how wonderful!"

"Well, I am sure of it, too," said Jucundus; "I'd stake the best image in my shop that she's not a Christian; but what if she is perverse enough to say she *is*? and such things are not uncommon. Then, I say, what in the world is to be done? If she says she is, why she is. There you are; and what can you do?"

"You don't mean to say," exclaimed Agellius, "that that sweet delicate child is in that horrible hole; impossible!" and he nearly shrieked at the thought. "What is the meaning of it all? dear, dear uncle, do tell me something more about it. Why did you not tell me before? What *can* be done?"

Jucundus thought he now had him in his hand. "Why, it's plain," he answered, "what can be *done*. She's no Christian, we both agree. It's certain, too, that she chooses to say she is, or something like it. There's just one person who has influence with her, to make her tell the truth."

"Ha!" cried Agellius, starting as if an asp had bitten him.

Jucundus kept silence, and let the poison of the said asp work awhile in his nephew's blood.

Agellius put his hands before his eyes; and with his elbows on his knees, began moving to and fro, as if in intense pain.

"I repeat what I have said," Jucundus observed at length; "I do really think that she imagines a certain young gentleman is likely to be in trouble, and that she is determined to share the trouble with him."

"But it isn't true," cried Agellius with great vehemence; "it's not true.... If she really is not a Christian, O my dear Lord, surely they won't put her to death as if she was?"

"But if she has made up her mind to be in the same boat with you, and *will* be a Christian while you are a Christian, what on earth can we do, Agellius?" asked Jucundus. "You have the whole matter in a nutshell."

"She does not love me," cried Agellius; "no, she has given me no reason to think so. I am sure she does not. She's nothing to me. That cannot be the reason of her conduct. *I* have no power over her; *I* could not persuade her.

What, what *does* all this mean? and I shut up here?" and he began walking about the little room, as if such locomotion tended to bring him out of it.

"Well," answered Jucundus, "it is easy to ascertain. I suppose you *could* be let out to see her."

But he was going on too fast; Agellius did not attend to him. "Poor, sweet Callista," he exclaimed, "she's innocent, she's innocent; I mean she's not a Christian. Ah!" he screamed out in great agony, as the whole state of the case unrolled itself to his apprehension, "she will die though not a Christian; she will die without faith, without love; she will die in her sins. She will die, done to death by false report of accepting that, by which alone she could be carried safely through death unto life. O my Lord, spare me!" and he sank upon the ground in a collapse of misery.

Jucundus was touched, and still more alarmed. "Come, come, my boy," he said, "you will rouse the whole neighbourhood. Give over; be a man; all will be right. If she's not a Christian (and she's not), she shall not die a Christian's death; something will turn up. She's not in any hole at all, but in a decent lodging. And you shall see her, and console her, and all will be right."

"Yes, I will see her," said Agellius, in a sort of musing manner; "she is either a Christian, or she is not. If she is a Christian ..." and his voice faltered; "but if she is not, she shall live till she is."

"Well said!" answered Jucundus, "*till* she is. She shall live *till* she is. Yes, I can get you to see her. You shall bring her out of prison; a smile, a whisper from you, and all her fretfulness and ill-humour will vanish, like a mist before the powerful burning sun. And we shall all be as happy as the immortal gods."

"O my uncle!" said Agellius, gravely. The language of Jucundus had shocked him, and brought him to a better mind. He turned away from Jucundus, and leant his face against the wall. Then he turned round again, and said, "If she *is* a Christian, I ought to rejoice, and I do rejoice; God be praised. If she is not a Christian, I ought at once to make her one. If she has already the penalty of a Christian, she is surely destined for the privilege. And how should I go," he said, half speaking to himself, "how should I go to tell her that she is not yet a Christian, and bid her swear by Jupiter, because that is her god, in order that she may escape imprisonment and death? Am I to do the part of a heathen priest or infidel sophist? O Cæcilius, how am I forgetting your lessons! No; I will go on no such errand. Go, I will, if I may, Jucundus, but I will go on no conditions of yours. I go on no promise to try to get her out of prison anyhow, poor child. I will not go to make her sacrifice to a false god; I go to persuade her to stay in prison, by deserving to stay. Perhaps I am not the best person to go; but if I go, I go free. I go willing to die myself for my Lord; glad to make her die for Him."

Agellius said this in so determined a way, so calmly, with such a grasp of the existing posture of affairs, and of the whole circumstances of the case, that it was now Jucundus's turn to feel surprise and annoyance. For a time he did not take in what Agellius meant, nor could he to the last follow his train of feeling. When he saw what may be called the upshot of the matter, he became very angry, and spoke with great violence. By degrees he calmed; and then the strong feeling came on him again that it was impossible, if a meeting took place between the two, that it could end in any way but one. He defied any two young people who loved each other, to come to any but one conclusion. Agellius's mood was too excited, too tragic to last. The sight of Callista in that dreadful prison, perhaps in chains, waiting, in order to be free, for ability to say the words, "I am not a Christian;" and that ability waiting for the same words from himself, would bring the affair to a very speedy issue. As if he could love a fancy better than he loved Callista! Agellius, too, had already expressed a misgiving himself on that head; so far they were agreed. And, to tell the truth, it was a very difficult transaction for a young man; and giving our poor Agellius all credit for pure intention and firm resolve, we really should have been very sorry to see him involved in a trial, which would have demanded of him a most heroic faith and the detachment of a saint. We, therefore, are not sorry that in matter of fact he gained the merit of so virtuous a determination, without being called on to execute it. For it so happened, that a most unexpected event occurred to him not many hours afterwards, which will oblige us to take up here rather abruptly the history of one of our other personages.

# Chapter Twenty-three

# GURTA

I N THE BOSOM of the woods which stretched for many miles from the immediate environs of Sicca, and placed on a gravel slope reaching down to a brook, which ran in a bottom close by, was a small, rude hut, of a kind peculiar to Africa, and commonly ascribed to the wandering tribes, who neither cared, nor had leisure for a more stable habitation. Some might have called it a tent, from the goat's-hair cloth with which it was covered; but it looked, as to shape, like nothing else than an inverted boat, or the roof of a house set upon the ground. Inside it was seen to be constructed of the branches of trees, twisted together or wattled, the interstices, or rather the whole surface, being covered with clay. Being thus stoutly built, lined, and covered, it was proof against the tremendous rains, to which the climate, for which it was made, was subject. Along the centre ridge or backbone, which varied in height from six to ten feet from the ground, it was supported by three posts or pillars; at one end it rose conically to an open aperture, which served for chimney, for sky-light, and for ventilator. Hooks were suspended from the roof for baskets, articles of clothing, weapons, and implements of various kinds; and a second cone, excavated in the ground with the vertex downward, served as a storehouse for grain. The door was so low, that an ordinary person must bend double to pass through it.

However, it was in the winter months only, when the rains were profuse, that the owner of this respectable mansion condescended to creep into it.

In summer she had a drawing-room, as it may be called, of nature's own creation, in which she lived, and in one quarter of which she had her lair. Close above the hut was a high plot of level turf, surrounded by old oaks, and fringed beneath with thick underwood. In the centre of this green rose a yew-tree of primeval character. Indeed, the whole forest spoke of the very beginnings of the world, as if it had been the immediate creation of that Voice which bade the earth clothe itself with green life. But the place no longer spoke exclusively of its Maker. Upon the trees hung the emblems and objects of idolatry, and the turf was traced with magical characters. Littered about were human bones, horns of wild animals, wax figures, spermaceti taken from vaults, large nails, to which portions of flesh adhered, as if they had had to do with malefactors, metal plates engraved with strange characters, bottled blood, hair of young persons, and old rags. The reader must not suppose any incantation is about to follow, or that the place we are describing will have a prominent place in what remains of our tale; but even if it be the scene of only one conversation, and one event, there is no harm in describing it, as it appeared on that occasion.

The old crone, who was seated in this bower of delight, had an expression of countenance in keeping, not with the place, but with the furniture with which it was adorned; that furniture told her trade. Whether the root of superstition might be traced deeper still, and the woman and her traps were really and directly connected with the powers beneath the earth, it is impossible to determine; it is certain she had the will, it is certain that that will was from their inspiration; nay, it is certain that she thought she really possessed the communications which she desired; it is certain, too, she so far deceived herself as to fancy that what she learned by mere natural means came to her from a diabolical source. She kept up an active correspondence with Sicca. She was consulted by numbers; she was up with the public news, the social gossip, and the private and secret transactions of the hour; and had, before now, even interfered in matters of state, and had been courted by rival political parties. But in the high cares and occupations of this interesting person, we are not here concerned; but with a conversation which took place between her and Juba, about the same hour of the evening as that of Cæcilius's escape, but on the day after it, while the sun was gleaming almost horizontally through the tall trunks of the trees of the forest.

"Well, my precious boy," said the old woman, "the choicest gifts of great Cham be your portion! You had excellent sport yesterday, I'll warrant. The rats squeaked, eh? and you beat the life out of them. That scoundrel sacristan, I suppose, has taken up his quarters below."

"You may say it," answered Juba. "The reptile! he turned right about, and would have made himself an honest fellow, when it couldn't be helped."

"Good, good!" returned Gurta, as if she had got something very pleasant in her mouth; "ah! that is good! but he did not escape on that score, I do trust."

"They pulled him to pieces all the more cheerfully," said Juba.

"Pulled him to pieces, limb by limb, joint by joint, eh?" answered Gurta. "Did they skin him?—did they do anything to his eyes, or his tongue? Anyhow, it was too quickly, Juba. Slowly, leisurely, gradually. Yes, it's like a glutton to be quick about it. Taste him, handle him, play with him,—that's luxury! but to bolt him,—faugh!"

"Cæso's slave made a good end," said Juba: "he stood up for his views, and died like a man."

"The gods smite him! but he has gone up—up!" and she laughed. "Up to what they call bliss and glory;—such glory! but he's out of our domain, you know. But he did not die easy?"

"The boys worried him a good deal," answered Juba: "but it's not quite in my line, mother, all this. I think you drink a pint of blood morning and evening, and thrive on it, old woman. It makes you merry; but it's too much for my stomach."

"Ha, ha, my boy!" cried Gurta; "you'll improve in time, though you make wry faces, now that you're young. Well, and have you brought me any news from the capitol? Is any one getting a rise in the world, or a downfall? How blows the wind? Are there changes in the camp? This Decius, I suspect, will not last long."

"They all seem desperately frightened," said Juba, "lest they should not smite your friends hard enough, Gurta. Root and branch is the word. They'll have to make a few Christians for the occasion, in order to kill them: and I almost think they're about it," he added, thoughtfully. "They have to show that they are not surpassed by the rabble. 'Tis a pity Christians are so few, isn't it, mother?"

"Yes, yes," she said, "but we must crush them, grind them, many or few: and we shall, we shall! Callista's to come."

"I don't see they are worse than other people," said Juba; "not at all, except that they are commonly sneaks. If Callista turns, why should not I turn too, mother, to keep her company, and keep your hand in?"

"No, no, my boy," returned the witch, "you must serve *my* master. You are having your fling just now, but you will buckle to in good time. You must one day take some work with my merry men. Come here, child," said the fond mother, "and let me kiss you."

"Keep your kisses for your monkeys and goats and cats," answered Juba; "they're not to my taste, old dame. Master! my master! I won't have a master! I'll be nobody's servant. I'll never stand to be hired, nor cringe to a bully, nor quake before a rod. Please yourself, Gurta; I am a free man. You're my mother by courtesy only."

Gurta looked at him savagely. "Why, you're not going to be pious and virtuous, Juba? A choice saint you'll make! You shall be drawn for a picture."

"Why shouldn't I, if I choose?" said Juba. "If I must take service, willy nilly, I'd any day prefer the other's to that of your friend. I've not left the master to take the man."

"Blaspheme not the great gods," she answered, "or they'll do you a mischief yet."

"I say again," insisted Juba, "if I must lick the earth, it shall not be where your friend has trod. It shall be in my brother's fashion, rather than in yours, Gurta."

"Agellius!" she shrieked out with such disgust, that it is wonderful she uttered the name at all. "Ah! you have not told me about him, boy. Well, is he safe in the pit, or in the stomach of an hyena?"

"He's alive," said Juba; "but he has not got it in him to be a Christian. Yes, he's safe with his uncle."

"Ah! Jucundus must ruin him, debauch him, and then we must make away with him. We must not be in a hurry," said Gurta, "it must be body and soul."

"No one shall touch him, craven as he is," answered Juba. "I despise him, but let him alone."

"Don't come across me," said Gurta, sullenly; "I'll have my way. Why, you know I could smite you to the dust, as well as him, if I chose."

"But you have not asked me about Callista," answered Juba. "It is really a capital joke, but she has got into prison for certain, for being a Christian. Fancy it! they caught her in the streets, and put her in the guard-house, and have had her up for examination. You see they want a Christian for the nonce: it would not do to have none such in prison; so they will flourish with her till Decius bolts from the scene."

"The Furies have her!" cried Gurta: "she *is* a Christian, my boy: I told you so, long ago!"

"Callista a Christian!" answered Juba, "ha! ha! She and Agellius are going to make a match of it, of some sort or other. They're thinking of other things than paradise."

"She and the old priest, more likely, more likely," said Gurta. "He's in prison with her—in the pit, as I trust."

"Your master has cheated you for once, old woman," said Juba.

Gurta looked at him fiercely, and seemed waiting for his explanation. He began singing,—

> "She wheedled and coaxed, but he was no fool;
> He'd be his own master, he'd not be her tool;
> Not the little black moor should send him to school.
>
> "She foamed and she cursed—'twas the same thing to him;
> She laid well her trap; but he carried his whim;—
> The priest scuffled off, safe in life and in limb."

Gurta was almost suffocated with passion. "Cyprianus has not escaped, boy?" she asked at length.

"I got him off," said Juba, undauntedly.

A shade, as of Erebus, passed over the witch's face; but she remained quite silent.

"Mother, I am my own master," he continued, "I must break your assumption of superiority. I'm not a boy, though you call me so. I'll have my own way. Yes, I saved Cyprianus. You're a bloodthirsty old hag! Yes, *I've* seen your secret doings. Did not I catch you the other day, practising on that little child? You had nailed him up by hands and feet against the tree, and were cutting him to pieces at your leisure, as he quivered and shrieked the while. You were examining or using his liver for some of your black purposes. It's not in my line; but you gloated over it; and when he wailed, you wailed in mimicry. You were panting with pleasure."

Gurta was still silent, and had an expression on her face, awful from the intensity of its malignity. She had uttered a low piercing whistle.

"Yes!" continued Juba, "you revelled in it. You chattered to the poor babe when it screamed, as a nurse to an infant. You called it pretty names, and squeaked out your satisfaction each time you stuck it. You old hag! I'm not of your breed, though they call us of kin. *I* don't fear you," he said, observing the expression of her countenance, "I don't fear the immortal devil!" And he continued his song—

> "She beckoned the moon, and the moon came down;
> The green earth shrivelled beneath her frown;
> But a man's strong will can keep his own."

While he was talking and singing, her call had been answered from the hut. An animal of some wonderful species had crept out of it, and proceeded to creep and crawl, moeing and twisting as it went, along the trees and shrubs which rounded the grass plot. When it came up to the old woman, it crouched at her feet, and then rose up upon its hind legs and begged. She took hold of the uncouth beast and began to fondle it in her arms, muttering something in its ear. At length, when Juba stopped for a moment in his song, she suddenly flung it right at him, with great force, saying, "Take that!" She then gave utterance to a low inward laugh, and leaned herself back against the trunk of the tree upon which she was sitting, with her knees drawn up almost to her chin.

The blow seemed to act on Juba as a shock on his nervous system, both from its violence and its strangeness. He stood still for a moment, and then, without saying a word, he turned away, and walked slowly down the hill, as if in a maze. Then he sat down....

In an instant up he started again with a great cry, and began running at the top of his speed. He thought he heard a voice speaking in him; and, however fast he ran, the voice, or whatever it was, kept up with him. He rushed through the underwood, trampling and crushing it under his feet, and scaring the birds and small game which lodged there. At last, exhausted, he stood still for breath, when he heard it say loudly and deeply, as if speaking with his own organs, "You cannot escape from yourself!" Then a terror seized him; he fell down and fainted away.

# Chapter Twenty-four

# A MOTHER'S BLESSING

WHEN HIS SENSES RETURNED, his first impression was of something in him not himself. He felt it in his breathing; he tasted it in his mouth. The brook which ran by Gurta's encampment had by this time become a streamlet, though still shallow. He plunged into it; a feeling came upon him as if he ought to drown himself, had it been deeper. He rolled about in it, in spite of its flinty and rocky bed. When he came out of it, his tunic sticking to him, he tore it off his shoulders, and let it hang round his girdle in shreds, as it might. The shock of the water, however, acted as a sedative upon him, and the coolness of the night refreshed him. He walked on for a while in silence.

Suddenly the power within him began uttering, by means of his organs of speech, the most fearful blasphemies, words embodying conceptions which, had they come into his mind, he might indeed have borne with patience before this, or uttered in bravado, but which now filled him with inexpressible loathing, and a terror to which he had hitherto been quite a stranger. He had always in his heart believed in a God, but he now believed with a reality and intensity utterly new to him. He felt it as if he saw Him; he felt there was a world of good and evil beings. He did not love the good, or hate the evil; but he shrank from the one, and he was terrified at the other; and he felt himself carried away, against his will, as the prey of some dreadful, mysterious power, which tyrannised over him.

The day had closed—the moon had risen. He plunged into the thickest wood, and the trees seemed to him to make way for him. Still they seemed to moan and to creak as they moved out of their place. Soon he began to see that they were looking at him, and exulting over his misery. They, of an inferior nature, had had no gift which they could abuse and lose; and they remained in that honour and perfection in which they were created. Birds of the night flew out of them, reptiles slunk away; yet soon he began to be surrounded, wherever he went, by a circle of owls, bats, ravens, crows, snakes, wild cats, and apes, which were always looking at him, but somehow made way, retreating before him, and yet forming again, and in order, as he marched along.

He had passed through the wing of the forest which he had entered, and penetrated into the more mountainous country. He ascended the heights; he was a taller, stronger man than he had been; he went forward with a preternatural vigour, and flourished his arms with the excitement of some vinous or gaseous intoxication. He heard the roar of the wild beasts echoed along the woody ravines which were cut into the solid mountain rock, with a reckless feeling, as if he could cope with them. As he passed the dens of the lion, leopard, hyena, jackal, wild boar, and wolf, there he saw them sitting at the entrance, or stopping suddenly as they prowled along, and eyeing him, but not daring to approach. He strode along from rock to rock, and over precipices, with the certainty and ease of some giant in Eastern fable. Suddenly a beast of prey came across him; in a moment he had torn up by the roots the stump of a wild vine plant, which was near him; had thrown himself upon his foe before it could act on the aggressive, had flung it upon its back, forced the weapon into its mouth, and was stamping on its chest. He knocked the life out of the furious animal; and crying "Take that," tore its flesh, and, applying his mouth to the wound, sucked a draught of its blood.

He has passed over the mountain, and has descended its side. Bristling shrubs, swamps, precipitous banks, rushing torrents, are no obstacle to his course. He has reached the brow of a hill, with a deep placid river at the foot of it, just as the dawn begins to break. It is a lovely prospect, which every step he takes is becoming more definite and more various in the daylight. Masses of oleander, of great beauty, with their red blossoms, fringed the river, and tracked out its course into the distance. The bank of the hill below him, and on the right and left, was a maze of fruit-trees, about which nature, if it were not the hand of man, had had no thought except that they should be all together there. The wild olive, the pomegranate, the citron, the date, the mulberry, the peach, the apple, and the walnut, formed a sort of spontaneous orchard. Across the water, groves of palm-trees waved their long and graceful branches in the morning breeze. The stately and solemn ilex, marshalled into long avenues, showed the way to substantial granges or luxurious villas. The green turf or grass was spread out beneath, and here and there flocks and herds were emerging out of the twilight, and growing distinct upon the eye. Elsewhere the ground rose up into sudden eminences crowned with chestnut woods, or with plantations of cedar and acacia, or wildernesses of the cork-tree, the turpentine, the carooba, the white poplar, and the Phenician juniper, while overhead ascended the clinging tendrils of the hop, and an underwood of myrtle clothed their stems and roots. A profusion of wild flowers carpeted the ground far and near.

Juba stood and gazed till the sun rose opposite to him, envying, repining, hating, like Satan looking in upon Paradise. The wild mountains, or the locust-smitten track would have better suited the tumult of his mind. It would have been a relief to him to have retreated from so fair a scene, and to have retraced his steps, but he was not his own master, and was hurried on. Sorely against his determined strong resolve and will, crying out and protesting and shuddering, the youth was forced along into the fulness of beauty and blessing with which he was so little in tune. With rage and terror he recognised that he had no part in his own movements, but was a mere slave. In spite of himself he must go forward and behold a peace and sweetness which witnessed against him. He dashed down through the thick grass, plunged into the water, and without rest or respite began a second course of aimless toil and travail through the day.

The savage dogs of the villages howled and fled from him as he passed by; beasts of burden, on their way to market, which he overtook or met, stood still, foamed and trembled; the bright birds, the blue jay and golden oriole, hid themselves under the leaves and grass; the storks, a religious and domestic bird, stopped their sharp clattering note from the high tree or farmhouse turret, where they had placed their nests; the very reptiles skulked away from his shadow, as if it were poisonous. The boors who were at their labour in the fields suspended it, to look at one whom the Furies were lashing and whirling on. Hour passed after hour, the sun attained its zenith, and then declined, but this dreadful compulsory race continued. Oh, what would he have given for one five minutes of oblivion, of slumber, of relief from the burning thirst which now consumed him! but the master within him ruled his muscles and his joints, and the intense pain of weariness had no concomitant prostration of strength. Suddenly he began to laugh hideously; and he went forward dancing and singing loud, and playing antics. He entered a hovel, made faces at the children, till one of them fell into convulsions, and he ran away with another; and when some country people pursued him, he flung the child in their faces, saying, "Take that," and said he was Pentheus, king of Thebes, of whom he had never heard, about to solemnise the orgies of Bacchus, and he began to spout a chorus of Greek, a language he had never learnt or heard spoken.

Now it is evening again, and he has come up to a village grove, where the rustics were holding a feast in honour of Pan. The hideous brutal god, with yawning mouth, horned head, and goat's feet, was placed in a rude shed, and a slaughtered lamb, decked with flowers, lay at his feet. The peasants were frisking before him, boys and women, when they were startled by the sight of a gaunt, wild, mysterious figure, which began to dance too. He flung and capered about with such vigour that they ceased their sport to look on, half with awe and half as a diversion. Suddenly he began to groan and to shriek, as if contending with himself, and willing and not willing some new act; and the struggle ended in his falling on his hands and knees, and crawling like a quadruped towards the idol. When he got near, his attitude was still more servile; still groaning and shuddering, he laid himself flat on the ground, and wriggled to the idol as a worm, and lapped up with his tongue the mingled blood and dust which lay about the sacrifice. And then again, as if nature had successfully asserted her own dignity, he jumped up high in the air, and, falling on the god, broke him to pieces, and scampered away out of pursuit, before the lookers-on recovered from their surprise.

Another restless, fearful night amid the open country; ... but it seemed as if the worst had passed, and, though still under the heavy chastisement of his pride, there was now more in Juba of human action and of effectual will. The day broke, and he found himself on the road to Sicca. The beautiful outline of the city was right before him. He passed his brother's cottage and garden; it was a wreck. The trees torn up, the fences broken down, and the room pillaged of the little that could be found there. He went on to the city, crying out "Agellius"; the gate was open, and he entered. He went on to the Forum; he crossed to the house of Jucundus; few people as yet were stirring in the place. He looked up at the wall. Suddenly, by the help of projections, and other irregularities of the brickwork, he mounted up upon the flat roof, and dropped down along the tiles, through the *impluvium*[111] into the middle of the house. He went softly into Agellius's closet, where he was asleep, he roused him with the name of Callista, threw his tunic upon him, which was by his side, put his boots into his hands, and silently beckoned him to follow him. When he hesitated, he still whispered to him "Callista," and at length seized him and led him on. He unbarred the street door, and with a movement of his arm, more like a blow than a farewell, thrust him into the street. Then he barred again the door upon him, and lay down himself upon the bed which Agellius had left. His good Angel, we may suppose, had gained a point in his favour, for he lay quiet, and fell into a heavy sleep.

---

111   "pool"

# Chapter Twenty-five

# CALLISTA IN DURANCE

W E WILL HOPE that the reader, as well as Agellius, is attracted by the word Callista, and wishes to know something about her fate; nay, perhaps finds fault with us as having suffered him so long to content himself with the chance and second-hand information which Jucundus or Juba has supplied. If we have been wanting in due consideration for him, we now trust to make up for it.

When Callista, then, had so boldly left the cottage to stop the intruders, she had in one important point reckoned without her host. She spoke Latin fluently, herself, and could converse with the townspeople, most of whom could do the same; but it was otherwise with the inhabitants of the country, numbers of whom, as we have said, were in Sicca on the day of the outbreak. The two fellows, whom she went out to withstand, knew neither her nor the Latin tongue. They were of a race which called itself Canaanite, and really was so; huge, gigantic men, who looked like the sons of Enac, described in Holy Writ. They knew nothing of roads or fences, and had scrambled up the hill as they could, the shortest way, and, being free from the crowd, with far more expedition than had they followed the beaten track. She and they could not understand each other's speech; but her appearance spoke for her, and, in consequence, they seized on her as their share of the booty, and without more ado, carried her off towards Sicca. As they came up by a route of their own, so they returned, and entered the city by a gate more to the south, not the Septimian; a happy circumstance, as otherwise she would have stood every chance of being destroyed in that wholesale massacre which the soldiery inflicted on the crowd as it returned.

These giants, then, got possession of Callista, and she entered Sicca upon the shoulder of one of them, who danced in with no greater inconvenience than if he was carrying on it a basket of flowers, or a box of millinery. Here the party met with the city police, who were stationed at the gate.

"Down with your live luggage, you rascals," they said, in their harsh Punic; "what have you to do with plunder of this kind? and how came you by her?"

"She's one of those Christian rats, your worship," answered the fellow, who, strong as he was, did not relish a contest with some dozen of armed men. "Long live the Emperor! We'll teach her to eat asses' heads another time, and brew fevers. I found her with a party of Christians. She's nothing but a witch, and she knows the consequences."

"Let her go, you drunken animal!" said the constable, still keeping his distance. "I'll never believe any woman is a Christian, let alone so young a one. And now I look at her, so far as I can see by this light, I think she's priestess of one of the great temples up there."

"She can turn herself into anything," said the other of her capturers, "young or old. I saw her one night near Madaura, a month ago, in the tombs in the shape of a black cat."

"Away with you both, in the name of the Suffetes[112] of Sicca and all the magistracy!" cried the official. "Give up your prisoner to the authorities of the place, and let the law take its course."

But the Canaanites did not seem disposed to give her up, and neither party liking to attack the other, a compromise took place. "Well," said the guardian of the night, "the law must be vindicated, and the peace preserved. My friends, you must submit to the magistrates. But since she happens to be on your shoulder, my man, let her even remain there, and we depute you, as

---

112  "magistrates governing a city-state," derived from the Hebrew *Shōphtim*, "Judges"

a beast of burden, to carry her for us, thereby to save us the trouble. Here, child," he continued, "you're our prisoner; so you shall plead your own cause in the *popina*[113] there. Long live Decius, pious and fortunate! Long live this ancient city, colony and municipium! Cheer up, my lass, and sing us a stave or two, as we go; for I'll pledge a *cyathus*[114] of unmixed, that, if you choose, you can warble notes as sweet as the manna gum."

Callista was silent, but she was perfectly collected, and ready to avail herself of any opportunity to better her condition. They went on towards the Forum, where a police-office, as we now speak, was situated, but did not reach it without an adventure. The Roman military force at Sicca was not more than a century of men; the greater number were at this moment at the great gate, waiting for the mob; a few, in parties of three and four, were patrolling the city. Several of these were at the entrance of the Forum when the party came up to it; and it happened that a superior officer, who was an assistant to what may be called the military resident of the place, a young man, on whom much of the duty of the day had devolved, was with the soldiers. She had known him as a friend of her brother's, and recognised him in the gloom, and at once took advantage of the meeting.

"Help," she said, "gentlemen! help, Calphurnius! these rascals are carrying me off to some den of their own."

The tribune at once knew her voice. "What!" he cried, with great astonishment, "what, my pretty Greek! You most base, infamous, and unmannerly scoundrels, down with her this instant! What have you to do with that young lady? You villains, unless you would have me crack your African skulls with the hilt of my sword, down with her, I say!"

There was no resisting a Roman voice, but prompt obedience is a rarity, and the ruffians began to parley. "My noble master," said the constable, "she's our prisoner. Jove preserve you, and Bacchus and Ceres bless you, my lord tribune! and long life to the Emperor Decius in these bad times. But she is a rioter, my lord, one of the ringleaders, and a Christian and a witch to boot."

113 "restaurant"
114 "ladle" for wine

"Cease your vile gutturals, you animal!" cried the officer, "or I will ram them down your throat with my pike to digest them. Put down the lady, beast. Are you thinking twice about it? Go, Lucius," he said to a private, "kick him away, and bring the woman here."

Callista was surrendered, but the fellow, sullen at the usage he had met with, and spiteful against Calphurnius, as the cause of it, cried out maliciously, "Mind what you are at, noble sir, it's not our affair; you can fry your own garlic. But an Emperor is an Emperor, and an Edict is an Edict, and a Christian is a Christian; and I don't know what high places will say to it, but it's your affair. Take notice," he continued, as he got to a safer distance, raising his voice still higher, that the soldiers might hear, "yon girl is a Christian priestess, caught in a Christian assembly, sacrificing asses and eating children for the overthrow of the Emperor, and the ruin of his loyal city of Sicca, and I have been interrupted in the discharge of my duty—I, a constable of the place. See whether Calphurnius will not bring again upon us the plague, the murrain, the locusts, and all manner of *larvæ* and *maniæ* before the end of the story."

This speech perplexed Calphurnius, as it was intended. It was impossible he could dispose of Callista as he wished, with such a charge formally uttered in the presence of his men. He knew how serious the question of Christianity was at that moment, and how determined the Imperial Government was on the eradication of its professors; he was a good soldier, devoted to head-quarters, and had no wish to compromise himself with his superiors, or to give bystanders an advantage over him, by setting a prisoner at liberty without inquiry, who had been taken in a Christian's house. He muttered an oath, and said to the soldiers, "Well, my lads, to the Triumviri with her, since it must be so. Cheer up, my star of the morning, bright beam of Hellas, it is only as a matter of form, and you will be set at liberty as soon as they look on you." And with these words he led the way to the *Officium*.

But the presiding genius of the *Officium* was less accommodating than he had anticipated. It might be that he was jealous of the soldiery, or of their particular interference, or indignant at the butchery at the great gate, of which the news had just come, or out of humour with the day's work, and especially with the Christians; at any rate, Calphurnius found he had better have taken a bolder step, and have carried her as a prisoner to the camp. However, nothing was now left for him but to depart; and Callista fell again into the hands of the city, though of the superior functionaries, who procured her a lodging for the night, and settled to bring her up for examination next morning.

The morning came, and she was had up. What passed did not transpire; but the issue was that she was remanded for a further hearing, and was told she might send to her brother, and acquaint him where she was. He was allowed one interview with her, and he came away almost out of his senses, saying she was bewitched, and fancied herself a Christian. What precisely she had said to him, which gave this impression, he could hardly say; but it was plain there must be something wrong, or there would not be that public process and formal examination which was fixed for the third day afterwards.

# Chapter Twenty-six

# WHAT CAN IT ALL MEAN?

WERE THE ORIGIN OF Juba's madness (or whatever the world would call it) of a character which admitted of light writing about it, much might be said on the surprise of the clear-headed, narrow-minded, positive, and easy-going Jucundus, when he found one nephew substituted for another, and had to give over his wonder at Agellius, in order to commence a series of acts of amazement and consternation at Juba. He summoned Jupiter and Juno, Bacchus, Ceres, Pomona, Neptune, Mercury, Minerva, and great Rome, to witness the marvellous occurrence; and then he had recourse to the infernal gods, Pluto and Proserpine, down to Cerberus, if he be one of them; but, after all, there the portent was, in spite of all the deities which Olympus, or Arcadia, or Latium ever bred; and at length it had a nervous effect upon the old gentleman's system, and, for the first evening after it, he put all his good things from him, and went to bed supperless and songless. What had been Juba's motive in the exploit which so unpleasantly affected his uncle, it is of course quite impossible to say. Whether his mention of Callista's name was intended to be for the benefit of her soul, or the ruin of Agellius's, must be left in the obscurity in which the above narrative presents it to us; so far alone is certain, though it does not seem to throw light on the question, that, on his leaving his uncle's house in the course of the forenoon, which he did, without being pressed to stay, he was discovered prancing and gesticulating in the neighbourhood of Callista's prison, so as to excite the attention of the *apparitor*, or constable, who guarded the entrance, and who, alarmed at his wildness, sent for some of his fellows, and, with their assistance, repelled the intruder, who, thereupon, scudding out at the eastern gate, was soon lost in the passes of the mountain.

To one thing, however, we may pledge ourselves, that Juba had no intention of shaking, even for one evening, the nerves of Jucundus; yet shaken they were till about the same time twenty-four hours afterwards. And when in that depressed state, he saw nothing but misery on all sides of him. Juba was lost; Agellius worse. Of course, he had joined himself to his sect, and he should never see him again; and how should he ever hold up his head? Well, he only hoped Agellius would not be boiled in a caldron, or roasted at a slow fire. If this were done, he positively must leave Sicca, and the most thriving trade which any man had in the whole of the Proconsulate. And then that little Callista! Ah!—what a real calamity was there! Anyhow he had lost her, and what should he do for a finisher of his fine work in marble, or metal? She was a treasure in herself. Altogether the heavens were very dark; and it was scarcely possible for any one who knew well his jovial cast of countenance, to keep from laughing, whatever his real sympathy, at the unusual length and blankness which were suddenly imposed upon it.

While he sat thus at his shop window, which, as it were, framed him for the contemplation of passers-by, on the day of the escape of Agellius, and the day before Callista's public examination, Aristo rushed in upon him in a state of far more passionate and more reasonable grief. He had called, indeed, the day before, but he found a pleasure in expending his distress upon others, and he came again to get rid of its insupportable weight by discharging it in a torrent of tears and exclamations. However, at first the words of both "moved slow," as the poet says, and went off in a sort of dropping fire.

"Well," said Jucundus, in a depressed tone; "he's not come to *you*, of course?"

"Who?"

"Agellius."

"Oh! Agellius! No, he's not with me." Then, after a pause, Aristo added, "Why should he be?"

"Oh, I don't know. I thought he might be. He's been gone since early morning."

"Indeed! No, I don't know where he is. How came he with you?"

"I told you yesterday; but you have forgotten. I was sheltering him; but he's gone for ever."

"Indeed!"

"And his brother's mad!—horribly mad!" and he slapped his hand against his thigh.

"I always thought it," answered Aristo.

"Did you? Yes, so it is; but it's very different from what it ever was. The furies have got hold of him with a vengeance! He's frantic! Oh, if you had seen him! Two boys, both mad! It's all the father!"

"I thought you'd like to hear something about dear, sweet Callista," said her brother.

"Yes, I should indeed!" answered Jucundus. "By Esculapius! they're all mad together!"

"Well, it is like madness!" cried Aristo, with great vehemence.

"The world's going mad!" answered Jucundus, who was picking up, since he began to talk, an exercise which was decidedly good for him. "We are *all* going mad! *I* shall get crazed. The townspeople are crazed already. What an abominable, brutal piece of business was that three days ago! I put up my shutters. Did it come near you?—all on account of one or two beggarly Christians, and my poor boy. What harm could two or three, toads and vipers though they be, do here? They might have been trodden down easily. It's another thing at Carthage. Catch the ringleaders, I say; make examples. The foxes escape, and our poor ganders suffer!"

Aristo, pierced with his own misery, had no heart or head to enter into the semi-political ideas of Jucundus, who continued,—

"Yes, it's no good. The empire's coming to pieces, mark my words! I told you so, if those beasts were let alone. They *have* been let alone. Remedies are too late. Decius will do no good. No one's safe! Farewell, my friends! I am going. Like poor dear Callista, I shall be in prison, and, like her, find myself dumb!... Ah! yes, Callista; how did you find her?"

"O dear, sweet, suffering girl!" cried her brother.

"Yes, indeed!" answered Jucundus; "yes!" meditatively. "She *is* a dear, sweet, suffering girl! I thought he might perhaps have taken her off—that was my hope. He was so set upon hearing where she was, whether she could be got out. It struck me he had made the best of his way to *her*. She could do anything with him. And she loved him, she did!—I'm convinced of it!— nothing shall convince me otherwise! 'Bring them together,' I said, 'and they will rush into each other's arms.' But they're bewitched!—The whole world's bewitched! Mark my words,—I have an idea who is at the bottom of this."

"Oh!" groaned out Aristo; "I care not for top or bottom!—I care not for the whole world, or for anything at all but Callista! If you could have seen the dear, patient sufferer!" and the poor fellow burst into a flood of tears.

"Bear up! bear up!" said Jucundus, who by this time was considerably better; "show yourself a man, my dear Aristo. These things must be;—they are the lot of human nature. You remember what the tragedian says: stay! no!—it's the comedian,—it's Menander"——

"To Orcus and Erebus with all the tragedy and comedy that ever was spouted!" exclaimed Aristo. "Can you do nothing for me? Can't you give me a crumb of consolation or sympathy, encouragement or suggestion? I am a stranger in the country, and so is this dear sister of mine, whom I was so proud of; and who has been so good, and kind, and gentle, and sweet. She loved me so much, she never grudged me anything; she let me do just what I would with her. Come here, go there,—it was just as I would. There we were, two orphans together, ten years since, when I was double her age. She wished to stay in Greece; but she came to this detestable Africa all for me. She would be gay and bright when I would have her so. She had no will of her own; and she set her heart upon nothing, and was pleased anywhere. She had not an enemy in the world. I protest she is worth all the gods and god-desses that ever were hatched! And here, in this ill-omened Africa, the evil eye has looked at her, and she thinks herself a Christian, when she is just as much a hippogriff, or a chimæra."

"Well, but, Aristo," said Jucundus, "I was going to tell you who is at the bottom of it all. Callista's mad; Agellius is mad; Juba is mad; and Strabo was mad;—but it was his wife, old Gurta, that drove him mad;—and there, I think, is the beginning of our troubles.——Come in! come in, Cornelius!" he cried, seeing his Roman friend outside, and relapsing for the moment into his lugubrious tone; "Come in, Cornelius, and give us some comfort, if you can. Well, this is like a friend! I know if you can help me, you will."

Cornelius answered that he was going back to Carthage in a day or two, and came to embrace him, and had hoped to have a parting supper before he went.

"That's kind!" answered Jucundus: "but first tell me all about this dreadful affair; for you are in the secrets of the Capitol. Have they any clue what has become of my poor Agellius?"

Cornelius had not heard of the young man's troubles, and was full of consternation at the news.

"What! Agellius really a Christian?" he said, "and at such a moment? Why, I thought you talked of some young lady who was to keep him in order?"

"She's a Christian too," replied Jucundus; and a silence ensued. "It's a bad world!" he continued. "She's imprisoned by the Triumviri. What will be the end of it?"

Cornelius shook his head, and looked mysterious.

"You don't mean it?" said Jucundus. "Not anything so dreadful, I do trust, Cornelius. Not the stake?"

Cornelius still looked gloomy and pompous.

"Nothing in the way of torture?" he went on; "not the rack, or the pitchfork?"

"It's a bad business, on your own showing," said Cornelius: "it's a bad business!"

"Can you do nothing for us, Cornelius?" cried Aristo. "The great people in Carthage are your friends. O Cornelius! I'd do anything for you!—I'd be your slave! She's no more a Christian than great Jove. She has nothing about her of the cut;—not a shred of her garment, or a turn of her hair. She's a Greek from head to foot—within and without. She's as bright as the day! Ah! we have no friends here. Dear Callista! you will be lost because you are a foreigner!" and the passionate youth began to tear his hair. "O Cornelius!" he continued, "if you can do anything for us! Oh! she shall sing and dance to you; she shall come and kneel down to you, and embrace your knees, and kiss your feet, as I do, Cornelius!" and he knelt down, and would have taken hold of Cornelius's beard.

Cornelius had never been addressed with so poetical a ceremonial, which nevertheless he received with awkwardness indeed, but with satisfaction. "I hear from you," he said with pomposity, "that your sister is in prison on suspicion of Christianity. The case is a simple one. Let her swear by the genius of the Emperor, and she is free; let her refuse it, and the law must take its course," and he made a slight bow.

"Well, but she is under a delusion," persisted Aristo, "which cannot last long. She says distinctly that she is *not* a Christian, is not that decisive? but then she won't burn incense; she won't swear by Rome. She tells me she does not *believe* in Jupiter, nor I; can anything be more senseless? It is the act of a mad woman. I say, 'My girl, the question is, Are you to be brought to shame? are you to die by the public sword? die in torments?' Oh, I shall go mad as well as she!" he screamed out. "She was so clever, so witty, so sprightly, so imaginative, so versatile! why, there's nothing she couldn't do. She could model, paint, play on the lyre, sing, act. She could work with the needle, she could embroider. She made this girdle for me. It's all that Agellius, it's Agellius. I beg your pardon, Jucundus; but it is;" and he threw himself on the ground, and rolled in the dust.

"I have been telling our young friend," said Jucundus to Cornelius, "to exert self-control, and to recollect Menander, 'Ne quid nimis.'[115] Grieving does

---

115 "Nothing to excess," the second of three proverbs over the doors of the Delphic Oracle.

no good; but these young fellows, it's no use at all speaking to them. Do you think you could do anything for us, Cornelius?"

"Why," answered Cornelius, "since I have been here, I have fallen in with a very sensible man, and a man of remarkably sound political opinions. He has a great reputation, he is called Polemo, and is one of the professors at the Mercury. He seems to me to go to the root of these subjects, and I'm surprised how well we agreed. He's a Greek, as well as this young gentleman's sister. I should recommend him to go to Polemo; if any one could disabuse her mind, it is he."

"True, true," cried Aristo, starting up, "but, no, *you* can do it better; you have power with the government. The Proconsul will listen to you. The magistrates here are afraid of *him*; *they* don't wish to touch the poor girl, not they. But there's such a noise everywhere, and so much ill blood, and so many spies and informers, and so much mistrust—but why should it come upon *Callista*? Why should *she* be a sacrifice? But you'd oblige the Duumvirs as much as me in getting her out of the scrape. But what good would it do, if they *took* her dear life? Only get us the respite of a month; the delusion would vanish in a month. Get two months, if you can; or as long as you can, you know. Perhaps they would let us steal out of the country, and no one the wiser; and no harm to any one. It was a bad job our coming here."

"We know nothing at Rome of feelings and intentions, and motives and distinctions," said Cornelius; "and we know nothing of understandings, con-nivances, and evasions. We go by facts; Rome goes by facts. The question is, What is the fact? Does she burn incense, or does she not? Does she worship the ass, or does she not? However, we'll see what can be done." And so he went on, informing the pair of mourners that, as far as his influence extend-ed, he would do something in behalf both of Agellius and Callista.

# Chapter Twenty-seven

# AM I A CHRISTIAN?

THE SUN HAD NOW descended for the last time before the solemn day which was charged with the fate of Callista, and what was the state of mind of one who excited such keen interest in the narrow circle within which she was known? And how does it differ from what it was some weeks before, when Agellius last saw her? She would have been unable to say herself. "So is the kingdom of God: as if a man should cast seed into the earth, and should sleep and rise night and day, and the seed should spring and grow up, whilst he knoweth not." She might, indeed, have been able afterwards, on looking back, to say many things of herself; and she would have recognised that while she was continually differing from herself, in that she was changing, yet it was not a change which involved contrariety, but one which expanded itself in (as it were) concentric circles, and only fulfilled, as time went on, the promise of its beginning. Every day, as it came, was, so to say, the child of the preceding, the parent of that which followed; and the end to which she tended could not get beyond the aim with which she set out. Yet, had she been asked, at the time of which we speak, where was her principle and her consistency, what was her logic, or whether she acted on reason, or on impulse, or on feeling, or in fancy, or in passion, she would have been reduced to silence. What did she know about herself, but that, to her surprise, the more she thought over what she heard of Christianity, the more she was drawn to it, and the more it approved itself to her whole soul, and the more it seemed to respond to all her needs and aspirations, and the more intimate was her presentiment that it was true? The longer it remained on her mind as an object, the more it seemed (unlike the mythology or the philosophy of her country, or the political religion of Rome) to have an external reality and substance, which deprived objections to it of their power, and showed them to be at best but difficulties and perplexities.

But then again, if she had been asked, what was Christianity, she would have been puzzled to give an answer. She would have been able to mention some particular truths which it taught, but neither to give them their definite and distinct shape, nor to describe the mode in which they were realised. She would have said, "I believe what has been told me, as from heaven, by Chione, Agellius, and Cæcilius:" and it was clear she could say nothing else. What the three told her in common and in concord was at once the measure of her creed and the ground of her acceptance of it. It was that wonderful unity of sentiment and belief in persons so dissimilar from each other, so distinct in their circumstances, so independent in their testimony, which recommended to her the doctrine which they were so unanimous in teaching. She had long given up any belief in the religion of her country. As to philosophy, it dwelt only in conjecture and opinion; whereas the very essence of religion was, as she felt, a recognition of the worshippers on the part of the Object of it. Religion could not be without hope. To worship a being who did not speak to us, recognise us, love us, was not religion. It might be a duty, it might be a merit; but her instinctive notion of religion was the soul's response to a God who had taken notice of the soul. It was loving intercourse, or it was a name. Now the three witnesses who had addressed her about Christianity had each of them made it to consist in the intimate Divine Presence in the heart. It was the friendship or mutual love of person with person. Here was the very teaching which already was so urgently demanded both by her reason and her heart, which she found nowhere else; which she found existing one and the same in a female slave, in a country youth, in a learned priest.

This was the broad impression which they made upon her mind. When she turned to consider more in detail what it was they taught, or what was implied in that idea of religion which so much approved itself to her, she understood them to say that the Creator of heaven and earth, Almighty, All-good, clothed in all the attributes which philosophy gives Him, the Infinite, had loved the soul of man so much, and her soul in particular, that He had come upon earth in the form of a man, and in that form had gone through sufferings, in order to unite all souls to Him; that He desired to love, and to be loved; that He had said so; that He had called on man to love Him, and did actually bring to pass this loving intercourse of Him and man in those souls who surrendered themselves to Him. She did not go much further than this; but as much as this was before her mind morning, noon, and night. It pleaded in her; it importuned her; it would not be rebuffed. It did not mind her moods, or disgusts, or doubts, or denials, or dismissals, but came again and again. It rose before her, in spite of the contempt, reproach, and persecution which the profession of it involved. It smiled upon her; it made promises to her; it opened eternal views to her; and it grew upon her convictions in clearness of perception, in congruity, and in persuasiveness.

Moreover, the more she thought of Chione, of Agellius, and of Cæcilius the more surely did she discern that this teaching wrought in them a something which she had not. They had about them a simplicity, a truthfulness, a decision, an elevation, a calmness, and a sanctity to which she was a stranger, which spoke to her heart and absolutely overcame her. The image of Cæcilius, in particular, came out prominently and eloquently in her memory,—not in his words so much as in his manner. In spite of what she had injuriously said to him, she really felt drawn to worship him, as if he were the shrine and the home of that Presence to which he bore such solemn witness.

O the change, when, as if in punishment for her wild words against him, she found herself actually in the hands of lawless men, who were as far below her in sentiment as he was above her! O the change, when she was dizzied by their brutal vociferations and rapid motion, and that breath and atmosphere of evil which steamed up from the rankness of their impiety! O the thankfulness which rose up in her heart, though but vaguely directed to an object, when she found the repose and quiet, though it was that of a prison! for young as she was, she had become tired of all things that were seen, and had no strong desire, except for meditation on the great truths which she did not know.

One day passes and then another; and now the morning and the hour is come when she must appear before the magistrates of Sicca. With dread, with agitation, she looks forward to the moment. She has not yet a peace within her. Her peace is the stillness of the room in which she is imprisoned. She knows it will pass away when she leaves it; she knows that again she must be in the hands of cruel, godless men, with whom she has no sympathy; but she has no stay whereon to lean in the terrible trial. Her brother comes to her: he affects to forget her perverseness or delusion. He comes to her with a smile, and throws his arms around her; and Callista repels, from some indescribable feeling, his ardent caress, as if she were no longer his. He has come to accompany her to court, by an indulgence which he had obtained; to support her there,—to carry her through, and to take her back in triumph home. My sister,—why that strange, piteous look upon thy countenance?— why that paleness of thy cheek?—why that whisper of thy lips?—why those wistful, gentle pleadings of thine eyes? Sweet eyes, and brow, and cheek, in which I have ever prided myself! Why so backward?—why so distant and unfriendly? Am I not come to rescue thee from a place where thou never shouldst have been?—where thou ne'er shalt be again? Callista, what is this mystery?—speak!

Such as this was the mute expostulation conveyed in Aristo's look, and in the fond grasp of his hand; while treading down forcibly within him his memory and his fears of her great change, he determined she should be to him still all that she had ever been. But how altered was that look, and how relaxed that grasp, when at length her misery found words, and she said to him in agitation, "My time is short: I want some Christian, a Christian priest!"

It was as though she had never shown any tendency before to the proscribed religion. The words came to him with the intensity of something new and unimagined hitherto. He clasped his hands in emotion, turned white, and could but say, "Callista!" If she had made confession of the most heinous of crimes,—if she had spoken of murder, or some black treachery against himself,—of some enormity too great for words, it might have been; but his sister!—his pride and delight, after all and certainly a Christian! Better far had she said she was leaving him for ever, to abandon herself to the degrading service of the temples; better had she said she had taken hemlock, or had an asp in her bosom, than that she should choose to go out of the world with the tortures, the ignominy, the malediction of the religion of slaves.

Time waits for no man, nor does the court of justice, nor the *subsellia*[116] of the magistrate. The examination is to be held in the Basilica at the Forum, and it requires from us a few words of explanation beforehand. The local magistrates then could only try the lesser offences, and decide civil suits; cases of suspected Christianity were reserved for the Roman authorities. Still, preliminary examinations were not unfrequently conducted by the city Duumvirs, or even in what may be called the police courts. And this may have especially been the case in the Proconsulates. Propraetors and Presidents were in the appointment of the Emperor, and joined in their persons the supreme civil and military authority. Such provinces, perhaps, were better administered; but there would be more of arbitrariness in their rule, and it would not be so acceptable to the ruled. The Proconsuls, on the other hand, were representatives of the Senate, and had not the military force directly in their hands. The natural tendency of this arrangement was to create, on the one hand, a rivalry between the civil and military establishments; and, on the other, to create a friendly feeling between the Proconsul and the local magistracy. Thus, not long before the date of this history, we read of Gordian, the Proconsul, enjoying a remarkable popularity in his African province; and when the people rose against the exactions of the imperial Procurator, as referred to in a former page, they chose and supported Gordian against him. But however this might be in general, so it was at this time at Sicca, that the Proconsular *Officium* and the city magistrates were on a good understanding with each other, whereas there was some collision be-

---

116 "court benches"

tween the latter and the military. Not much depends in the conduct of our story upon this circumstance; but it must be taken to account for the examination of Callista in the Forum, and for some other details which may follow before we come to the end of it.

The populace was collected about the gates and within the ample space of the Basilica, but they gave expression to no strong feeling on the subject of a Christian delinquent. The famine, the sickness, and, above all, the lesson which they had received so lately from the soldiers, had both diminished their numbers and cowed their spirit. They were sullen, too, and resentful; and, with the changeableness proverbial in a multitude, had rather have witnessed the beheading of a magistrate, or the burning of a tribune, than the torture and death of a dozen of wretched Christians. Besides, they had had a glut of Christian blood; a reaction of feeling had taken place, and, in spite of the suspicion of witchcraft, the youth and the beauty of Callista recommended her to their compassion.

The magistrates were seated on the *subsellia*, one of the Duumvirs presiding, in his white robe bordered with purple; his lictors, with staves, not fasces, standing behind him. In the vestibule of the court, to confront the prisoner on her first entrance, were the usual instruments of torture. The charge was one which can only be compared, in the estimation of both state and people in that day, to that of witchcraft, poisoning, parricide, or other monstrous iniquity in Christian times. There were the heavy *boiæ*, a yoke for the neck, of iron, or of wood; the fetters; the *nervi*, or stocks, in which hands and feet were inserted, at distances from each other which strained or dislocated the joints. There, too, were the *virgæ*, or rods with thorns in them; the *flagra, lori,* and *plumbati,* whips and thongs, cutting with iron or bruising with lead; the heavy clubs; the hook for digging into the flesh; the *ungula,* said to have been a pair of scissors; the *scorpio,* and *pecten,* iron combs or rakes for tearing. And there was the wheel, fringed with spikes, on which the culprit was stretched; and there was the fire ready lighted, with the water hissing and groaning in the large caldrons which were placed upon it. Callista had lost for ever that noble intellectual composure of which we have several times spoken; she shuddered at what she saw, and almost fainted, and, while waiting for her summons, leaned heavily against the merciless *cornicularius*[117] at her side.

At length the judge began—"Let the servant from the *Officium* stand forth." The *officialis* answered that he had brought a prisoner charged with Christianity; she had been brought to him by the military on the night of the riot.

The *scriba* then read out the deposition of one of the *stationarii*,[118] to the effect that he and his fellow-soldiers had received her from the hands of the civic force on the night in question, and had brought her to the office of the Triumvirs.

"Bring forward the prisoner," said the judge; she was brought forward.

"Here she is," answered the *officialis*,[119] according to the prescribed form.

"What is your name?" said the judge.

She answered, "Callista."

The judge then asked if she was a freewoman or a slave.

She answered, "Free; the daughter of Orsilochus, lapidary, of Proconnesus."

Some conversation then went on among the magistrates as to her advocate or *defensor*. Aristo presented himself, but the question arose whether he was *togatus*.[120] He was known, however, to several magistrates, and was admitted to stand by his sister.

Then the *scriba* read the charge—viz., that Callista was a Christian, and refused to sacrifice to the gods.

It was a plain question of fact, which required neither witnesses nor speeches. At a sign from the Duumvir in came two priests, bringing in between them the small altar of Jupiter; the charcoal was ready lighted, the incense at the side, and the judge called to the prisoner to sprinkle it upon the flame for the good fortune of Decius and his son. All eyes were turned upon her.

---

117 "adjutant"
118 "guards"
119 "official"
120 "in a toga"

"I am not a Christian," she said; "I told you so before. I have never been to a Christian place of worship, nor taken any Christian oath, nor joined in any Christian sacrifice. And I should lie did I say that I was in any sense a Christian."

There was a silence; then the judge said, "Prove your words; there is the altar, the flame, and the incense; sacrifice to the genius of the Emperor."

She said, "What can I do? I am not a Christian." The judges looked at each other, as much as to say, "It is the old story; it is that inexplicable, hateful obstinacy, which will neither yield to reason, common sense, expediency, or fear."

The Duumvir only repeated the single word, "Sacrifice."

She stopped awhile; then she came forward with a hurried step. "O my fate!" she cried, "why was I born? why am I in this strait? I have no god. What can I do? I am abandoned; why should I not do it?" She stopped; then she went right on to the altar; she took the incense: suddenly she looked up to heaven and started, and threw it away. "I cannot! I dare not!" she cried out. There was a great sensation in court. "Evidently insane," said some of the more merciful of the Decurions; "poor thing, poor thing!" Her brother ran up to her; talked to her, conjured her, fell down on his knees to her; took her hand violently, and would have forced her to offer. In vain; all he could get from her was, "I am not a Christian; indeed, I am not a Christian. I have nothing to do with them. O the misery!"

"She is mad!" cried Aristo; "my lord judges, listen to me. She was seized by brutal ruffians during the riot, and the fright and shock have overcome her. Give her time, oh! give her time, and she will get right. She's a good religious girl; she has done more work for the temples than any girl in Sicca; half the statues in the city are her finishing. Many of you, my lords, have her handiwork. She works with me. Do not add to my anguish in seeing her deranged, by punishing her as a criminal, a Christian: do not take her from me. Sentence her, and you end the whole matter; give her a chance, and she will certainly be restored to the gods and to me. Will you put her to death because she is mad?"

What was to be done? The court was obsequious to the Proconsul, afraid of Rome; jealous that the mob should have been more forward than the magistracy. Had the city moved sooner, as soon as the edict came, there would have been no rising, no riot. Already they had been called on for a report about that riot and an explanation; if ever they had need to look sharp what they were doing, it was now. On the other hand, Callista and her brother had friends among the judges, as we have said, and their plea was at once obvious and reasonable. "If she persists, she persists, and nothing can be said; we don't wish to be disloyal, or careless of the emperor's commands. If she is obstinate, she must die; but she dies quite as usefully to us, with quite as much effect, a month hence as now. Not that we ask you to define a time on your own authority; simply do this, write to Carthage for advice. The government can answer within an hour, if it chooses. Merely say, 'Here is a young woman, who has ever been religious and well conducted, of great accomplishments, and known especially for her taste and skill in religious art, who since the day of the riot has suddenly refused to take the test. She can give no reason for her refusal, and protests she is not a Christian. Her friends say that the fright has turned her brain, but that if kindly treated and kept quiet, she will come round, and do all that is required of her. What are we to do?'"

At last Callista's friends prevailed. It was decided that the judges should pass over this examination altogether, as if it had been rendered informal by Callista's conduct. Had they recognised it as a proper legal process, they must have sentenced and executed her. Such a decision was of this further advantage to her, that nothing was altered as to her place of confinement. Instead of being handed over to the state prison, she remained in her former lodging, though in custody, and was allowed to see her friends. There had been very little chance of her recovery, supposing she was mad, or of ever coming out, if she had once gone into the formidable *Carcer*.[121] Meanwhile the magistrates sent to Carthage for instructions.

---

121 "Prison"

# Chapter Twenty-eight

# A SICK CALL

Aristo was not a fellow to have very long distresses; he never would have died of love or of envy, for honour or for loss of property; but his present calamity was one of the greatest he could ever have, and weighed upon him as long as ever any one could. His love for his sister was real, but it would not do to look too closely into the grounds of it; if we are obliged to do so, we must confess to a suspicion that it lay rather in certain outward, nay, acciden-tal attributes of Callista, than in Callista herself. Did she lose her good looks, or her amiable unresisting submission to his wishes, whatever they were, she would also lose her hold upon his affections. This is not to make any severe charge against him, considering how it is with the common run of brothers and sisters, husbands and wives; at the same time, most people certainly are haunted by the memory of the past, and love for "Auld lang syne," and this Aristo might indeed have had, and perhaps had not. He loved chiefly for the present, and by the hour.

However, at the present time he was in a state of acute suffering, and, under its paroxysm, he be thought him again of Cornelius's advice, which he had rejected, to betake himself to Polemo. He had a distant acquaintance with him, sufficient for his purpose, and he called on him at the Mercury after the latter's lecture. Polemo was no fool, though steeped in affectation and self-conceit, and Aristo fancied that his sister might be more moved by a philosophical compatriot than any one else. Polemo's astonishment, however, when the matter was proposed to him surpassed words, and it showed how utterly Aristo was absorbed in his own misery, that the possibility of such a reception should not have occurred to him. What, he, the friend of Plotinus, of Rogatian, and the other noble men and women who were his fellow-disciples at Rome; he, a member of the intellectual aristocracy of the metropolis of the world; what, he to visit a felon in prison! and when he found the felon was a Christian, he fully thought that Aristo had come to insult him, and was on the point of bidding him leave him to himself. Aristo, however, persisted; and his evident anguish, and some particulars which came out, softened him. Callista was a Greek; a literate, or blue stocking. She had never indeed worn the philosophic pallium[122] (as some Christian martyrs afterwards, if not before, have done—St. Catherine and St. Euphemia), but there was no reason why she should not do so. Polemo recollected having heard of her at the Capitol, and in the triclinium of one of the Decurions, as a lady of singular genius and attainments; and he lately had made an attempt to form a female class of hearers, and it would be a feather in his cap to make a convert of her. So, not many days after, one evening, accompanied by Aristo, he set out in his litter to the lodging where she was in custody; not, however, without much misgiving when it came to the point, some shame, and a consequent visible awkwardness and stiffness in his manner. All the perfumes he had about him could not hinder the disgust of such a visit rising up into his nostrils.

Callista's room was very well for a prison; it was on the ground-floor of a house of many stories, close to the *Officium* of the Triumvirate. Though not any longer under their strict jurisdiction, she was allowed to remain where she had first been lodged. She was in one of the rooms belonging to an apparitor of that *Officium*, and, as he had a wife, or at least a partner, to take care of her, she might consider herself very well off. However, the reader must recollect that we are in Africa, in the month of July, and our young Greek was little used to heats, which made the whole city nothing less than

---

122  "wollen cloak," a vestment of authority

one vast oven through the greater part of the twenty-four hours. In lofty spacious apartments the resource adopted is to exclude the external air, and to live as Greenlanders, with closed windows and doors; this was both impossible, and would have been unsuccessful, if attempted in the small apartment of Callista. But fever of mind is even worse than the heat of the sky; and it is undeniable that her health, and her strength, and her appearance are affected by both the physical and the moral enemy. The beauty, which was her brother's delight, is waning away; and the shadows, if not the rudiments of a diviner loveliness, which is of expression, not of feature, which inspires not human passion, but diffuses chaste thoughts and aspirations, are taking its place. Aristo sees the change with no kind of satisfaction. The room has a bench, two or three stools, and a bed of rushes in one corner. A staple is firmly fixed in the wall; and an iron chain, light, however, and long, if the two ideas can be reconciled, reaches to her slender arm, and is joined to it by an iron ring.

On Polemo's entering the room, his first exclamation was to complain of its closeness; but he had to do a work, so he began it without delay. Callista, on her part, started; she had no wish for his presence. She was reclining on her couch, and she sat up. She was not equal to a controversy, nor did she mean to have one, whatever might be the case with *him*.

"Callista, my life and joy, dear Callista," said her brother, "I have brought the greatest man in Sicca to see you."

Callista cast upon him an earnest look, which soon subsided into indifference. He had a rose of Cyrene in his hand, whose perfume he diffused about the small room.

"It is Polemo," continued Aristo, "the friend of the great Plotinus, who knows all philosophies and all philosophers. He has come out of kindness to you."

Callista acknowledged his presence; it was certainly, she said, a great kindness for any one to visit her, and there.

Polemo replied by a compliment; he said it was Socrates visiting Aspasia. There had always been women above the standard of their sex, and they had ever held an intellectual converse with men of mind. He saw one such before him.

Callista felt it would be plunging her soul still deeper into shadows, when she sought realities, if she must take part in such an argument. She remained silent.

"Your sister has not the fit upon her?" asked Polemo of Aristo aside, neither liking her reception of him, nor knowing what to say. "Not at all, dear thing," answered Aristo; "she is all attention for you to begin."

"Natives of Greece," at length said he, "natives of Greece should know each other; they deserve to know each other; there is a secret sympathy between them. Like that mysterious influence which unites magnet to magnet; or like the echo which is a repercussion of the original voice. So, in like manner, Greeks are what none but they can be," and he smelt at his rose and bowed.

She smiled faintly when he mentioned Greece. "Yes," she said, "I am fonder of Greece than of Africa."

"Each has its advantages," said Polemo; "there is a pleasure in imparting knowledge, in lighting flame from flame. It would be selfish did we not leave Greece to communicate what they have not here. But you," he added, "lady, neither can learn in Greece nor teach in Africa, while you are in this vestibule of Orcus. I understand, however, it is your own choice; can that be possible?"

"Well, I wish to get out, if I could, most learned Polemo," said Callista sadly.

"May Polemo of Rhodes speak frankly to Callista of Proconnesus?" asked Polemo. "I would not speak to every one. If so, let me ask, what keeps you here?"

"The magistrates of Sicca and this iron chain," answered Callista. "I would I could be elsewhere; I would I were not what I am."

"What could you wish to be more than you are?" answered Polemo; "more gifted, accomplished, beautiful than any daughter of Africa."

"Go to the point, Polemo," said Aristo, nervously, though respectfully; "she wants home-thrusts."

"I see my brother wants you to ask how far it depends on me that I am here," said Callista, wishing to hasten his movements; "it is because I will not burn incense upon the altar of Jupiter."

"A most insufficient reason, lady," said Polemo.

Callista was silent.

"What does that action mean?" said Polemo; "it proposes to mean nothing else than that you are loyal to the Roman power. You are not of those Greeks, I presume, who dream of a national insurrection at this time? then you are loyal to Rome. Did I believe a Leonidas could now arise, an Harmodius, a Miltiades, a Themistocles, a Pericles, an Epaminondas, I should be as ready to take the sword as another; but it is hopeless. Greece, then, makes no claim on you just now. Nor will I believe, though you were to tell me so yourself, that you are leagued with any obscure, fanatic sect who desire Rome's downfall. Consider what Rome is;" and now he had got into the magnificent commonplace, out of his last panegyrical oration with which he had primed himself before he set out. "I am a Greek," he said, "I love Greece, but I love truth better; and I look at facts. I grasp them, and I confess to them. The wide earth, through untold centuries, has at length grown into the imperial dominion of One. It has converged and coalesced in all its various parts into one Rome. This, which we see, is the last, the perfect state of human society. The course of things, the force of natural powers, as is well understood by all great lawyers and philosophers, cannot go further. Unity has come at length, and unity is eternity. It will be for ever, because it is a whole. The principle of dissolution is eliminated. We have reached the *apotelesma*[123] of the world. Greece, Egypt, Assyria, Libya, Etruria, Lydia, have all had their share in the result. Each of them, in its own day, has striven in vain to stop the course of fate, and has been hurried onwards at its wheels as its victim or its instrument. And shall Judæa do what profound Egypt and subtle Greece have tried in vain? If even the freedom of thought, the liberal scepticism, nay, the revolutionary theories of Hellas have proved unequal to the task of splitting up

---

123   Greek: "the end destined by the stars"

the Roman power, if the pomp and luxury of the East have failed, shall the mysticism of Syria succeed?"

"Well, dear Callista, are you listening?" cried Aristo, not over-confident of the fact, though Polemo looked round at him with astonishment.

"Ten centuries," he continued, "ten centuries have just been completed since Rome began her victorious career. For ten centuries she has been fulfilling her high mission in the dispositions of Destiny, and perfecting her maxims of policy and rules of government. For ten centuries she has pursued one track with an ever-growing intensity of zeal, and an ever-widening extent of territory. What can she not do? just one thing; and that one thing which she has not presumed to do, you are attempting. She has maintained her own religion, as was fitting; but she has never thrown contempt on the religion of others. This you are doing. Observe, Callista, Rome herself, in spite of her great power, has yielded to that necessity which is greater. She does not meddle with the religions of the peoples. She has opened no war against their diversities of rite. The conquering power found, especially in the East, innumerable traditions, customs, prejudices, principles, superstitions, matted together in one hopeless mass; she left them as they were; she recognised them; it would have been the worse for her if she had done otherwise. All she said to the peoples, all she dared say to them, was, 'You bear with me, and I will bear with you.' Yet this you will not do; you Christians, who have no pretence to any territory, who are not even the smallest of the peoples, who are not even a people at all, you have the fanaticism to denounce all other rites but your own, nay, the religion of great Rome. Who are you? upstarts and vagabonds of yesterday. Older religions than yours, more intellectual, more beautiful religions, which have had a position, and a history, and a political influence, have come to nought; and shall you prevail, you, a *congeries*, a hotch-potch of the leavings, and scraps, and broken meat of the great peoples of the East and West? Blush, blush, Grecian Callista, you with a glorious nationality of your own to go shares with some hundred peasants, slaves, thieves, beggars, hucksters, tinkers, cobblers, and fishermen! A lady of high character, of brilliant accomplishments, to be the associate of the outcasts of society!"

Polemo's speech, though cumbrous, did execution, at least the termination of it, upon minds constituted like the Grecian. Aristo jumped up, swore an oath, and looked round triumphantly at Callista, who felt its force also. After all, what did she know of Christians?—at best she was leaving the known for the unknown: she was sure to be embracing certain evil for contingent good. She said to herself, "No, I never can be a Christian." Then she said aloud, "My Lord Polemo, I am not a Christian;—I never said I was."

"That is her absurdity!" cried Aristo. "She is neither one thing nor the other. She won't say she's a Christian, and she won't sacrifice!"

"It is my misfortune," she said, "I know. I am losing both what I see, and what I don't see. It is most inconsistent: yet what can I do?"

Polemo had said what he considered enough. He was one of those who sold his words. He had already been over-generous, and was disposed to give away no more.

After a time, Callista said, "Polemo, do you believe in one God?"

"Certainly," he answered; "I believe in one eternal, self-existing something."

"Well," she said, "I feel that God within my heart. I feel myself in His presence. He says to me, 'Do this: don't do that.' You may tell me that this dictate is a mere law of my nature, as is to joy or to grieve. I cannot understand this. No, it is the echo of a person speaking to me. Nothing shall persuade me that it does not ultimately proceed from a person external to me. It carries with it its proof of its divine origin. My nature feels towards it as towards a person. When I obey it, I feel a satisfaction; when I disobey, a soreness—just like that which I feel in pleasing or offending some revered friend. So you see, Polemo, I believe in what is more than a mere 'something.' I believe in what is more real to me than sun, moon, stars, and the fair earth, and the voice of friends. You will say, Who is He? Has He ever told you anything about Himself? Alas! no!—the more's the pity! But I will not give up what I have, because I have not more. An echo implies a voice; a voice a speaker. That speaker I love and I fear."

Here she was exhausted, and overcome too, poor Callista! with her own emotions.

"O that I could find Him!" she exclaimed, passionately. "On the right hand and on the left I grope, but touch Him not. Why dost Thou fight against me?—why dost Thou scare and perplex me, O First and Only Fair? I have Thee not, and I need Thee." She added, "I am no Christian, you see, or I should have found Him; or at least I should say I had found Him."

"It is hopeless," said Polemo to Aristo, in much disgust, and with some hauteur of manner: "she is too far gone. You should not have brought me to this place."

Aristo groaned.

"Shall I," she continued, "worship any but Him? Shall I say that He whom I see not, whom I seek, is our Jupiter, or Cæsar, or the goddess Rome? They are none of them images of this inward guide of mine. I sacrifice to Him alone."

The two men looked at each other in amazement: one of them in anger.

"It's like the demon of Socrates," said Aristo, timidly.

"I will acknowledge Cæsar in every fitting way," she repeated; "but I will not make him my God."

Presently she added, "Polemo, will not that invisible Monitor have something to say to all of us,—to you,—at some future day?"

"Spare me! spare me, Callista!" cried Polemo, starting up with a violence unsuited to his station and profession. "Spare my ears, unhappy woman!—such words have never hitherto entered them. I did not come to be insulted. Poor, blind, hapless, perverse spirit—I separate myself from you for ever! Desert, if you will, the majestic, bright, beneficent traditions of your forefathers, and live in this frightful superstition! Farewell!"

He did not seem better pleased with Aristo than with Callista, though Aristo helped him into his litter, walked by his side, and did what he could to propitiate him.

# Chapter Twenty-nine

# CONVERSION

I F THERE IS A STATE of mind utterly forlorn, it is that in which we left the poor prisoner after Polemo had departed. She was neither a Christian, nor was she not. She was in the midway region of inquiry, which as surely takes time to pass over, except there be some almost miraculous interference, as it takes time to walk from place to place. You see a person coming towards you, and you say, impatiently, "Why don't you come faster?—why are you not here already?" Why?—because it takes time. To see that heathenism is false,—to see that Christianity is true,—are two acts, and involve two processes. They may indeed be united, and the truth may supplant the error; but they may not. Callista obeyed, as far as truth was brought home to her. She saw the vanity of idols before she had faith in Him who came to destroy them. She could safely say, "I discard Jupiter:" she could not say, "I am a Christian." Besides, what did she know of Christians? How did she know that they would admit her, if she wished it? They were a secret society, with an election, an initiation, and oaths;—not a mere philosophical school, or a profession of opinion, open to any individual. If they were the good people that she fancied them to be,—and if they were not, she would not think of them at all,—they were not likely to accept of her.

Still, though we may account for her conduct, its issue was not, on that account, the less painful. She had neither the promise of this world, nor of the next, and was losing earth without gaining heaven. Our Lord is reported to have said, "Be ye good money-changers." Poor Callista did not know how to turn herself to account. It had been so all through her short life. She had ardent affections, and keen sensibilities, and high aspirations; but she was not fortunate in the application of them. She had put herself into her brother's hands, and had let him direct her course. It could not be expected that he would be very different from the world. We are cautioned against "rejoicing in our youth." Aristo rejoiced in his without restraint; and he made his sister rejoice in hers, if enjoyment it was. He himself found in the pleasures he pointed out a banquet of fruits:—she dust and ashes. And so she went on; not changing her life, from habit, from the captivity of nature, but weary, disappointed, fastidious, hungry, yet not knowing what she would have; yearning after something, she did not well know what. And as heretofore she had cast her lot with the world, yet had received no price for her adhesion, so now she had bid it farewell; yet had nothing to take in its place.

As to her brother, after the visit of Polemo, he got more and more annoyed—angry rather than distressed, and angry with her. One more opportunity occurred of her release, and it was the last effort he made to move her. Cornelius, in spite of his pomposity, had acted the part of a real friend. He wrote from Carthage, that he had happily succeeded in his application to government, and, difficult and unusual as was the grace, had obtained her release. He sent the formal documents for carrying it through the court, and gained the eager benediction of the excitable Aristo. He rushed with the parchments to the magistrates, who recognised them as sufficient, and got an order for admission to her room.

"Joy, my dearest," he cried; "you are free! We will leave this loathsome country by the first vessel. I have seen the magistrates already."

The colour came into her wan face, she clasped her hands together, and looked earnestly at Aristo. He proceeded to explain the process of liberation. She would not be called on to sacrifice, but must sign a writing to the effect that she had done so, and there would be an end of the whole matter. On the first statement she saw no difficulty in the proposal, and started up in animation. Presently her countenance fell; how could she say that she had done what it was treason to her inward Guide to do? What was the difference between acknowledging a blasphemy by a signature or by incense? She smiled sorrowfully at him, shook her head, and lay down again upon her rushes. She had anticipated the Church's judgment on the case of the *Libellatici.*[124]

Aristo could not at first believe he heard aright, that she refused to be saved by what seemed to him a matter of legal form; and his anger grew so high as to eclipse and to shake his affection. "Lost girl," he cried, "I abandon you to the Furies!" and he shook his clenched hand at her. He turned away, and said he would never see her again, and he kept his word. He never came again. He took refuge, with less restraint than was usual to him, in such pleasures as the city could supply, and strove to drive his sister from his mind by dissipation. He mixed in the games of the Campus Martius under the shadow of the mountain; took part with the revellers in the Forum, and ended the evening at the Thermæ. Sometimes the image of dear Callista, as once she looked, would rush into his mind with a force which would not be denied, and he would weep for a whole night.

At length he determined to destroy himself, after the example of so many great men. He gave a sumptuous entertainment, expending his means upon it, and invited his friends to partake of it. It passed off with great gaiety; nothing was wanting to make it equal to an occasion so special and singular. He disclosed to his guests his purpose, and they applauded; the last libations were made—the revellers departed—the lights were extinguished. Aristo disappeared that night: Sicca never saw him again. After some time it was found that he was at Carthage, and he had been provident enough to take with him some of his best working tools, and some specimens of his own and poor Callista's skill.

Strange to say, Jucundus proved a truer friend to the poor girl than her brother. In spite of his selfishness and hatred of Christians, he was considerably affected as her case got more and more serious, and it became evident

---

124   Christians who had acquired certificates of conformity to the state religion

that only one answer could be returned to the magistrates from Carthage. He was quite easy about Agellius, who had, as he considered, successfully made off with himself, and he was reconciled to the thought of never seeing him again. Had it not been for this, one might have fancied that some lurking anxiety about the fate of his nephew might have kept alive the fidget which Callista's dismal situation gave him, for the philosopher tells us, that pity always has something in it of self; but, under the circumstances, it would be rash judgment to have any such suspicion of his motives. He was not a cruel man: even the "hoary-headed Fabian," or Cyprian, or others whom he so roundly abused, would have found, when it came to the point, that his bluster was his worst weapon against them; at any rate he had enough of the "milk of human kindness" to feel considerable distress about that idiotic Callista.

Yet what could he do? He might as well stop the passage of the sun, as the movements of mighty Rome, and a rescript would be coming to a certainty in due time from Carthage, and would just say one thing, which would forthwith be passing into the region of fact. He had no one to consult, and to tell the truth, Callista's fate was more than acquiesced in by the public of Sicca. Her death seemed a solution of various perplexities and troubles into which the edict had brought them; it would be purchasing the praise of loyalty cheaply. Moreover, there were sets of men actually hostile to her and her brother; the companies of statuaries, lapidaries, and goldsmiths, were jealous of foreign artists like them, who showed contempt for Africa, and who were acquainted, or rather intimate, with many of the higher classes, and even high personages in the place. Well, but could not some of those great people help her now? His mind glanced towards Calphurnius, whom he had heard of as in some way or other protecting her on the evening of the riot, and to him he determined to betake himself.

Calphurnius and the soldiery were still in high dudgeon with the populace of Sicca, displeased with the magistrates, and full of sympathy for Callista. Jucundus opened his mind fully to the tribune, and persuaded him to take him to Septimius, his military superior, and in the presence of the latter many good words were uttered both by Calphurnius and Jucundus. Jucundus gave it as his opinion that it was a very great mistake to strike at any but the leaders of the Christian sect; he quoted the story of King Tarquin and the poppies, and assured the great man that it was what he had always said and always prophesied, and that, depend upon it, it was a great mistake not to catch Cyprianus.

"The strong arm of the law," he said, "should not, on the other hand, be put forth against such butterflies as this Callista, a girl who, he knew from her brother, had not yet seen eighteen summers. What harm could such a poor helpless thing possibly do? She could not even defend herself, much less attack anybody else. No," he continued, "your proper policy with these absurd people is a smiling face and an open hand. Recollect the fable of the sun and the wind; which made the traveller lay aside his cloak? Do you fall in with some sour-visaged, stiff-backed worshipper of the Furies? fill his cup for him, crown his head with flowers, bring in the flute-women. Observe him—he relaxes; a smile spreads on his countenance; he laughs at a jest; 'captus est; habet:'[125] he pours a libation. Great Jove has conquered! he is loyal to Rome; what can you desire more? But beat him, kick him, starve him, turn him out of doors; and you have a natural enemy to do you a mischief whenever he can."

Calphurnius took his own line, and a simple one. "If it was some vile slave or scoundrel African," he said, "no harm would have been done; but, by Jupiter Tonans, it's a Greek girl, who sings like a Muse, dances like a Grace, and spouts verses like Minerva. 'Twould be sacrilege to touch a hair of her head; and we forsooth are to let these cowardly dogs of magistrates entrap Fortunianus at Carthage into this solecism."

Septimius said nothing, as became a man in office; but he came to an understanding with his visitors. It was plain that the Duumvirs of Sicca had no legal custody of Callista; in a criminal matter she might seem to fall under the jurisdiction of the military; and Calphurnius gained leave to claim his

---

125  "He is taken: he has it," a phrase used by spectators of gladiatorial contests when one gladiator had smitten or netted the other

right at the proper moment. The rest of his plan the tribune kept to himself, nor did Septimius wish to know it. He intended to march a guard into the prison shortly before Callista was brought out for execution, and then to make it believed that she had died under the horrors of the Barathrum. The corpse of another woman could without difficulty be found to be her representative, and she herself would be carried off to the camp.

Meanwhile, to return to the prisoner herself, what was the consolation, what the occupation of Callista in this waiting time, ere the Proconsul had sent his answer? Strange to say, and, we suppose, from a sinful waywardness in her, she had, up to this moment, neglected to avail herself of a treasure, which by a rare favour had been put into her possession. A small parchment, carefully written, elaborately adorned, lay in her bosom, which might already have been the remedy of many a perplexity, many a woe. It is difficult to say under what feelings she had been reluctant to open the Holy Gospel, which Cæcilius had intrusted to her care. Whether she was so low and despondent that she could not make the effort, or whether she feared to convince herself further, or whether she professed to be waiting for some calmer time, as if that were possible, or whether her unwillingness was that which makes sick people so averse to eating, or to remedies which they know would be useful to them, cannot well be determined; but there are many of us who may be able, from parallel instances of infirmity, to enter into that state of mind, which led her at least to procrastinate what she might do any minute. However, now left absolutely to herself, Aristo gone, and the answer of the government to the magistracy not having yet come, she recurred to the parchment, and to the Bishop's words, which ran, "Here you will see who it is we love," or language to that effect. It was tightly lodged under her girdle, and so had escaped in the confusion of that terrible evening. She opened it at length and read.

It was the writing of a provincial Greek; elegant, however, and marked with that simplicity which was to her taste the elementary idea of a classic author. It was addressed to one Theophilus, and professed to be a carefully digested and verified account of events which had been already attempted by others. She read a few paragraphs, and became interested, and in no long time she was absorbed in the volume. When she had once taken it up, she did not lay it down. Even at other times she would have prized it, but now, when she was so desolate and lonely, it was simply a gift from an unseen world. It opened a view of a new state and community of beings, which only seemed too beautiful to be possible. But not into a new state of things alone, but into the presence of One who was simply distinct and removed from anything that she had, in her most imaginative moments, ever depicted to her mind as ideal perfection. Here was that to which her intellect tended, though that intellect could not frame it. It could approve and acknowledge, when set before it, what it could not originate. Here was He who spoke to her in her conscience; whose Voice she heard, whose Person she was seeking for. Here was He who kindled a warmth on the cheek of both Chione and Agellius. That image sank deep into her; she felt it to be a reality. She said to herself, "This is no poet's dream; it is the delineation of a real individual. There is too much truth and nature, and life and exactness about it, to be anything else." Yet she shrank from it; it made her feel her own difference from it, and a feeling of humiliation came upon her mind, such as she never had had before. She began to despise herself more thoroughly day by day; yet she recollected various passages in the history which reassured her amid her self-abasement, especially that of His tenderness and love for the poor girl at the feast, who would anoint His feet; and the full tears stood in her eyes, and she fancied she was that sinful child, and that He did not repel her.

O what a new world of thought she had entered! it occupied her mind from its very novelty. Everything looked dull and dim by the side of it; her brother had ever been dinning into her ears that maxim of the heathen, "Enjoy the present, trust nothing to the future." She indeed could not enjoy the present with that relish which he wished, and she had not any trust in the future either; but this volume spoke a different doctrine. There she learned the very opposite to what Aristo taught—viz., that the present must be sacrificed for the future; that what is seen must give way to what is believed. Nay, more, she drank in the teaching which at first seemed so paradoxical, that even present happiness and present greatness lie in relinquishing what at first sight seems to promise them; that the way to true pleasure is, not through self-indulgence, but through mortification; that the way to power is weakness, the way to success failure, the way to wisdom foolishness, the way to glory dishonour. She saw that there was a higher beauty than that which the order and harmony of the natural world revealed, and a deeper peace and calm than that which the exercise, whether of the intellect or of the purest human affection, can supply. She now began to understand that strange, unearthly composure, which had struck her in Chione, Agellius, and Cæcilius; she understood that they were detached from the world, not because they had not the possession, nor the natural love of its gifts, but because they possessed a higher blessing already, which they loved above everything else. Thus, by degrees, Callista came to walk by a new philosophy; and had ideas, and principles, and a sense of relations and aims, and a susceptibility of arguments, to which before she was an utter stranger. Life and death, action and suffering, fortunes and abilities, all had now a new meaning and application. As the skies speak differently to the philosopher and the peasant, as a book of poems to the imaginative and to the cold and narrow intellect, so now she saw her being, her history, her present condition, her future, in a new light, which no one else could share with her. But the ruling sovereign thought of the whole was He, who exemplified all this wonderful philosophy in Himself.

# Chapter Thirty

# TORRES VEDRAS

T HERE WERE THOSE, however, whom Callista could understand, and who could understand her; there were those who, while Aristo, Cornelius, Jucundus, and Polemo were moving in her behalf, were interesting themselves also in her, and in a more effectual way. Agellius had joined Cæcilius, and, if in no other way, by his mouth came to the latter and his companions the news of her imprisonment. On the morning that Agellius had been so strangely let out of confinement by his brother, and found himself seated at the street-door, with his tunic on his arm and his boots on the ground before him, his first business was to recollect where he was, and to dispose of those articles of dress according to their respective uses. What should he do with himself, was of course his second thought. He could not stay there long without encountering the early risers of Sicca, the gates being already open. To attempt to find out where Callista was, and then to see her or rescue her, would have ended at once in his own capture. To go to his own farm would have been nearly as dangerous, and would have had less meaning. Cæcilius too had said, that they were not long to be separated, and had given him directions for finding him.

Immediately then he made his way to one of the eastern gates, which led to Thibursicumbur. There was indeed no time to be lost, as he soon had indications; he met several men who knew him by sight, and one of the apparitors of the Duumviri, who happily did not. An apostate Christian, whose zeal for the government was notorious, passed him and looked back after him. However, he would soon be out of pursuit, if he had the start of them until the sun got round the mountains he was seeking. He walked on through a series of rocky and barren hills, till he got some way past the second milestone. Before he had reached the third he had entered a defile in the mountains. Perpendicular rocks rose on each side of him, and the level road, reaching from rock to rock, was not above thirty feet across. He felt that if he was pursued here, there was no escape. The third milestone passed, he came to the country road; he pursued it, counting out his thousand steps, as Cæcilius had instructed him. By this time it had left the stony bottom, and was rising up the side of the precipice. Brushwood and dwarf pines covered it, mingled with a few olives and caroubas. He said out his seven pater nosters[126] as he walked, and then looked around. He had just passed a goatherd, and they looked hard at each other. Agellius wished him good morning.

"You are wishing a kid for Bacchus, sir," said the man to him as he was running his eye over the goats. On Agellius answering in the negative, he said in a clownish way, "He who does not sacrifice to Bacchus does not sacrifice goats."

Agellius, bearing in mind Cæcilius's directions, saw of course there was something in the words which did not meet the ear, and answered carelessly, "He who does not sacrifice, does not sacrifice to Bacchus."

"True," said the man, "but perhaps you prefer a lamb for a sacrifice."

Agellius replied, "If it is the right one; but the one I mean was slain long since."

The man, without any change of manner, went on to say that there was an acquaintance of his not far up the rock, who could perhaps satisfy him on the point. He said, "Follow those wild olives, though the path seems broken, and you will come to him at the nineteenth."

Agellius set out, and never was path so untrue to its own threats. It seemed ending in abrupt cliffs every turn, but never fulfilled the anticipa-

---

126 "Our Fathers"

tion; that is, while he kept to the olive-trees. After ascending what was rather a flight of marble steps, washed and polished by the winter torrents, than a series of crags, he fulfilled the number of trees, and looked round at the man sitting under it. O the joy and surprise! it was his old servant Aspar.

"You are safe, then, Aspar," he said, "and I find you here. O what a tender Providence!"

"I have taken my stand here, master," returned Aspar, "day after day, since I got here, in hopes of seeing you. I could not get back to you from Jucundus's that dreadful morning, and so I made my way here. Your uncle sent for you in my presence, but at the time I did not know what it meant. I was able to escape."

"And now for Cæcilius," said Agellius.

Behind the olive-tree a torrent's bed descended; the descent being so easy, and yet so natural, that art had evidently interfered with nature, yet concealed its interference. After tracing it some yards, they came to a chasm on the opposite side; and, passing through it, Agellius soon found himself, to his surprise, on a bleak open hill, to which the huge mountain formed merely a sort of *façade*. Its surface was half rock, half moor, and it was surrounded by precipices. It was such a place as some hermit of the middle ages might have chosen for his solitude. The two walked briskly across it, and at length came to a low, broad yawning opening, branching out into several passages which, if pursued, would have been found to end in nothing. Aspar, however, made straight for what appeared a dead wall of rock, in which, on his making a signal, a door, skilfully hidden, was opened from within, and was shut behind them by the porter. They now stood in a gallery running into the mountain. It was very long, and a stream of cold air came along it. Aspar told him that at the extremity of it they should find Cæcilius.

Agellius was indeed in the vestibule of a remarkable specimen of those caves which had been used for religious purposes, first by the aborigines of the country, then by the Phœnician colonists, and in the centuries which had just passed, for the concealment of the Christians. The passage along which they were proceeding might itself be fitly called a cave, but still it was only one of several natural subterraneans, of different shapes, and opening into each other. Some of them lay along the face of a ravine, from which they received light and air; and here in one place there were indications of a fortified front. They were perfectly dry, though the water had at some re-mote period filtered through the roof, and had formed pendants and pillars of semi-transparent stalactite, of great beauty. It was another and singular advantage that a particular spot in one of the caverns, which bordered on the ravine, was the focus of an immense ear or whispering-gallery, such, that whatever took place in the public road in which the ravine terminated, could be distinctly heard there, and thus they were always kept on guard against the attack of an enemy, if expected. Had either Agellius or Aspar been curious about such a matter, the latter might have pointed out the place where a Punic altar once had been discovered, with a sort of *tumulus* of bones of mice near at hand, that animal coming into the list of victims in the Phœnician worship.

But the two Christians were engaged, as they first halted, and then walked along the corridor, in other thoughts, than in asking and answer-ing questions about the history of the place of refuge in which they found themselves. We have already remarked on the central position of Sicca for the purpose of missionary work and of retreat in persecution; such a dwell-ing in the rocks did but increase its advantageousness, and in consequence at this moment many Christians had availed themselves of it. It is an English proverb that three removes are as bad as a fire; and so great were the perils and the hardships of flight in those times, that it was a question, in a merely earthly point of view, whether the risk of being apprehended at home was not a far less evil than the evils which were certain upon leaving it. There was nothing, then, ungenerous in the ecclesiastical rule that they alone should flee, in persecution, who were marked out for death, if they stayed. The la-ity, private families, and the priests, on whose ministrations they depended, remained; bishops, deacons, and what may be called the staff of the episco-pate, notaries, messengers, seminarists, and ascetics, would disappear from the scene of persecution.

Agellius learned from his slave that the cave had been known to him from the time he was a boy, and that it was one of the secrets which all who shared it religiously observed. Holy men, it seemed, had had intimations of the present trial for several years past; and it was the full persuasion of the heads of the Church, that, though it might blow over for a short time, it would recur at intervals for many years, ending in a visitation so heavy and long, that the times of Antichrist would seem to have arrived. However, the impression upon their minds was, that then would come a millennium, or, in some sort, a reign of the saints upon the earth. That, however, was a date which even Agellius himself, young as he was, would not be likely to reach; indeed, who could expect to escape, who might not hope to gain, a Martyr's death, in the interval, in the series of assaults, between which Christianity had to run the gauntlet? Aspar said, moreover, that some martyrs lay in the chapels within, and that various confessors had ended their days there. At the present time there were representatives, there collected, of a large portion of the Churches of the Proconsulate. A post, so to call it, went between them and Carthage every week, and his friend and father, the bishop of that city, was especially busy in correspondence.

Moreover, Agellius learned from him that they had many partisans, well-wishers, and sympathizers, about the country, whom no one suspected; the families of parents who had conformed to the established worship, nay, sometimes the apostates themselves, and that this was the case in Sicca as well as elsewhere. For himself, old and ignorant as he was, the persecution had proved to him an education. He had been brought near great men, and some who, he was confident, would be martyrs in the event. He had learned a great deal about his religion which he did not know before, and had drunk in the spirit of Christianity, with a fulness which he trusted would not turn to his ultimate condemnation. He now too had a consciousness of the size and populousness of the Church, of her diffusion, of the promises made to her, of the essential necessity of what seemed to be misfortune, of the episcopal regimen, and of the power and solidity of the see of Peter afar off in Rome, all which knowledge had made him quite another being. We have put all this into finer language than the good old man used himself, and we have grouped it more exactly, but this is what his words would come to, when explained.

Coming down to sublunary matters, Aspar said the cave was well provisioned; they had bread, oil, figs, dried grapes, and wine. They had vessels and vestments for the Holy Sacrifice. Their serious want was a dearth of water at that season, but they relied on Divine Providence to give them by miracle, if in no other way, a supply. The place was piercingly cold too in the winter.

By this time they had gained the end of the long gallery, and passed through a second apartment, when suddenly the sounds of the ecclesiastical chant burst on the ear of Agellius. How strange, how transporting to him! he was almost for the first time coming home to his father's house, though he had been a Christian from a child, and never, as he trusted, to leave it, now that it was found. He did not know how to behave himself, nor indeed where to go. Aspar conducted him into the seats set apart for the faithful; he knelt down and burst into tears.

It was approaching the third hour, the hour at which the Paraclete originally descended upon the Apostles, and which, when times of persecution were passed, was appointed in the West for the solemn mass of the day. In that early age, indeed, the time of the solemnity was generally midnight, in order to elude observation; but even then such an hour was considered of but temporary arrangement. Pope Telesphorus is said to have prescribed the hour, afterwards in use, as early even as the second century; and in a place of such quiet and security as the cavern in which we just now find ourselves, there was no reason why it should not be selected. At the lower end of the chapel was a rail extending across it, and open in the middle, where its two portions turned up at right angles on each side towards the altar. The enclosure thus made was the place proper for the faithful, into which Agellius had been introduced, and about fifty persons were collected about him. Where the two side-rails which ran up the chapel ceased, there was a broad step; and upon it two pulpits, one on each side. Then came a second elevation, carrying the eye on to the extremity of the upper end.

In the middle of the wall at that upper end is a recess, occupied by a tomb. On the front of it is written the name of some glorious champion of the faith who lies there. It is one of the first bishops of Sicca, and the inscription attests that he slept in the Lord under the Emperor Antoninus. Over the sacred relics is a slab, and on the slab the Divine Mysteries are now to be celebrated. At the back is a painting on the wall, very similar to that in Agellius's cottage. The ever-blessed immaculate Mother of God is exercising her office as the Advocate of sinners, standing by the sacrifice as she stood at the cross itself, and offering up and applying its infinite merits and incommunicable virtue in union with priest and people. So instinctive in the Christian mind is the principle of decoration, as it may be called, that even in times of suffering, and places of banishment, we see it brought into exercise. Not only is the arch which overspans the altar ornamented with an arabesque pattern, but the roof or vault is coloured with paintings. Our Lord is in the centre, with two figures of Moses on each side, on the right unloosing his sandals, on the left striking the rock. Between the centre figure and the altar may be seen the raising of Lazarus; in the opposite partition the healing of the paralytic; at the four angles are men and women alternately in the attitude of prayer.

At this time the altar-stone was covered with a rich crimson silk, with figures of St. Peter and St. Paul worked in gold upon it, the gift of a pious lady of Carthage. Beyond the altar, but not touching it, was a cross; and on one side of the altar a sort of basin or *piscina* cut in the rock, with a linen cloth hanging up against it. There were no candles upon the altar itself, but wax lights fixed into silver stands were placed at intervals along the edge of the presbytery or elevation.

The mass was in behalf of the confessors for the faith then in prison in Carthage; and the sacred ministers, some half-hour after Agellius's entrance, made their appearance. Their vestments already varied somewhat from the ordinary garments of the day, and bespoke antiquity; and, though not so simply *sui generis*[127] as they are now, they were so far special, that they were

---

127  "one of a kind"

never used on any other occasion, but were reserved for the sacred service. The neck was bare, the amice being as yet unknown; instead of the stole was what was called the *orarium*, a sort of handkerchief resting on the shoulders, and falling down on each side. The alb had been the inner garment, or *camisium*, which in civil use was retained at night when the other garments were thrown off; and, as at the present day, it was confined round the waist by a zone or girdle. The maniple was a napkin, supplying the place of a handkerchief; and the chasuble was an ample *pænula*,[128] such as was worn by the judges, a cloak enveloping the whole person round, when spread out, with an opening in the centre, through which the head might pass. The deacon's dalmatic was much longer than it is now, and the subdeacon's tunicle resembled the alb. All the vestments were of the purest white.

The mass began by the bishop giving his blessing; and then the Lector, a man of venerable age, taking the roll called *Lectionarium*,[129] and proceeding to a pulpit, read the Prophets to the people, much in the way observed among ourselves still on holy Saturday and the vigil of Pentecost. These being finished, the people chanted the first verse of the *Gloria Patri*,[130] after which the clergy alternated with the people the *Kyrie*,[131] pretty much as the custom is now.

Here a fresh roll was brought to the Lector, then or afterwards called *Apostolus*, from which he read one of the canonical epistles. A psalm followed, which was sung by the people; and, after this, the Lector received the *Evangeliarium*,[132] and read a portion of the Gospel, at which lights were lighted, and the people stood. When he had finished, the Lector opened the roll wide, and, turning round, presented it to bishop, clergy, and people to kiss.

The deacon then cried out, "Ite in pace, catechumeni," "Depart in peace, catechumens;" and then the kiss of peace was passed round, and the people began to sing some psalms or hymns. While they were so engaged, the dea-

---

128  "cloak," resembling a poncho
129  "Lectionary"
130  "Glory to the Father," the liturgical prayer begiing with those words.
131  Greek: "Lord," the first word of the liturgical prayer "Lord, have mercy; Christ, have mercy; Lord, have mercy."
132  "Evangeliary," a book of Goepel passage for public reading

con received from the acolyte the *sindon*,[133] or corporal, which was of the length of the altar, and perhaps of greater breadth, and spread it upon the sacred table. Next was placed on the *sindon* the *oblata*,[134] that is, the small loaves, according to the number of communicants, with the paten, which was large, and a gold chalice, duly prepared. And then the *sindon*, or corporal, was turned back over them, to cover them as a pall.

The celebrant then advanced: he stood at the further side of the altar, where the candles are now, with his face to the people, and then began the holy sacrifice. First he incensed the *oblata*, that is, the loaves and chalice, as an acknowledgment of God's sovereign dominion, and as a token of uplifted prayer to Him. Then the roll of prayers was brought him, while the deacon began what is sometimes called the bidding prayer, being a catalogue of the various subjects for which intercession is to be made, after the manner of the *Oremus dilectissimi*,[135] now used on Good Friday. This catalogue included all conditions of men, the conversion of the world, the exaltation of Holy Church, the maintenance of the Roman empire, the due ripening and gathering of the fruits of the earth, and other spiritual and temporal blessings,—subjects very much the same as those which are now called the Pope's intentions. The prayers ended with a special reference to those present, that they might persevere in the Lord even to the end. And then the priest began the *Sursum corda*,[136] and said the *Sanctus*.[137]

The Canon or *Actio*[138] seems to have run, in all but a few words, as it does now, and the solemn words of consecration were said secretly. Great stress was laid on the Lord's prayer, which in one sense terminated the function. It was said aloud by the people, and when they said, "Forgive us our trespasses," they beat their breasts.

---

133  Greek: "a cloth covering," usually a shroud, but in this case the altar cloth likened to the shroud of Christ
134  "offerings"
135  "Let us pray, dearly beloved"
136  "Lift up your hearts"
137  "Holy," the first word of the liturgical prayer "Holy, holy, holy, Lord God of hosts…"
138  "Action," a name for the essential components of the liturgy

It is not wonderful that Agellius, assisting for almost the first time at this wonderful solemnity, should have noted everything as it occurred; and we must be considered as giving our account of it from his mouth.

It needs not to enlarge on the joy of the meeting which followed between Cæcilius and his young penitent. "O my father," he said, "I come to thee, never to leave thee, to be thy dutiful servant, and to be trained by thee after the pattern of Him who made thee what thou art. Wonderful things have happened; Callista is in prison on the charge of Christianity; I was in a sort of prison myself, or what was worse for my soul; and Juba, my brother, in the strangest of ways, has this morning let me out. Shall she not be saved, my father, in God's own way, as well as I? At least we can all pray for her; but surely we can do more—so precious a soul must not be left to herself and the world. If she has the trials, she may claim the blessings of a Christian. Is she to go back to heathenism? Is she, alas! to suffer without baptism? Shall we not hazard death to bestow on her that grace?"

# Chapter Thirty-one

# THE BAPTISM

WE HAVE ALREADY had occasion to mention that there were many secret well-wishers, or at least protectors, of Christians, as in the world at large, so also in Sicca. There were many persons who had received benefits from their charity, and had experience of the scandalous falsehood of the charges now circulated against them. Others would feel a generosity towards a cruelly persecuted body; others, utterly dead to the subject of religion, or rather believing all religions to be impostures, would not allow it to be assumed that only one was worthy of bad treatment. Others liked what they heard of the religion itself, and thought there was truth in it, though it had no claim to a monopoly of truth. Others felt it to be true, but shrank from the consequences of openly embracing it. Others, who had apostatised through fear of the executioner, intended to come back to it at the last. It must be added that in the African Church confessors in prison had, or were considered to have, the remarkable privilege of gaining the public forgiveness of the Church for those who had lapsed; it was an object, then, for all those who, being in that miserable case, wished some day to be restored, to gain their promise of assistance, or their good-will. To these reasons was added, in Callista's case, the interest which naturally attached to a woman, young and defenceless.

The burning sun of Africa is at the height of its power. The population is prostrated by heat, by scarcity, by pestilence, and by the decimation which their riot brought upon them. They care neither for Christianity, nor for anything else just now. They lie in the porticoes, in the caverns under the city, in the baths. They are more alive at night. The *apparitor*, in whose dwelling Callista was lodged, who was himself once a Christian, lies in the shade of the great doorway, into which his rooms open, asleep, or stupefied. Two men make their appearance about two hours before sunset, and demand admittance to Callista. The jailor asks if they are not the two Greeks, her brother and the rhetorician, who had visited her before. The junior of the strangers drops a purse heavy with coin into his lap, and passes on with his companion. When the mind is intent on great subjects or aims, heat and cold, hunger and thirst, lose their power of enfeebling it; thus perhaps we must account for the energy now displayed both by the two ecclesiastics and by Callista herself.

She too thought it was the unwelcome philosopher come again; she gave a start and a cry of delight when she saw it was Cæcilius. "My father," she said, "I want to be a Christian, if I may; He came to save the lost sheep. I have learnt such things from this book—let me give it you while I can. I am not long for this world. Give me Him who spoke so kindly to that woman. Take from me my load of sin, and then I will gladly go." She knelt at his feet, and gave the roll of parchment into his hand.

"Rise and sit," he answered. "Let us think calmly over the matter."

"I am ready," she insisted. "Deny me not my wish, when time is so urgent—if I may have it."

"Sit down calmly," he said again; "I am not refusing you, but I wish to know about you." He could hardly keep from tears, of pain, or of joy, or of both, when he saw the great change which trial had wrought in her. What touched him most was the utter disappearance of that majesty of mien, which once was hers, a gift, so beautiful, so unsuitable to fallen man. There was instead of it a frank humility, a simplicity without concealment, an unresisting meekness, which seemed as if it would enable her, if trampled on, to smile and to kiss the feet that insulted her. She had lost every vestige of what the world worships under the titles of proper pride and self-respect. Callista was now living, not in the thought of herself, but of Another.

"God has been very good to you," he continued; "but in the volume you have returned to me He bids us 'reckon the charges.' Can you drink of His chalice? Recollect what is before you."

She still continued kneeling, with a touching earnestness of face and demeanour, and with her hands crossed upon her breast.

"I *have* reckoned," she replied; "heaven and hell: I prefer heaven."

"You are on earth," said Cæcilius; "not in heaven or hell. You must bear the pangs of earth before you drink the blessedness of heaven."

"He has given me the firm purpose," she said, "to gain heaven, to escape hell; and He will give me too the power."

"Ah, Callista!" he answered, in a voice broken with distress, "you know not what you will have to bear, if you join yourself to Him."

"He has done great things for me already; I am wonderfully changed; I am not what I was. He will do more still."

"Alas, my child!" said Cæcilius, "that feeble frame, ah! how will it bear the strong iron, or the keen flame, or the ruthless beast? My child, what do *I* feel, who am free, thus handing you over to be the sport of the evil one?"

"Father, I have chosen Him," she answered, "not hastily, but on deliberation. I believe Him most absolutely. Keep me not from Him; give Him to me, if I may ask it; give me my Love."

Presently she added, "I have never forgotten those words of yours since you used them; 'Amor meus crucifixus est.'"[139]

She began again, "I will be a Christian; give me my place among them. Give me my place at the feet of Jesus, Son of Mary, my God. I wish to love Him. I think I can love Him. Make me His."

"He has loved you from eternity," said Cæcilius, "and, therefore, you are now beginning to love Him."

She covered her eyes with her hands, and remained in profound meditation. "I am very ignorant—very sinful," she said at length; "but one thing I know, that there is but One to love in the whole world, and I wish to love

---

139  "My love is crucified."

him. I surrender myself to Him, if He will take me; and He shall teach me about Himself."

"The angry multitude, their fierce voices, the brutal executioner, the prison, the torture, the slow, painful death." He was speaking, not to her, but to himself. She was calm, in spite of her fervour; but he could not contain himself. His heart melted within him; he felt like Abraham, lifting up his hand to slay his child.

"Time passes," she said; "what may happen? you may be discovered. But, perhaps," she added, suddenly changing her tone, "it is a matter of long initiation. Woe is me!"

"We must gird ourselves to the work, Victor," he said to his deacon who was with him. Cæcilius fell back and sat down, and Victor came forward. He formally instructed her so far as the circumstances allowed. Not for baptism only, but for confirmation, and Holy Eucharist; for Cæcilius determined to give her all three sacraments at once.

It was a sight for angels to look down upon, and they did; when the poor child, rich in this world's gifts, but poor in those of eternity, knelt down to receive that sacred stream upon her brow, which fell upon her with almost sensible sweetness, and suddenly produced a serenity different in kind from anything she had ever before even had the power of conceiving.

The bishop gave her confirmation, and then the Holy Eucharist. It was her first and last communion; in a few days she renewed it, or rather completed it, under the very Face and Form of Him whom she now believed without seeing.

"Farewell, my dearest of children," said Cæcilius, "till the hour when we both meet before the throne of God. A few sharp pangs which you can count and measure, and all will be well. You will be carried through joyously, and like a conqueror. I know it. You could face the prospect before you were a Christian, and you will be equal to the actual trial, now that you are."

"Never fear me, father," she said in a clear, low voice. The bishop and his deacon left the prison.

The sun had all but set, when Cæcilius and Victor passed the city gate; and it was more than twilight as they crossed the wild hills leading to the precipitous pass. Evil men were not their only peril in this work of charity. They were also in danger from wild beasts in these lone wastes, and, the heathen would have added, from bad spirits. Bad spirits Cæcilius recognised too; but he would not have granted that they were perilous. The two went forward, saying prayers lowly, and singing psalms, when a sudden cry was heard, and a strong tall form rushed past them. It might be some robber of the wild, or dangerous outcast, or savage fanatic, who knew and hated their religion; however, while they stopped and looked, he had come, and he was gone. But he came again, more slowly; and from his remarkable shape Cæcilius saw that it was the brother of Agellius. He said, "Juba;" Juba started back, and stood at a distance. Cæcilius held out his hand, and called him on, again mentioning his name. The poor fellow came nearer: Cæcilius's day's work was not at an end.

Since we last heard of him, Juba had dwelt in the mountainous tract over which the two Christians were now passing; roaming to and fro, or beating himself in idle fury against the adamantine rocks, and fighting with the stern necessity of the elements. How he was sustained can hardly be guessed, unless the impulse, which led him on the first accession of his fearful malady, to fly upon the beasts of the desert, served him here also. Roots too and fruits were scattered over the wild; and still more so in the ravines, wherever any quantity of soil had been accumulated. Alas! had the daylight lasted, in him too, as well as in Callista, Cæcilius would have found changes, but of a very different nature; yet even in him he would have seen a change for the better, for that old awful expression of pride and defiance was gone. What was the use of parading a self-will, which every moment of his life belied? His actions, his words, his hands, his lips, his feet, his place of abode, his daily course, were in the dominion of another, who inexorably ruled him. It was not the gentle influence which draws and persuades; it was not the power which can be propitiated by prayer; it was a tyranny which acted without reaction, energetic as mind, and impenetrable as matter.

"Juba," said Cæcilius a third time. The maniac came nearer, and then again suddenly retreated. He stood at a short distance from Cæcilius, as if afraid to come on, and cried out, tossing his hands wildly, "Away, black hypocrite, come not near me! Away! hound of a priest, cross not my path, lest I tear you to shreds!" Such visitations were no novelties to Cæcilius; he raised his hand and made the sign of the cross, then he said, "Come." Juba advanced, shrieked, and used some terrible words, and rushed upon Cæcilius, as if he would treat him as he had treated the savage wolf. "Come?" he cried, "yes, I come!" and Victor ran up, fearing his teeth would be in Cæcilius's throat, if he delayed longer. The latter stood his ground, quailing neither in eye nor in limb; he made the sign of the cross a second time; and in spite of a manifest antagonism within him, the stricken youth, with horrid cries, came dancing after him.

Thus they proceeded, with some signs of insurrection from time to time on Juba's part, but with a successful reduction of it as often on the part of Cæcilius, till they got to the ascent by the olive-trees, where careful walking was necessary. Then Cæcilius turned round, and beckoned him. He came. He said, "Kneel down." He knelt down. Cæcilius put his hand on his head, saying to him, "Follow me close and without any disturbance." The three pursued their journey, and all arrived safe at the cavern. There Cæcilius gave Juba in charge to Romanus, who had been intrusted with the *energumens*[140] at Carthage.

---

140 "possesed person"

# Chapter Thirty-two

# THE IMPERIAL RESCRIPT

HAD THE IMPERIAL EDICT been acted on by the magistrates of Sicca, without a reference to Carthage, it is not easy to suppose that Callista would have persevered in her refusal to commit the act of idolatry required of her. But, to speak of second causes, the hesitation of her judges was her salvation. Once baptised, there was no reason she should desire any further delay of her conflict. Come it must, and come it did. While Cæcilius was placing her beyond danger, the rescript of the Proconsul had been received at the office of the Duumvirs.

The absence of the Proconsul from Carthage had been the cause of the delay; and then, some investigation was needed to understand the relation of Callista's seizure to the riot on the one hand, and to the strong act of the military on the other, in quelling it. It was thought that something or other might come to light to account for the anomalous and unaccountable position which she had taken up. The imperial government considered it had now a clear view of her case, and its orders were distinct and peremptory. Christianity was to cease to be. It was a subtle foe, sapping the vitals of the state. Rome must perish, or this illegal association. Such evasions as Callista had used were but instances of its craft. Its treason lay, not in its being Christianity, but in its not sacrificing to the gods of Rome. Callista was but throwing dust in their eyes. There had been no blow struck against the treason in inland Africa. Women had often been the most dangerous of

conspirators. As she was a stranger, there was more probability of her connection with secret societies, and also less inconvenience in her execution.
Whatever happened, she was to be got rid of; but first her resolution was to
be broken, for the sake of the example. First, let her be brought before the
tribunal and threatened: then thrust into the Tullianum[141]; then put upon
the rack, and returned to prison; then scorched over a slow fire; last of all,
beheaded, and left for beasts of prey. She would sacrifice ere the last stage
was reached. When she had given way, let her be given up to the gladiators.
The message ended by saying that the Proconsular Procurator, who came by
the same carriages, would preside at the process.

O wisdom of the world! and strength of the world! what are you when
matched beside the foolishness and the weakness of the Christian? You are
great in resources, manifold in methods, hopeful in prospects; but one thing
you have not,—and that is peace. You are always tumultuous, restless, ap-
prehensive. You have nothing you can rely upon. You have no rock under
your feet. But the humblest, feeblest Christian has that which is impossible
to you. Callista had once felt the misery of maladies akin to yours. She had
passed through doubt, anxiety, perplexity, despondency, passion; but now
she was in peace. Now she feared the torture or the flame as little as the
breeze which arose at nightfall, or the busy chatter of the grasshoppers at the
noonday. Nay, rather, she did not think of torture and death at all, but was
possessed by a peace which bore her up, as if bodily, on its mighty wings. For
hours she remained on her knees, after Cæcilius left her: then she lay down
on her rushes and slept her last sleep.

She slept sound; she dreamed. She thought she was no longer in Africa,
but in her own Greece, more sunny and bright than before; but the inhabitants were gone. Its majestic mountains, its rich plains, its expanse of waters,
all silent: no one to converse with, no one to sympathize with. And, as she
wandered on and wondered, suddenly its face changed, and its colours were
illuminated tenfold by a heavenly glory, and each hue upon the scene was of

---

141 "Mamertine Prison"

a beauty she had never known, and seemed strangely to affect all her senses at once, being fragrance and music, as well as light. And there came out of the grottoes and glens and woods, and out of the seas, myriads of bright images, whose forms she could not discern; and these came all around her, and became a sort of scene or landscape, which she could not have described in words, as if it were a world of spirits, not of matter. And as she gazed, she thought she saw before her a well-known face, only glorified. She, who had been a slave, now was arrayed more brilliantly than an oriental queen; and she looked at Callista with a smile so sweet, that Callista felt she could but dance to it.

And as she looked more earnestly, doubting whether she should begin or not, the face changed, and now was more marvellous still. It had an innocence in its look, and also a tenderness, which bespoke both Maid and Mother, and so transported Callista, that she must needs advance towards her, out of love and reverence. And the lady seemed to make signs of encouragement: so she began a solemn measure, unlike all dances of earth, with hands and feet, serenely moving on towards what she heard some of them call a great action and a glorious consummation, though she did not know what they meant. At length she was fain to sing as well as dance; and her words were, "In the name of the Father, and of the Son, and of the Holy Ghost;" on which another said, "A good beginning of the sacrifice." And when she had come close to this gracious figure, there was a fresh change. The face, the features were the same; but the light of Divinity now seemed to beam through them, and the hair parted, and hung down long on each side of the forehead; and there was a crown of another fashion than the Lady's round about it, made of what looked like thorns. And the palms of the hands were spread out as if towards her, and there were marks of wounds in them. And the vestment had fallen, and there was a deep opening in the side. And as she stood entranced before Him, and motionless, she felt a consciousness that her own palms were pierced like His, and her feet also. And she looked round, and saw the likeness of His face and of His wounds upon all that company. And now they were suddenly moving on, and bearing something or some one, heavenwards; and they too began to sing, and their words seemed to be, "Rejoice with Me, for I have found My sheep," ever repeated. They went up through an avenue or long grotto, with torches of diamonds, and amethysts, and sapphires, which lit up its spars and made them sparkle. And she tried to look, but could not discover what they were carrying, till she heard a very piercing cry, which awoke her.

# Chapter Thirty-three

# A GOOD CONFESSION

THE CRY CAME from the keeper's wife, whom we have described as kindly disposed to her. She was a Lybo-Phœnician, and spoke a broken Latin; but the language of sympathy is universal, in spite of Babel. "Callista," she exclaimed; "girl, they have sent for you; you are to die. O frightful! worse than a runaway slave,—the torture! Give in. What's the harm? you are so young: those terrible men with the pincers and hot bars!"

Callista sat up, and passed from her vision to her prison. She smiled and said, "I am ready; I am going home." The woman looked almost frightened, and with some shade of disgust and disappointment. She, as others, might have thought it impossible, as it was unaccountable, that when it came to the point Callista would hold out. "She's crazed," she said. "I am ready, mother," Callista said, and she got up. "You have been very good to me," she continued; "I have been saying many prayers for you, while my prayers were of no good, for then He was not mine. But now I have espoused Him, and am going to be married to-day, and He will hear me." The woman stared at her stupidly, as much as to make it evident that if afterwards a change took place in her, as in Callista, that change too, though in so different a soul, must come of something beyond nature. She had something in her hand, and said, "It's useless to give a mad woman like her the packet, which my man has brought me."

Callista took the packet, which was directed to her, and broke the seal. It was from her brother. The little roll of worn parchment opened; a dagger fell out. Some lines were written on the parchment; they were dated Carthage, and ran as follows:—

"Aristo to his dearest Callista. I write through Cornelius. You have not had it in your power to kill me, but you have taken away half my life. For me, I will cherish the other half, for I love life better than death. But you love annihilation; yet, if so, die not like a slave. Die nobly, mindful of your country; I send you the means."

Callista was beyond reflecting on anything around her, except as in a sort of dream. As common men think and speak of heaven, so she now thought and spoke of earth. "I wish *Him* to kill me, not myself," she said. "I am His victim. My brother! I have no brother, except One, who is calling me."

She was carried to court, and the examination followed. We have already given a specimen of such a process; here it will be sufficient to make use of two documents, different in kind, as far as they go, which have come down to us. The first is an alto-relief, which once was coloured, not first-rate in art or execution, and of the date of the Emperor Constantius, about a century later. It was lately discovered in the course of excavations made at El Kaf, the modern Sicca, on the ruins of a church or Roman basilica, for the building in question seems to have served each purpose successively. In this sculpture the prætorium is represented, and the tribunal of the president in it. The tribunal is a high throne, with wings curving round on each side, making the whole construction extend to almost a semicircle, and it is ascended by steps between the wings. The curule chair[142] is at the top of the steps; and in the middle and above it are purple curtains, reaching down to the platform, drawn back on each side, and when drawn close together running behind the chair, and constituting what was called the *secretarium*.[143] On one side of the tribunal is a table covered with carpeting, and looking something like a modern ottoman, only higher, and not level at top; and it has upon it the Book of Mandates, the sign of jurisdiction.

---

142  A chair with a curved seat and legs representing military power
143  "hiding place"

The sword too is represented in the sculpture, to show a criminal case is proceeding. The procurator is seated on the chair; he is in purple, and has a gold chain of triple thread. We can also distinguish his lawyers, whether assessors or *consiliarii*[144]; also his lictors and soldiers. There, too, are the notaries in a line below him; they are writing down the judge's questions and the prisoner's answers: and one of them is turning round to her, as if to make her speak more loudly. She herself is mounted upon a sort of platform, called *catasta*, like that on which slaves were put up for sale. Two soldiers are by her, who appear to have been dragging her forwards. The executioners are also delineated, naked to the waist, with instruments of torture in their hands.

The second document is a fragment of the *Acta Proconsularia*[145] of her Passion. If, indeed, it could be trusted to the letter, as containing Callista's answers word for word, it would have a distinctly sacred character, in consequence of our Lord's words, "It shall be given you in that hour what to speak." However, we attach no such special value to this document, since it comes to us through heathen notaries, who may not have been accurate reporters; not to say that before we did so we ought to look very carefully into its genuineness. As it is, we believe it to be as true as any part of our narrative, and not truer. It runs as follows:—

"Cneius Messius Decius Augustus II., and Gratus, Consuls, on the seventh before the Calends of August, in Sicca Veneria, a colony, in the Secretary at the Tribunal, Martianus, procurator, sitting; Callista, a maker of images, was brought up by the Commentariensis on a charge of Christianity, and when she was placed,

"MARTIANUS, the procurator, said: This folly has been too long; you have made images, and now you will not worship them.

"CALLISTA answered: For I have found my true Love, whom before I knew not.

---

144 "counsellors"
145 "Record of the Proconsul"

"MARTIANUS, the procurator, said: Your true love is, I ween, your last love; for all were true in their time.

"CALLISTA said: I worship my true Love, who is the Only True; and He is the Son of God, and I know none but Him.

"MARTIANUS, the procurator, said: You will not worship the gods, but you are willing to love their sons.

"CALLISTA said: He is the true Son of the True God; and I am His, and He is mine.

"MARTIANUS, the procurator, said: Let alone your loves, and swear by the genius of the emperor.

"CALLISTA said: I have but one Lord, the King of kings, the Ruler of all.

"MARTIANUS, the procurator, turned to the lictor and said: This folly is madness; take her hand, put incense in it, and hold it over the flame.

"CALLISTA said: You may compel me by your great strength, but my own true Lord and Love is stronger.

"MARTIANUS, the procurator, said: You are bewitched; but we must undo the spell. Take her to the Lignum (the prison for criminals).

"CALLISTA said: He has been there before me, and He will come to me there.

"MARTIANUS, the procurator, said: The jailer will see to that. Let her be brought up to-morrow.

"On the day following, Martianus, the procurator, sitting at the tribunal, called up Callista. He said: Honour our lord, and sacrifice to the gods.

"CALLISTA said: Let me alone; I am content with my One and only Lord.

"MARTIANUS, the procurator, said: What? did he come to you in prison, as you hoped?

"CALLISTA said: He came to me amid much pain; and the pain was pleasant, for He came in it.

"MARTIANUS, the procurator, said: You have got worn and yellow, and he will leave you.

"CALLISTA said: He loves me the more, for I am beautiful when I am black.

"MARTIANUS, the procurator, said: Throw her into the Tullianum; perhaps she will find her god there also.

"Then the procurator entered into the Secretary, and drew the veil; and dictated the sentence for the tabella.[146] Then he came out, and the præco[147] read it:—Callista, a senseless and reprobate woman, is hereby sentenced to be thrown into the Tullianum; then to be stretched on the equuleus[148]; then to be placed on a slow fire; lastly, to be beheaded, and left to the dogs and birds.

"CALLISTA said: Thanks to my Lord and King."

Here the Acta end: and though they seem to want their conclusion, yet they supply nearly every thing which is necessary for our purpose. The one subject on which a comment is needed, is the state prison, which, though so little is said of it in the above Report, is in fact the real *medium*, as we may call it, for appreciating its information; a few words will suffice for our purpose.

The state prison, then, was arranged on pretty much one and the same plan through the Roman empire, nay, we may say, throughout the ancient world. It was commonly attached to the government buildings, and consisted of two parts. The first was the vestibule, or outward prison, which was a hall, approached from the prætorium, and surrounded by cells, opening into it. The prisoners, who were confined in these cells, had the benefit of the air and light, which the hall admitted. Such was the place of confinement allotted to St. Paul at Cæsarea, which is said to be the "prætorium of Herod." And hence, perhaps, it is that, in the touching Passion of St. Perpetua and St. Felicitas, St. Perpetua tells us that, when permitted to have her child, though she was in the inner portion, which will next be described, "suddenly the prison seemed to her like the prætorium."

---

146   "writing tablet"
147   "herald"
148   "torture rack"

From this vestibule there was a passage into the interior prison, called Robur or Lignum, from the beams of wood, which were the instruments of confinement, or from the character of its floor. It had no window or outlet, except this door, which, when closed, absolutely shut out light and air. Air, indeed, and coolness might be obtained for it by the *barathrum*,[149] presently to be spoken of, but of what nature we shall then see. The apartment, called Lignum, was the place into which St. Paul and St. Silas were cast at Philippi, before it was known that they were Romans. After scourging them severely, the magistrates, who nevertheless were but the local authorities, and had no proper jurisdiction in criminal cases, "put them in prison, bidding the jailer to keep them carefully; who, on receiving such a command, put them in the inner prison, and fastened them in the lignum." And in the Acts of the Scillitane Martyrs we read of the Proconsul giving sentence, "Let them be thrown into prison, let them be put into the Lignum, till to-morrow."

The utter darkness, the heat, and the stench of this miserable place, in which the inmates were confined day and night, is often dwelt upon by the martyrs and their biographers. "After a few days," says St. Perpetua, "we were taken to the prison, and I was frightened, for I never had known such darkness. O bitter day! the heat was excessive by reason of the crowd there." In the Acts of St. Pionius, and others of Smyrna, we read that the jailers "shut them up in the inner part of the prison, so that, bereaved of all comfort and light, they were forced to sustain extreme torment, from the darkness and stench of the prison." And, in like manner, other martyrs of Africa, about the time of St. Cyprian's martyrdom, that is, eight or ten years later than the date of this story, say, "We were not frightened at the foul darkness of that place; for soon that murky prison was radiant with the brightness of the Spirit. What days, what nights we passed there no words can describe. The torments of that prison no statement can equal."

Yet there was a place of confinement even worse than this. In the floor of this inner prison was a sort of trap-door, or hole, opening into the *barath-*

---

149  A pit into which criminals were thrown

*rum*, or pit, and called, from the original prison at Rome, the Tullianum. Sometimes prisoners were confined here, sometimes despatched by being cast headlong into it through the opening. It was into this pit at Rome that St. Chrysanthus was cast; and there, and probably in other cities, it was nothing short of the public cesspool.

It may be noticed that the Prophet Jeremiah seems to have had personal acquaintance with Vestibule, Robur, and Barathrum. We read in one place of his being shut up in the "atrium," that is, the vestibule, "of the prison, which was in the house of the king." At another time he is in the "ergastulum,"[150] which would seem to be the inner prison. Lastly his enemies let him down by ropes into the lacus or pit, in which "there was no water, but mud."

As to Callista, then, after the first day's examination, she was thrown for nearly twenty-four hours into the stifling Robur, or inner prison. After the sentence, on the second day, she was let down, as the commencement of her punishment, that is, of her martyrdom, into the loathsome Barathrum, lacus, or pit, called Tullianum, there to lie for another twenty hours before she was brought out to the equuleus or rack.

---

150 "dungeon"

# Chapter Thirty-four

# THE MARTYRDOM

CALLISTA HAD SIGHED for the bright and clear atmosphere of Greece, and she was thrown into the Robur and plunged into the Barathrum of Sicca. But in reality, though she called it Greece, she was panting after a better country and a more lasting home, and this country and home she had found. She was now setting out for it.

It was, indeed, no slight marvel that she was not already there. She had been lowered into that pit of death before noon on the day of her second examination, and, excepting some unwholesome bread and water, according to the custom of the prison, had had no food since she came into the custody of the *commentariensis*[151] the day before. The order came from the magistrates to bring her out earlier in the morning than was intended, or the prison might have really effected that death which Calphurnius had purposed to pretend. When the apparitors attempted to raise her, she neither spoke or moved, nor could well be seen. "Black as Orcus," said one of the fellows, "another torch there! I can't see where she nestles." "There she is, like a bundle of clothes," said another. "Madam gets up late this morning," said a third. "She's used to softer couches," said a fourth. "Ha! ha! 'tis a spoiler of beauty, this hole," said a fifth. "She is the demon of stubbornness, and must be crushed," said the jailer; "she likes it, or she would not choose it." "The plague take the

---

151 "prison keeper"

witch," said another; "we shall have better seasons when a few like her are ferreted out."

They got her out like a corpse, and put her on the ground outside the prison. When she still did not move, two of them took her between them on their shoulders and arms, and began to move forward, the instrument of torture preceding her. The fresh air of the morning revived her; she soon sat up. She seemed to drink in life again, and became conscious. "O beautiful Light!" she whispered, "O lovely Light, my light and my life! O my Light and my Life, receive me!" Gradually she became fully alive to all that was going on. She was going to death, and that rather than deny Him who had bought her by His own death. He had suffered for her, and she was to suffer for Him. He had been racked on the Cross, she too was to have her limbs dislocated after His pattern. She scarcely rested on the men's shoulders; and they vowed afterwards that they thought she was going to fly away, vile witch as she was.

"The witch, the witch," the mob screamed out, for she had now come to the place of her conflict. "We'll pay you off for blight and pestilence! Where's our bread, where's the maize and barley, where are the grapes?" And they uttered fierce yells of execration, and seemed disposed to break through the line of apparitors, and to tear her to pieces. Yet, after all, it was not a very hearty uproar, but got up for the occasion. The populace had spent their force, not to say their lives, in the riot in which she was apprehended. The priests and priestesses of the temples had sent the poor wretches and paid them.

The place of execution was on the north-east of the city, outside the walls, and towards the mountain. It was where slaves were buried, and it was as hideous as such spots usually were. The neighbourhood was wild, open to the beasts of prey, who at night used to descend and feast upon the corpses. As Callista approached to the scene of her suffering, the expression of her countenance had so altered that a friend would scarce have known it. There was a tenderness in it and a modesty which never had been there in that old time. Her cheek had upon it a blush, as when the rising sun suddenly touches some grey rock or tower yet it was white and glistening too, so much so that others might have said it was like silver. Her eyes were larger than they had been, and gazed steadfastly, as if at what the multitude did not see. Her lips spoke of sweet peace and deep composure. When at length she came close upon the rabble, who had been screaming and yelling so fiercely, men, women, and boys suddenly held their peace. It was first from curiosity, then from amazement, then from awe. At length a fear smote through them, and a strange pity and reverence. They almost seemed inclined to worship what stirred them so much, they knew not how; a new idea had visited those poor ignorant souls.

A few minutes sufficed to put the rack into working order. She was laid down upon its board in her poor bedimmed tunic, which once flashed so bright in the sun,—she who had been ever so delicate in her apparel. Her wrists and ankles were seized, extended, fastened to the moveable blocks at the extremities of the plank. She spoke her last word, "For Thee, my Lord and Love, for Thee!... Accept me, O my Love, upon this bed of pain! And come to me, O my Love, make haste and come!" The men turned round the wheels rapidly to and fro; the joints were drawn out of their sockets, and then snapped in again. She had fainted. They waited for her coming-to; they still waited; they got impatient.

"Dash some water on her," said one. "Spit in her face, and it will do," said a second. "Prick her with your spike," said a third. "Hold your wild talk," said a fourth; "she's gone to the shades." They gathered round, and looked at her attentively. They could not bring her back. So it was: she had gone to her Lord and her Love.

"Lay her out for the wolves and vultures," said the *cornicularius*,[152] and he was going to appoint guards till nightfall, when up came the *stationarii*[153] and Calphurnius in high wrath.

"You dogs!" he cried, "what trick have you been practising against the soldiers of Rome?" However, expostulation and reproach were bootless; nor would it answer here to go into the quarrel which ensued over the dead body.

---

152 "adjutant"
153 "guards"

The magistrates, having got scent of Calphurnius's scheme, had outwitted the tribune by assigning an earlier hour than was usual for the execution. Life could not be recalled; nor did the soldiers of course dare publicly to disobey the Proconsul's order for the exposure of the corpse. All that could be done, they did. They took her down with rude reverence from the rack, and placed her on the sand; and then they set guards to keep off the rabble, and to avail themselves of any opportunity which might occur to show consideration towards her.

# Chapter Thirty-five

# THE CORPO SANTO

THE SUN OF AFRICA has passed over the heavens, but has not dared with one of his fierce rays to profane the sacred relics which lie out before him. The mists of evening rise up, and the heavy dews fall, but they neither bring the poison of decay to that gracious body, nor receive it thence. The beasts of the wild are roaming and roaring at a distance, or nigh at hand: not any one of them presumes to touch her. No vultures may promise themselves a morning meal from such a victim, as they watch through the night upon the high crags which overlook her. The stars have come out on high, and, they too look down upon Callista, as if they were funeral lights in her honour. Next the moon rises up to see what has been going on, and edges the black hangings of the night with silver. Yet mourning and dirge are but of formal observance, when a brave champion has died for her God. The world of ghosts has as little power over such an one as the world of nature. No evil spirit has aught to say to her, who has gone in her baptismal white before the Throne. No penal fire shall be her robe, who has been carried in her bright *flammeum*[154] to the Bridal Chamber of the Lamb. A divine odour fills the air, issuing from that senseless, motionless, broken frame. A circle of light gleams round her brow, and, even when the daylight comes again, it there is faintly seen.

---

154 "bridal veil"

Her features have reassumed their former majesty, but with an expression of childlike innocence and heavenly peace. The thongs have drawn blood at the wrists and ankles, which has run and soaked into the sand; but angels received the body from the soldiers when they took it off the rack, and it lies, sweetly and modestly composed, upon the ground.

Passers-by stand still and gaze; idlers gather round. The report spreads in Sicca that neither sun by day, nor moon by night, nor moist atmosphere, nor beast of prey, has power over the wonderful corpse. Nay, that they cannot come near it without falling under some strange influence, which makes them calm and grave, expels bad passions, and allays commotion of mind. Many come again and again, for the mysterious and soothing effect she exerts upon them. They cannot talk freely about it to each other, and are seized with a sacred fear when they attempt to do so. Those who have merely heard their report without seeing her, say that these men have been in a grove of the Eumenides, or have suddenly encountered the wolf. The popular sensation continues and extends; some say it is magical, others that it is from the great gods. Day sinks again into evening, evening becomes night; the night wears out, and morning is coming again.

It begins to dawn: a glimmer is faintly spread abroad, and, mixing with the dark, makes twilight, which gradually brightens, and the outlines of nature rise dimly out of the night. Gradually the sacred body comes to sight; and, as the light grows stronger around it, gradually too the forms of five men emerge, who had not been there the night before. One is in front; the rest behind with a sort of bier or litter. They stand on the mountain side of her, and must have come from the country. It has been a bold enterprise theirs, to expose themselves to the nightly beasts, and now again to the rabble and the soldiers. The soldiers are at some little distance, silent and watchful; such of the rabble as have passed the night there have had some superstitious object in their stay. They have thought to get portions of the flesh for magical purposes; a finger, or a tooth, or some hair, or a portion of her tunic, or the blood-stained rope which was twisted round her wrist and ankle.

As the light makes her at length quite visible to the youth on the other side, who stands by himself with clasped hands and tearful eyes, he shrinks from the sight. He turns round to his companions who are provided with a large winding-sheet or pall, and with the help of one of them, to the surprise of the populace, he spreads it all over the body. And having done this, he stands again trembling, just for a few seconds, absorbed in his meditations, praying and weeping, and nerving himself for what is to follow. Ah, poor Agellius! you have not risen yet to the pitch of triumph; and other thoughts must be let to range through your breast, other emotions must spend themselves, before you are prepared simply to rejoice, exult, and glory in the lifeless form which lies before you. You are upon a brave work, but your heart is torn while you set hand to it, and you linger before you begin.

It was in the pride of her earthly beauty and the full vigour and elevation of her mind, that he last had seen her. It seemed an age since that morning, as if a chasm ran between the now and the then, when she so fascinated him with her presence, and so majestically rebuked him for bowing to that fascination. Yet on his memory every incident of that interview was fixed, and was indelible. O why should the great Creator shatter one of His most admirable works! If the order of the sun and stars is adorable, if the laws by which earth and sea are kept together mark the Hand of supreme Wisdom and Power, how much nobler perfection of beauty is manifested in man! And of human nature itself here was the supereminent crown, a soul full of gifts, full of greatness, full of intellect, placed in an outward form, equally surpassing in its kind, and still more surpassingly excellent from its intimate union and subordination to the soul, so as almost to be its simple expression; yet this choicest, rarest specimen of Almighty skill, the Almighty had pitilessly shattered, in order that it might inherit a higher, an eternal perfection. O mystery of mysteries, that heaven should not be possibly obtained without such grinding down and breaking up of our original nature! O mysterious, that principle in us, whatever it is, and however it came there, which is so antagonistic to God, which has so spoilt what seems so good, that all must be undone, and must begin anew! "An enemy hath done this;" and, knowing as much as this, and no more, we must leave the awful mystery to that day when all things shall be made light.

Agellius has not been idle while these thoughts pass through his mind. He has stooped down and scooped up such portions of the sand as are moistened with her blood, and has committed them to a small bag which he has taken out of his bosom. Then without delay, looking round to his attendants, and signing to them, with two of the party he resolutely crossed over to the other side of the corpse, covering it from attack, while his two assistants who were left proceeded quickly to lay hold of it. They had raised it, laid it on the bier, and were setting off by an unusual track across the waste, while Agellius, Aspar, and the third were grappling with some ruffians who had rushed upon them. Few, however, were there as yet to take part against them, but their cries of alarm were bringing others up, and the Christians were in growing danger of being worsted and carried off, when suddenly the soldiers interfered. Under pretence of keeping the peace, they laid about them with their heavy maces; and so it was, the blows took effect on the heads and shoulders of the rabble, with but slight injury to Agellius and his companions. The latter took instant advantage of the diversion, and vanished out of view by the same misleading track which their comrades had already chosen. If they, or the party who had preceded them, came within the range of sight of any goatherds upon the mountains, we must suppose that angels held those heathen eyes that they should not recognise them.

# Chapter Thirty-six

# LUX PERPETUA
# SANCTIS TUIS, DOMINE

THE BIER AND ITS BEARERS, and its protectors, have reached the cave in safety, and pace down the gallery, preceded by its Christian hosts, with lighted tapers, singing psalms. They place the sacred body before the altar, and the mass begins. St. Cyprian celebrates, and after the Gospel, he adds a few words of his own.

He said that they were engaged in praising, blessing, and exalting the adorable Grace of God, which had snatched so marvellously a brand out of the furnace. Benedicamus Patrem et Filium cum Sancto Spiritu. Benedictus, et laudabilis, et gloriosus, et superexaltatus in sæcula.[155] Every day doing marvels and exceeding all that seemed possible in power and love, by new and still newer manifestations. A Greek had come to Africa to embellish the shrines of heathenism, to minister to the usurpation of the evil one, and to strengthen the old ties which connected genius with sin; and she had suddenly found salvation. But yesterday a poor child of earth, and to-day an inhabitant of the heavens. But yesterday without God and without hope; and to-day a martyr with a green palm and golden vestment, worshipping before the Throne. But yesterday the slave of Satan, and spending herself on the vanities of time; and to-day drinking of the never-cloying torrents of bliss everlasting. But yesterday one of a number, a grain of a vast heap, destined indiscriminately for the

---

155 "Let us bless the Father, and the Son, and the Holy Spirit. Blessed, and laudible, and glorious, and exalted above all forever."

flame; to-day one of the elect souls, written from eternity in the book of life, and predestined to glory. But yesterday, hungry and thirsty, and restless for some object worthy an immortal spirit; to-day enjoying the ineffable ecstasy of the Marriage Feast and the espousals of Emmanuel. But yesterday tossed about on a sea of opinion; and to-day entranced in the vision of infallible truth and immutable sanctity. And yet what was she but only one instance out of ten thousand, of the Almighty and All-manifold Grace of the Redeemer? And who was there of all of them, there assembled, from the most heroic down to the humblest beginner, from the authoritative preacher down to the slave or peasant, but was equally, though in his own way, a miracle of mercy, and a vessel, once of wrath, if now of glory? Only might he and all who heard him persevere as they had begun, so that if (as was so probable) their trial was to be like hers, its issue might be like hers also.

St. Cyprian ceased; and, while the deacon opened the *sindon* for the offertory, the faithful took up alternately the verses of a hymn, which we here insert in a most unworthy translation:—

> "The number of Thine own complete,
>     Sum up and make an end;
> Sift clean the chaff, and house the wheat,—
>     And then, O Lord, descend.
>
> "Descend, and solve by that descent,
>     This mystery of life;
> Where good and ill, together blent,
>     Wage an undying strife.
>
> "For rivers twain are gushing still,
>     And pour a mingled flood;
> Good in the very depths of ill—
>     Ill in the heart of good.
>
> "The last are first, the first are last,
>     As angel eyes behold;
> These from the sheepcote sternly cast,
>     Those welcomed to the fold.
>
> "No Christian home, no pastor's eye,
>     No preacher's vocal zeal,
> Moved Thy dear martyr to defy
>     The prison and the wheel.

"Forth from the heathen ranks she stepped
   The forfeit throne to claim
Of Christian souls who had not kept
   Their birthright and their name.

"Grace formed her out of sinful dust;
   She knelt a soul defiled;
She rose in all the faith and trust
   And sweetness of a child.

"And in the freshness of that love
   She preached by word and deed,
The mysteries of the world above—
   Her new-found glorious creed.

"And running, in a little hour,
   Of life the course complete,
She reached the throne of endless power,
   And sits at Jesus' feet.

"Her spirit there, her body here,
   Make one the earth and sky;
We use her name, we touch her bier,
   We know her God is nigh."

The last sentiment of the yet unfinished hymn was receiving an answer while they sang it. Juba had been brought into the chapel in the hands of his brother and the exorcists. Since he had been under their care, he had been, on the whole, calm and manageable, with intervals of wild tempest and mad terror. He spoke, at times, of an awful incubus weighing on his chest, which he could not throw off, and said he hoped that they would not think all the blasphemies he uttered were his own. On this occasion, he struggled most violently, and shook with distress; and, as they brought him towards the sacred relics, a thick, cold dew stood upon his brow, and his features shrank and collapsed. He held back, and exerted himself with all his might to escape, foaming at the mouth, and from time to time uttering loud shrieks and horrible words, which disturbed, though they could not interrupt, the hymn. His bearers persevered; they brought him close to Callista, and made him touch her feet with his hands. Immediately he screamed fearfully, and was sent up into the air with such force that he seemed discharged from some engine of war: then he fell back upon the earth apparently lifeless.

The long prayer was ended; the *Sursum corda* was uttered. Juba raised himself from the ground. When the words of consecration had been said, he adored with the faithful. After the mass, his attendants came to him; he was quite changed; he was quiet, harmless, and silent: the evil spirit had gone out; but he was an idiot.

This wonderful deliverance was but the beginning of the miracles which followed the martyrdom of St. Callista. It may be said to have been the resurrection of the Church at Sicca. In not many months Decius was killed, and the persecution ceased there. Castus was appointed bishop, and numbers began to pour into the fold. The lapsed asked for peace, or at least such blessings as they could have. Heathens sought to be received. When asked for their reason, they could only say that Callista's history and death had affected them with constraining force, and that they could not help following her steps. Increasing in boldness, as well as numbers, the Christians cowed both magistrates and mob. The spirit of the populace had been already broken; and the continual change of masters, and measures with them, in the imperial government, inflicted a chronic timidity on the magistracy. A handsome church was soon built, to which Callista's body was brought, and which remained till the time of the Diocletian persecution.

Juba attached himself to this church; and, though he could not be taught even to sweep the sacred pavement, still he never was troublesome or mischievous. He continued in this state for about ten years. At the end of that time, one morning, after mass, which he always attended in the church porch, he suddenly went to the bishop, and asked for baptism. He said that Callista had appeared to him, and had restored to him his mind. On conversing with him, the holy Castus found that his recovery was beyond all doubt: and not knowing how long his lucid state would last, he had no hesitation, with such instruction as the time admitted, in administering the sacred rite, as Juba wished. After receiving it, he proceeded to the tomb, within which lay St. Callista, and remained on his knees before his benefactress till nightfall. Not even then was he disposed to rise; and so he was left there for the night. Next morning he was found still in the attitude of prayer, but lifeless. He had been taken away in his baptismal robe.

As to Agellius, if he be the bishop of that name who suffered at Sicca in his old age, in the persecution of Diocletian, we are possessed in this circumstance of a most interesting fact to terminate his history withal. What makes this more likely is, that this bishop is recorded to have removed the body of St. Callista from its original position, and placed it under the high altar, at which he said mass daily. After his own martyrdom, St. Agellius was placed under the high altar also.

# THE END

# POSTSCRIPTS TO LATER EDITIONS

*February 8, 1856.*—Since the volume has been in print, the Author finds that his name has got abroad. This gives him reason to add, that he wrote great part of Chapters I., IV., and V., and sketched the character and fortunes of Juba, in the early spring of 1848. He did no more till the end of last July, when he suddenly resumed the thread of his tale, and has been successful so far as this, that he has brought it to an end.

Without being able to lay his finger upon instances in point, he has some misgiving lest, from a confusion between ancient histories and modern travels, there should be inaccuracies, antiquarian or geographical, in certain of his minor statements, which carry with them authority when they cease to be anonymous.

*February 2, 1881.*—October, 1888.—In a tale such as this, which professes in the very first sentence of its Advertisement to be simple fiction from beginning to end, details may be allowably filled up by the writer's imagination and coloured by his personal opinions and beliefs, the only rule binding on him being this—that he has no right to contravene acknowledged historical facts. Thus it is that Walter Scott exercises a poet's licence in drawing his Queen Elizabeth and his Claverhouse, and the author of "Romola" has no misgivings in even imputing hypothetical motives and intentions to Savonarola. Who, again, would quarrel with Mr. Lockhart, writing in Scotland, for excluding Pope, or Bishops, or sacrificial rites from his interesting Tale of Valerius?

Such was the understanding, as to what I might do and what I might not, with which I wrote this story; and to make it clearer, I added in the later editions of this Advertisement, that it was written "from a Catholic point of view;" while in the earlier, bearing in mind the interests of historical truth, and the anachronism which I had ventured on at page 82 [57] in the date of Arnobius and Lactantius, I said that I had not "admitted any actual interference with known facts without notice," questions of religious controversy, when I said it, not even coming into my thoughts. I did not consider my Tale to be in any sense controversial, but to be specially addressed to Catholic readers, and for their edification.

This being so, it was with no little surprise I found myself lately accused of want of truth, because I have followed great authorities in attributing to Christians of the middle of the third century what is certainly to be found in the fourth,—devotions, representations, and doctrines, declaratory of the high dignity of the Blessed Virgin. If I had left out all mention of these, I should have been simply untrue to my idea and apprehension of Primitive Christianity. To what positive and certain facts do I run counter in so doing, even granting that I am indulging my imagination? But I have allowed myself no such indulgence; I gave good reasons long ago, in my "Letter to Dr. Pusey" (pp. 53–76), for what I believe on this matter and for what I have in "Callista" described.

www.ingramcontent.com/pod-product-compliance
Lightning Source LLC
Chambersburg PA
CBHW071128260626
47162CB00003B/709